GREAT
TALES
of the SEA

GREAT TALES
of the SEA

Selected and condensed by
the Editors of The Reader's Digest

VOLUME ONE

With an Introduction
BY DOUGLAS REEMAN

THE READER'S DIGEST ASSOCIATION
LONDON, SYDNEY, CAPE TOWN

FIRST EDITION
Published by
The Reader's Digest Association Limited
25 Berkeley Square, London W1X 6AB

For information as to ownership of copyright
in the material in this book see last page

Filmset by Typesetting Services Ltd.,
Glasgow and Edinburgh

Printed by South China Printing Co. Ltd.
Hong Kong

CONTENTS

SEA FEVER

*I must go down to the seas again, to the lonely sea and
    the sky,*
And all I ask is a tall ship and a star to steer her by;
*And the wheel's kick and the wind's song and the white
    sail's shaking,*
And a grey mist on the sea's face and a grey dawn breaking.

*I must go down to the seas again, for the call of the
    running tide*
Is a wild call and a clear call that may not be denied;
And all I ask is a windy day with the white clouds flying,
*And the flung spray and the blown spume, and the sea-
    gulls crying.*

I must go down to the seas again, to the vagrant gypsy life,
*To the gull's way and the whale's way where the wind's
    like a whetted knife;*
*And all I ask is a merry yarn from a laughing fellow-
    rover,*
*And quiet sleep and a sweet dream when the long trick's
    over.*

JOHN MASEFIELD

INTRODUCTION
by Douglas Reeman

DOWN OVER THE CENTURIES the oceans of the world have provoked interest, and the tales written of ships and the men who serve them have grown rather than diminished in popularity. As a sea story writer, both under my own name and also the pseudonym of Alexander Kent, I receive many letters from readers all over the world—some to ask about a particular incident or theme, others to share an experience or vivid memory with me, but all to tell of their fascination for the sea.

In the case of my own race, an island race, it is perhaps understandable. It has been said often enough that we British have salt in our blood. When you consider that it is impossible for any of us to be born more than eighty miles from the sea, this comment gathers a certain authority.

Since man first challenged the deep waters, ships have left our ports to explore, to fish, to wage war and restore peace. Events both momentous and tiny have been woven together as part of our heritage—like the little vessels which sailed to meet the Spanish Armada, or went with Nelson to the Nile; or the lonely men who perished in the ice while they searched for some new route or a fresh source of prosperity.

To us then the sea has been more of an ally than an enemy. In times of war some nations have been beaten back to a coastline and have seen it as a barrier, a final defeat. But what British soldier, slogging through France, ever doubted that he could get home, if only he could find the friendly sea at a place called Dunkirk? And later, at Singapore, after what is still remembered as the worst defeat in our history, there were men who took to the water as a means of survival, even though the nearest land thought to be free of enemy domination was six hundred miles away in Java. Many made the distance—not great navigators or experienced sailors but ordinary men, islanders.

But why this fascination amongst many nations where the sea is, more often than not, just a holiday memory? Perhaps it is because of the world we live in. On film and television we can watch the launching of space craft and follow their journeys on the screen or through the dialogue of their masters on the ground. We can even see those first cautious steps of the young astronauts as they test the moon's surface, their triumph complete. But we are nevertheless excluded. We can never be a part of it.

If you question the average man or woman it is doubtful if you will find one who can tell you the names of the astronauts, the order they landed on the moon or made a rendezvous in space. But just mention a name like Thor Heyerdahl and it is a different story—because he is a *real* person, a part of our time. You see that same dreamy look which you might notice at a boat show or around some harbour, as if to say, "I shall get a boat one day. I could do what he did." A dream perhaps, but the sea is always there, waiting.

I believe that people like to read about those who have accepted the sea's challenge, for their stories are as many and as varied as the tides. Nowadays we tend to take travel for granted and can reach almost anywhere in hours by air. Before the Second World War, however, travel was still very much restricted by cost, confined usually to the prosperous, the diplomats and the military. The sailor—with his blue jacket and brass buttons, his rolling walk and tales of far-off places and awful ships aboard which he would *never* set foot again (until the next time!)—was a figure of mystery and romance.

In spite of all the obvious changes and advancement, the image of today's sailor is not much altered. He still personifies man against the elements, with little but his courage and skill to sustain him.

I am thankful that I had no part in choosing the titles for these two volumes. It must have been a formidable and challenging task, but one with an excellent result. The stories are spread over history and are as varied as the oceans. They give us a taste of everything from the square-rigger to the nuclear submarine.

There are some items in the collection which have been a part of my life since I can remember, such as Slocum's *Sailing Alone Around the World*, a far cry from today's heavily subsidized and sponsored yachtsman, and Melville's *The Great White Whale* which was a part of one of the earliest tales I can recall. I still re-read it with pleasure and admiration.

The Ra Expeditions, the story of Thor Heyerdahl's attempt to cross the great wastes of the Atlantic in a flimsy papyrus hull of the kind used by the ancient Egyptians is a proof that when the sea offers a challenge, there will always be somebody to accept it. It is a story of our times, of a man turning his back on the accepted world in his search for adventure and the truth.

And then we have examples of books by that special breed of author, the ex-sailor. In this selection Dudley Pope and Alistair MacLean write with different styles, one fact, the other fiction, but each man with the familiarity and awareness of ships and the sea.

I was particularly glad to find *Surface at the Pole* included. It is a true story of underwater courage and determination which any novelist would find hard to match.

Some years ago I was a guest of the United States Navy and during my stay in America I was invited to the Naval Academy at Annapolis. It was during June Week, that bustling time when another batch of would-be admirals parade for the last time before joining their first ships. The superintendent of Annapolis must always be carefully chosen —a man who can inspire his youthful charges, and by his own past example make them into naval officers.

He certainly impressed me. He was Rear Admiral James Calvert, who as commander of the nuclear submarine *Skate* fought the Arctic ice and won. He was also the author of this fine book.

And who but Conrad could bring a rusty old tramp steamer to life so vividly? *Youth* is a sea story of the lasting kind, of a young man's involvement with a clapped-out ship.

There is a moving account of the *Titanic*'s loss, that great unsinkable ship whose memory seems to grow sharper with the years. Another story, *An Iceland Fisherman*, is about men who fought the bitter waters around their island for the sea's harvest.

I have left Alan Villiers' book *Captain Cook, the Seamen's Seaman* until the last. The others I picked at random from each volume and can safely leave a choice of favourites to the readers.

But Alan Villiers holds a firm place in my life. As a sailor and now as a writer I have always admired the work of this rugged Australian.

If I had to choose a "man of the sea" Alan Villiers would fit exactly. His interesting life and his valuable contributions to maritime affairs are remarkable. He has sailed in square-riggers and served at sea in time of war. From his pen, and in the sound of his voice or the pitch of his words on his many radio talks I have *heard* the sea. Villiers has the ability of being able to share his experiences with others, surely the true gift of a writer. It is a rare thing to know a man so well without ever meeting him or speaking with him—a man whom Captain Cook would certainly have appreciated.

In this lively collection, there are stories of make-believe and hard fact but all are true of the sea itself. There may be some which the reader will want to buy unabridged, perhaps one about a special event or a particular hero. Be that as it may, I know of no better way than this to gather up the seven seas in one collection and present them for the enjoyment of so many.

Douglas Reeman

ENGLAND EXPECTS
by Dudley Pope

England Expects

A condensation of the book by
Dudley Pope

In January 1805, Napoleon was at the height of his power in Europe. All that stood between him and his dreams of further conquest was his arch rival, perfidious Albion. For nearly two years the Royal Navy had been maintaining a ceaseless blockade of French ports. Now, at last, Napoleon had a master plan that would not only break this stranglehold but also bring Britain to her knees. This is the heroic story, brilliantly related, of how the intrepid Admiral Lord Nelson and his mighty ships-of-the-line smashed to pieces that plan—and the combined fleets of France and her ally Spain—off the rocky coast of Cape Trafalgar, and so won immortality.

DUDLEY POPE was wounded when serving as a Merchant Navy midshipman in the Battle of the Atlantic After the war, he took up journalism but the success of *England Expects* enabled him to concentrate on writing the books that have made him famous—scholarly naval histories and the novels about his Nelsonic hero, Ramage.

CHAPTER 1

Two hoists of flags quivered in the moaning wind as they streamed out from the signal halyards of the 38-gun frigate *Euryalus*, which was, on this stormy October day in 1805, serving as the flagship of Cuthbert Collingwood, vice admiral of the blue.

For the past five days Collingwood had been in command of the victorious British fleet now fighting for its life in a gale only a few miles off the Spanish coast at Cape Trafalgar. He had seen many of its battle prizes, vast French and Spanish three-deckers which had been the pride of the Emperor, Napoleon, and of His Catholic Majesty, Charles IV, smashed by the heavy seas.

The sixty-knot winds and great singing waves had blunted the fleet's progress north towards England; yet Collingwood could no longer delay informing the Admiralty in London of the best news—that the Combined Fleet of France and Spain had been defeated five days before, and the worst—that Lord Nelson, commander in chief of the British Mediterranean fleet, had died in battle.

Downwind from the *Euryalus*, the tiny schooner *Pickle*, sails reefed, hatches battened down, was lying hove to while some of her thirty-two crewmen tried to snatch some rest. Her lookout spotted the pennants flying from the yardarms of the *Euryalus*, indicating the signal, "Pass within hail."

Wearily the *Pickle*'s commander, thirty-five-year-old Lieutenant John Richards Lapenotière, gave the order to get under way. Each crewman used one hand for his task and the other to hold on, for the ship was rolling and pitching like a log in a mountain torrent.

Slowly the *Pickle* began to work her way across to the *Euryalus*, where Collingwood was waiting. His dispatch, addressed to William Marsden, the secretary to the Board of Admiralty, and dated October 22, 1805, the day after the great battle, was ready in his cabin. He had since written a second letter to Mr. Marsden, describing the damage wrought by the gale. He had already been forced to scuttle some of the captured ships, including the *Santissima Trinidad*, the greatest warship ever built, and to set others afire. Of the remaining prizes, he had observed, "Unless the weather moderates, I doubt whether I shall be able to carry a ship of them into port."

Captain Henry Blackwood, commanding the *Euryalus*, had hoped that he would have the honour of carrying home news of the battle. But Collingwood had decided instead to send his dispatches in the fast-sailing *Pickle*, as a reward to her commander. Several years earlier Collingwood had been travelling in a ship when young Lapenotière, although only a passenger, had saved it from going on the rocks. A grateful Collingwood had said then, "If ever I have the opportunity, I will do you a service." Now that opportunity had come, and when Lapenotière scrambled on board the *Euryalus* from his jolly boat, Collingwood reminded the young lieutenant of his promise and said, "Take these dispatches to England; you will receive five hundred pounds and your commander's commission. Now I have kept my word."

Lapenotière went back on board the *Pickle*. With more than a thousand miles to go from Trafalgar, the *Pickle* had a long and dangerous voyage ahead of her. Enemy ships might fall upon her from Spanish and French ports, yet Lapenotière knew that the weather would probably turn out to be his worst enemy.

By the following Monday, however, the winds had moderated, and with more canvas set, Lapenotière decided to muster the crew. In addition to checking the ship's company against the ship's books, form number 15 had to be filled in. This had several columns with different headings—the date a man joined the ship, whether press-ganged or a volunteer, name, rating, age, stature, etc. There was one column headed ominously "D., D.D., R., or R.A.R."—discharged, discharged dead, "run" (deserted), or returned after run. Of the ship's complement of forty sailors from many nations, there were now only thirty-two on board; the rest had run or been discharged.

The steady weather, which allowed for orderly routine, did not last long. On Thursday morning, as the *Pickle* was rounding Cape Finisterre before entering the Bay of Biscay, a heavy sea swept the ship, wrenching away the jib-boom and spritsail yard. By nightfall the *Pickle*'s position had become critical. Somewhere below the waterline she had sprung a leak, and the more the ship laboured the worse it got. The wind increased in the darkness, whipping up vicious seas on the heavy swells already rolling in from a great storm centre in the heart of the Atlantic. The ship reared and plunged, sending great shudders through her timbers.

By the morning of Friday, November 1, the wind was so strong that when the ship rolled to leeward she hung there sluggishly, seemingly reluctant to roll back. Lapenotière ordered four carronades, each weighing six hundredweight, to be heaved over the side. Lightened by more than a ton, the *Pickle* seemed to ride easier.

At noon the wind eased slightly, then veered and dropped to a fresh breeze. By dark the *Pickle* had all her working canvas set, the leak had been stopped and the men who were off watch wriggled into their sodden hammocks for their first decent sleep in eleven days.

The next day the *Pickle* reached the entrance of the English Channel. By now she was no longer alone; on the horizon all around were sails of ships entering or leaving English ports, and by sunset the ship had made her way into the narrow channel between England and France. At two o'clock the next morning a sharp-eyed lookout spotted the Lizard lighthouse on England's southernmost tip.

Sailing ships had made this very landfall for centuries, returning from the four corners of the earth with the rare cargoes that had made England rich, or limping home from sea battles which maintained her greatness. Even as the Lizard was Drake's last glimpse of England before he died off Portobelo in 1596, so it had been Nelson's a bare few weeks before his victory at Trafalgar.

Reaching Falmouth Bay on November 4, with the winds light and the tide foul, Lapenotière went below and struggled into his best uniform, mildewed and creased as it was, before giving orders to swing the jolly boat over the side to row him ashore.

Gales and calms, head winds and leaks had conspired to slow the

Pickle; now at last, a full two weeks after Britain's victory at Trafalgar, Lapenotière stepped onto dry land and began to arrange for a post chaise to take him and his precious dispatches the two hundred and sixty-six miles to the Admiralty in London.

THE TALL LIEUTENANT was glad the roads were dry—it had not rained for five days—and his coachmen kept up a good speed. At the Royal Hotel in Truro the hostlers were ready with four fresh horses, and as soon as they were changed, the coach clattered on.

At Basingstoke, some fifty miles from London, by late afternoon the weather gave a warning of fog to come, and as the weary Lapenotière approached the outskirts of the great capital, the sheets of mist gradually thickened into banks of fog, yellowed with the throat-catching tang of sulphur. The coachman slowed the horses from a gallop to a trot, from a trot to a walk and from a walk to a crawl.

It was the worst fog London had seen in years. By the time Lapenotière approached Whitehall, stiff and jaded from nearly thirty-seven hours' hard driving, midnight had struck and November 6 had been ushered in.

IN THE ADMIRALTY the silver-haired Lord Barham, now eighty and first lord, had retired to bed. Working late in the Board Room, however, was Secretary Marsden, the son of an Irish banker with shipping interests.

The room where Marsden worked had been the centre of Britain's dominion of the seas since Thomas Ripley constructed the building in 1725. From here the orders had gone out which sent Anson on his great voyage of exploration in 1740; Cook on the three voyages which opened up the entire Pacific; and Nelson himself to the great victories of the Nile, Copenhagen, and against the Combined Fleet of France and Spain at Trafalgar.

The Board Room was rectangular, with a high white ceiling decorated with gilt roses, and walls heavily panelled with oak. A log fire burned in the grate, which still bore the arms of Charles II, and on the wall over the fireplace were several charts, wound on rollers so that they looked like sunblinds. On the north wall, flanked by bookcases, was what appeared to be a huge clockface; it was a circular map depicting Europe from the Baltic to Spain, the North Sea bearing the name The British Ocean. In its centre was fixed a gilded pointer, and around the edge were marked the points of the compass. The pointer was geared to a wind vane on top of the Admiralty building. Sitting around the heavy mahogany table in the middle of the room, members could see which way the wind was blowing and thus whether or not a fleet could sail.

The fire glowed, and a stately grandfather clock in a corner of the room ticked away the passing minutes. Marsden was just finishing his work when the night porter knocked and announced an officer bearing dispatches. Lapenotière, unshaven, uniform crumpled, his face lined with fatigue, strode into the candlelit room. Without any preamble, he said, "Sir, we have gained a great victory; but we have lost Lord Nelson." He then handed over the dispatches.

Shocked as he was by this double-edged news, Marsden remembered he was the secretary to the board. There were many people as well as the first lord to inform—among them the King, at Windsor, the Prince of Wales, the Duke of York, Prime Minister William Pitt in Downing Street, other ministers and the lord mayor of London. A notice for the royal salutes was also necessary, and preparations had to be made for a *Gazette* extraordinary.

The night porter was sent around the Admiralty building to rouse anyone who could help. A copy of Collingwood's dispatch was sent by a messenger to the prime minister, who had just gone to sleep. Pitt had been awakened at various hours during his eventful life by the arrival of news; but whether good news or bad he could always lay his head on his pillow and sink into a sound sleep again. "On *this occasion*, however," wrote the diplomat Lord Malmesbury, "he could not calm his thoughts, but at length got up, though it was three in the morning."

At Windsor Castle, George III was so deeply affected on hearing of Nelson's death "that a profound silence of nearly five minutes ensued before he could give utterance to his feelings." Queen Charlotte called the weeping princesses around her and read Collingwood's dispatch to them. "The whole Royal group shed tears to the memory of Lord Nelson."

Despite the fog, rumours of Nelson's great victory and of his death spread across London like wildfire. The Park and Tower guns boomed out at ten o'clock, while the London *Gazette*'s compositors worked hurriedly to set up Collingwood's dispatch in type. Crowds besieged the newspaper offices, clamouring for news of Nelson, of husbands, brothers and sons.

By late afternoon shop windows had been draped with purple cloth. That evening "the Metropolis was very generally and brilliantly illuminated . . . yet there was a damp upon the public spirit, which it was impossible to overcome," reported the *Naval Chronicle*. "The loss of Lord Nelson was more lamented than the victory was rejoiced at." The illuminations were discontinued, and in many ships of the Royal Navy hardened seamen broke down and wept openly.

Frances (Fanny), the wife from whom Nelson had been separated since 1801, had the news of her husband's death direct from the Admiralty. Although Lord Barham was more than busy the day Collingwood's dispatches arrived, he found a few minutes to write to Lady Nelson. "Madam," his letter began. "It is with the utmost concern that in the midst of victory I have to inform Your Ladyship of the death of your illustrious partner, Lord Viscount Nelson . . . it is the death he wished for and less to be regretted on his own account."

At Merton, the home he had left for the battle, Nelson's beloved mistress, Emma Hamilton, was grief-stricken, sending messages to her friends that she was very ill. Her lover and protector was dead.

Honours were soon awarded. Three days after Collingwood's dispatches arrived, Nelson's brother and heir, the Reverend William, received an earldom. Later there was a parliamentary grant of one hundred and twenty thousand pounds to the Nelson family. An income of five thousand pounds a year was granted to those who succeeded to the title, and Nelson's widow received two thousand pounds a year. But Nelson's last wishes were ignored. In a codicil to his will, written moments before engaging the enemy at Trafalgar, he had detailed Emma's "eminent services" to her King, and said, "Could I have rewarded these services, I would not now call upon my Country, but as that has not been in my power, I leave Emma Hamilton therefore a legacy to my King and Country, that they will give her an ample provision to maintain her rank in life."

There remained one other dearly loved person to be cared for— Horatia, Nelson's daughter by Lady Hamilton. But to the ruling class in England, Nelson and Emma had committed the greatest sin of all—

openly living together unwed at Merton; and Emma and Horatia were left to their own devices. By 1807, Lady Hamilton was so badly in debt that she had to sell Merton. Harried by creditors, she fled to France, where she died in misery and poverty in 1815.

NELSON WAS THE possessor of perhaps the most contradictory personality in British history, yet his death was felt in England as something more than a public calamity. What was it about "that

Lady Nelson

Lord Nelson

cripple-gaited, one-eyed, one-armed little naval critter" that gave him such a hold on the emotions of the British people? The legend of Nelson as the greatest sailor-warrior in a navy of great sailor-warriors has tended to obscure the Nelson known to the men who fought with him, the women who loved him, and the ladies and gentlemen who met him on his rare appearances in the gay and gossipy salons that were the centres of London society.

Nelson's face had none of the sternness of purpose or steadfastness that are associated with military heroism. Instead of a square jaw and firm lips, his face was narrow and boyish, with sensitive lips forming a pouting mouth. In fact, at first glance his head, with its careless hair and mobile, almost womanish features lined with pain and anxiety, might be that of a restless poet.

Of a race that prided itself on never revealing its feelings, Nelson was a melodramatic exception. Moody and temperamental, he was one

21

moment suicidally depressed and the next almost childishly elated. His whole personality appears to have been unstable—yet he rarely made a wrong decision, whether it was one long debated or suddenly arrived at in the heat of battle. It seemed as if he had two distinct personalities—the hot-blooded, hypersensitive and erratic one which manifested itself in his relations with people, and the steely, questing and unswerving personality which turned him into the perfect fighter when his ears were deafened by the thunder of guns and his nostrils dilated with the smoke of powder.

Born a weakling, Nelson was constantly ill when at sea. ("Dreadfully seasick," he wrote the year before Trafalgar; "always tossed about, and always seasick.") His health had been ruined by fever in the West Indies; he had lost the sight of his right eye off Corsica in 1794, and had lost his right arm three years later, after a vicious night attack at the battle of Santa Cruz de Tenerife. Wounded and exhausted, he had broken down after his victory at the Nile in 1798—"I never expect to see your face again," he wrote to Lord Jervis, his commander in chief in the Mediterranean. And during the British blockade of France in 1803, his thin body was racked with spasms of perpetual coughing, his muscles were knotted with rheumatism, and his head buzzed with toothache. He had a regular pain in the chest, and also appears to have had nervous dyspepsia almost without pause.

But his were not the moanings of a hypochondriac. When being given a pension in 1797, Nelson had first to present a memorial outlining his service. "Your memorialist has been in four actions with the fleets of the enemy, in three actions with frigates, in six engagements against batteries, in ten actions in boats.... He has assisted in the capture of seven sail of the line, six frigates, four corvettes, eleven privateers, and taken and destroyed near fifty sail of merchantmen. [He] has been actually engaged against the enemy upwards of one hundred and twenty times." When that was written, Nelson had just celebrated his thirty-ninth birthday; the battles at the Nile, Copenhagen and Trafalgar were yet to be fought.

Though constantly subject to illness, he retained an ironic sense of humour. "I have all the diseases there are," he once wrote, "but there is not enough in my frame for them to fasten on." To the future William IV he wrote after losing his arm: "I assure your

Royal Highness that not a scrap of that ardour with which I served our King has been shot away!" And it was during the landing assault at Santa Cruz that Nelson, his right arm shattered, was rowed to Thomas Fremantle's *Seahorse*, half unconscious and in urgent need of medical attention. But he refused to go on board because Fremantle's new bride was there, anxiously awaiting her husband's return. "I will die rather than alarm Mrs. Fremantle by her seeing me in this state when I can give her no tidings of her husband," he said.

Nelson could be petty, to be sure, and there was often a hint of shrewishness in his temper, usually where little things were concerned. Yet it was his humanity which endeared him to his officers and men. When he was ill, hard-bitten seamen nursed him with all the tenderness they might have lavished on a woman. From the Baltic in 1801, he wrote: "All the fleet are so truly kind to me that I should be a wretch not to cheer up."

Warmhearted with those he liked and respected, Nelson also had a tremendous loyalty—whether to a man, a ship or a fleet. Merely because one was his, then each was of the best. His ships of the Mediterranean fleet were "the best commanded and the best manned afloat." That warm loyalty was, of course, returned, and it was often returned in a spontaneous and dramatic way. Thomas Troubridge, for instance, a fine seaman with vast experience, was so upset at something Nelson had written to him that he sat down and replied: "Your letter has really so unhinged me that I am quite unmanned and crying. I would sooner forfeit my life—my everything—than be deemed ungrateful to an officer and a friend I feel I owe so much. Pray, pray acquit me."

If it seems strange that among Nelson's dying words were "Kiss me, Hardy," it should be remembered that this was the grave and kindly captain, Sir Thomas Masterman Hardy, who had lowered a boat from Nelson's frigate *Minerve* and rowed after a seaman who had fallen over the side at a moment when Spanish battleships were in fast pursuit. Though Nelson was faced with the danger that the *Minerve* would be captured before the boat could get back, he did not hesitate. "By God, I'll not lose Hardy! Back the mizzen topsail." The *Minerve* lay to while Hardy's boat caught up. The nearest Spanish battleship, fearing a trap, backed a topsail as well, giving

Nelson time to get Hardy and his boat's crew on board, and the *Minerve* escaped.

Nelson's leadership was that of example and trust accompanied with a warm smile—the rarest kind of all, the most easily abused and yet the most successful.

CHAPTER 2

THE BATTLE OF Trafalgar was not only the greatest sea victory ever won by British arms but the climax of the greatest campaign fought up to that time in British history.

After a long and bitter struggle against France, which had started in 1793, the Treaty of Amiens in 1802 had brought England a brief fourteen months of peace. During that time Napoleon, first consul of France, swiftly tidied up after the war and the Revolution. He had every reason to be pleased with himself; victorious in his land battles against the best troops in Europe, he had also won a diplomatic victory, for under the terms of the Amiens treaty the African, Indian and West Indian colonies were returned to him. But while Napoleon put all his efforts into filling his arsenals and restocking storehouses that had been emptied by years of British blockade, most of Britain sighed with relief and sat back to enjoy the peace.

The British prime minister, Henry Addington, halved the size of the army, demobilized the volunteers and paid off more than sixty of the navy's hundred battleships. Worse than that, more than forty thousand veteran seamen were discharged, and surplus war stores were sold to the highest bidders—often French agents who gleefully shipped them across the Channel.

France was, without question, the most powerful nation the world had ever seen. And though outwardly peaceful, her navy and army were still mobilized, biding their time and gathering their strength. And while newly arrived British tourists gazed in awe and admiration at the priceless paintings and statues in the Louvre—many of them plundered from palaces and castles all over Europe—the first consul, plainly dressed in a simple blue uniform, strode through his magnificent apartments in the Palais des Tuileries, planning and plotting new conquests.

As an insignificant Corsican boy, knowing scarcely a word of French, taciturn, and small in stature, born on an island where an insult could be answered only with a dagger, Napoleon had gone to the Paris cadets' school. After graduating and becoming an artillery sublieutenant, he had then but a single dream—of freeing Corsica from the bondage of France. Now, amid the splendour of his home in the Tuileries, he had another dream—of conquering a world whose sun would rise and set over Paris.

Only one country apparently stood in his way—England, that damnable nation of shopkeepers and her thrice-damned navy. However much Napoleon might overrun Europe, defeating or double-crossing kings, making promises and treaties he never intended to honour, Britain stood firm behind her moat, and her navy had cast a net around his great continental conquests, preventing him from breaking out to conquer other lands.

Now he turned greedy eyes towards the riches of the East—to India—and to the great continents of America and Australia. The world, Napoleon thought, was a ripe fruit waiting for him to pluck. But the ships of the Royal Navy had to be destroyed before he could extend France's colonial greatness.

Being a land animal, he could visualize only one sure way in which France, the greatest of land powers, could fight and defeat the greatest of the maritime powers—by invasion. If the Royal Navy was a thousand-headed hydra (and he began to think that it was), then its heart was London. Destroy that heart, he decided, and the heads would wither and die of their own accord.

BECAUSE THE BRITISH had failed to evacuate Malta, as arranged under the terms of the Treaty of Amiens, war broke out again between France and England in 1803, before Napoleon was ready. He was quick to recover his stride. "They want us to jump the ditch," he declared, "and we *will* jump it." With all the zest and fire that had lifted him to be first consul, Napoleon set his nation to work. She was to produce the craft which would set the Grand Army ashore on the Kent coast for its triumphal march to London.

Several hundred barges, sloops, pinnaces and gunboats were to be built at Dunkerque and Cherbourg, and assembled at Boulogne, where the Grand Army was now camped over one hundred and fifty thousand strong. Later, Napoleon ordered more craft to be built in twenty other Channel ports, with the minister of marine, Admiral Denis Decrès, bearing the brunt of his broadside of instructions.

In the Channel ports the shipyards echoed to the rhythmic thud of shipwrights' adzes and the hoarse cough of ripsaws as they shaped great balks of oak and pine into planks and beams and masts. In the forest clearings ovens glowed and turned wood into charcoal. Skilled men mixed the charcoal with saltpetre and sulphur to make gunpowder, and in the foundries perspiring men worked day and night casting cannon and shot.

That summer Napoleon, accompanied by his wife, Josephine, went on a grand tour of the invasion ports. He was not at all pleased with what he saw at Boulogne. As if to display how the Royal Navy ruled the Channel, one of his frigates came close in to attack seven landing craft which were sailing into the port. The guns of Boulogne opened fire, but their shot fell short, infuriating the first consul, who had all the pride of an old artilleryman. According to a Briton living in Boulogne at the time, Napoleon "became fidgety [and] uttered a few sacrés." Then, discovering that the guns had accidentally been loaded with saluting charges instead of full charges, he flew into a fury, tearing the epaulets from the shoulders of the officer responsible, and telling him he was no longer in the French army.

The summer of 1803 gave way to autumn. Although the adze sliced trunk and bough into frames and timbers, and the furnaces ran hot metal into the moulds of great guns, there was a sobering difference between Napoleon's plan to have some twenty-five hundred landing craft and a thousand transports moored in the Channel ports and the actual craft on the moorings. The inspector general of flotillas had to report a deficit of a thousand craft.

September brought vicious equinoctial gales in the Channel. Napoleon waited. Slowly but reluctantly he began to see some of the snags in his invasion plan. He had reckoned on rowing his army across to the Kent beaches when the sea was calm and the Channel thick with fog. Then, he had reasoned, the British fleet would be becalmed, and he would not have to risk his own fleet as a covering force. But as he stood on the cliffs overlooking the sea at Boulogne, he realized that the ideal weather conditions he sought rarely occurred. His ships *would* have to wrest control of the Channel from the Royal Navy.

ACROSS THE CHANNEL, meanwhile, Britain quickly roused—and fright-ened—itself, and the government under Addington tried to arm the country overnight. As George Cruickshank, the famous cartoonist of the period, wrote: "Every town was, in fact, a sort of garrison—in one place you might hear the tattoo of some youths learning to beat the drum, at another some march or national air being practised upon the fife, and every morning at five o'clock the bugle horn was sounded . . . to call Volunteers to a two-hour drill."

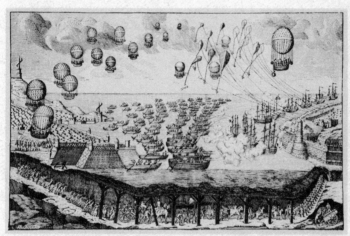

A British conception of Napoleon's plans

From the time the war against France began again in May 1803 until the battle of Trafalgar was fought in October 1805, the "Corsican ogre" dominated the lives of the people in Britain. Napoleon's villainy grew in the telling—he poisoned the sick to save food, he gloated over corpses scattered on the battlefields. Now he was variously building a massive bridge from Calais to Dover, across which his army would march; searching the English shore with his spyglass; and digging a tunnel under the Channel to the Kentish meadows.

When invasion failed to materialize in the summer or autumn of 1803, it was assumed that Napoleon would arrive in the summer of 1804. In southeast England invasion scares were frequent. Beacons made of brush and cordwood and tar were set up all around the coasts, ready to be lighted at night as a warning visible for at least three miles. In daylight wet hay was to be burned to make smoke signals. Inevitably some of the beacons were lighted by accident or because of a false alarm. Seventy-four towers, looking like inverted flowerpots, were built. The great flat beaches of Romney Marsh, reckoned an ideal place for a landing, were cut off by a deep canal.

Under Addington's vacillating leadership, however, Britain stayed on the defensive, and the people lost what little trust they had in his government. William Pitt the Younger was the only man who could give them the fighting leadership they wanted. So Pitt became prime minister on May 18, 1804—on the same day that Napoleon was declared the Emperor of France. Pitt knew that the sole hope for Britain lay in gaining allies on the Continent. He therefore began negotiations with young Alexander, the Czar of all the Russias, to form the third of the four European coalitions organized against the Corsican.

Meanwhile, Napoleon had tantalizing glimpses of his objective. He liked to ride along the beaches around Calais and Boulogne, where the waters of the Channel seemed to mock him. "From the heights of Ambleteuse I have seen the coast of England as one sees the Calvary from the Tuileries," he wrote. "One could distinguish the houses and the bustle. It is a ditch that shall be leaped when one is daring enough to try."

THE GREATEST DEFEAT suffered by the French navy up to the eve of Trafalgar had been at the hands of its own people. While a king sat on the throne of France, service as an officer in the navy had been a noble profession, but during the Revolution of 1789, which dragged Louis XVI from the throne to the guillotine, almost every officer, from admiral to the most junior ensign, who had the taint of blue blood in his veins was arrested and guillotined or forced to flee.

On board the ships the revolutionary cry of *"Liberté, égalité, fraternité"* had put the heaviest emphasis on *égalité*, and in place of the "aristos" had come men whose devotion to the Revolution far outweighed their abilities as seamen. Inevitably discipline vanished, and any attempts by newly appointed officers to enforce it put them in peril of being denounced. Sailors ashore found their new freedom heady, but it gave them no stomach for going to sea.

After Napoleon had lifted himself to power, he saw the reason for the navy's weakness and restored some of the surviving former officers to high commands. But by 1798 the French navy's position had improved only slightly when its fleet was attacked in Abukir Bay by fourteen British ships under Nelson's command. When the battle of the Nile had ended, nine of the French ships had been captured, two more destroyed, and nearly nine thousand men killed, wounded or taken prisoner. The French navy had suffered a terrible blow to its self-confidence.

Many years later, in exile at St. Helena, a sadder, defeated and perhaps wiser Napoleon said that he had been unable to find a man sufficiently strong to raise the character of the French navy. "There is in the navy a peculiarity," he declared, "a technicality that impeded all my conceptions. If I proposed a new idea, immediately the whole Marine Department were against me. 'Sire, that cannot be.' 'Why not?' 'Sire, the winds do not admit of it.' Then objections were started respecting calms and currents, and I was obliged to stop short." Hitler, just a century and a quarter later, also blamed the navy for not performing the miracles that his own orders precluded.

It was not only the leadership problem that bedevilled Napoleon's efforts. The French dockyards were inefficient, short of everything needed to make them function. The mountings of guns in the forts protecting the harbours were rotten and the guns themselves unfit to be used. Seamen were deserting, and soldiers had to be drafted to man the ships.

Yet it would be wrong to assume that because its victory at Trafalgar was so overwhelming the British navy was faultless. On paper it had a total of 181 battleships. But of this number, 26 were on order, 39 on harbour service, 33 in need of major repair, and only 83 were in commission. And since the British ships had to stay at sea almost continuously to contain Napoleon's fleet, even they were often damaged by "fair wear and tear". But there was also corruption in every service. Perhaps most of the blame for this must be put on the men in authority—including ministers of the Crown—who, as rewards for votes in Parliament or the exercise of some favour, gave contracts to unqualified and unscrupulous men. The net effect was that many ships sailed from English dockyards incompletely repaired or equipped.

There were, moreover, many bad constructional practices in the famous yards at Deptford and Woolwich on the Thames, at Chatham on the Medway, and at Plymouth. Too often the great oaken planks had started to rot even before the ships had been launched, and at least one great three-decker was condemned within a year of being launched. To make matters worse, ships were built in the open air and the frame exposed "for a twelvemonth or a little more" before being planked, so it was not unusual to have the whole frame covered with growing spores of rot before the planking-up was even started.

Some of the fastest ships in the Royal Navy were, ironically enough, those captured from the enemy. The *Tonnant*, after she had her tricolour changed for the British ensign, was considered "the finest two-decker ever seen in the Royal Navy," and the *Egyptian* "the finest ship on one deck we ever had." But English builders failed to learn anything from enemy prizes, and their conservative methods meant they continued to design ships that were frequently slow, difficult to manoeuvre and not particularly good in heavy weather.

It might seem strange, then, that the Royal Navy was so successful in battle. The answer lies in the superior training and experience of the British officers and men. British gunnery was superb, and in addition they had plenty of carronades—short-barrelled guns, rather like mortars, with a very big bore. These were easily handled and very destructive at short range.

Battles were fought at close quarters, with ships sometimes lashed together. Thus manoeuvrable ships with fine lines counted for little in action. Once the opposing fleets had closed with each other, warfare was reduced to a battle of broadsides. The ships that could fire the fastest won the battle, and because of the superior training and discipline of their crews, these were usually British ships.

Still, manning the great ships of the Royal Navy (a three-decker needed some eight hundred and fifty officers and men) was always a problem, especially in wartime, when there were rival claims from the mercantile marine—in which discipline was less harsh and the pay higher—and the army. Some of the navy's seamen had joined as boys and stayed on, but many of the men were pressed, according to a practice that is believed to date back to the days of King John.

By law the whole of the seafaring population of Britain was liable to serve the King at sea. If a man was given an "imprest" or advance payment by an agent of the King's—"taking the King's shilling"—he had to serve. In practice this meant that a captain short of crew—and captains were always in this unhappy state—would send out a dozen or so strong and reliable seamen under a lieutenant. Armed with clubs and cutlasses, they would make their way ashore, and any able-bodied man drinking a glass of beer with his friends at the local inn was liable to be seized and carried off.

A press-gang could also go to the local court and have the prisoners in gaol turned over to it. But it must not be thought that the gaolbirds pressed into the Royal Navy were criminals in the modern sense of the word. In Nelson's day men were given heavy sentences for even the most trivial offences. The laws of George III's reign allowed a man to be hanged for stealing a handkerchief from another's pocket. So it was not a constant stream of hardened criminals who left dank stone cells to serve in the King's navy; it was, instead, the agile young poacher, with plenty of initiative and a light tread, who frequently made a good topman, or the deft pickpocket who soon learned to turn a neat splice.

Nevertheless, the hard core of the Royal Navy consisted of tough, skilled and honest seamen. The fact that a raw recruit came on board verminous and hungry from one of His Majesty's gaols mattered not at all to captain, bosun or the old hands. What did matter was whether or not he would make a good seaman. And even the hardened criminal found that the seaman's own rough-and-ready justice helped to make him once again an honest man.

As ENGLISHMEN RAISED their glasses to toast the New Year of 1805, the future seemed like a long dark tunnel with no light at its end. Napoleon's invasion force was poised on the eastern flank of the Channel. Holland, Switzerland and northern Italy were mere subject territories of France, while Napoleon was threatening southern Italy—endangering Britain's whole position in the Mediterranean—and Turkey. Anticipating that Spain would eventually come into the war on France's side, Pitt had earlier ordered the seizure of homecoming Spanish treasure ships carrying silver from Montevideo. Spain in turn had declared war against England in December 1804, joining her fleet with France's.

Napoleon was now at the height of his power. And yet, despite the cheers of his massed armies and the flattery of his generals and admirals, he still had to face the problem of England. His Grand Army had been constantly drilling with its landing craft, and all France was waiting for the masterstroke. But Britain's great blockade of France's ports, which began in May 1803, had gone on ever since, and she continued to control the seas. Napoleon had delayed in 1803 and 1804. What had he in mind for 1805? With Spain now on his side, he could count on another thirty-two battleships to back up his fleet, making him powerful enough to challenge Britain at sea or at least to protect an invasion force crossing the Channel. But Spain had already warned him that, because Britain had caught her unawares, twenty-five of those Spanish ships would not be ready for sea until March. Thus Napoleon could not act until the spring. In the meantime, he had to do something to keep Britain occupied.

He therefore decided to make a peace offer to the British, and at the same time to launch a heavy attack on their rich sugar islands in the West Indies. This sudden assault, he guessed, would throw the merchants of the City of London into a panic and create a clamour for peace at any price, which would probably topple Prime Minister Pitt's government. In addition, he thought, the Royal Navy's strength would be drawn away from his Atlantic coast in a hurried dash to the West Indies.

Napoleon's peace offer was sent off on January 2, 1805. But belying his earnest declarations were two sets of orders that went out that same day. The first was to Rear Admiral Missiessy at Rochefort, on the Bay of Biscay, the second to Vice Admiral Pierre Charles Villeneuve, at Toulon, on the Mediterranean. They were to take on troops and sail independently for the West Indies, where they were to conduct operations against British possessions, and then return to Rochefort. Thus the first move in the train of events that was to lead directly and inexorably to the battle of Trafalgar began on January 11, when Admiral Missiessy's fleet of five battleships and five other warship's evaded the British blockade in a snowstorm and sailed for the West Indies.

The French admiral had been at sea three days when Britain's reply to Napoleon's peace offer arrived in Paris. Addressed simply to "The Head of the French Government"—a deliberate insult which successfully infuriated the Emperor—it said Britain was not prepared to negotiate without consulting with the other powers, particularly with the Russian Czar. Once bitten—by the Treaty of

Amiens—Britain was twice shy. Far from being ready to sue for peace, she realized that there could be no peace in the world while Napoleon was alive.

ADMIRAL VILLENEUVE HAD been unable to get far from Toulon—not because of Nelson's blockading force waiting over the horizon to fall on him but because of a gale that tattered sails, tore rigging, broke spars and scattered his fleet. He gave up, and unknown to Nelson, he and the remains of his squadron returned to Toulon.

Nelson, meanwhile, combed the Mediterranean from end to end for Villeneuve. It was not until February 19 that he learned that Villeneuve was back in port. "Those gentlemen are not accustomed to a Gulf of Lyons gale," he wrote, "which we have buffeted for twenty-one months, and not carried away a spar."

As for Napoleon, he was furious at Villeneuve's failure. "What is to be done with admirals who allow their spirits to sink and resolve to be beaten home at the first damage they suffer?" he asked.

AT THE PALAIS des Tuileries in early 1805, most of the outward signs of the Revolution had gone. In place of boots, men wore stockings and buckled shoes; elaborately wrought ceremonial swords replaced clumsy sabres. Men addressed each other as *monsieur* instead of *citoyen*. But if the Tuileries was a place where Napoleon lived in great splendour, it was also the place where he worked hard. Two or three secretaries were always at hand in his study, pens ready to fly across paper, as their master dictated letters to kings and princes, orders to his generals and admirals, plans for new conquests. Maps and army and navy reports were kept handy for instant reference. Each day he was up by seven in the morning, reading his own correspondence—and that of several other select people whose mail had been intercepted by his postmaster general. While he dressed, a secretary would read aloud from the newspapers. Breakfast, usually eaten alone and always hurriedly, followed. And then the real work of the day began.

On February 5 he cancelled orders for an anticipated campaign against Austria, a cancellation forced upon him by the Austrians' placatory reply to a provocative note he had sent in January. He began to formulate another plan.

On March 2, bathed, shaved and breakfasted, with his secretaries before him in the study, the Emperor began dictating some of the most fantastic orders he had ever given. His first move was to send new orders to Admiral Missiessy, instructing him to wait in the West Indies until June. His next was to order Vice Admiral Honoré Ganteaume to take his twenty-one battleships out of the Channel port of Brest and sail for El Ferrol, on Spain's Atlantic coast, where he was to beat off the blockading British and fetch out Rear Admiral Gourdon's four battleships and the Spanish squadron. He was then to sail across the Atlantic to the French island of Martinique, where he would find Villeneuve and Missiessy. Corresponding orders were drawn up for Villeneuve—he was to sail to the Spanish port of Cádiz, pick up a French 74-gun ship and the Spanish admiral Federico Carlos de Gravina with as many of his fifteen battleships as were ready, then sail direct to the West Indies to join Missiessy and wait for Ganteaume. Once at Martinique, the total force of over forty French battleships, plus the Spanish squadron, was to return to Europe as a single fleet, destroy the British ships off Ushant, at the western approach to the English Channel, then sail to Boulogne, where Napoleon's invasion force was poised.

This was Napopeon's great plan, yet seldom had an operation been planned with so little regard for what the enemy might do. His fleets would first have to fight their way out of port. Then there would be three separate groups of French ships crossing the Atlantic to the West Indies, plus a minimum wait of a month while the fleets concentrated; and Napoleon assumed that the British would not attack even one of them.

THE EMPEROR'S BRAVE new plan soon started to go adrift. At Brest, Ganteaume set to work getting his ships manned, and by March 24 he was ready to sail. There was only one snag. Seventeen British battleships were waiting for him outside the harbour. What should he do? "Go out without fighting," Napoleon ordered. Three days later Ganteaume made a halfhearted attempt to *"Sortez sans combat,"* but the British battleships soon persuaded him to return, and by March 29 his ships were once more safely moored up in harbour.

On March 30, Villeneuve made his second attempt to leave Toulon with his eleven battleships, some frigates and two brigs. Two British frigates kept watch, but Nelson was not in sight, for he wanted to destroy the squadron, not frighten it into staying in port.

The British frigates shadowed Villeneuve for a short time and then went off to report to Nelson that the French fleet was sailing south. Nelson was confident that Villeneuve would head for Egypt. But Villeneuve, having learned that Nelson was south of Sardinia, had altered course and headed direct for the Strait of Gibraltar. He passed through the strait April 9, picked up Admiral Gravina and six Spanish ships of the line that had evaded the blockade and soon was heading southwest for the West Indies.

When the news reached Nelson, he was sailing west from Sicily, a sad and bitter man. Because of strong headwinds, it was May 4 before he arrived at Gibraltar. Provisioning and refitting took another six days, and on May 11, Nelson's ten battleships and three frigates weighed anchor and set sail in pursuit. The chase was on, but Villeneuve had a full month's start.

Villeneuve arrived in Martinique on May 16 and settled down to wait for the others. Ganteaume, of course, was bottled up in Brest, and Missiessy, having missed the latest instructions from France, was on his way back to Europe. But Rear Admiral Charles Magon arrived from Rochefort on June 4 with two battleships, bringing Villeneuve's Combined Fleet up to twenty ships of the line. On that day, however, another fleet appeared in the West Indies, and shortly afterwards Villeneuve heard the dreadful news: Nelson had arrived, like an avenging angel, "with twelve or fourteen of the line."

"In this dilemma," Villeneuve wrote, "I found [Admiral Gravina] fully agreed as to the necessity of immediately making our way back." And on June 11, a week after Nelson's arrival, Villeneuve and his Combined Fleet were heading eastward to attempt the ordered rendezvous at the Spanish port of El Ferrol, before proceeding up the Channel to join Napoleon at Boulogne.

In the meantime, Nelson had searched for the French fleet to the south. But on June 13 he guessed that they had turned back towards Europe, and he sailed in pursuit. He knew that he was close behind the Combined Fleet; the gap of thirty-two days between them had in fact been reduced to two days. But once again he was to be unlucky. Though he crossed Villeneuve's tracks one night, for the rest of the voyage the Combined Fleet was to the north of him.

SAILING BACK ACROSS THE ATLANTIC, Nelson prayed that he would catch up with Villeneuve. Nearly a month later, with the African shore close by, he wrote in his private diary: "No French fleet, nor any information about them—how sorrowful this makes me...." After finally anchoring at Gibraltar on July 19, where he went ashore for the first time in nearly two years, he learned of the Combined Fleet's northerly course.

He immediately set sail—running into strong head winds—to join

View of Merton Place, Surrey

the Brest fleet off Ushant. But Nelson was too late: by the time he reached Admiral Cornwallis's force there, Villeneuve was already safe in Vigo. Worn out, and with an ever-increasing sense of failure weighing him down, Nelson left his ships under Cornwallis's command and sailed for Portsmouth in the *Victory*.

CHAPTER 3

THE WIND WAS VERY light, and with irritating slowness the *Victory* worked her way up the Channel on August 17. It was dark by the time she nosed past St. Catherine's Point and then anchored off Dunnose Head.

When Nelson's barge reached shore the next day, a large crowd had gathered to cheer him, and rain was pouring down. He finally climbed into a carriage for the wearisome journey up the London road. By dawn the following day, he had his first sight for many months of the lush green fields of England, and at six a.m. he reached Merton Place, where his beloved Emma was waiting for him.

Merton was a red brick, two-storey house, a home at long last befitting his position. A tributary of the river Wandle—Lady Hamilton called it "the Nile"—passed through the grounds, and a previous owner had built an elaborate Italian-style bridge across it. Many strange trees

Lady Hamilton

Horatia Nelson

grew around the house, and Virginia creeper climbed over the porch. And now his dreams had come true—he was back again, with Emma to welcome him. Soon they were laughing with their daughter, Horatia, now four and a half.

The next three weeks were perhaps the happiest of Nelson's life. He loved a woman deeply and was deeply loved in return, and the fact that the woman was not his wife did not damage that love. Horatia had been born and successfully passed off as his adopted daughter. He knew, moreover, that he had the love and respect of his captains, and his circle of friends was a large one.

He was also to be kept busy discussing high policy with the nation's leaders, knowing his opinion was wanted and listened to with great interest. And yet is is unlikely that Nelson was looking forward to his first meeting with Lord Barham. The first lord was almost a complete stranger, and there is no doubt that he was, not unreasonably, suspicious of the vain and colourful young admiral. Had Nelson's conduct in his long and fruitless chase of Villeneuve been all that it should have been? Could he be trusted again with command in the Mediterranean during the extremely critical days ahead?

Barham was determined not to let Nelson's previous victories at the Nile and Copenhagen blind him to possible errors of judgment. In fact, Nelson had been greeted on arriving in England with a request that he forward journals for the first lord's inspection. He apparently read into the request a possible criticism of his conduct, for he replied to Secretary William Marsden: "I beg leave to acquaint you that never having been called upon . . . to furnish their Lordships with a journal of my proceedings, none has been kept for that purpose, except for different periods the fleet under my command was in pursuit of the enemy . . . which I herewith transmit for the information of the Lords Commissioners of the Admiralty."

The happy result is reported by Nelson's biographers. "Lord Barham afterwards liberally declared he had not before sufficiently appreciated [the admiral's] extraordinary talents. This opinion . . . was immediately communicated to the Cabinet, with an assurance from Lord Barham that unbounded confidence ought to be placed in Nelson. . . ." Every door in Whitehall was opened to him. He saw Prime Minister Pitt and the war secretary, Lord Castlereagh, almost immediately, and later reported to his friend and favourite captain, Sir Richard Keats, that "as I am now set up for a *Conjuror*, and God knows they will very soon find out I am far from being one, I was asked my opinion, against my inclination, for if I make one wrong guess the charm will be broken."

The discussions during the next few days covered a wide range of subjects, for Nelson's knowledge of the Mediterranean in general and the kingdom of Naples in particular was invaluable. But he had other calls to make and people to see. One visit was to a Mr. Peddison, an upholsterer off Regent Street, who had in his care Nelson's coffin. This was a gift from Captain Benjamin Hallowell, who was a devoted friend of Nelson's. Hallowell had commanded the *Swiftsure* at the battle of the Nile, where part of the French *L'Orient*'s mainmast was brought on board after the ship itself blew up. Hallowell ordered a coffin to be made from it. He then sent it to Nelson with a covering letter:

My Lord, Herewith I send you a coffin made of part of the *L'Orient*'s mainmast, that when you are tired of this life you may be buried in one of your own trophies—but may that period be far distant, is the sincere wish of your obedient and much obliged servant, Ben Hallowell.

Nelson was delighted. Far from being disturbed by a constant reminder of his mortality, he had the coffin placed upright against the bulkhead of his cabin. It was finally removed after "the entreaties of an old servant," and ended up in Mr. Peddison's care until its owner was ready for it. Now Nelson went to inspect the upholstery, "for," he told Mr. Peddison, "I think it highly probable that I may want it on my return."

Among his many visits, he found time to entertain a Danish author, Andreas Andersen Feldborg, an erudite man who had published a slim book on the battle of Copenhagen and had sent a presentation copy to the victor. Nelson invited him to call at Merton, and Feldborg's description of his visit offers a glimpse of Nelson at the height of his power.

Merton Place is not a large, but a very elegant structure; in the balconies I observed a great number of ladies, who I understood to be Lord Nelson's relations. Entering the house . . . I was ushered into a magnificent apartment, where Lady Hamilton sat at the window; I at first scarcely observed his Lordship, he having placed himself immediately at the entrance on the right. The Admiral wore a uniform emblazoned with different orders of knighthood; he received me with the utmost [kindliness].

As frequently as he was able, the Dane closely observed the man who, on the eve of Good Friday four years earlier, had sailed past Kronborg Castle to attack nineteen ships and floating batteries off Copenhagen in a battle which broke up one of Napoleon's most cherished ambitions—a northern coalition against Britain. Feldborg wrote:

Lord Nelson was in his person of a middle stature, a thin body, and an apparently delicate constitution. The lines of his face were hard; but the penetration of his eye threw a kind of light on his countenance which tempered its severity, and rendered his harsh features in some measure agreeable. His luxuriant hair flowed in graceful ringlets down his temples, and his aspect commanded the utmost veneration, especially when he looked upward. Lord Nelson had not the least pride of rank; but combined with that degree of dignity, which a man of quality should have, the most engaging address in his air and manners.

In the evenings Nelson found time for entertainment. The vivacious Lady Bessborough reported the gossip from one dinner table:

Bess and Ca din'd at Crawford's Tuesday to meet him. Both she and he say that so far from appearing vain and full of himself, as one has always heard, he was perfectly unassuming and natural. Talking of . . . his having been mobbed and huzza'd in the City, Lady Hamilton wanted him to give an account of it, but he stopped her: "Why," she said, "you like to be applauded—you cannot deny it." "I own it," he answered, "popular applause is very acceptable and grateful to me, but no man ought to be too much elated by it; it is too precarious to be depended upon, and as it may be my turn to feel the tide set as strong against me as ever it did for me."

Later, Lady Bessborough wrote: "Lady Hamilton [says] that if she could be Lord Nelson's wife for one hour she should die contented, and that he always invokes her in his prayers before action, and during the battle cries out very often, 'For Emma and England'."

When Captain Keats arrived at Merton Place, he and Nelson walked through the grounds together, talking cheerfully as they skirted "the Nile", with its ornate bridge. The two old friends were soon speaking of naval battles. "No day can be long enough to arrange a couple of fleets, and fight a decisive battle, according to the old system," Nelson said, referring to the traditional way of drawing up fleets into long parallel lines. "When *we* meet the enemy, for meet them we shall, I shall form the fleet into three lines and attack at right angles. . . . It will confound and surprise the enemy. They won't know what I am about. It will bring forward a pell-mell battle, and that is what I want." Thus it appears that Richard Keats, although he was destined to miss the battle, was the first to have heard of Nelson's revolutionary plan of attack.

THE NOISE OF A POST CHAISE clattering up the drive at five o'clock in the morning on Monday, September 2, warned Nelson that either urgent orders were coming from the Admiralty or an important and unexpected visitor was arriving at Merton. It turned out to be Captain Henry Blackwood of the *Euryalus*, at thirty-five years of age one of the greatest frigate captains in the Royal Navy.

As Blackwood gripped Nelson's left hand in greeting, the admiral exclaimed, "I am sure you bring me news of the French and Spanish fleets, and I think I shall yet have to beat them!"

And that was, indeed, why Blackwood had called. Searching for the Combined Fleet, which had again put to sea, he had found it off Cape St. Vincent and shadowed it. He had been chased but held on until he was sure it had gone into Cádiz. Then Blackwood hurried north to raise the alarm.

Once Blackwood's brief message had been delivered and the post chaise had started off again for the Admiralty, Nelson had to break to Emma the news which she had been dreading to hear yet knew must arrive. Whatever her reply, Nelson's response is on record: "Brave Emma! Good Emma!" he said. "If there were more Emmas there would be more Nelsons."

"I am again heartbroken," Emma wrote two days later, "as our dear Nelson is immediately going. It seems as though I have had a fortnight's dream, and am awoke to all the misery of this cruel separation. But what can I do? His powerful arm is of so much consequence to his country."

Lord Barham was in his little office at the Admiralty when Nelson arrived later that morning. The old first lord and the young admiral sat down to discuss plans upon which, quite simply, the whole safety and future of Britain depended, plans which would affect the future of the world for more than a century.

The precise problem facing them was how to deal with the new situation brought about by Villeneuve's move to Cádiz with a total of thirty-three battleships, while Admiral Allemand, who had succeeded Missiessy, was at sea with four more and Ganteaume lay in Brest with twenty-one. With Nelson resuming his role of commander in chief in the Mediterranean, which would include the Cádiz area, he had two bare alternatives—to blockade the Combined Fleet in Cádiz throughout the coming winter or to lure Villeneuve to sail, and then fight a completely decisive action, in order to put an end once and for all to Napoleon's threats at sea.

But how was he to get Villeneuve out of Cádiz? Ironically enough, the very weakness of the British fleet there might give the French admiral enough courage to sail, even if it might also prevent Nelson from delivering a decisive blow. To offset this weakness, Barham would send out every ship he could repair or refit to join Nelson's force at Cádiz.

Once again Barham showed his admiration for Nelson's leadership. He gave him the latest edition of the *List of the Navy* and told him to choose the officers he wanted. Nelson handed it back. "Choose yourself, my Lord, the same spirit actuates the whole profession; you cannot choose wrong."

Although Nelson had gallantly refused Barham's offer to choose his own captains, undoubtedly he did name a few. One was Captain Sir Edward Berry, a fearless fighter who was never happier than when leading hand-to-hand fighting across the decks of an enemy ship. Nelson was able to give him command of the *Agamemnon*, which was considered by the French admiral Allemand to be "England's fastest ship". Orders to place themselves under Nelson's command also went out to Henry Blackwood, commanding the *Euryalus*, to Richard Keats and his *Superb* and to the faithful Thomas Hardy in the *Victory*, among many others.

The remaining days that Nelson spent in England were busy with preparations. On September 5 his steward and valet left Merton for Portsmouth and the *Victory* with Nelson's heavy baggage. On Saturday a letter arrived from Marsden, saying that Nelson's orders were ready and asking him to call at the Admiralty to collect them. The admiral went straightaway, to find that the first lord had given him a free hand for all intents and purposes. While at the Admiralty, Nelson wrote a short note to reassure Collingwood. "My dear Coll," he said, "I shall be with you in a very few days, and I hope you will remain second-in-command. You will change the *Dreadnought* for *Royal Sovereign*, which I hope you will like."

The following Thursday, Nelson went to say his official farewells to Pitt and Castlereagh, after which he left for Merton, where dinner guests were waiting for him, among them Lord Minto, who thoroughly disliked Lady Hamilton. When she finally came into the room, eyes puffed and red from crying, Lord Minto had an uneasy feeling that it was to be a strained and uncomfortable evening. Sitting at the place of honour beside her, he was shocked to find that "she could not eat, and hardly drink, and near swooning, and all at table." This was a somewhat arid judgment on Nelson's mistress. It is clear that Nelson felt that he would die in the inevitable battle ahead, and however much he tried, it is doubtful that he could hide this premonition from Emma. Nor did she have the comfort of being Nelson's wife, and to someone of Emma's background (she was reputed to have become the aged Sir William Hamilton's wife after being cast off as a mistress by his nephew) this would be of great importance. The dinner guests departed early.

Friday, September 13—the day of his departure—dawned, and as usual Nelson was up early. In the soft sunshine of an English autumn, he took his last stroll around the grounds, seeing the house and graceful cedars, drinking in the quiet beauty of the day. Perhaps he shook off the black thoughts which were creeping into his mind like a cold evening mist.

The day was soon over. Dinner was served, and it stuck in the throats of his sister Catherine and her husband, George Matcham, for they felt helpless to alter destiny. Candles flickered as people moved about restlessly in the drawing room while they listened for the clatter of the coach that was to arrive for the admiral.

Upstairs, Nelson went quietly to the bedside of his daughter, conceived aboard the *Foudroyant* in the warm Mediterranean more than five years earlier. Resting his head in his hand, he said a quiet prayer, and tiptoed out of the room and out of Horatia's life forever. Finally, having said farewell to a distraught Emma and to his sister and brother-in-law with as much cheerfulness as he could muster, he walked to the carriage.

In the solitude of the long night spent on the Portsmouth road, Nelson had time for reflection. A prayer in his private diary, written in the upright, jerky script that he contrived with his left hand, provides a clear insight into his feelings.

At half past ten, drove from dear, dear Merton, where I left all which I hold dear in this world, to go to serve my King and country. May the Great God whom I adore, enable me to fulfil the expectations of my country; and if it is His good pleasure that I should return, my thanks will never cease being offered up to the throne of His Mercy. If it is His good Providence to cut short my days upon earth, I bow with the greatest submission, relying that He will protect those so dear to me, that I may leave behind. His will be done. Amen. Amen. Amen.

At six o'clock next morning the carriage arrived at the George Inn, Portsmouth. Nelson, tired and stiff, went in to find his friend George Rose, George Canning—a friend of Pitt's—and Captain Hardy. As he left the inn for his last brief walk on English soil, the people of Portsmouth gathered around him. Some cheered; others knelt in the dirty street and clasped their hands in prayer as he passed; many more stood unashamedly weeping.

Finally, Nelson reached the sea, where his barge waited at the bottom of the steps to the landing stage. As soon as he was seated, the coxswain gave the order, "Shove off," and within a few moments the crew were pulling at their oars, keeping perfect time, and the crowd redoubled its cheering. Nelson raised his hat, and turning to Hardy, said, "I had their huzzas before—I have their hearts now."

Soon his barge was alongside the *Victory*, anchored off St. Helens, and his flag—white, with a red Saint George's cross—was hoisted once again. Rose and Canning had dinner with Nelson while the *Victory* prepared to sail.

Next morning her log reported with stark brevity the beginning of Nelson's last voyage: "Sunday 15th. 8 a.m. weighed and made sail to the S.S.E. *Euryalus* in company."

The wind was foul, however, and by next day the two ships had got only as far west as Portland. On Tuesday, Nelson wrote to Emma:

> I intreat, my dear Emma, that you will cheer up; and we will look forward to many, many happy years, and be surrounded by our children's children. God Almighty can, when he pleases, remove the impediment. My heart and soul is with you and Horatia.

On Thursday the *Victory*, with the *Euryalus, Ajax* and *Thunderer* in company, took her departure from Lizard Point, following in the wake of Sir Francis Drake, when he went off to "Singe the King of Spain's beard" at Cádiz in 1587; of the gallant Sir Richard Grenville, who sailed in the *Revenge* to meet a brave death "at Flores, in the Azores", and of Sir Walter Raleigh, who went to find El Dorado. So Nelson sailed to meet his destiny with open arms but with occasional half-ashamed backward glances. He seemed to know that in this last and greatest battle he would be the victor, but also the victim.

CHAPTER 4

ADMIRAL VILLENEUVE HAD worked swiftly at Vigo, and after warning Rear Admiral Gourdon at El Ferrol to make ready to join the Combined Fleet, he sailed again. But when he arrived at the entrance to the Spanish port, a boat came alongside with orders from Napoleon prohibiting him from putting into El Ferrol. Instead, he was, with the Rochefort and Brest squadrons, to "make himself master of the Strait of Dover, were it only for four or five days". However, in a covering letter the minister of marine, Admiral Decrès, had added an important point. The Emperor had anticipated that in certain circumstances "the situation of the Fleet would not allow of our carrying out his designs . . . and in this case alone the Emperor desires to assemble an imposing array of forces in Cadiz."

Villeneuve took up his pen and dispatched a tale of woe to Decrès. Had he made a fast Atlantic crossing and joined with Ganteaume at Brest, "I should be the foremost man in France," he said. "Well, all this should have happened—but . . . two gales damaged us because we have bad sails, bad rigging, bad officers and bad seamen. The enemy had been warned, they have been reinforced."

On August 13 the Combined Fleet of twenty-nine battleships (eighteen French and eleven Spanish) finally sailed westward from El Ferrol. That evening, according to Villeneuve, some battleships were sighted, followed next day by a report of fourteen more, then eight others.

Ironically enough, it is now known that the only battleships in the area were those of Allemand, who was waiting to rendezvous with the Combined Fleet off El Ferrol and to whom Villeneuve had sent the frigate *Didon* with dispatches and orders.

The next evening one of Villeneuve's frigates reported sighting a ship with another in tow. Villeneuve did nothing about identifying them, but they were in fact the British *Phoenix*, towing the *Didon*, which she had captured after a bitter fight. Without the *Didon*'s dispatches from Villeneuve, Allemand was without information or new orders. Thus his squadron and the Combined Fleet were destined never to meet.

Another British ship, Captain Griffith's *Dragon*, also played a part in deciding Villeneuve's destiny. Griffith had boarded a Danish merchantman and had said, quite casually, that his ship was part of a

Captain Sir Thomas Hardy

fleet of twenty-five British battleships. Later on, a French frigate commander boarded the Danish merchantman and asked if the Danes had seen any British ship. Indeed they had, the Danes told the Frenchman, reporting Griffith's visit and "intelligence".

This news was hurriedly relayed to Villeneuve, who immediately assumed that Captain Griffith's imaginary fleet had been sent out to chase him. He continued steering towards the intended rendezvous with Ganteaume and Allemand at Brest, but that same evening, August 15, he made his great decision. He based it on two factors—the battleships which he had sighted but had failed to identify and the threat of Captain Griffith's twenty-five-ship fleet. As night fell, a signal from Villeneuve's flagship, the *Bucentaure*, turned the Combined Fleet southward for Cádiz.

Napoleon had been waiting at Boulogne since August 2, impatiently riding up and down the beach on his famous horse, Marengo. Events were moving fast. Along the French coast facing England, his great army was waiting. Yet while Napoleon and his lookouts watched the Channel for the squadrons of Villeneuve, Ganteaume and Allemand to come sailing up, the new coalition between England, Russia and Austria was growing stronger. Suddenly, Napoleon was beginning to have to face both ways—eastward to Austria and Russia and westward to Britain.

Where was Villeneuve? For several days the Emperor ranted and raged; then on August 22 he heard that Villeneuve and the Combined Fleet had been at sea for more than a week. The fact that he had not yet appeared off Brest, explained Decrès, was because the wind was foul. However, Napoleon was not convinced, and gave instructions in case Villeneuve had gone to Cádiz. He was to reinforce his Combined Fleet with the six battleships there, then "proceed up to the Channel". This brought an agonized wail from Decrès, who

The *Victory*, Nelson's flagship, at anchor in right foreground, with other ships of the fleet

believed that if Villeneuve had gone to Cádiz, the great invasion scheme should be abandoned. "I implore you on no account to order it to come round from Cádiz to the Channel," he wrote to Napoleon, "because if the attempt is made at this moment it will only be attended with misfortune."

By now Napoleon apparently had no further patience to waste on Villeneuve. The day after Decrès made his plea, the Emperor wrote to his foreign minister, the lame and brilliant aristocrat, Talleyrand, a man as cultured as he was rakish, that by the following April he would find himself in a critical situation, surrounded by Russians, Englishmen and Austrians. "My decision is made." His army of England, camped on the cliffs before him, was to break camp and march swiftly and secretly across Europe to deal the impertinent Austrians a crushing blow before they realized what was happening.

Yet Napoleon did not entirely wash his hands of Villeneuve. "If he follows his instructions," he continued, "joins the Brest squadron, and enters the Channel, there is still time; I am master of England."

On September 2, the same day Blackwood arrived in England with the news that Villeneuve had reached Cádiz, Napoleon left the seashore, that now mocked him, for Paris. For two days the Emperor was silent on the subject of Villeneuve. Then he wrote to Decrès:

> Admiral Villeneuve has filled the cup to overflowing.... It is treason beyond all doubt.... Villeneuve is a scoundrel who must be dismissed from the service in disgrace ... he would sacrifice everything to save his own skin.

On September 14, the same day Nelson boarded the *Victory* to sail for Cádiz, Napoleon drew up new orders for the Combined Fleet. They were based on the fear of a joint British-Russian operation in southern Italy, which he saw as an attack on his "soft under-belly" and a threat to his Austrian campaign. To crush it he ordered the fleet to sail around Gibraltar into the Mediterranean. Villeneuve was to go to Naples, land the troops he had on board, then take the fleet back to Toulon. Napoleon thus proposed to use the major part of his available fleet— some thirty-three battleships—to carry out a comparatively unimportant landing of four thousand troops.

Decrès forwarded the Emperor's orders to Villeneuve with a covering letter which contained this strong hint: "I cannot too highly recommend you, M. *L'Amiral*, to seize the first favourable opportunity to effect your departure; and I repeat my most earnest wishes for your success." He did not tell Villeneuve the vital news that Napoleon already had decided to sack him and place Admiral Rosily in command of the Combined Fleet. In fact, the letter relieving Villeneuve of command and ordering him to Paris "to give an account of the campaign on which you have been recently employed" was given to Rosily to deliver personally, even though he was not leaving until September 24. But rumours that he was to be replaced reached Villeneuve through unofficial channels, and they drove him to such a desperate act that Napoleon's letter never reached him.

In Paris the Emperor had packed his bags and left for Austria. By transferring his Grand Army secretly from the Channel to the Danube, he had the chance to fling two hundred thousand highly trained veterans against seventy thousand Austrian troops officered by elegant but inefficient amateurs. On October 7, Napoleon struck his blow. By the seventeenth the Austrian general Mack was surrounded at Ulm. By the twentieth the Austrians had surrendered.

IN THE GREAT Spanish port of Cádiz, meanwhile, the Combined Fleet was in a poor state. "My lord," Villeneuve had written to Decrès, "...the lack of funds, the poverty of the port, the great requirements of the ships, and those of the crews, increase in proportion to the time passing and to the season that is approaching."

The lack of funds reached almost farcical proportions. Villeneuve needed cash to supply seventeen thousand men for at least fifty days, but the French agent-general in Cádiz warned him that he had no money and that his credit was exhausted. Even the inspector of artillery refused to supply any powder or shot unless it was paid for with cash. Fortunately for Villeneuve, the French ambassador in Madrid finally managed to get some financial help from a French banker.

Apart from supplying the ships with food, powder and shot, it was a massive task to get them ready for sea again. The frigates were all short of sails; one battleship needed a new main yard, another had lost part of her rudder, a third had a broken bowsprit, and a fourth had crumpled her sternworks in a collision. The ships' crews, too, were decimated by illness, and hundreds of seamen had deserted. Altogether Villeneuve was short of more than two thousand men.

The Spaniards were in no better condition. One of Gravina's battleships had been left behind in El Ferrol, and three more at Vigo. There should have been six fresh battleships waiting for him at Cádiz, but in fact there were only two. In addition, the Spanish navy had great difficulty in manning their ships. Reporting to Decrès on the Spanish squadron, Villeneuve said, "It is very distressing to see such fine and powerful ships manned with herdsmen and beggars."

WHEN NAPOLEON'S ORDERS to sail for Naples finally arrived in Cádiz on September 27, the French and Spanish admirals received them without fuss. Villeneuve reported that "the captains in command will realize from the position and strength of the enemy before this port that an engagement must take place the very same day that the Fleet puts to sea." Then with a sudden burst of confidence, he added:

"The Fleet will see with satisfaction the opportunity that is offered to . . . revenge the insults offered to its Flag, and lay low the tyrannical domination of the English upon the seas. Our Allies will fight at our side, under the walls of Cadiz and in sight of their fellow citizens; the Emperor's gaze is fixed upon us."

But the news he sent to Decrès some hours later must have tempered his earlier elation. "I have just been informed that the enemy squadron has just been joined by three sail of the line . . . coming from the west. There are now thirty-one line-of-battle ships well known to be in these waters." The three ships were the *Ajax, Thunderer* and *Victory*.

September 28 brought a fresh northwesterly breeze in the morning, and the *Victory*, with the *Ajax* and *Thunderer* in company, ran before it across the Bay of Cádiz. The effect on the fleet of Nelson's arrival was instantaneous. Captain Sir Edward Codrington, of the *Orion*, wrote to his wife: "Lord Nelson is arrived. A sort of general joy has been the consequence, and many good effects will shortly arise from our change of system."

The next day was Nelson's forty-seventh birthday, an appropriate day to take command of the fleet. And one of Nelson's first visitors was his old friend Vice Admiral Cuthbert Collingwood. These two very different men had served together for many years, Collingwood following in Nelson's footsteps, taking over Nelson's command and rank as Nelson rose from lieutenant to commander to post captain to admiral. And so it was to be at Trafalgar.

Collingwood was fifty-five, of medium height, thin, with a small head and a round face. In a crowd he would pass without notice but for his penetrating blue eyes and his thin lips, which betrayed a firm and unruffled character. He had gone to sea at eleven and at twenty-four had led a party of seamen at Bunker Hill. By now a weary man, his thoughts were constantly turning to his native Northumberland, where his wife, Sarah, had waited so long for his return. He had married her fifteen years earlier, and they had had two daughters, yet most of his married life had been spent at sea. A week before Nelson's arrival he had written: "How happy I should be, could I but hear from home, and know how my dear girls are going on! I am fully determined, if I can get home and manage it properly, to go on shore next spring for the rest of my life; for I am very weary."

Although he was not to die until five years after Trafalgar, Collingwood was doomed never to see England or his family again. Succeeding to the command of the Mediterranean fleet on Nelson's death, he was left at sea despite his protestations. The year after Trafalgar he wrote: "Fame's trumpet makes a great noise, but the notes do not dwell long on the ear."

AFTER MEETING COLLINGWOOD and receiving from him the various un-executed Admiralty orders, Nelson proposed changing the whole system of blockade. By shifting his fleet over the horizon, he would take it out of the sight of the telescopes of French and Spanish lookouts ashore and perhaps lure Villeneuve out of Cádiz.

By staying fifty miles to the west in the Gulf of Cádiz, he could watch over the Combined Fleet whether it went northwest towards the Channel, south to Gibraltar or west into the broad Atlantic. More important, he would be sufficiently far offshore that a westerly gale would not force his square-riggers to run before it through the Strait of Gibraltar and into the Mediterranean, leaving the Combined Fleet free to bolt before he could get back on station again.

On this day nearly all his captains, wearing their best uniforms, with swords at their sides, left their ships and were rowed across to the *Victory* to meet their new commander in chief. It might be thought that most of these men were simply renewing their acquaintanceship with Nelson. But of the twenty-seven British battleships which were to fight at Trafalgar, only five belonged to Nelson's own Mediterranean fleet and only eight of the twenty-seven captains had previously served with him. Thus Nelson had quickly to get to know them, gain their confidence and train them as a fleet.

One by one the captains clambered up the *Victory*'s towering sides and, turning aft, walked a few feet to the ladder leading to the upper deck and Nelson's quarters. His day cabin ran the width of the stern. Its deck was covered in canvas painted with a black-and-white chessboard pattern. A large table dominated the cabin; several armchairs were scattered about, among them a particularly deep one, leather-covered, which was Nelson's favourite. Incongruous among the finely carved pieces of furniture and the paintings on the bulkheads (among them one of Horatia) were two 12-pounder cannons mounted on carriages, one on each side of the cabin. The sun, sparkling on the sea under the *Victory*'s massively ornate stern, reflected up through the windows to make dancing patterns on the white deckhead.

One by one the officers strode into the cabin to greet Nelson and wish him a happy birthday. Very soon it was echoing to the sound of their voices, and the talk was young men's talk, for few of them had reached their mid-forties. Nelson was well pleased with the way he was received. "The officers who came on board to welcome my return forgot my rank as Commander-in-Chief in the enthusiasm with which they greeted me," he wrote later. "As soon as these emotions were past I laid before them the plan I had previously arranged for attacking the enemy; and it was not only my pleasure to find it generally approved, but clearly perceived and understood." And to Lady Hamilton he described it more jubilantly: "When I came to explain to them the *Nelson Touch* it was like an electric shock. Some shed tears, all approved—'It was new—it was singular—it was simple!' and, from Admirals downwards, it was repeated— 'It must succeed if ever they will allow us to get at them!'"

Vice Admiral Cuthbert Collingwood

Next day, Monday, presented several new and varied difficulties for the attention of the commander in chief. Foremost among these was the problem of Vice Admiral Sir Robert Calder, who was writing to the Admiralty demanding an inquiry into his conduct against Villeneuve's fleet off Cape Finisterre. He had just "learnt with astonishment . . . that there has been a most unjust and wicked endeavour to prejudice the public mind against me as an officer." His decision to ask for an inquiry seems to have been based on a talk with Collingwood and Nelson. Now he was asking that Captains William Brown, William Lechmere and Philip Durham, who were with him in the action, be allowed to return home with him as witnesses, though Durham had in fact not yet joined the fleet.

Nelson was touched by Calder's anguish and reported to Lord Barham: "It will give your Lordship pleasure to find, as it has me, that an inquiry is what the Vice-Admiral wishes." He then went on to explain that he could not insist on Calder's leaving his *Prince of Wales* for a smaller ship for the voyage home. Although he could ill afford the loss of such a powerful 90-gun ship, "I trust that I shall be considered to have done right as a man, and to a brother officer in affliction—my heart could not stand it, and so the thing must rest."

Tuesday, October 1, found the crews of most of the ships in the British fleet hard at work with scrapers, paintpots and brushes. The

Nelson's cabin in the *Victory*

Victory's hull was painted in the Nelson style—in black with three horizontal yellow bands. Each yellow band was at the same level as a tier of gunports, but since the port lids were painted black on the outside, when they were closed the lids gave a chessboard effect. This looked smart and impressive and, what was more important, it was the Nelson style. Individual captains were quick to emulate it, although many of them probably had to foot the paint bill themselves.

Nelson himself, lying in his cot in the *Victory*, was weak and weary after a "dreadful spasm" during the night, but he got up early as usual to attend to the day's business. He was worried about his fleet's supply situation. It needed more than eight hundred bullocks, plus a transport laden with wine and water each month; so he must arrange regular convoys to Gibraltar and Tetuán, on the African coast.

Captain Blackwood, in the frigate *Euryalus*, watching along with the *Hydra* every movement of the Combined Fleet from close in to Cádiz, was warned by Nelson of "the importance of not letting these rogues escape us without a fair fight, which I pant for by day, and dream of by night." A string of additional ships was needed to stretch from the lookout frigates across the fifty-odd miles to the west where the fleet waited, so that as soon as the *Euryalus* ran up a flag signal, it could be repeated from ship to ship until it reached the *Victory*. To provide this link Nelson required at least three more ships. He had already appealed to the Admiralty for more frigates, but until they arrived he had to use battleships.

On Friday the wind went round to the east—the wind with which the Combined Fleet could sail—and Nelson sent the schooner *Pickle* to help Blackwood's two frigates off Cádiz. "The French and Spanish ships have taken the troops on board," he wrote to Lord Barham, "and it is said they mean to sail the first Levant [strong easterly] wind." On Sunday the wind was still in the east, and with the Combined Fleet embarking troops, Nelson was a very anxious man. "It is . . . ." he wrote, "annihilation that the country wants, and not merely a splendid victory of twenty-three [against] thirty-six—honourable to the parties concerned, but absolutely useless in the extended scale to bring Bonaparte to his marrow-bones."

On Monday the 74-gun *Defiance*, commanded by Captain Philip Durham, arrived from England to join Nelson's fleet, and the next day the *Royal Sovereign*, freshly repaired, arrived. She brought secret orders from the Admiralty, which told Nelson that in addition to dealing with the Combined Fleet of Cádiz, he was to cover a small troop convoy due to sail from Gibraltar for Italy with reinforcements for an expeditionary force under General Sir James Craig; Nelson would have to detach battleships to guard it.

Even as Nelson read his new orders, events reached a crisis aboard Villeneuve's flagship anchored in Cádiz.

ON THE DAY Captain Durham joined the British fleet, Villeneuve paced up and down on board the *Bucentaure*, a lonely man, prey to many emotions. He knew he had little or no sympathy from the Emperor. His own flag officers, Rear Admiral Magon and Rear Admiral Dumanoir, were not giving him the support he expected, and the French and Spanish captains were saying openly that they stood very little chance against the British under Nelson. Friction was growing between the French and Spanish squadrons. Stories that the French had treacherously abandoned two Spanish warships in an earlier action were spreading through Cádiz, and French sailors were being murdered in the streets.

The wind had been in the west—foul for getting the Combined Fleet out of Cádiz; but later that Monday afternoon it went round to the northeast. At last they could leave. Villeneuve made his decision, and within a few minutes the signal for the Combined Fleet to put to sea was run up aboard the *Bucentaure*. At once there was a great deal of bustle aboard all the ships. Then more flag hoists were run up from the *Bucentaure*; the order was cancelled. The fleet would not sail after all.

Next day Villeneuve wrote his excuses in a letter to Decrès. A gale had blown up, he wrote, and the very wind which would take him out of Cádiz also threatened to prevent his getting through the Strait of Gibraltar to Naples. As if that were not enough, Villeneuve added another reason for not sailing: "I could not turn a deaf ear to the observations which reached me from every side, as to the inferiority of our force in comparison with that of the enemy . . . to put to sea in such circumstances has been termed an act of despair."

So Villeneuve that Tuesday morning called a council of war of all the flag officers of the Combined Fleet and the senior captains, of whom seven were French and seven Spanish. At the head of the council was Villeneuve, now aged forty-one, who had fought at the Nile and was later to be described by Admiral Collingwood as "a well-bred man, and I believe, a good officer: he has nothing in his manners of the offensive vapouring and boasting which we, perhaps too often, attribute to Frenchmen." A thousand years before, one of Villeneuve's ancestors had fallen at the side of Roland in the Pass of Roncesvalles; another had charged beside Richard Coeur de Lion in the Holy Land. The admiral himself was a Knight of Malta—the ninety-first member of the family to belong to the order—and had gone to sea when very young. He was one of the few members of the nobility who did not leave the navy at the Revolution. Like Collingwood, Villeneuve thought longingly of his wife and his home. But like Collingwood, he was never again to see his village among the pine trees in Provence.

The Spaniards were led by Don Federico Carlos de Gravina, a

grandee of old Spain, with the right to wear his hat in the presence chamber of the King. Now forty-nine, he had been at sea since he was twelve, and he was the most highly regarded officer in the Spanish navy.

Villeneuve opened the council of war by saying that the Emperor's instructions were that the Combined Fleet should weigh anchor at the first favourable opportunity. From various sources it had been discovered, however, that the British had between thirty-one and thirty-three battleships. Would everyone, Villeneuve asked, "be so good as to give his opinion upon the situation in which the Combined Fleet is placed?"

Some of the French officers declared that there was no doubt about the proposal to sail. The result would be the rout of the British and "the consequent ease" of carrying out their orders to make for Naples.

The Spanish officers, who had the advantage of having talked among themselves before boarding the *Bucentaure*, replied simply that they agreed with Rear Admiral Escaño, their chief of staff. Escaño made several comments on "the difference between the skilled seamanship of those [British] who had been at sea ... without the least intermission since 1793 and those who had spent eight years without putting to sea...." He then concluded, "Superior orders cannot bind us to attempt the impossible, as nothing would serve as an excuse in the event of a disaster, which I see to be inevitable if we weigh."

Rear Admiral Magon, an impetuous Breton, immediately leaped up, angry and red in the face, to contradict Escaño. He spoke so hotly that within a few moments there was uproar in Villeneuve's cabin. Finally, Admiral Gravina stood up and, quieting them all, requested that they vote—without any further arguing—on the question. Should or should not the Combined Fleet put to sea, considering that it had not a superiority of force to make up for its inherent inferiority? Villeneuve took a vote—and the majority verdict of the French and Spanish senior officers was that they should stay at anchor. They concluded with a sop to the Emperor: "In all these observations, the officers of the two nations composing this assembly have borne witness to the desire that they will always feel of going out to engage the enemy, whatever his force, as soon as His Majesty desires it...."

ON THE DAY OF THIS TURBULENT council of war, Nelson sat down at his desk in the great day cabin aboard the *Victory*, took up his pen and started to write laboriously with his left hand. Heading his message with the two words "Secret" and "Memorandum", he wrote:

> Thinking it almost impossible to bring a Fleet of forty Sail of the Line into a Line of Battle in variable winds thick weather and other circumstances without such a loss of time that the opportunity would probably be lost ... to make the business decisive. I have therefore made up my mind to keep the fleet ... in two Lines of Sixteen Ships each, with an advanced Squadron of Eight. ...
>
> The Second in Command will, after my intentions are made known to him, have the entire direction of His Line to make the attack upon the Enemy, and to follow up the Blow until they are Capturd or destroy'd.

Nelson was writing his famous "Nelson Touch" memorandum of October 9, 1805, which was to establish a tradition of bold tactics and a standard of bravery that have become a part of the British character.

Describing how Collingwood's division was to break through the enemy's single line of battle about the twelfth ship from the rear and his own division would break through about the centre, he emphasized that "the whole impression of the British Fleet" must be to overpower a part of the enemy line, from two or three ships ahead of their commander in chief—whom he supposed would be in the centre—to its rear. In this way the whole of the British fleet would be concentrated on half the Combined Fleet. The rest of the enemy ships would require time to regroup and join the battle.

Nelson was determined to force the enemy to fight the battle he wanted, even though he ran the risk of having his ships dismasted by enemy broadsides before they could break the line and bring their own guns to bear. "The risk he took of having the heads of his two columns ... crushed prematurely by the concentration to which he exposed them naked, almost passed the limits of sober leading," wrote the naval historian Sir Julian Corbett. Yet Nelson knew from long experience that the enemy gunnery tended to be wild—and it was. "Something must be left to chance," he wrote; "nothing is sure in a sea fight beyond all others."

More ships were now coming out to reinforce Nelson's fleet. In addition to the *Royal Sovereign*, which had joined on October 8, the *Belleisle* arrived on the tenth. Two frigates which arrived on the eleventh were sent on to Gibraltar to help escort the convoy being sent to join Craig's expeditionary force. When the *Agamemnon* was signalled on October 13, Nelson slapped his thigh and exclaimed with glee, "Here comes Berry; now we shall have a battle!"

Captain Sir Edward Berry had indeed only just avoided a battle with Allemand, who was still at sea with his battleships, a constant threat to Nelson's communications. Berry reported that he had been chased, a three-decker getting within gunshot on the weather quarter and an 80-gun ship on the lee, and had only escaped after a seventy-mile dash.

On October 14 the *Africa* joined the fleet. The little *Africa*, with sixty-four guns and a crew of only four hundred and ninety, was the smallest battleship at Trafalgar and was commanded by one of the most successful of captains. Going to sea at the age of thirteen, Henry Digby was as brave as he was successful. Despite her size, the little *Africa* was to tackle the biggest ship in the world, the 130-gun *Santissima Trinidad*, in the battle now impending.

The October days were passing quickly, with the fleet constantly taking on stores from transport ships. Nelson's plans were made; it only remained to wait patiently for the enemy to make the first move, and to hope they did so before winter gales came whirling in from the Atlantic. "Touch and Take," Nelson said, was to be his motto; but for the time being it might well have been "Watch and Wait."

Early on Saturday morning, October 19, the British fleet was sailing in two divisions, the one to windward led by Nelson, the other by Collingwood. Nelson wrote to Collingwood: "What a beautiful day! Will you be tempted out of your ship?" A boat took this letter across to the *Royal Sovereign*. While Collingwood was reading it, William Cumby, first lieutenant on the *Bellerophon*, the fourth ship in Collingwood's division, spotted the nearest lookout battleship, the *Mars*, flying a hoist of flags from her masthead. Putting his telescope to his eye, he read them—signal 370.

In the *Signal Book for the Ships of War* the meaning given number 370 is: "The Enemy's ships are coming out of port, or are getting under sail."

CHAPTER 5

VILLENEUVE WAS A man for whom the future now held little promise. On October 15 he had heard from Bayonne, on the Franco-Spanish border, that Vice Admiral Rosily had passed through on his way to Cádiz. A few hours later he learned that Rosily was in fact coming to take over command of the Combined Fleet. It was now quite clear to him that, whatever Rosily's mission, Decrès and the Emperor were deliberately keeping him in ignorance of it, and that in itself was significant.

Swiftly, and without telling anyone, Villeneuve made his plans. His orders to sail for Naples still held good, and if he carried them out before Rosily arrived, he could not be blamed—and his honour would be satisfied. His order of battle, moreover, had been distributed on October 6, before the council of war had taken place.

Villeneuve's final instructions to the Combined Fleet—his equivalent of the Nelson Touch—was an extraordinary document. It showed that he had in fact correctly penetrated Nelson's mind. "The enemy will not confine himself to forming on a line of battle parallel with our own and with engaging us in an artillery duel, in which success lies frequently with the more skilful but always with the more fortunate," Villeneuve had written. "He will endeavour to envelop our rear, to break through our line and to direct his ships in groups upon such of ours as he shall have cut off, so as to surround them and defeat them."

Villeneuve was like a mesmerized rabbit which knows it will be killed by the weasel but is powerless to move, and in place of a defensive measure, he ordered: "A captain in command must consult his own daring and love of honour far more than the signals of the Admiral, who being perhaps engaged himself and shrouded in smoke, may no longer have the power of making any." He had rounded off the instructions with some wishful thinking. "Nothing in the sight of an English Squadron should daunt us . . . they are worn out with a two years' cruise; they are not braver than we and have infinitely less feeling of enthusiasm and patriotism. . . . Everything unites to give us the firm hope of the most glorious victories and of a new era for the seamen of the Empire."

With these orders in the hands of all the French and Spanish captains, Villeneuve now planned a night attack by a squadron of seven battleships, under Admiral Magon, on the British frigates waiting outside Cádiz. With Nelson's "eyes" captured, Magon would then be able to reconnoitre to see where the British fleet was and what was its strength. Then, if Magon's report was favourable, the Combined Fleet would sail immediately. But on Friday, as the wind veered to the east, enabling Magon to sail, Villeneuve received a message that

Vice Admiral Villeneuve

His flagship, the *Bucentaure*

had been passed up the Spanish coast from one lookout post to another. The British convoy waiting at Gibraltar to reinforce Craig in Italy had at last sailed, with an escort of four battleships under Rear Admiral Thomas Louis. A fifth battleship was at Gibraltar, with her mainmast out, and a sixth was steering up the strait to anchor in the port.

Realizing that Nelson's fleet was now weakened by six battleships, Villeneuve knew he had to seize his chance. He called on Gravina and told him he had made up his mind to sail with the entire Combined Fleet the next day. Signal flags were soon fluttering at the masthead of the *Bucentaure*. Each ship was ordered to summon its crew on board, and then to hoist in their boats and to be ready to weigh anchor. But Villeneuve did not attempt to get to sea under the welcome cover of darkness.

Saturday broke with a clear sky and the wind variable, little more than a balmy breeze. Between five and six a.m. Villeneuve hoisted the signal for the ships to sail, but although some of the battleships and frigates managed to sail out or were towed out by their boats before the young flood tide became too strong, most ships of the Combined Fleet did not have enough breeze to warrant their weighing anchor. Gravina's flagship, the *Principe de Asturias*, Villeneuve's *Bucentaure* and the great 130-gun *Santissima Trinidad* stayed where they were.

By that evening only seven battleships and three frigates had managed to get out of port. Magon, in the *Algésiras*, ordered this motley squadron to form a line of battle. But by ten p.m., to Magon's annoyance, the breeze faded until his ships barely had steerageway, and in the darkness they lost each other. Two of them anchored for the rest of the night.

All this time the British ships had kept discreetly to seaward. But now, with most of his ships still at anchor in Cádiz harbour, Villeneuve knew that the alarm had been raised throughout the enemy fleet. What would Nelson do?

NELSON HAD REACTED quickly to signal 370 by ordering the fleet for a "General chase southeast," his plan being to steer immediately for the Strait of Gibraltar to cut off the Combined Fleet and prevent its sailing through into the Mediterranean.

At three p.m. Captain James Morris's *Colossus*, the ship beyond the *Mars* in the communication chain, had come hurrying up, all sails set, and firing guns to draw attention. From her mastheads flew signals reporting—inaccurately—that the enemy's fleet was at sea.

Captain Blackwood, on the *Euryalus*, in the meantime, was still watching those enemy ships that were slowly working their way out of the bay. The breeze faded, and along with the enemy ships, the *Euryalus* and *Sirius* wallowed and drifted, sails hanging limply from the yards. Blackwood took the opportunity to go down to his cabin and write a letter to his wife:

> What think you, my own dearest love? At this moment the enemy are coming out, as if determined to have a fair fight.... They have thirty-four sail of the line and five frigates. Lord Nelson has but twenty-seven sail of the line with him; the rest are at Gibraltar, getting water.

Not that he has not enough to bring them to close action; but I want him to have so many as to make this the most decisive battle that was ever fought, and which may bring us lasting peace and all its blessings.

That Saturday evening Nelson formed the advanced squadron visualized in his memorandum, by putting eight of his fastest ships under the command of Captain George Duff in the *Mars*. They were to burn lights during the night, and some of them were to keep to the eastward and maintain contact with the frigates that were shadowing the Combined Fleet.

DAWN ON SUNDAY, October 20, brought with it dull weather; thick clouds masked the sun, and what wind there was came up from the south. About six a.m. Villeneuve once again ordered the Combined Fleet to weigh anchor and make for the open sea, and by eight a.m. all the ships were under sail.

Ashore, the quays and roads overlooking the anchorage were thronged with people—many of them in tears—to bid the Combined Fleet farewell. Mothers and fathers, wives and sweethearts of the Spanish crews queued outside the Iglesia del Carmen, the old sailors' church, to be admitted in relays; at the high altar of the Oratorio de San Felipe Neri, Archbishop Utrera spent the day on his knees, pleading with his God for the safety of the great ships.

By ten a.m. the weather was rapidly worsening; the wind went round to the southwest and increased, bringing heavy seas and rain-squalls. Outside the harbour, Villeneuve ordered his fleet to shorten sail. Raw seamen, hastily trained while the ships were at anchor, were now having to scramble aloft a hundred and fifty feet above sea level, with strong winds tearing at them. Stiff canvas flogged and thrashed as they tried to tie reef points, tearing the nails from their fingers and stripping off the skin. The result was that several of the ships sagged off to leeward; and in the midst of the confusion, a man fell overboard from the *Bucentaure*, to be rescued by her next astern, the *Redoutable*.

At about noon the wind swung round to the west, and Villeneuve ordered the fleet to steer for the strait. But as he saw his half-formed fleet milling around the *Bucentaure* like a flock of startled sheep, he must have known in his heart that the dice were loaded against him.

Villeneuve had no news of Nelson's whereabouts until six o'clock that evening, when the *Achille* reported sighting eighteen ships in the distance. The French admiral promptly ordered his fleet to form a line of battle. The result was something approaching chaos. The ships could not sort themselves out before night came down. Thus it was, with his ships moving southward in a vast, uncoordinated mass, lights showing from their ports and windows, that Villeneuve spent the night. Round the fleet, hidden in the darkness, Blackwood's frigates watched.

THAT SAME SUNDAY morning the British fleet was located a dozen miles west of Cape Trafalgar and thirty miles from the Strait of Gibraltar. Nelson's earlier cheerfulness quickly disappeared. The strong winds, rough seas and heavy rain was just the kind of weather to send the Combined Fleet scurrying back to Cádiz with broken topmasts, torn sails and seasick crews.

Admiral Nelson knew that if Villeneuve had sailed on Saturday, as the *Colossus* had signalled, the Combined Fleet would now be very near, and that was quite clearly not the case. He was probably making up his mind to take the fleet back the way they had just sailed when the *Mars*, closely followed by the *Defiance, Defence* and *Phoebe*, signalled that the enemy was to the northward. Nelson gave the order for the fleet to turn around and sail back to the northwest.

In the afternoon Nelson walked restlessly up and down the windward side of the poop deck, fitting the scraps of information together in his mind like a jigsaw puzzle. Still, he had time to remember the smaller details which contribute to victory. Midshipman Richard Roberts recorded it thus: "*Victory* tellegraphed to the *Africa* to paint the hoops of her mast yellow." Nelson knew that it was a French custom to paint the mast hoops black, and in the thick smoke of battle their colour might be the only way of distinguishing a ship before pouring a broadside into her. He had already said to both Captain Hardy and the Reverend A. J. Scott that "the twenty-first of October will be our day." Now, to a group of young midshipmen standing near him, he said with a smile, "This day or tomorrow will be a fortunate one for you young men." It was a grim jest, but one they understood. Heavy casualties in the fleet, especially among the lieutenants, would mean promotion to acting rank for some fortunate midshipmen.

Nelson's night orders were: "If the enemy are standing to the southward, or towards the Strait, burn two blue lights together, every hour, in order to make the greater blaze. If the enemy are standing to the westward three guns, quick, every hour."

As Sunday drew to a close for the British fleet, the *Naiad* reported that the Combined Fleet was steering to the south. Nelson did not want to get too close, in case Villeneuve was frightened back to Cádiz. He therefore signalled the fleet to come around again and head south, putting them in a commanding position, ten miles to windward and five miles ahead of the enemy, ready to counter any move Blackwood's frigates might report. One ship missed the signal—the little *Africa*, commanded by Captain Digby—and continued sailing north.

Everything was now ready. In the *Neptune*, young Midshipman William Lovell, little guessing that one day he would become a vice admiral, was excited. "When night closed in," he wrote, "the rockets and blue lights . . . informed us that the inshore squadron still kept sight of our foes, and, like good and watchful dogs, our ships continued to send forth occasionally a growling cannon to keep us alert, and to cheer us with a hope of a glorious day on the morrow."

CHAPTER 6

ON MONDAY, OCTOBER 21, while men of many nations waited impatiently, the dawn seemed reluctant to lighten the black of night, as if unwilling to begin such a dreadful day. In the darkness the British fleet tacked around and began sailing slowly northward. Some fifteen miles inshore the Combined Fleet, on an almost opposite course, was still being dogged by Blackwood's frigates, dark phantoms which lit blue flares from time to time that bathed the French and Spanish ships in an eerie light and brought disquiet to French and Spanish hearts.

In the *Victory*, Nelson's slender body lay in the narrow cot slung from the deckhead, half hidden by the hangings which Emma had embroidered. The cot swung from side to side as the ship pitched and rolled in the heavy swell which was welling up under a calm sea.

Two decks below and farther forward, the men who were off watch slept in the fetid hold, their hammocks swinging in unison, their snores punctuating the creaking of the timbers. Whether British or foreign, press-ganged or volunteers, each man had taken the oath to serve his Sovereign Lord King George III, and they were now being borne along towards a great battle, where death waited to look them over. They had long since ceased to be masters of their fate.

DAWN BEGAN AS A small band of black on the horizon, diluted into a grey that began to spread outward and upward. British ships suddenly came to life. In his cabin, Nelson scrambled awkwardly from his cot and began to wash, while his steward, Henry Chevalier, brought him a hot drink. Gradually the fleet moved into the greyness of morning twilight. As it grew lighter, the waves seemed to grow bigger, a common optical illusion.

The first sight of the enemy was thus described by Able Seaman J. Brown, on the *Victory*: "At day light the french and Spanish fleets was like a great wood on our lee bow which cheered the hearts of every british tar in the *Victory* like lions Anxious to be at it. . . ."

Nelson, a small figure with an empty sleeve dangling from his usual threadbare frock coat, stepped on deck and surveyed the enemy ships. Although to leeward, as he intended, they were not as he had pictured, "in the line of battle ready to attack"; instead, they appeared to be in no formation at all, simply a mass of ships scurrying southward towards the strait. With only a light wind now blowing, it would be several hours before they could be brought to action.

In the meantime, he set about putting his own fleet in order. At 6:10 a.m., before the sun had risen over Cape Trafalgar to the eastward, he gave instructions to hoist the signal for the fleet to form into only two columns, thus eliminating from his original plan of attack the eight-ship advanced squadron. His ships quickly hoisted the answering pennant and prepared to get into station astern either Nelson's *Victory* or Collingwood's *Royal Sovereign*.

Nelson had two main concerns now that he had spotted his quarry. Staying to windward was the first, allowing his fleet to manoeuvre much more freely and to disguise until the last moment exactly where it would attack the enemy. The second was to cut off the Combined Fleet from their bolt-hole of Cádiz, which was still only a bare twenty-five miles away to the north. If Nelson sailed to the east-northeast, he would both stay to windward *and* cut them off, so at 6:13 a.m. a second signal was run up aboard the *Victory* to bear up and sail on an east-northeasterly course. Then, at 6:46 a.m., he ordered the fleet to steer due east. Now Nelson's column was heading towards the rear of the enemy's line, while Collingwood's, a mile away to the south, was heading for the vanguard. Although it was given five and a quarter hours before the first British shot at the enemy, this was the last manoeuvring signal Nelson had to give to the fleet as a whole, a fact that shows how well his captains knew what was expected of them in carrying out the Nelson Touch.

BETWEEN MANOEUVRES THE *Victory* hoisted the signal which the fleet had been awaiting for many weary months. It was number 13—"Prepare for battle." Immediately, "Clear for action!" was shouted from quarterdecks throughout the fleet, and bosun's mates ran to the hatchways, their pipes sounding the call like a chorus of angry birds. At once the men went to work.

In the *Victory*, parties of men were detailed to clear away the bulkheads forming the cabins. If they were hinged at the top, they were swung up horizontally and secured out of the way; if they were not, they were knocked down section by section and carried below. In this way the decks were opened up from one end of the ship to the other. A man standing at the after end of Nelson's cabin at the stern could look right through to the forward end of the fo'c'sle.

The men took the furniture from the officers' cabins and carried it carefully down four ladders to the orlop, the lowermost deck, where it was lowered into the holds. On the mess decks the tables slung up between the guns were taken down and stowed, and all wooden ladders not needed in action were unshipped and taken below, rope ladders being fitted in their place. All this was done to protect the men, not the furniture; a shot hitting a bulkhead or a piece of furniture would shatter it into scores of splinters—sharp slivers which could kill as effectively as grapeshot or musket balls.

Meanwhile, William Willmet, the *Victory*'s bosun, collected his mates to reinforce the great yards on which the sails were set, to prevent them from crashing down in the thick of battle. They also arranged the rigging so that if some was cut, the rest would take the strain of holding the masts up. Grappling irons were ranged along the bulwarks, ready to clutch an enemy ship in a lethal embrace, and axes were placed around the upper deck, where they could be snatched up by men to cut away wreckage. Splinter nets were slung between the masts.

The *Victory*'s surgeon, Dr. William Beatty, went down to the cockpit, amidships on the orlop, with the two assistant surgeons. It was a dark and cheerless place, lighted only by a few dim lanterns, and now cleared of everything except for a few tables which stood starkly in the middle of the open space, like altars. Here the wounded men would be offered up to Beatty's skill; limbs would be amputated with only a stiff tot of rum for anaesthesia and the loblolly men holding down the patient.

Forward on the same deck, men were wrestling with the massive rope anchor cables (each twenty-four inches in circumference) to make them as level a surface as possible; awnings and spare sails would then be laid out flat on top, and here wounded men would lie awaiting their turn to be treated. To avoid favouritism it was a strict rule that the wounded were attended to in the same order they were brought down to the cable tier. In practice this rule meant that many of the most badly wounded died from loss of blood before their turns came.

The gunner, William Rivers, and his mates had tasks to perform on the ship's magazines. These gunpowder lockers were located in the most carefully protected parts of the vessel. Built below the waterline, where they could be quickly flooded in case of fire, the bulkheads were lined with felt. To provide light, small rooms with glass windows were built outside the magazines, where lanterns could be placed without danger of fire. Rivers and his mates put on soft leather or felt slippers—the nails in ordinary shoes might kick up sparks—before unlocking the doors and going inside to check the charges, arranged in hundreds of flannel bags filled with gunpowder. The largest cartridges were for the thirty 32-pounders, the biggest guns in the *Victory*, which because of their weight were kept on the lower deck. With a distant charge for maximum range, they could fire a 32-pound shot more than a mile; at a range of three hundred and fifty yards, such a shot could penetrate three feet of solid oak.

In peace or war, fire was the great enemy in a wooden ship, and in action the main danger was that loose grains of gunpowder, falling along passageways or around the guns, would be ignited by a spark. To guard against this, the decks were washed down with water before the ship went into action. Now, while Rivers and his mates were making sure that there were plenty of charges ready, other men were letting down thick flannel screens with holes through which charges would be passed to the powder monkeys, whose task was to carry them to the guns.

The lower gun deck of the *Victory*

On the gun decks, match tubs were dragged to each gun. Slow-burning matches—lengths of loose-laid rope steeped in nitre—were kept in casks, the burning ends hanging over water, ready in case the gun captain's flintlock should fail to produce a spark. Spare casks of water with swabs beside them were placed around the decks so that the men could snatch a quick drink or douse a small fire. Other casks by the guns were for soaking the sponges which would be rammed in after each firing to clean out any burning residue in the barrels.

William Bunce, the *Victory*'s carpenter, and his mates were down in their storerooms getting out the wooden plugs which would bung up any holes that the enemy's shot might tear in the *Victory*'s hull. Cone-shaped, covered with oakum and liberally spread with tallow, the plugs could be pushed into the smaller shot holes and hammered home. For the bigger, more jagged holes, sheets of lead and salted hides were made ready, along with nails and hammers to secure them.

While the specialists were methodically preparing the *Victory* for battle, dozens of landsmen, ordinary seamen, marines and volunteers were scrambling up the ladders, carrying extra shot. Rings of rope called garlands were in position behind the guns, and into them the men rolled the shot, an extra ten or dozen for each gun, in addition to those nestling like innocent black eggs in the racks. Other men dragged the fire engine into position. Looking like an ordinary pump

A carronade, for close-range fire

stolen from some village square, the rectangular wooden tank perched incongruously on small, thick wheels. It had four handles which, worked up and down vigorously by as many men as could crowd around, sent water spurting from the long brass nozzle fitted on a swivel at the top.

All the while, the marines under Captain William Adair were being inspected; William Elliott, the ship's policeman, walked along the decks keeping an eye on hundreds of men; lieutenants supervised the decks for which they were responsible; excited midshipmen dashed here and there, carrying orders to men old enough to be their fathers.

In every ship of the fleet the men were waiting for the staccato of the drum beating to quarters, a tattoo which was to surprise some because they found they were not frightened, and sicken others because it left them craven.

HAVING BEEN SIGNALLED BY THE *Victory* to come aboard, Henry Blackwood rowed across from the *Euryalus* to find Nelson "in good, but very calm, spirits." Blackwood had not been on board more than a few minutes when a shout made everyone look towards the enemy. The broadening sails of the Combined Fleet made it clear that Villeneuve had ordered his fleet to reverse course. Like a line of marching soldiers doing an about-face, they came off their southerly course towards the Strait of Gibraltar and headed towards Cádiz. What had been the rear ship now became the leader.

Although Nelson had anticipated this, he was far from pleased. Had the ships continued sailing south, they would have brought the Strait of Gibraltar under their lee, providing an escape route into the Mediterranean for British ships damaged in battle. But with the Combined Feet sailing north, the shoal-strewn and dangerous coast between Cape Trafalgar and Cádiz was close to leeward, a dreadful trap for crippled ships, particularly in rough weather. And with a westerly gale brewing, the weather was obviously going to get a great deal worse.

This was the time to attack. Nelson left the poop deck and went down to his day cabin, where he knelt at his desk, the chairs having already been removed. He took a pen and wrote a prayer in his private diary:

> May the Great God, whom I worship, grant to my Country, and for the benefit of Europe in general, a great and glorious Victory; and may no misconduct in any one tarnish it; and may humanity after Victory be the predominant feature in the British Fleet. For myself, individually, I commit my life to Him who made me, and may his blessing light upon my endeavours for serving my country faithfully. To Him I resign myself and the just cause which is entrusted to me to defend. Amen. Amen. Amen.

Now, Nelson took a sheet of paper and wrote a codicil to his will, calling on his country to provide for Emma and Horatia. "These are the only favours I ask my King and Country at this moment when I am going to fight their Battle. May God bless my King and Country, and all those I hold dear." Nelson then sent for Hardy and Blackwood to witness his signature.

A few minutes later Captain Hardy gave the order that the crews throughout the fleet had been awaiting all morning. "Mr. Quilliam," he called, "send the hands to quarters." The acting first lieutenant, John Quilliam, glanced around for the bosun and for the drummer. "Mr. Willmet! Hands to quarters! Drummer—beat to quarters!"

Within a few seconds the beat of the drum, to the tune of "Heart of Oak", reverberated across the upper deck, through the hatchways and down to the gun decks. Willmet and his mates ran to the hatches to sound their shrill pipes. "All hands to quarters! Rouse out there and look alive! All hands to quarters!"

The decks suddenly looked like a disturbed anthill. Men headed for the twelve 12-pounders on the quarterdeck and for the fo'c'sle, to handle the two 68-pounder carronades. Others ran to the thirty 12-pounders on the upper deck, and nearly two hundred more went below for the twenty-eight 24-pounders on the middle deck. The thirty 32-pounders on the lower deck and had more than two hundred men to load and fire them. Another fifty men went to the magazines and the passageways to fill or pass cartridges, and ten more made for the cockpit to help the surgeons and loblolly men.

In the galley the cook doused his fire as soon as he heard the first clatter of the drum. On all the decks sand was sprinkled to give a better grip for the men's feet. Most of the seamen were now stripped to the waist, with narrow bands of cloth bound around their heads to lessen the deafening effect of the guns and to prevent perspiration from running into their eyes.

As the gun crews fell in at their respective guns, the loader and the sponger went to the muzzle and took out the plug which sealed the barrel when the gun was not in use. Others hauled on tackle, raising the port lid, which let the sunlight stream in. With the guns unplugged and the port lids up, each of the lieutenants put a speaking trumpet to his mouth and shouted, "Load!"

Now each powder monkey slipped a bulky cartridge out of the carrying case and gave it to the assistant loader, who handed it to the loader as if it were a hot potato. The loader slid the cartridge into the barrel. The sponger took up the rammer and pushed the cartridge home, then a wad, then the shot, then another wad. As soon as the gun was loaded, the men stood back.

"Run out!"

All the gun crew except the captain and powder monkey grabbed the gun-tackle falls and hauled. The gun rumbled out until the forward edge of the carriage was hard up against the ship's side and the muzzle projected through the port.

"Prime!" bellowed the lieutenants.

The gun captain thrust the priming wire into the vent so hard that it made a small hole in the flannel covering the cartridge. He then pulled out the wire and slipped a thin tube—in effect a fuse—into the vent and poured some gunpowder into the pan of the lock.

Now Lieutenant Quilliam reported to Captain Hardy on the *Victory*'s quarterdeck that the ship was ready for action, her more than eight hundred men at general quarters. But since it was unlikely that firing would start for some time, Midshipman Richard Francis Roberts, in his *Remark Book*, noted the next thing that concerned the sailors: "At 11—Dinner and grog."

THE LOOKOUTS IN THE French frigate *Hermione* had spotted the British fleet to the west shortly after dawn, and Villeneuve, still sailing southward, had immediately ordered the frigates to reconnoitre. Once again he made signals to the fleet to form line of battle, but there was little chance of that happening.

A swell was coming in on the fleet's beam, making the ships roll badly; in addition, with the wind also on the beam, the swaying masts flung the wind out of their sails. While three out of the four squadrons (the lead squadron under Vice Admiral de Álava, in the *Santa Ana*; the centre squadron under Villeneuve, in the *Bucentaure*; and the rear squadron under Rear Admiral Dumanoir, in the *Formidable*) tried to get themselves into some semblance of a line, Admiral Gravina, in the *Principe de Asturias*, ordered his squadron of observation ships to take up a position in line ahead of the fleet, instead of staying to windward of it, as Villeneuve had ordered, available to reinforce the line anywhere it was threatened. For the moment Villeneuve did nothing about Gravina's altered position, and it was to have a great effect on the battle.

By 7:30 a.m. Villeneuve was in a difficult position. "The enemy squadron," he reported, ". . . appeared to me to be standing in a body for my rear, with the double intention of attacking it advantageously and of cutting off the retreat of the Combined Fleet on Cadiz." Ahead lay the Strait of Gibraltar and six more British battleships; to the east lay Cape Trafalgar and its line of dangerous shoals. With every moment that passed, he was drawing farther away from Cádiz, his only port of refuge, and Nelson was nearer to cutting it off as a line of retreat.

At eight a.m. Villeneuve finally made up his mind. He would turn about and steer back towards Cádiz, "my sole object being to protect the rear from the projected attack of the entire enemy force." By turning together, the ships would about-face in the line, so that the *Neptuno* to the north, which had been the last ship in the line, would now be the leader, and the *San Juan Nepomuceno*, which had recently been made the leader of Gravina's squadron, would now bring up the rear.

When he saw the signal, Commodore Churruca, commanding the *San Juan Nepomuceno*, and one of the most capable of the Spanish officers, turned to his second-in-command and said, "The fleet is doomed. The French admiral does not understand his business." The turnabout that Villeneuve had ordered, Churruca declared, was bound to throw the fleet into confusion. Since the Combined Fleet had not had time to form a proper line of battle on the former tack, only chaos could result by heading it in the opposite direction. Indeed, some ships sagged off to leeward, unable or unwilling to get into position, while others scrambled into the line wherever they could find a gap. To add to the confusion, a light wind came up from the southwest and reached the rear ships first, bunching them up. Thus the Combined Fleet formed its unruly line of battle.

Villeneuve's order to turn northward was finally completed by ten a.m., though there were large gaps in the line. The fleet had formed in a huge half-moon, the centre sagging away from the advancing British only five miles away. At 10:15 a.m. Villeneuve, trying to get it formed properly, signalled to the leading ship, the *Neptuno*, to hug the wind and for the others to follow in succession. But in hugging the wind, the lead ships slowed up, and those astern dropped farther to leeward. In addition, Villeneuve now realized that Gravina's squadron of observation ships was sailing to take position as the last ships in the line, instead of staying up to windward. He promptly signalled Gravina to keep up to windward "so as to be at hand to cover the centre of the fleet, which appears to be the point on which the enemy is desirous of concentrating his greatest effort." But it was too late. Gravina could not reach that position in time.

Churruca, whose ship was now the last in Gravina's squadron and therefore the most southerly of all, had been watching the *Bucentaure*, waiting patiently for Villeneuve to make the signal that he considered would foil Nelson's attack. "[The French admiral] has only to order the van ships to turn around at once and double on the rear squadron," he declared. "That will place the enemy between two fires." But the signal never came.

The British ships were now drawing very close. "I made the signal to commence the action as soon as within range," wrote Villeneuve. Meanwhile, the Imperial Eagle was paraded around the deck by Villeneuve, followed by his flag captain, Magendie; Major General Contamine, who was commanding the troops; and the rest of the *Bucentaure*'s officers.

"It is impossible," wrote Magendie, "to display greater enthusiasm and eagerness for the fray than was shown ... by all the officers, sailors and soldiers of the *Bucentaure*, each one of us putting our hands between the Admiral's and renewing our oath upon the Eagle entrusted to us by the Emperor, to fight to the last gasp; and shouts of '*Vive l'Empereur, vive l'Amiral Villeneuve*' were raised once more."

Intrepid little Captain Lucas—he was only four feet four inches tall —in the *Redoutable*, was close astern of the *Bucentaure*. He almost certainly commanded the best-trained crew in the Combined Fleet. His ideas "were always directed towards fighting by boarding.... All the men armed with swords were instructed in broadsword practice every day and pistols had become familiar arms to them. The grapnels were thrown aboard so skilfully that they succeeded in hooking a ship even though she was not exactly touching us." Allowing for Lucas's exaggerations—and they become clearer later when he describes how the *Redoutable* engaged the *Victory*—Villeneuve must have regretted not having more captains like him.

The huge *Santissima Trinidad*, just ahead of the *Bucentaure*, was painted in alternate bands of red and white; her figurehead, as befitted the largest ship in the world, was an imposing carving of figures representing the Holy Trinity, from whom she took her name. She had a crew of a thousand and forty-eight. One of them, going into action for the first time, wrote:

[When] the decks were cleared for action, I heard someone say: "The sand—bring the sand. . . ." Sacks of sand were emptied out on the decks and spread about. . . . My curiosity prompted me to ask a lad what this was for. "For the blood," he said very coolly. Unable to repress a shudder, I looked at the sand . . . and for a moment I felt I was a coward.

Thus the ships of the Combined Fleet waited, drums and fifes playing, the French tricolour or the yellow-and-red flag of Spain flying, and in every Spanish ship a large wooden cross, solemnly blessed by the chaplains, hanging from the boom and over the taffrail.

CHAPTER 7

WITH THE UNRUFFLED majesty of swans, the British battleships sailed down towards the Combined Fleet drawn up across their course. The frigates and the *Pickle* and *Entreprenante* were ranged to port like attendant cygnets. Leading the windward column was the *Victory*. Just astern of her was Captain Eliab Harvey's 98-gun *Téméraire*, nicknamed then the "Saucy" *Téméraire*—the prefix "Fighting" was not to be coined for another thirty-four years, when Turner sent his famous painting to the Royal Academy. Next astern of the *Téméraire* was the *Neptune*, commanded by Captain Sir Thomas Fremantle. One of the midshipmen serving on board, William Badcock, aged seventeen at the time, wrote: "The old *Neptune*, which was never a good sailer, took it into her head to sail better that morning than I ever remember to have seen her do before."

Close astern of the *Neptune* were the *Leviathan* and the *Conqueror*. The latter was commanded by Captain Israel Pellew, a name already famous enough to bring Cornishmen flocking to join his ship as volunteers. Astern of the *Conqueror* came the *Britannia*, the Earl of Northesk and Captain Bullen on her quarterdeck. Lieutenant John Pilford, the commanding officer of the *Ajax*, just astern, could be forgiven any nervousness he felt over a new command. The impetuous Sir Edward Berry, in the *Agamemnon*, followed the *Ajax*, and close to him was the *Orion*, commanded by Captain Codrington, who reported: "We were all fresh, hearty and in high spirits."

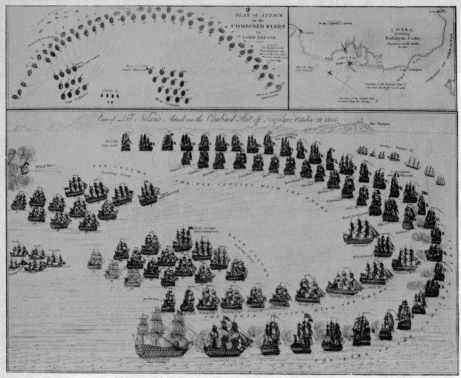

Diagram of Nelson's plan of attack against Villeneuve

A considerable distance behind the *Orion* was the *Prince*, commanded by Captain Richard Grindall. The 98-gun ship belonged at the head of Collingwood's division, but she was slow and had been forced to shift a topsail, and had thus lagged behind. The men of the *Minotaur*, next astern, listened to a rousing speech by Captain C. J. M. Mansfield. Their cheers carried across the water to the next ship astern, the *Spartiate*, commanded by Captain Sir Francis Laforey, the last ship in Nelson's division.

To port, the men on Blackwood's *Euryalus* had perhaps the best view of all the fleet. Midshipman Hercules Robinson wrote: "How well I remember the ports of our great ship hauled up, the guns run out, and as from the sublime to the ridiculous is but a step, the *Pickle*, schooner, close to our ship with her boarding nets up, her tampions out and her four guns (about as large and formidable as two pairs of Wellington boots) . . . as imposing as Gulliver waving his [sword] before the King and Queen of Brobdingnag."

Although Nelson's division was steering for the enemy in some semblance of a column, Collingwood's ships, following a signal from him that they were to proceed at a right angle to the enemy line, were sailing with each successive ship behind Collingwood's *Royal Sovereign* out on the starboard quarter of her next ahead. Astern and to starboard of the *Royal Sovereign* was the *Belleisle*, commanded by Captain William Hargood. She was a fast and powerful two-decker, captured from the French ten years earlier. To Hargood's delight he had been signalled to change places with the *Tonnant*, one of Nelson's French trophies from the Nile. As the *Belleisle* forged past her, Hargood ordered the band to play "Rule, Britannia". Not to be outdone, Captain Charles Tyler ordered the *Tonnant*'s band to reply with "Britons, Strike Home!" With the bands thumping away, the young officers were now considerably more cheerful. Their earlier feelings were described by Lieutenant Paul Harris Nicolas:

> The officers now met at breakfast; and though each seemed to exult in the hope of a glorious termination to the contest so near at hand, a fearful presage was experienced that all would not again unite at that festive board. . . . The sound of the drums, however, soon put an end to our meditations, and after a hasty and, alas, a final farewell to some, we repaired to our respective posts.

Captain George Duff, of the *Mars*, had been trying to give his ship wings. Every stitch of canvas was set. Studding sails hung out over the water at the end of the yards. The reason for this was that Nelson had just signalled Duff to go ahead, and thus be the first to break through the enemy line. But Duff could not manage to overtake the *Royal Sovereign*, and the descent on the enemy turned into a race between Nelson and Collingwood.

The *Bellerophon*—the "Billy Ruff'n"—was the next in Collingwood's division. Her captain, John Cooke, had always had one ambition: to serve under Nelson. Now he stood on the quarterdeck talking to William Cumby, his first lieutenant, and some of his other officers. Earlier that morning, Cooke had shown Cumby the Nelson Touch memorandum, explaining, as Cumby later wrote, that "he wished me to be made acquainted with it, that in the event of his being 'bowl'd out' I might know how to conduct the ship agreeable to the Admiral's wishes. On this I observed that it was very possible that the same shot which disposed of him might have an equally tranquillizing effect upon me, and under that idea I submitted to him the expediency of the [ship's] Master being also apprised. . . . To this Captain Cooke immediately assented. . . . And here I may be permitted to remark *en passant* that, of the three officers who carried the knowledge of this private Memorandum into action, I was the only one that brought it out [alive]."

Away to the westward were the rest of the ships of Collingwood's division. Among them were the 74-gun *Colossus*, commanded by Captain James Morris; the *Achille*, under Captain Richard King; and the *Revenge*, whose captain, Robert Moorsom, was a gunnery expert A long gap separated the next ship, Captain Durham's *Defiance*. The three ships following the *Defiance* were almost abreast of each other—the *Swiftsure, Dreadnought* and *Polyphemus*. The last two ships in the column, the *Thunderer* and *Defence*, were quite close to the last ships of Nelson's division.

There remained only the little 64-gun *Africa*, smallest of Nelson's battleships, which now appeared to the north, sailing down towards the British fleet and passing close to the leading ships of the Combined Fleet. Captain Digby had seen the French fleet's signals during the night and taken up "a station of discretion". It put him in a dangerous position, and a signal from the *Victory* was soon to test him and his ship's company.

LOOKING AT THE Combined Fleet spread out ahead of him, Nelson remarked to Blackwood, who had boarded the *Victory* for final orders, "They put a good face on it." But he quickly added, "I'll give them such a dressing as they never had before!" At that moment Blackwood, realizing that the *Victory* would bear the brunt of the enemy's fire, pointed out respectfully to Nelson the value of his life. "I proposed hoisting his flag in the *Euryalus*, whence he could better see what was going on . . ." Blackwood wrote, "but he would not hear of it, and gave as his reason the force of example; and probably he was right."

Several of the *Victory*'s officers had also worried over the fact that the various decorations on Nelson's frock coat would make him a conspicuous target for sharpshooters. Dr. Beatty, the ship's surgeon, suggested that the admiral should be asked to cover them up with a handkerchief, but Dr. Scott, the chaplain, and John Scott, Nelson's secretary, observed that Nelson would be extremely annoyed with anyone who suggested a change in his dress for this reason. "Take care, Doctor, what you are about," warned John Scott. "I would not be the man to mention such a matter to him."

Nelson had gone around the various decks, chatting with the men as they stood to their guns, warning them not to waste a single shot. Talking with Blackwood a little later, he had asked him what he would regard as a victory. "Considering the handsome way the enemy are offering battle," Blackwood replied, "and the nearness of the land, I should think that if fourteen ships are captured it would be a glorious result." Nelson answered. "I shall not, Blackwood, be satisfied with anything short of twenty."

The bustle aboard the *Victory* was quieting down now. The main task was to keep the ship sailing as fast as possible. There were still several signals to make, however. With the nearest enemy ships less than two miles ahead, Nelson walked across the poop deck to where Lieutenant John Pasco and his signalmen were waiting. He ordered a signal to be made to the *Africa*—sailing towards them on the port beam near the head of the enemy's line—to "engage the enemy more closely". Then he said, "Mr. Pasco, I wish to say to the fleet, 'England confides that every man will do his duty.'" Pasco thought for a moment, searching through the telegraphic vocabulary. Then he replied, "If your Lordship will permit me to substitute 'expects' for 'confides' the signal will soon be completed, because the word 'expects' is in the vocabulary, and 'confides' must be spelt."

"That will do, Pasco, make it directly," Nelson said hurriedly.

After the signalmen had bent the flags onto the halyards, Nelson said to Pasco, "Make the signal for Close Action, and *keep it up*." Turning away to Hardy and Blackwood after having ordered his last signal to the fleet, he remarked, "I can do no more. We must trust to the great Disposer of all events, and the justice of our cause. I thank God for this great opportunity of doing my duty."

COLLINGWOOD AND HIS fifteen ships were to attack the last twelve ships in the enemy's line, but Nelson had left Collingwood free to carry out the order as he thought best. Early on, Collingwood had ordered his ships to form up on a diagonal (whereas Nelson attacked in column),

with the *Royal Sovereign* to the north. But the line of bearing was never properly formed because he would not reduce sail to allow the others to get into position on his quarter; instead, he contented himself with signalling his ships to make more sail. The effect was to put the *Royal Sovereign*, fresh from the dockyard, well ahead, with seven more ships strung out astern and the rest of the division well behind them.

Although Collingwood later reported that he broke through the enemy line "about the twelfth from the rear", in fact, he broke through between the fifteenth ship and the sixteenth. Thus the first eight of Collingwood's division attacked sixteen ships of the Combined Fleet. Moreover, an hour was to elapse between the time the *Royal Sovereign* opened fire and the first of the remaining seven ships under his command managed to get into action.

Sailing with easy grace across the swell-waves, the eyes of the fleet upon her, the *Royal Sovereign* bore down on the *Santa Ana* and the *Fougueux*. Sextants measured the angle between the *Santa Ana*'s waterline and the truck of her mainmast, and reference to a table showed trigonometrically what the eye hardly detected. Three degrees fourteen minutes—she was thirteen hundred yards away . . . three degrees forty-nine minutes—eleven hundred yards. The enemy ships ahead would open fire any second now. Four degrees ten minutes—a range of a thousand yards. The time was 11:58 a.m.

The *Royal Sovereign* was now within a few hundred yards of what seemed to be a solid wall of enemy ships. Suddenly a row of glowing red dots rippled down their sides. The *Fougueux* had launched her first broadside at Collingwood's flagship, and the battle of Trafalgar had begun. As the rumble of the first broadside reached the *Royal Sovereign*, more flashes rippled from the *Santa Ana*, ahead of the *Fougueux*, and from the Spanish *Monarca* astern. Enemy shot fell round the British ship like hail on a pond, but magnificent in her stateliness, apparently unperturbed, the *Royal Sovereign* continued to head for the gap between the *Santa Ana* and the *Fougueux*.

"Steer for the Frenchman and carry away his bowsprit!" ordered Collingwood. Slowly the *Royal Sovereign*'s bowsprit began to swing to starboard as the ship's master selected a spot for the two ships to meet. Captain Baudouin, realizing that the British ship intended to smash her way through, quickly ordered the *Fougueux*'s main topsail to be

backed. His ship slowed up, leaving the *Royal Sovereign* just enough room to get past.

As she forged through the gap, the *Royal Sovereign*'s port guns fired a whole broadside into the unprotected stern of the *Santa Ana*, Vice Admiral de Álava's flagship. As successive guns bore and fired, the solid planking and rich carvings on the *Santa Ana*'s transom were smashed; shot and splinters spun onto the decks, cutting down men and overturning fourteen guns. The British worked swiftly in the choking smoke to reload as the *Royal Sovereign* swung round to port to come alongside. But as she turned, Captain Baudouin fired the *Fougueux*'s full broadside into her starboard quarter, as did the 80-gun *Indomptable*, only five hundred yards away.

The *Santa Ana*'s captain had guessed that the *Royal Sovereign* would swing round, and he had brought the port guns' crews over to reinforce those on the starboard side. When the British did come alongside, the Spanish gunners fired. At the same time, two more Spanish ships, the *San Justo* and the *San Leandro*, which were well ahead, swung round and also started firing into the *Royal Sovereign*; the French *Neptune*, which was in between them, followed suit. Collingwood's flagship was thus being engaged by three Spanish and three French ships at once.

Enemy shots cut through the *Royal Sovereign*'s rigging and slashed her studding sails to pieces. Collingwood, standing amid the smoke and noise as unconcerned as if he had been standing in his orchard at home, walked down to the quarterdeck and talked to the men at the guns, particularly praising a Negro seaman who, with the admiral beside him, fired ten rounds at the *Santa Ana*.

Though the *Royal Sovereign*'s port gunners did their best, the Spanish ship kept pounding away. Collingwood was wounded and the ship's master, William Chalmers, was killed. Describing his death, Collingwood wrote:

A great shot almost divided his body: he laid his head upon my shoulder, and told me he was slain. I supported him till two men carried him off. He could say nothing to me, but to bless me; but as they carried him down, he wished he could but live to read the account of the action in a newspaper. He lay in the cockpit, among the wounded, until the *Santa Ana* struck; and, joining in the cheer which they gave her, expired with it on his lips.

By this time the other ships in Collingwood's division were coming into action. Captain Hargood, of the *Belleisle*, had sent for his officers and declared, "Gentlemen, I have only this to say: that I shall pass under the stem of that ship." He pointed to the *Santa Ana*, whose great figurehead, an effigy of the mother of the Virgin, could now be clearly seen in the sunlight. "Put in two round shot and then a grape," he continued, "and give her *that*. Now go to your quarters and mind not to fire until each gun will bear with effect." With this laconic instruction, reported Lieutenant Paul Nicolas, of the Royal Marines, "the gallant little man posted himself on the slide of the foremast carronade on the starboard side of the quarter-deck."

Several ships had begun firing at the *Belleisle*, "[giving] us an intimation of what we should in a few minutes undergo," Lieutenant Nicolas wrote. "An awful silence prevailed in the ship, only interrupted by the commanding voice of Captain Hargood, 'Steady! Starboard a little! Steady so!'"

The shot were by now streaming in over the bow, tearing at the heavy timbers, the sails and the rigging, sending up sparks as they crashed into metal, and scooping up scores of splinters as they burrowed into wood. "My ears rang with the shrieks of the wounded and the moans of the dying," declared Lieutenant Nicolas, but "our energies became roused and the mind diverted from its appalling condition, by the order 'Stand to your guns!'"

It was 12:11 p.m., and by now the French and Spanish broadsides were beginning to tell against the *Belleisle*. "Although until that moment we had not fired a shot . . . our mizen-topmast was shot away and the ensign had been thrice re-hoisted," wrote the lieutenant. More than fifty men had been killed or wounded. But now the whole port broadside crashed out at the *Santa Ana*, and almost immediately the starboard broadside was fired into the *Fougueux*. Smoke drifted before the *Belleisle*, almost hiding the *Indomptable* ahead and the *San Justo* beyond.

With the *Fougueux* on her starboard quarter and the Spanish *San Justo* on her port bow, the *Belleisle*'s master earnestly addressed the captain, "Shall we go through, sir?"

"There's your ship, sir; place me alongside her!" was his energetic reply.

The master brought the *Belleisle* around to go under the *Indomptable*'s stern. Suddenly out of the great banks of smoke, sails hanging from masts like old clothes on a scarecrow, the *Fougueux* loomed up very close on the starboard quarter, and in a few moments her bow crashed against the *Belleisle*'s starboard gangway.

As the two ships drifted together, the conditions on the gun decks were appalling. One man wrote: "At every moment the smoke accumulated more and more thickly . . . often [blotting] out the men at the guns from those close at hand on each side. The guns had to be trained by means of orders passed down from above. . . . The only comfort from this serious inconvenience was that every man was so isolated from his neighbour that he was not . . . in danger [of] seeing his messmates go down all round."

The *Indomtable*, meanwhile, saved by the *Fougueux*, turned and fired a broadside into the *Belleisle*. Then as if she considered her part in the battle fulfilled, she drifted off into the smoke, leaving the *Fougueux* and the *Belleisle* locked together, hammering away at each other.

By now, Captain Duff's 74-gun *Mars* was in action. The *Fougueux*, having gone ahead to engage Collingwood's flagship and then the *Belleisle*, had left a gap which the Spanish *Monarca* was slow to close. Captain Duff planned to pass through there, but Captain Cosmao-Kerjulien in the 74-gun *Pluton* quickly set all possible sail, and within a few minutes had ranged ahead into the gap, nearly across the bows of the *Mars*. To avoid a raking broadside, Captain Duff put the *Mars* on a course parallel with the *Pluton*. But on this heading the *Mars* was fast approaching the *Santa Ana*, and Duff had to luff up and stop in order to avoid hitting the Spanish ship. With the *Mars* dead in the water, the *Pluton* was in an ideal position to rake the British ship, as was the *Fougueux*, after having shot away the *Belleisle*'s mizzenmast and drifted clear.

Captain Norman, commanding the marines on board the *Mars*, spotted the *Fougueux* through the swirling smoke and ran to the quarterdeck to warn Captain Duff, but the *Mars* was hemmed in and unable to manoeuvre. Duff could just see the *Fougueux* on the starboard quarter through the smoke, and he told his aide to go below and order the guns to be pointed farther aft. The boy was just turning away when the *Fougueux* fired a full broadside into the *Mars*. One shot

Trafalgar by Thomas Pocock depicts British ships breaking the line of the Combined Fleet

decapitated Duff and went on to kill two seamen who were standing just behind him.

Word was sent below to Duff's thirteen-year-old son, Norwich, that his father had been killed. The boy had joined the ship only a few weeks earlier. "He seems very well pleased with his choice of profession," Duff had written home proudly to his wife in Edinburgh. The *Mars* was something of a family ship, with two of Norwich's young cousins also newly aboard. When the men heard that their captain had been killed, wrote Midshipman Robinson, a family friend, "they held his body up and gave three cheers to show they were not discouraged by it, and then returned to their guns."

Lieutenant William Hennah was now in command. The ship's masts were riddled with shot and about to crash over the side; several guns had been smashed, and the stern quarter and rudder were badly damaged. Already killed, in addition to Norwich's father, were

Norwich's cousin Alexander, who died in his younger brother's arms, two midshipmen, seventeen seamen and eight marines. Another sixty-six men were wounded.

The stricken ship was out of control, with her damaged stern towards the *Pluton*. Captain Cosmao-Kerjulien raked the *Mars* with another broadside and turned away, drifting to leeward until he found the *Belleisle* lying helpless. He then hove to on the British ship's port quarter and opened fire.

THE *TONNANT*, under Captain Tyler, had followed the *Mars* into battle, breaking the line between the stern of the 74-gun *Monarca* and the bow of the French *Algésiras*, the flagship of Rear Admiral Magon. The captain had taken his ship "so close," according to the third lieutenant, Frederick Hoffman, "that a biscuit might have been thrown on either of them." He added: "Our guns were all double-shotted.

The order was given to fire; being so close, every shot was poured into their hulls, and down came the Frenchman's [*Algésiras's*] mizenmast, and after our second broadside the Spaniard's [*Monarca's*] fore and cross-jack yards." The *Monarca* was badly damaged and gradually dropped astern. The *Tonnant* went ahead, firing at the *Algésiras* to starboard.

Now, seeing the *Pluton* ahead, sending broadside after broadside into the helpless *Mars*, Tyler brought the *Tonnant* round to starboard and fired his port broadside into Cosmao-Kerjulien's ship. But this was the chance for which Magon, in the *Algésiras*, was waiting. He forged ahead to cross under the *Tonnant*'s stern and seize the chance to cripple her with a raking broadside. Tyler immediately brought the *Tonnant* round still farther, and before Magon could change course, the *Algésiras*'s bow had crashed into the *Tonnant* amidships. In this position none of the French guns could be brought to bear, but almost every one of the *Tonnant*'s starboard guns was able to rake the *Algésiras*.

Admiral Magon at once gave orders for the *Tonnant* to be boarded. But the moment the French boarding party tried to clamber onto the British ship, carronades and quarterdeck guns blasted them with grapeshot and musket balls, killing most of them.

The battle between the two ships went on for more than an hour. Passing British ships sent their broadsides into the *Algésiras*, which gradually swung round until she was alongside the *Tonnant*, and blazing wads from the *Tonnant*'s guns eventually started a fire in the French ship. "At length," the *Tonnant*'s Lieutenant Hoffman wrote later, "both ships caught fire. . . . Our firemen, with all the courage so inherent in British seamen . . . finally extinguished the flames, although two of them were severely wounded in doing so."

Firing with great coolness, the British gunners gradually got the upper hand. Commander Le Tourneur reported that on board the *Algésiras*, Magon, "feeling our position to be critical, went about everywhere encouraging us by his presence and displaying . . . heroic courage." While he was cheering his men, he was hit in the arm by a musket ball, and later by a splinter in the thigh. Finally, having refused the pleading of his officers that he should go below to have his wounds dressed, Magon collapsed onto the deck, killed by a bullet in the chest. "Our 18-pounder battery was at this time deserted and utterly silenced," says Le Tourneur. "We collected all our men in the 36-pounder battery, which continued to be served by them with the utmost activity."

These guns were doing considerable damage in the *Tonnant*. Captain Tyler had been carried below, wounded, leaving Lieutenant John Bedford in command. Down in the cockpit, the surgeon, Forbes Chevers, was amputating torn limbs by the dim and flickering light of tallow candles held by two assistants. (When later he washed his face, he found that the candles had completely burned off his eyebrows.) Chevers was being helped by "a very powerful and resolute woman", the wife of a petty officer, who had somehow contrived to be on board. But of the sixteen men on the *Tonnant* who were eventually to undergo amputations, only two survived.

Up on deck, wrote Lieutenant Hoffman, they had the satisfaction of seeing the *Algésiras*'s remaining mast "go by the board, ripping the partners up in their fall, as they had been shot through below the deck, and carrying with them all their sharpshooters to look sharper in the next world." The French ship was now so crippled that she was forced to cease fire. Waving cutlasses, pikes and tomahawks, sixty of the *Tonnant*'s crew scrambled on board, where they found that seventy-seven Frenchmen had been killed and one hundred and forty-two wounded.

But for the *Tonnant* the battle was not yet over. Commodore Churruca's *San Juan Nepomuceno*, already badly damaged in action with the *Defiance* and the *Dreadnought*, now appeared to the south. The *Algésiras* drifted away, and the *Tonnant* was able to use her whole starboard broadside to engage the Spanish vessel. "We returned her salute with interest, and her foremast went. . . . We cheered and gave her another broadside, and down came her colours."

CHAPTER 8

"SEE HOW THAT NOBLE fellow Collingwood carries his ship into action!" Nelson had exclaimed as the *Royal Sovereign* broke the enemy line. Fifteen minutes later the first of the enemy ships had opened fire at long range at the *Victory*. Rolling as they were, in the swell off the rocky shore of Cape Trafalgar, sighting was difficult for the inexperienced French and Spanish gunners on board. But even wildly inaccurate shooting steadied the men—and not only those in the enemy ships.

The time had now come for Nelson to send Captain Blackwood back to the *Euryalus*. On the quarterdeck of the *Victory*, Blackwood took Nelson's hand. "I trust, my Lord, that on my return . . . I shall find your Lordship well, and in possession of twenty prizes." Nelson looked at Blackwood, and a presentiment of death must have been gripping him now. "God bless you, Blackwood, I shall never speak to you again."

In the faltering breeze the *Victory* was sailing at the speed of a dawdling child. But with the *Téméraire, Neptune, Leviathan* and *Conqueror* following close astern, she seemed to the French the sharp end of a massive wedge driving down on them with the crushing inevitability of a glacier.

Directly ahead were four enemy ships. Captain Poulain, commanding the northernmost, the 74-gun *Héros*, gave orders to try the range again. From the *Victory* they could see red flame spitting from her gunports. The huge *Santissima Trinidad*, just astern of her, and Villeneuve's flagship, the *Bucentaure*, now opened fire. The shot splashed up well short of the *Victory*.

"Starboard a little," ordered Captain Hardy, and Thomas Atkinson, the master, repeated it to the quartermaster. On each of the gun decks the lieutenants put their speaking trumpets to their lips. Perspiration trickled down naked backs. There was no laughing and joking now, for each man was alone with himself.

The *Bucentaure* fired another few rounds. The *Victory* was now just over a mile away and still the shot fell short. But a few moments later the men on the *Victory*'s upper deck heard a whirring overhead. A hole suddenly appeared in the main-topgallant sail—a clear indication to the enemy that the *Victory* was now within range. The desultory firing stopped. There was a minute of awful silence.

Suddenly the outlines of the French ships were blurred by rolling banks of flame-tinged yellow smoke—nearly two hundred guns, the full broadsides of the *Héros, Santissima Trinidad, Bucentaure* and *Redoutable* had fired. Before the sound of their discharge reached the *Victory*, a hail of death smashed into her. Solid shot plunged through the hull, throwing out a hail of great splinters which cut men down like invisible scythes; straining ropes were slashed; holes pock-marked the sails. Men grunted and sat down abruptly, with death inside them; others fell shrieking. When the livid flame and smoke of the enemy guns stopped for a moment, it seemed incongruous that the weak sun still shone, that the sails still flapped with lazy majesty, and the sea continued to murmur its quiet song under bow and stern.

Again and again the enemy guns coughed. Nelson's secretary, John Scott, was talking to Hardy when he was suddenly flung to the deck, dead. "Is that Scott that is gone? Poor fellow!" said Nelson. A double-headed shot spun into the group of red-coated marines drawn up on the poop deck. Eight of them fell to the deck. Seeing this, Nelson called to Captain Charles Adair, their commanding officer, "Disperse your men round the ship." But for this order, which may have spared some lives, the marines would have cleared the sharpshooters from the enemy's tops—and perhaps saved Nelson's life.

Hardy glanced at his heavy gold watch. Barely 12:20 . . . they had been under fire for less than five minutes. A shot cut through rolled-up hammocks, smashed away part of the launch as it lay on the booms, hit the forebrace bitts on the quarterdeck and whined between himself and Nelson. A splinter tore away the ornate buckle of Hardy's shoe.

Nelson glanced up at Hardy and smiled. "This is too warm work to last long."

Again the enemy guns rumbled. A shot smashed the *Victory*'s wheel, and for a moment she was out of control, until emergency steering could be organized below. Suddenly there was a crash high above as a shot cut into the mizzen topmast and sent it toppling down. Forward, the foresail had been torn away from the yard, and within five minutes the studding sails had been ripped from the booms. Every other sail in the ship was pocked with holes. The *Victory* was now like a bird with its wings clipped.

Now the *Victory* was only a few hundred yards from the enemy. Hardy pointed out that it would not be possible to break through the almost solid wall of ships without running aboard one of them.

"I cannot help it," said Nelson. "Go on board where you please." Hardy chose to try to break through under the stern of Villeneuve's *Bucentaure* and ahead of Captain Lucas's *Redoutable*. Slowly, pounded

The *Battle of Trafalgar* by J. M. W. Turner
shows the *Victory* tangling with the *Bucentaure*

Nelson on the Quarterdeck of the Victory
after a painting by W. H. Overend

by the guns of the *Bucentaure* and *Redoutable*, the *Victory* swung round and headed for the gap.

Sixty yards to go . . . fifty yards . . . forty yards. Hardy was taking it very close. Thirty yards . . . now the *Victory*'s great long bowsprit was overlapping the *Bucentaure*'s stern . . . twenty yards, and bosun William Willmet took the strain on the trigger line of his carronade on the fo'c'sle. Ten yards. Willmet realized that in a moment or two he would almost be able to reach out and grasp the tricolour hanging limp over the taffrail of the *Bucentaure*.

Suddenly, Willmet's right hand jerked back. The thunder of the carronade gave way to a terrible clatter as five hundred musket balls smashed through the *Bucentaure*'s stern, cutting down the Frenchmen working the guns. The men on the British ship could hear the wild screams of the wounded and dying. But then, as the *Victory* passed the *Bucentaure*, she received a broadside from the French *Neptune*

waiting beyond, which damaged her foremast and bowsprit, and several shots damaged her anchors.

Hardy had decided to get alongside the *Redoutable*, on his starboard side, and ordered the helm to be put over. While the men at the port guns quickly sponged out and reloaded, the starboard gun captains waited for the *Victory* to come round far enough for them to fire their first broadside. In a moment or two they could see Lucas's ship. The captains jerked their trigger lines and the full starboard broadside smashed into the *Redoutable*. Willmet, who had run across to the starboard carronade, fired it down on the French sailors massed on the *Redoutable*'s decks as the two ships locked together.

While the *Victory*'s starboard guns pounded the *Redoutable*, the port guns kept firing at the *Bucentaure* as she drifted away. Villeneuve, meanwhile, had hoisted a belated signal. With the Combined Fleet's line broken in two, Villeneuve ordered "all those ships, which are not engaging, to take any such position as will bring them as speedily as possible into action." But Rear Admiral Dumanoir and his ships in the van, for whom the order was really intended, sailed majestically on towards Cádiz.

Meanwhile, Captain Lucas's well-trained sharpshooters, perched in the tops of the *Redoutable*, kept up a hail of musket fire down on the *Victory*'s decks. Most of the French guns were silent below, but the *Victory*'s guns were being constantly run out, their muzzles almost touching the French ship's side. It seemed likely that the *Redoutable* might be set on fire by the flash of their discharge. Since this would be a danger to the *Victory* as well, the crew flung buckets of water out of the ports to stifle any flames.

While the *Victory* and the *Redoutable* fought it out, Captain Eliab Harvey took the *Téméraire* round to break through the enemy line astern of the *Redoutable*. As Harvey's ship came slowly through the gap, the French *Neptune* launched a broadside at her that cut away her great foreyard and buckled her main topmast, which collapsed with a mass of rigging. Although she was almost out of control, her gunners fired broadside after broadside into the *Redoutable* until the French ship's gun ports slammed down shut.

The *Redoutable*, with the *Victory* locked alongside, was drifting towards the bow of the *Téméraire*, and a collision was unavoidable. The French ship's bowsprit crashed over the *Téméraire*'s deck just forward of the mainmast, and Captain Harvey ordered his men to lash it there. In this position the *Téméraire*'s gunners raked the *Redoutable* with their port broadside again and again, their shot hurling guns off their carriages, slashing rigging and sails and tearing up deck planking.

The *Redoutable*'s sharpshooters, however, were bringing terrible casualties to the *Victory*. Dr. Scott, the chaplain, was horrified by what he saw in the faint light of the lanterns in the cockpit, but he went around to each man, doing what he could to comfort him. One desperately wounded young lieutenant, realizing that he was dying, impatiently ripped his tourniquets off so that he would bleed to death more quickly. This so upset the frenzied Scott that he ran up the blood-stained hatchways to the upper deck. There a pall of smoke and dust hung so thickly that he could only just make out the figures of

Nelson and Hardy pacing up and down the quarterdeck between the shattered wheel and the hatchway.

Returning to his duties below, Scott was unaware that tragedy was about to strike. Nelson and Hardy had almost reached the hatch when Hardy turned to see Nelson on his knees, trying to support himself with his left hand. Before he could reach him, Nelson's one arm gave way and he collapsed. Hardy crouched down. "I hope you are not severely wounded, my Lord?" he inquired anxiously.

"They have done for me at last, Hardy," Nelson gasped. "My backbone is shot through."

Hardy called to three crewmen near by. "Take the admiral down to the cockpit immediately," he ordered. Gently they lifted the stricken Nelson in their arms and carried him to the hatchway. Somehow Nelson managed to take out a handkerchief and place it over his face so that no one should recognize him as he was taken below.

Moving carefully to avoid jolting him, the crewmen finally edged down the last ladder to the orlop and slowly made their way past the other wounded men. Several of them recognized Nelson from the decorations on his coat. "Mr. Beatty!" they cried. "Mr. Beatty! Lord Nelson is here! The admiral is wounded!"

Above the groans and cries of the wounded, Beatty heard their calls, and in the gloom he saw the three men stumbling along towards him, carrying Nelson's small figure. Quickly he and Walter Burke, the purser, took the admiral from the arms of the seamen and carried him to an empty space on the port side and put him down gently on a rough mattress, his back against one of the massive frames of the ship's side. They slipped off his coat and shirt and drew a sheet over him. Nelson said to Dr. Scott in a quiet voice, "Doctor, I told you so. Doctor, I am gone." Apparently convinced that he would die within a few minutes, he added, "I have to leave Lady Hamilton, and my adopted daughter, Horatia, as a legacy to my country."

Beatty was by now ready with his surgical instruments. The frame against which Nelson rested his back shivered and vibrated with the shock of battle as Lucas's *Redoutable* also fought a losing struggle for life. As he probed, Beatty realized that the musket ball had plunged deep into Nelson's chest and was now probably lodged in the spine. He examined Nelson's back, but there was no mark of a wound. "Tell me all your sensations, my Lord," he said.

"I feel a gush of blood every minute within my breast," replied Nelson. "I have no feeling in the lower part of my body . . . breathing is very difficult and gives me very severe pain about the part of the spine I am sure the ball has struck—for I felt it break my back."

Beatty heard the admiral list his symptoms with a sinking heart. They confirmed his suspicions. He wrote later:

> The gush of blood which his Lordship complained of, together with the state of his pulse, indicated . . . the hopeless situation of the case: but till after the victory was ascertained and announced to his Lordship, the true nature of his wound was concealed from all on board except Captain Hardy, Dr Scott, Mr Burke and Messrs Smith and Westemburg, the Assistant Surgeons.

ON THE UPPER DECKS of the *Victory* smoke swirled like fog on a moor, blinding men and making them cough. Casualties were so heavy that soon Hardy, striding about with his telescope under his arm, Captain Adair, the red-jacketed marine, and one or two other officers were the only men left alive on deck.

The *Redoutable*'s big guns had almost stopped firing, leading the *Victory*'s gunners to think she was about to surrender, so that they too stopped firing.

This momentary pause led to an extraordinary misunderstanding. Captain Lucas, describing the *Redoutable*'s point of view, wrote: "At last the *Victory*'s batteries were not able to reply to us; I perceived that they were preparing to board. . . . I ordered the trumpet to sound. . . . The boarding parties came up in such perfect order that one would have said that it was only a sham fight. . . ." Lucas followed with an imaginative touch: "Then there began a furious musketry fire in which Admiral Nelson was fighting at the head of his crew; our fire became so greatly superior that in less than fifteen minutes we had silenced that of the *Victory* and Admiral Nelson was killed. . . . Midshipman Yon and four seamen succeeded in getting on board the *Victory* by means of the anchor and informed us that there was not a soul on her decks."

Lucas had misread what was taking place on board the *Victory*. Once Hardy and Adair had called up men from below, the French attack was quickly beaten off, but twenty-two officers and men were wounded and nineteen killed, including Captain Adair, who was hit by a musket ball as he encouraged his men up the gangway.

Although the *Redoutable*'s sharpshooters kept up their fire, the arrival of the *Téméraire* changed the picture. "It would be difficult to describe the horrible carnage caused by the murderous broadsides," wrote Lucas. "More than 200 of our brave lads were killed or wounded. I was wounded at the same instant but not so seriously as to prevent me remaining at my post. . . . In this state the *Téméraire* hailed us to strike. . . . I ordered several soldiers who were near me to answer this summons with musket shots, which was performed with great zeal." But it was a hopeless gesture in view of the damage to the *Redoutable* Lucas describes:

> The decks were all torn open by the fire of the *Victory* and the *Téméraire*; all the guns were shattered or dismounted. . . . Our decks were covered with dead, buried beneath the debris and the splinters from different parts of the ship. Out of the ship's company of 643 men we had 522 disabled, 300 being killed and 222 wounded . . . in the midst of this horrible carnage the brave lads who had not yet succumbed and those who were wounded . . . still cried "Vive l'Emperor! We're not taken yet; is our Captain still alive?"

There was little point in holding out any longer. Lucas had no sooner ordered the colours to be hauled down than the mizzenmast from which they were flying collapsed across the *Téméraire*'s poop deck. Fire had also broken out aboard the *Redoutable*, and without bothering to take possession of her, Captain Hardy ordered several hands to go aboard and put it out. To their surprise they were well received by the French.

As to the *Victory*, she had lost her mizzen topmast at the beginning of the action, and now the other masts and much of the rigging were badly damaged. Her hull, too, was badly damaged, and more than fifty officers and men had been killed and another hundred wounded.

Hardy now wanted to get his ship clear. He set men pushing her off with fire booms. A few moments earlier a lieutenant, hearing the *Téméraire*'s guns firing on the other side, looked aft and saw another French two-decker lying close on the *Téméraire*'s starboard side. Soon he could read the name on the stern. It was the *Fougueux*.

Overleaf: detail from *The Battle of Trafalgar As Seen From the Mizzen Starboard Shrouds of the Victory* by J. M. W. Turner

CHAPTER 9

T HE *VICTORY* HAD forced a big gap in the enemy line. And although
the *Téméraire* could not take advantage of it in time, the third
ship in Nelson's division, Captain Thomas Fremantle's *Neptune*, could
and did.

The *Neptune*'s band had been playing bravely as the enemy's guns
started the overture to their thunderous symphony; Fremantle found
the excitement "entirely drove away the bile" which had been troubl-
ing him earlier. He had watched the *Victory* rake the *Bucentaure* and
then run alongside the *Redoutable*, and he immediately decided to go
through the gap between the *Victory* and the *Bucentaure*.

Villeneuve's flagship was still reeling from the *Victory*'s broadsides
when Fremantle took the *Neptune* across her stern. On the gun decks
the lieutenants were shouting themselves hoarse. "Make ready!...
Don't fire until your guns bear!" One after another the gunners tugged
the trigger lines, and treble-shotted guns belched smoke and flame. This
hail of nearly a hundred and fifty shot pouring in through the
Bucentaure's stern flung almost every remaining gun off its carriage; the
crews were cut down where they stood, by solid shot or splinters.
Fremantle then brought the *Neptune* round to port, and as she swung,
the whole broadside once again smashed into the French flagship,
wounding her captain, Jean Magendie.

Ahead and to the right of the now helpless *Bucentaure* was the
Santissima Trinidad, her red-and-white topsides gleaming through the
clouds of smoke. She was still heading north, which allowed
Fremantle to sail the *Neptune* across her unprotected stern and give her
a devastating raking. The *Neptune* then advanced to within less than a
hundred yards of the great ship.

The fourth ship in Nelson's line, Captain Bayntun's *Leviathan*,
followed through the gap in the wake of the *Neptune*. Like Fremantle,
Bayntun took his ship across the *Bucentaure*'s stern and fired off two
raking broadsides. He then looked for another opponent. After chasing
away the French *Neptune*, which had until then been firing into the
Téméraire, he raked the *Santissima Trinidad* and headed north towards
the French ships he saw in the distance.

THE 74-GUN *CONQUEROR*, under Captain Israel Pellew, fifth in Nelson's line, arrived at the gap, and Pellew took his ship under the stern of the *Bucentaure* as his three predecessors had done. "A cannonading commenced at so short a distance that every shot flew winged with death and destruction," wrote one of Pellew's lieutenants, and he did not exaggerate. More than thirty treble-shotted guns smashed in through the *Bucentaure*'s stern.

A few moments earlier Villeneuve had again hoisted a signal ordering Dumanoir to bring his van squadron into action. When the *Conqueror*'s broadside tore into the *Bucentaure*, shot splintered the mizzenmast and toppled the mainmast just above the upper deck, taking Villeneuve's signal to Dumanoir with it.

Aboard the *Bucentaure* the end was very near. "I had kept a boat lowered, foreseeing the possibility of being dismasted, with the intention of going aboard another vessel," Villeneuve later wrote. "As soon as the mainmast fell I gave orders for it to be made ready, but whether it had been sunk by shot or crushed by the falling of the masts, it could not be found.

"I had the *Santissima Trinidad* . . . hailed to know if she could send a boat [but] I had no reply; this ship was herself engaging vigorously with a three-decker [*Neptune*] that was firing into her quarter.

"In the end, surrounded by the enemy ships . . . powerless to do them any injury, the upper works and the 24-pounder gun deck being deserted and strewn with dead and wounded; the lower-deck guns dismounted or masked by the fallen masts and rigging . . . I was obliged to yield to my fate and put an end to a slaughter already vast." A white handerkerchief was waved in token of surrender.

Pellew was impatient to be on his way to join the attack on the *Santissima Trinidad* and did not want to weaken his own ship by putting a large boarding crew aboard the *Bucentaure*. Without realizing that it was the French commander-in-chief who had just surrendered— for Villeneuve's flag was not flying—he ordered Captain James Atcherley, commanding the *Conqueror*'s marines, to take a few men in a cutter and receive the French ship's surrender.

The *Conqueror*'s cutter was rowed across to the *Bucentaure*, and Atcherley made his way to the quarterdeck. Three French officers slowly walked towards him. Their leader was a tall, thin-faced man in the uniform of an admiral—a long-tailed coat with a high collar, and greenish-coloured corduroy trousers with a wide stripe down each side.

"To whom," asked Villeneuve, in English, "have I the honour of surrendering?"

"To Captain Pellew of the *Conqueror*," replied the awed Atcherley.

"It is a satisfaction to me," Villeneuve said courteously, "that it is to one so fortunate as Sir Edward Pellew that I have lowered my flag."

Atcherley looked startled. "It is his brother, sir."

"His brother? What, are there two of them? *Hélas!*"

The short, jocund-looking man at Villeneuve's side, who had already been taken to England twice before as a prisoner, shook his head philosophically. "*Fortune de la guerre,*" said the bloodstained Magendie. Atcherley politely suggested that all kept their swords and surrender them to an officer of a higher rank than his own.

As he led his captives down to the cutter waiting alongside, Atcherley saw that Captain Pellew had gone on ahead with the *Conqueror*, so he looked around for the nearest British ship. This was the *Mars*. A few minutes later her surprised commanding officer was receiving the sword of Vice Admiral Pierre Charles Jean Baptiste Sylvestre de Villeneuve, commander of the Combined Fleet of France and Spain.

THE *SANTISSIMA TRINIDAD* was putting up a brave and lonely fight against the *Neptune* on her starboard quarter when the *Conqueror* came up on her other side. Their combined broadsides smashed into the great ship; several shot bit into the massive mizzenmast below decks, and slowly it toppled over the side, taking the red-and-yellow flag of Spain with it. More shot cut into the mainmast, which crashed down like a great branch-laden tree. The men who had been perched in the tops with muskets were catapulted into the water, where their cries for help went unheard or unheeded.

"Her immense topsails had every reef out," wrote one of the *Conqueror*'s officers. "The falling of this majestic mass of spars, sails and rigging plunging into the water at the muzzles of our guns, was one of the most magnificent sights I ever beheld."

By now the little 64-gun *Africa* had joined the fray. On her way to rejoin Nelson she had passed the eight ships of Dumanoir's van squadron and exchanged broadsides with them. Now, finding the largest battleship in the action, Captain Digby brought to on her weather bow and began firing broadsides into her.

At the beginning of the battle, the proud flagship of Rear Admiral Don Baltazar Hidalgo Cisneros had poured devastating broadsides into the *Victory* as she came to break the line, but the fire from Fremantle's *Neptune* had been the beginning of her defeat. Soon everyone on the upper deck with the exception of her captain, Commodore de Uriarte, had been killed or wounded. Lying in heaps, trapped under gun carriages and caught by falling masts and yards were more than two hundred dead Spanish seamen and soldiers. "Blood ran in streams about the deck, and in spite of the sand, the rolling of the ship carried it hither and thither until it made strange patterns on the deck," says a Spanish account.

Now the broadsides of the *Neptune* and the *Conqueror*, helped by the *Africa*, were hitting the ship's most vulnerable part—her underwater sections. Shorn of her sails, the *Santissima Trinidad* was rolling considerably in the swell; first one side and then the other of her weed-stained hull showed above water, exposing it to shot from the British guns. Water flooded into her hold.

A splinter hit Commodore de Uriarte in the head and knocked him unconscious; the second-in-command was also wounded within a few moments. Admiral Cisneros, who lay wounded in the cockpit, sent orders to the third-in-command that he was not to surrender before consulting with the surviving officers still at their posts. These saw that further resistance would be useless, but how were they to surrender? There was no mast, not even a stump, from which a white flag could be flown. Someone discovered a British flag and ran to the gangway, waving it. At last the guns of the *Neptune* and *Conqueror* stopped firing.

Fremantle, on the *Neptune*, and Pellew, on the *Conqueror*, both noticed that Dumanoir's squadron was now less than two miles away, coming southward towards them as if to join in the battle. Bayntun's *Leviathan* was already boldly steering northward to meet the enemy, and they too followed.

It was left to Digby, in the *Africa*, to take possession of the surrendered *Santissima Trinidad*. He sent Lieutenant John Smith to board her with a boat crew. Making his way through the wreckage to the quarterdeck, Smith asked a Spanish officer if his ship had struck. Despite the previous flag-waving, the Spaniard pointed to Dumanoir's squadron, by now drawing closer, and replied, "No, no!" Smith left and rowed back to the *Africa*, where Digby was preparing to join the *Neptune* and the *Conqueror* in dealing with the approaching ships that had changed surrender to hope on board the great *Santissima Trinidad*.

IN THE GLOOM OF the *Victory*'s cockpit, Nelson was still half lying, half sitting against the thick oak frame in the only position that gave him any relief from the gnawing pain in his chest. Dr. Scott and Burke, the purser, squatted down on either side, supporting him. They were soon joined by Henry Chevalier and Gaetano Spedilo, Nelson's servants.

The flickering lanterns cast eerie shadows which lengthened and shortened with the ship's roll. Beatty and his two assistant surgeons hurried from one wounded man to the next. There were groans from some men; screams came from others. More, who had been waiting for the surgeons to reach them, were silent, for death had already stopped their pain.

There were faint cheers from the decks above. "What is that?" asked Nelson. "Why are they cheering?" Lieutenant Pasco, lying wounded nearby, raised himself on his elbow. "Another enemy ship has struck, my Lord."

Nelson settled back, apparently well satisfied. Occasionally, when particularly sharp spasms of pain twisted his emaciated body, he would gasp, "Fan, fan," and Burke or Scott would wave a cloth in front of him. The air seemed to give him relief. Then he would whisper, "Drink, drink," and they would give him sips of lemonade, or wine and water. Frequently he would ask how the battle was going, his voice revealing his apprehension. Burke, trying to comfort him, said, "The enemy are decisively defeated, and I hope your Lordship will live to be yourself the bearer of the joyful tidings to our country."

But Nelson, who had seen a sailor fall and break his back in the *Victory* only a month earlier and had often questioned Beatty in detail about the man's symptoms (for the unfortunate sailor had taken thirteen days to die), was not to be fooled by such well-meant words. "It is nonsense, Mr. Burke," he gasped, "to suppose I can live. My sufferings are great, but they will soon be over."

For some time Nelson had been worried about Captain Hardy, and had sent several messengers to fetch him. But the burly Hardy had his hands full dealing with the *Redoutable* alongside and dared not leave the quarterdeck. Nelson became more and more anxious about the friend who had served him so faithfully. "Will no one bring Hardy to me? He is surely destroyed!" A few minutes later a midshipman arrived fresh from the quarterdeck with a message.

"Circumstances respecting the fleet require Captain Hardy's presence on deck," he said, carefully repeating the message, "but he will avail himself of the first favourable moment to visit his Lordship."

From the moment Nelson had fallen wounded, Hardy had in fact been acting as commander-in-chief, and the "circumstances respecting the fleet" that now detained him were the ships of Dumanoir's squadron, which looked as if they were finally about to enter the battle.

THE 74-GUN *Fougueux*, commanded by Captain Baudouin, had been immediately astern of Vice Admiral de Álava's 112-gun flagship, the *Santa Ana*, at the beginning of the action. In going to the *Santa Ana*'s assistance, the *Fougueux* had been raked by the 100-gun *Royal Sovereign* and two seventy-fours, the *Belleisle* and the *Mars*. With topsail and lower yards shot away, she had drifted to the northwest in thick smoke. This cleared in a gentle breeze just when Harvey noticed her from the *Téméraire*. His powerful starboard broadside had not yet been fired, and Harvey paused until the *Fougueux* came slowly into his sights; then a devastating wall of round shot and grape smashed into her. The *Fougueux*'s main- and mizzenmasts began to totter; Captain Baudouin collapsed, dying, on the quarterdeck; the carriages of many guns were smashed to matchwood; and scores of seamen and soldiers were cut down.

Commander Bazin, the second-in-command, took over; but the *Fougueux* was out of control, and glided on towards the *Téméraire* through the smoke of the first broadside, as another broadside flung solid shot and grape screaming into her. Then, with a rending crash, the *Fougueux* ran into the *Téméraire*. The impact snapped her wobbling main- and mizzenmasts and they collapsed over the side.

Commander Bazin sent for the third-in-command to help him fight off the boarders who would soon be invading his ship. But word came back that the third-in-command had been killed and that the fourth-in-command was dying. Finally, Bazin's messenger found one surviving lieutenant, who told him that nearly every man who had been serving the lower-deck guns was dead. By this time shouting British seamen and marines were swarming over the bulwarks, lashing out with their cutlasses, stabbing with short-handled boarding pikes and using their muskets as clubs.

"Seeing the impossibility of repelling boarding, or of defending the ship against the number . . . who were getting aboard," wrote Bazin, "I gave orders to cease firing and dragged myself, in spite of my wounds, as far as the Captain's cabin to get and throw into the sea the [leaden] box containing the signals and instructions for the ship, and, reappearing on the quarter-deck, I was taken and conveyed on board the English ship; the enemy hauled down the colours and gradually the slaughter ceased entirely."

To the south, Captain John Cooke's 74-gun *Bellerophon* was just coming down to the Combined Fleet's line. Her black-and-yellow sides gleaming, the *Bellerophon* was ready for battle. At 12:10 p.m., just after the *Royal Sovereign* had broken through the enemy line, one of the *Bellerophon*'s midshipmen tripped over a trigger line and a gun went off. The enemy ships ahead apparently thought that this was some signal prearranged among the British ships, and four seventy-fours—the *Aigle*, *Bahama*, *Montañes* and *Swiftsure*—opened fire on the *Bellerophon* together. As the enemy shots whined into his ship, Captain Cooke ordered his forward guns to be fired so that the *Bellerophon* would be partly hidden in her own smoke from the French and Spanish ships.

Now there was almost a calm; the *Bellerophon* was down to under two knots in the rapidly falling wind. Slowly she bore down on the enemy line until she finally had the *Bahama* coming into the sights of her port guns and the *Montañes* into those to starboard. There was a brief pause as the gunners waited for the ship's roll, and then, with shattering suddenness, the *Bellerophon*'s broadsides smashed into the Spanish ships.

While the guns on both sides were being reloaded, Captain Cooke ordered the ship brought round to range up alongside the *Bahama*. But in the dirty yellow smoke to leeward, he saw the topgallants of another ship, very close on the starboard side. The quartermasters spun the wheel while sail trimmers scrambled to get the sails aback in order to check the *Bellerophon*'s way through the water. They just had time to read the name *Aigle* before the *Bellerophon*'s starboard bow crashed into the French ship.

The French *Swiftsure* had, in the meantime, come up astern of the *Aigle*, and the *Bellerophon* was now caught between four of the enemy: the *Aigle* alongside to starboard, the *Swiftsure* on the starboard quarter, the *Bahama* away on the port bow and the *Montañes* on the port quarter. All kept up a brisk fire on the British ship.

The *Bellerophon* concentrated most of her efforts on the *Aigle*. A rain of musket balls and shot smashed across the *Aigle*'s decks, cutting down men in swathes. Her commanding officer, Captain Gourrège, lay dying, leaving Commander Tempié in charge.

Aboard the *Bellerophon*, Captain Cooke ordered his chief lieutenant, William Cumby, to keep the starboard guns firing at all costs and to elevate them so that the shot would smash upward through the *Aigle*'s decks and cause maximum damage. Scrambling up to the main deck after giving his instructions to the officers on the gun deck, Cumby saw Overton, the master, dying, one of his legs shattered by a shot. Then, before he reached the quarterdeck ladder, a quartermaster shouted to him, "The captain's been wounded, sir! I believe he's dead!"

Captain Cooke had been firing his pistols at the *Aigle*'s quarterdeck and was reloading them when two musket balls hit him in the chest. Before a minute passed he had died.

On the lower decks the French and British gun crews were fighting through the ports, battering each other with rammers, slashing out with cutlasses, firing muskets and hurling grenades. French officers could be heard shouting "*A l'abordage!*" The space between the two ships was so narrow that French sailors and soldiers could leap across and grab a handhold. "Their hands received some severe blows from whatever the English could lay their hands on. In this way hundreds of Frenchmen fell between the ships and were drowned," wrote Midshipman John Franklin.

Heavy fire from the *Aigle* was slashing the *Bellerophon*'s rigging.

Among the ropes cut were those carrying her colours. When they came down for the third time, the yeoman of signals, Christopher Beatty, searched for and found an ensign, flung it over his shoulders and clambered up the tattered mizzen rigging. As soon as he began his hand-over-hand scramble, a hail of musket balls whistled around him. Several feet above the deck he took the flag from his shoulders and began to spread it on the shrouds. Almost at once the French sharp-shooters stopped firing, as if they understood his motives and admired his courage. The ensign lashed, he climbed down to the deck again, unharmed.

By now the other enemy ships were closing in around the *Bellerophon*. The *Bahama* was only a few score yards away to windward, firing slowly but with deadly effect. The *Bellerophon*'s main-topmast tumbled down, dragging a tangled mass of rigging with it. The topsail fell on the starboard side, hanging over the guns as they pounded the *Aigle*. In a few moments the flash from the muzzles set the canvas ablaze, and the flames threatened to set both ships on fire. Cumby soon had the sail trimmers cutting it free with axes, and the burning sail dropped into the sea. By then, with sails and rigging slashed and the hull riddled with shot holes, the *Bellerophon* was "an unmanageable wreck".

Although the French sharpshooters packed in her tops were still busy, the *Aigle*'s gunfire, like that of the *Bellerophon*'s, was beginning to ease up appreciably. Each ship's guns had taken a heavy toll; at least half the *Aigle*'s crew had been killed or wounded, while by now more than twenty in the *Bellerophon* had been killed and a hundred wounded. Within a few minutes the *Aigle* had had enough. French seamen hoisted a jib and sheeted it home. Slowly the *Aigle* dragged herself clear and sagged away to leeward. "Her quarter was entirely beaten in," wrote an officer on the *Bellerophon*. "I have no doubt she would have struck had we been able to follow and engage her for a quarter of an hour longer."

The *Bellerophon*, however, was still in grave danger. Before her encounter with the *Tonnant*, Churruca's *San Juan Nepomuceno* had come out of the smoke and manoeuvered into position to fire a broad-side into the *Bellerophon*'s stern, which might well have put her out of action altogether. But a huge British three-decker, the 98-gun *Dreadnought*, loomed up alongside her just in time, and a few seconds later the pulsing darts of flame and spurts of smoke heralded a devastating broadside at Churruca's ship.

As the smoke cleared away, Cumby wrote: "We observed that the *Aigle* was engaged by the *Defiance* and soon after two o'clock she struck." He could see that several other enemy ships had also struck, including the Spanish *Monarca*, which was lying nearby, by now a shattered hulk, with one hundred and one men dead and another one hundred and fifty-four wounded. He sent a boarding party to take possession of her.

CAPTAIN JAMES MORRIS, of the *Colossus*, got into close action five minutes behind his next ahead, the *Bellerophon*. The first ship she met was the French *Swiftsure*, which was falling away after her encounter with the *Bellerophon*. Morris managed to fire a broadside into her before sailing on into a great cloud of smoke. Suddenly out of the murk on the starboard side the French *Argonaute* appeared on a converging course. In a few seconds the two ships crashed with a rending and splintering of wood.

Swiftly the seamen on the *Colossus* opened fire on the *Argonaute*, loading and firing double-shotted broadsides, while on the poop deck the marines kept up a fusillade with their muskets. Within ten minutes, according to the British accounts, the *Argonaute*'s guns were almost silent, and the swell, which had been lifting the two ships and crashing them together, finally drew them apart, and the French ship drifted clear. Almost the last shot fired by the *Argonaute* hit Captain Morris above the knee, wounding him badly. He refused to be taken down to the cockpit, lashing a tourniquet around his thigh to stop the bleeding.

By this time Commodore Alcala Galiano, of the Spanish *Bahama*, who had previously hauled clear of the onslaught of the *Bellerophon*, now opened fire on the *Colossus*. A few minutes later the French *Swiftsure* rejoined the fray, forging between the two ships to mask the *Bahama*'s fire and take the full force of the *Colossus*'s broadside. The British gunners fired so rapidly and with such accuracy that she soon dropped astern, leaving the *Bahama* once again in the line of fire.

Rapid broadsides from the *Colossus* slashed the *Bahama*'s rigging and crashed through her hull. One shot flung a splinter which hit

Galiano on the foot, and a few minutes later another gashed his scalp. Still he refused to go below to the surgeon. "Alcala Galiano gave his orders and directed his guns as if the ship had been firing salutes at a review," says one Spanish account. But the British gunners were firing faster than the Spaniards, and more accurately.

Now a shot spun the telescope out of Galiano's hand and made him stagger. When a coxswain hurried to his side, Galiano gave a re-assuring smile. At that moment a cannonball hit the coxswain; a second later Galiano was hit in the head and fell dead. Although a flag was flung over his body so that the men should not know their fearless captain had perished, the news spread rapidly through the whole crew, and the heart went out of them.

The *Bahama*'s surviving officers held a rapidly summoned council of war. Some seventy-five officers and men had been killed and sixty-six wounded out of a crew of six hundred and ninety. While the officers of the council deliberated, the mizzenmast crashed down about their ears. Within a few minutes the *Bahama* "gave signs, by showing an English jack, that she had surrendered".

There was no time to send a prize crew across from the *Colossus*. The French *Swiftsure*, which had dropped astern, began to turn under the Britisher's stern to pour in a raking broadside. But Captain Morris, although faint from loss of blood, was too alert to be caught. He gave the order to come round, and the *Colossus* swung even faster than the *Swiftsure*. A few of the *Swiftsure*'s port guns fired before a broadside from the *Colossus* toppled her mizzenmast and knocked her main-topmast over the side.

Then Codrington's *Orion*, half-hidden in the smoke, came in astern of the *Swiftsure* and fired three broadsides into her. Their effect was disastrous. The *Swiftsure*'s foremast followed the other two over the side. "Having no longer any hope of being supported..." wrote Captain Villemadrin, "and [having] five feet of water in the hold—I gave orders to cease fire and I hauled down my colours."

THE SEVENTH SHIP IN Collingwood's division to get into action was Captain Richard King's 74-gun *Achille*. King brought his ship down to pass through the enemy's line astern of the *Montañes* and ahead of the *San Ildefonso*. He chose the *Montañes* for his victim, steered boldly under her stern and fired a broadside into her quarter as he passed, then brought the *Achille* alongside her. Wreathed in thick smoke, the two ships lay close to each other, firing broadsides as boxers might exchange punches.

Within half an hour the *Montañes*'s Captain Salzedo was killed and his second-in-command wounded. On the quarterdeck "the crews of all the guns aft were out of action, many being stretched dead and dying on the deck; the same thing was apparent in the chief guns on the quarter-deck. . . ."

The *Montañes* sheered off out of the fight, and Captain King turned the *Achille* away to starboard. A few minutes later he found another Spanish ship, the *Argonauta*, in the smoke to his right. He promptly hove to on her port bow, and for the best part of an hour British gunners fired broadside after broadside into the Spanish ship. According to her wounded commanding officer, Captain Pareja, the *Argonauta* had "a great number of guns in the batteries out of action, as much as on account of the pieces [being damaged] as from the want of crews . . . the whole rigging was destroyed, so that there were no shrouds left to the masts. . . .

"In this situation," he adds, "it was very evident that the ship could make but slight and feeble resistance. . . . With these inexpressible feelings I was taken below to have my wounds dressed, expecting every minute to find myself brought to the grievous point of having to surrender." But for the moment the *Argonauta* had won a brief reprieve. The French *Achille* (which had been in action down the line with the *Revenge*) arrived on the British *Achille*'s port side and opened fire.

A short while afterwards the French *Berwick* sailed up on the British *Achille*'s other side, and for a few minutes the British ship was sandwiched between two of the enemy while the *Argonauta* drifted away to leeward. Her masts tottering, and with three hundred and three men killed or wounded out of a total crew of seven hundred and eighty, the stricken *Argonauta* was more like a floating coffin than a ship of war. She surrendered to the *Belleisle* a half hour later.

The French *Achille* went ahead, leaving the British *Achille* and the *Berwick* to fight it out. Although King and his men had already silenced two ships, the *Montañes* and the *Argonauta*, they still had plenty of fight left in them, and within half an hour they forced the *Berwick* to strike.

The wounded in the *Berwick* amounted to nearly two hundred; her loss in officers was very severe, "the quarter-deck having thrice been cleared".

At 12:35 p.m. Captain Robert Moorsom brought the 74-gun *Revenge* into action.

The *Revenge*, a new ship launched only a few months earlier, had come up to the line obliquely, running almost parallel to the *San Ildefonso* and the French *Achille*. When Captain Moorsom ordered the *Revenge*'s gunners to open fire on both ships, shot from their opening broadsides topped the *Achille*'s mizzenmast. She had been sailing very close to the stern of the *San Ildefonso*, but as the mizzen went by the board, she slowed down, and Moorsom seized the opportunity to break through the line. He went close to the French ship, then luffed up and put his ship on the *Achille*'s starboard bow, where he could fire his port guns into her and aim his starboard broadside at the stern of the *San Ildefonso*.

Just astern, Admiral Gravina's flagship, the *Principe de Asturias*, bore away so that she could rake the *Revenge*. The British 74-gun ship now found herself in a triangle of fire from the *San Ildefonso*, *Achille* and *Principe de Asturias*. It was nearly twenty minutes before help arrived from four of the last ships in Collingwood's division, led by Captain Durham in the *Defiance*. This gallant Scot tried to pass under the stern of the *Principe de Asturias*, but the next in line, the French *Berwick* (as yet unwounded), closed the gap and ran into his ship, damaging the rigging.

Gravina's flagship turned away to pass astern of the *Revenge* and rake her, but Durham extricated the *Defiance* from the *Berwick*'s clutches and went off in pursuit of the *Principe de Asturias*. The *Berwick*, apparently unwilling to be left alone (for there were three more British ships coming up astern), followed the *Principe de Asturias*'s example and also turned away. But as we have seen, she was to fall victim to the British *Achille*.

Durham's *Defiance* had to break off her chase of the *Principe de Asturias* because of her damaged rigging. Shortly afterwards the *Defiance* met the *Aigle*, fresh from her shattering encounters with the *Bellerophon* and the *Belleisle*. According to Durham's biographer, although severely damaged, the *Aigle* "was, however, quite ready for action, and defended herself most gallantly for some time; at length her fire began to slacken, and Captain Durham, thinking she had surrendered, called up his boarders to take possession."

Every one of the *Defiance*'s boats was riddled with shot, and there was little breeze to get the British ship alongside the *Aigle*. This situation inspired young Midshipman Jack Spratt, described as a "high-spirited Irishman", to volunteer to swim over to the *Aigle*. Sticking an axe in his belt, he "took his cutlass between his teeth, called upon the boarders to follow, [and] leapt overboard." Scrambling up the French ship by means of the rudder chains, Spratt quickly discovered that she had not surrendered after all. He managed to disable three French soldiers before his shipmates from the *Defiance* came to his rescue.

But Spratt's adventures were not ended. A French soldier aimed a musket at his chest and squeezed the trigger. Spratt knocked the musket barrel down as it fired, so that the ball hit his right leg just below the knee, breaking both bones. Managing to avoid falling, Spratt hopped between two quarterdeck guns to get his back against the bulwarks and thus prevent the French soldiers from cutting him down from behind.

Fortunately the boarding party had managed to get lines across to the *Defiance* from the *Aigle*, so that Captain Durham could warp both ships together. One of the first people that Durham saw through the smoke was Spratt, who had dragged himself to the side by then. Holding his bleeding limb over the rail, he called out, "Captain, poor old Jack Spratt is done up at last!" He was brought on board and taken below to the cockpit, where he steadfastly refused to allow the surgeons to amputate his wounded leg.

Sharpshooters in the tops kept firing down on the boarding party, and many more were busy throwing grenades through the *Defiance*'s gun ports. Captain Durham, rather than lose any more of his men, called the boarding party back on board the *Defiance* and ordered the lines holding the *Aigle* to be cut. When the two ships had drifted a few yards apart, the guns on the *Defiance* opened fire. Shot after shot crashed with great precision into the *Aigle*.

"We held out for some time," reported Lieutenant Asmus Classen, now in command, "but the enemy's flaming sulphur-saturated wads having set the gun room on fire ... we decided to haul down our colours in order to extinguish the flames and to preserve for the Emperor the scanty number of the gallant defenders who remained." Classen had not exaggerated. "The decks were covered with dead and wounded," wrote one of the *Defiance*'s crew. "They never heave their dead overboard in time of action as we do." The *Defiance* had seventeen men killed and fifty-three wounded.

CHAPTER 10

NELSON'S MAIN PURPOSE had now been achieved. The van of the Combined Fleet, under Dumanoir, had been prevented for more than two hours from taking any effective part in the battle; Villeneuve had been captured, and those battleships around him which had not surrendered had been driven off to leeward, out of the way. The rear ships, under Gravina, were still being savagely handled by the rest of Collingwood's ships as they came into action.

The 98-gun *Dreadnought* was slow, but when she finally arrived, Captain Conn quickly brought her alongside Churruca's *San Juan Nepomuceno*. The British three-decker's attack was overwhelming, and although bravely fought, the *San Juan Nepomuceno* had to surrender. Commander Churruca, according to one Spanish account, had "directed the battle with gloomy calmness. Knowing that only care and skill could supply the place of strength, he economized our fire, trusting entirely to careful aim. . . . He saw to everything, settled everything, and the shot flew round him and over his head without his ever once even changing colour. . . .

"It was not the will of God, however, that he should escape alive from that storm of fire. . . . He was returning to the quarter-deck [from the gun deck] when a cannon ball hit his right leg with such violence as almost to take it off. He fell to the ground, but the next moment he made an effort to raise himself. His face was as white as death, but he said, in a voice that was scarcely weaker than his ordinary tones: 'It is nothing—go on firing.'

"He did all he could to conceal the terrible sufferings of his cruelly mangled frame. At last he yielded to our entreaties and seemed to understand that he must give up the command. . . . He was going fast. He specially desired that the men should be thanked for their heroic courage. Then, after sending a farewell message to his poor young wife, whom he had married only a few days before he sailed, he fixed his thoughts on God. So with the calm resignation of a good man and the fortitude of a hero, Churruca passed away."

When the Spanish ship surrendered, Captain Conn brought the *Dreadnought* round and joined in the pursuit of the *Principe de Asturias*, which was the only ship in Gravina's squadron which had not surrendered or quit the battle by running to leeward.

The *Santa Ana*, flagship of Admiral de Álava, was just surrendering to the *Royal Sovereign* when a boat from the *Victory* arrived alongside. Admiral Collingwood, his leg swollen and bleeding under its bandage, was told by Lieutenant Alexander Hills, of the *Victory*, that Nelson had been wounded. "I asked the officer if his wound was dangerous," Collingwood later wrote. "He hesitated; then said he hoped it was not; but I saw the fate of my friend in his eye; for his look told what his tongue could not utter."

For the moment the *Royal Sovereign* was helpless, having lost her main- and mizzenmasts. Blackwood's *Euryalus* was signalled to take her in tow. With his ship finally under way again, Collingwood hailed Blackwood and told him to go aboard the *Santa Ana* and "Bring me the admiral."

Blackwood found Admiral de Álava too badly wounded to be moved and brought Captain Gardoqui back with him instead. When the Spanish captain came on board the *Royal Sovereign*, on being told the name of the ship, he said in broken English, "I think she should be called the *Royal Devil*."

DUMANOIR, MEANWHILE, had received Villeneuve's last signal just before the *Bucentaure*'s masts toppled over the side. "The over-light breeze checked the speed with which I desired to bear down to his assistance," Dumanoir later said in a report aimed at justifying his tardiness. "I had still a hope that I might take him [Villeneuve] in tow and endeavour to get him out of [the line of] fire."

When Captain Hardy, from the bloodstained decks of the *Victory*, noticed Dumanoir's ships turning back as though to join in the battle, he hoisted the signal for the British ships to come north on a port tack, thus getting into a position to beat off the new threat while at the same time guarding the prizes to leeward. A similar signal by

Collingwood to the British ships to the south ordered them to leave off their pursuit of Gravina and bear north to join battle with Dumanoir.

Dumanoir's squadron had by now split itself into three distinct groups—Dumanoir's *Formidable* was followed by four ships sailing southward about half a mile to windward of the *Bucentaure* and towards the British *Spartiate* and *Minotaur*, the last ships in Nelson's division, just now coming into the battle. The second group, the *Intrépide* and *San Augustin*, were heading bravely down towards the battle. The third group, made up of three more ships, were to leeward, unashamedly about to steer away for Cádiz. In other words, out of the ten fresh and undamaged French and Spanish ships, only two were attempting to go directly to Villeneuve's rescue.

Dumanoir's descent with his five ships on the two lone British ships was a curious parallel with Nelson's right-angle approach to the enemy line. But whereas Nelson succeeded, Dumanoir had to report afterwards that "the two vessels that I had intended to cut off managed to pass ahead of me at pistol shot and damaged me greatly." Even with the odds at five to two, he had failed to make an impression. His last in line, moreover, the Spanish *Neptuno*, was surrounded and captured.

The admiral bemoaned his fate; reasonably enough, he felt the lack of the five ships which had failed to follow him. "If I had had with me ten ships, however, desperate our position, I should have been able to bear down on the scene of the action and fight the enemy to a finish . . . and perhaps it would have been reserved for me to have made the day glorious for the Allied Fleet." But he appeared to have forgotten that this opportunity had existed from the moment the action began, and that two hours earlier his intervention might well have had a considerable effect.

Of the four ships now left to him—well, "to bear down on the enemy at this moment would . . . have only served to increase the number of our losses and augment the advantages to the enemy to whom, on account of the depletion of my division, I could not have done much damage." So Dumanoir's quartet sailed on to the south, apparently satisfied. Two weeks later Dumanoir was to meet Sir Richard Strachan's squadron in the Mediterranean and have his four ships captured.

MEANWHILE, CAPTAIN LOUIS INFERNET's *Intrépide* was steering for the enemy to fight one of the most gallant actions of the whole battle. "We could hardly make out in the midst of the smoke and confusion of the battle," wrote the Marquis Gicquel des Touches, a young lieutenant on board, "the situation of our flagship [*Bucentaure*], surrounded as she was by the enemy . . . [and] it was into the thick of this fray that our Captain Infernet led us. He wanted, he said, to rescue Admiral Villeneuve and then to rally round ourselves the ships that were still in a fit state to fight. . . . It was a noble madness, but though we knew it, we all supported him with joyful alacrity—and would that others had imitated his example!"

While Infernet steered the *Intrépide* down towards the new line of British ships, the *San Augustin* steered a parallel course to leeward. The *Leviathan*, leading the British line, was the first to engage the *San Augustin*, turning out of the line to run alongside her, and Infernet seized the opportunity to pour a raking broadside into her bow. The little 64-gun *Africa* quickly turned up under the *Intrépide*'s stern and opened fire. Next the *Britannia*, *Ajax*, *Agamemnon* and *Neptune* fired into the *Intrépide* as they passed northward in pursuit of the ships steering for Cádiz. Finally, Codrington brought the *Orion* up to rake the French ship.

Young Marquis des Touches in the *Intrépide* was having a busy time. He wrote:

> While the fighting was very hot the British *Orion* crossed our bows. . . . I got my men ready to board and sent [a midshipman] to the Captain with a request to have the ship laid on board the *Orion*. Seeing the ardour of my men, I already imagined myself master of the British 74 and taking her into Cadiz with her colours under ours. With keen anxiety I waited; but there was no change in the *Intrépide*'s course.
>
> Then I dashed off to the quarter-deck myself. On the way I found my [emissary] lying flat on the deck, terrified at the sight of the *Britannia* thundering into us from her lofty batteries. . . . I gave him a hearty kick —and then I hurried aft to explain my project personally to the Captain. It was then, though, too late. The *Orion* swept forward across our bows, letting fly a murderous broadside—and no second chance presented itself.
>
> At the moment I reached the poop the brave Infernet was brandish-

ing a small curved sabre. . . . The blade went close to my face, and I said laughingly, "Do you went to cut my head off, Captain?"

"No, certainly not you, my friend," was the reply, "but that's what I mean to do to the first man who speaks to me of surrender."

Infernet, a Provençal by birth, rough in manner and uneducated, wrote a report which gives some idea of the odds he was by now fighting:

At four o'clock* I was dismantled to such a degree that all my rigging was cut to pieces and several guns dismounted. At 4:45 I ordered the few hands remaining on deck to go below to the batteries in order to engage to starboard and larboard. . . . At five o'clock the wheel and the tiller were shattered. I at once had the spare tiller rigged and steered with it, always fighting desperately. At 5:15 the mizzenmast fell; four or five minutes later the mainmast did the same; I still fought—and I am able to say so to the honour of those whom I commanded—undauntedly. . . .

At 5:53 p.m. the foremast fell; I was then left without masts or sails; not being able to escape, having, moreover, no French ships in sight to come to my assistance. . . . I was obliged to yield to the seven enemy ships that were engaging me.

Although British reports do not bear out Infernet's report that there were seven ships engaging him sumultaneously, Senhouse, of the *Conqueror*, wrote that the French captain surrendered "after one of the most gallant defences I ever witnessed. The Frenchman's name was Infernet . . . and it deserves to be recorded in the memory of those who admire true courage."

Gravina's *Principe de Asturias*, in the meantime, was rolling and lurching her way north in company with three French ships. At 4:30 p.m. the admiral had ordered the remaining French and Spanish ships to rally and steer towards Cádiz. At 5:00 p.m. the frigate *Themis* took the flagship in tow, and on their way they were joined by six other ships of the Combined Fleet. Dumanoir was already well clear with his four ships. But the drama off Cape Trafalgar was not yet over.

*Infernet's time was an hour ahead of that used by the British ships.

WHILE MEN OF MANY NATIONS were fighting for their lives around the *Victory*, Horatio Nelson lay with his back against the ship's side, feeling death within him yet keeping a tenuous but painful grasp on life. Burke had his arm around his shoulders; Scott, the chaplain, knelt to massage his chest or offer a drink. The steward, Chevalier, and Spedilo, Nelson's valet, crouched nearby, anxious for a task that would ease their helplessness.

Looking pathetically small and helpless, his face white and his breathing shallow, Nelson waited for Hardy to appear. More than an hour had passed since he had been carried below from the quarter-deck. For the whole of that time he had been without news of what was happening in this, his last and his greatest battle.

Finally, Hardy scrambled down the ladder. Crouching to avoid banging his head on the beams, he went over to the admiral and shook hands affectionately.

"Well, Hardy, how goes the battle? How goes the day with us?"

"Very well, my Lord. We have got twelve or fourteen of the enemy's ships in our possession."

"I hope," said Nelson, "none of *our* ships have struck, Hardy."

"No, my Lord, there is no fear of that."

Then Nelson said, "I am a dead man, Hardy, I am going fast; it will be all over with me soon. Come nearer to me. . . ."

Sensing that whatever Nelson was about to say would be private, Burke made to move away, but he was motioned to stay.

"Pray let my dear Lady Hamilton have my hair, and all other things belonging to me," whispered Nelson.

Hardy, distressed at this turn in the conversation, said that he hoped that Beatty could hold out some prospect of life.

"Oh no," replied Nelson with what vehemence he could muster. "It is impossible. My back is shot through. Beatty will tell you so."

Hardy's presence was wanted on the quarterdeck. He again shook hands with Nelson and with a sad heart climbed back up the ladder. Soon after his departure the surgeon was summoned to Nelson's side.

"Ah, Mr. Beatty," said Nelson quietly, "I have sent for you to say what I forgot to tell you before, that all power of motion and feeling below my breast are gone; and *you* very well *know* I can live but a short time."

Beatty knew that Nelson had in his mind the seaman who had broken his back the previous July, and he realized that it was pointless to comfort his admiral. "My Lord, unhappily for our country, nothing can be done for you." As if saying aloud what he had tried to conceal had broken his professional reserve, tears came to his eyes, and he turned quickly and walked a few paces so that he could not be seen.

Burke and Scott kept giving Nelson sips of lemonade from time to time, but his brow was cold and his breathing uneven and painful. Beatty came back and asked if the pain was still very bad. "It continues so severe," was the reply, "that I wish I was dead. Yet," he said, his voice dropping, as a confiding child might reveal a secret wish, "one would like to live a little longer, too."

Another hour went by. During that time Dumanoir's ships had passed to windward. Hardy now had a few minutes to spare for another visit, as described by Beatty:

> Lord Nelson and Captain Hardy shook hands again, and while the Captain retained his Lordship's hand, he congratulated him, even in the arms of death, on his brilliant victory, which, he said, was complete; though he did not know how many of the enemy were captured . . . he was certain of fourteen or fifteen.
>
> "That is well, but I bargained for twenty," said Nelson; then, gripping Hardy's hand tighter, he exclaimed with sudden emphasis, "*Anchor*, Hardy, anchor!"

Nelson recalled the long white clouds which had, from early morning, spread like feathers from the west; coupled with the heavy swell, Nelson knew that a storm was coming up from the direction of the setting sun. With the shoals of Cape Trafalgar and the rock-grit coast close under their lee, the British fleet and the prizes were in great danger.

Hardy evidently considered that the time had come for Collingwood to take over command, but it was a difficult suggestion to make to a dying man, and particularly to Nelson. So he said, with as much tact as he could muster, "I suppose, my Lord, Admiral Collingwood will now take upon himself the direction of affairs."

The effect on Nelson was startling. He reacted violently, trying to struggle up from the mattress. "Not while I live, I hope, Hardy!" He added, "No, do *you* anchor, Hardy!"

"Shall we make the signal, sir?"

"Yes—for if I live, I'll anchor."

Beatty says that "the energetic manner in which [Nelson] uttered these his last orders to Captain Hardy, accompanied by his efforts to raise himself, evinced his determination never to resign the command while he retained the exercise of his transcendent faculties...."

But as if this last effort had taken him a few steps nearer to the end he said to Hardy, "I feel that in a few moments I shall be no more. Don't throw me overboard, Hardy."

"Oh no, certainly not."

"Then," whispered Nelson, "you know what to do; and take care of my dear Lady Hamilton.... Kiss me, Hardy."

Hardy knelt and kissed his cheek. With every beat of his heart, Nelson's life was ebbing away fast. He looked up at Hardy's strained face and whispered, "Now I am satisfied. Thank God I have done my duty."

Hardy stood up and made his way back to the quarterdeck.

The *Victory*'s log recorded: "Partial firing continued until 4:30, when a victory having been reported to the Right Honourable Lord Viscount Nelson, he then died of his wound."

THE FRENCH *Achille*, which had been burning for over an hour, blew up at 5:30 p.m., and thus signalled the end of the battle. Admiral Collingwood, now in command, had already transferred from the badly damaged *Royal Sovereign* to the *Euryalus*, where he was accompanied by Admiral Villeneuve.

When the sun went down that evening, it left behind a scene of grandeur and of desolation. The Combined Fleet of France and Spain, which a few hours earlier had been drawn up in fine array, was now so badly mauled as to be powerless. Seventeen French and Spanish ships had been captured and the eighteenth had blown up—just two short of the twenty for which Nelson had "bargained". Dumanoir, with four ships, was sailing off to eventual destruction, and Gravina, with the remaining eleven, was heading for the safety of Cádiz. Not one of the British fleet of twenty-seven ships which had gone into action against the thirty-three of the enemy had been sunk or forced to strike.

But the great swells which now rolled across the scene of battle, and

the fronds of high cloud which had finally merged into an ominous grey sheet were no idle portents. By the next day there was a gale blowing, and the day after that, October 23, great seas were sweeping in from the west, rolling along before the screaming winds. It was into this that Captain Cosmao-Kerjulien, of the *Pluton*, led twelve French and Spanish ships out of Cádiz to try to recapture some of the prizes which were now drifting at the mercy of the weather.

The remaining British ships in the area rallied, but the weather was too bad for battle. Cosmao-Kerjulien managed to get the *Santa Ana* and French *Neptune* in tow and take them back to Cádiz, but the sally cost him three of his five battleships—two to the storm and one, forced to anchor, captured by the British next day. Of the fifteen prizes that remained, six were eventually wrecked and another five were scuttled or burned, because Collingwood thought he could not save them in the gale.

The Death of Nelson by Arthur Devis

At left, *The Battle of Trafalgar*
by J. R. Luna—a Spanish artist's view

Of the French and Spanish admirals who had engaged in the battle, one was now dead and five were wounded. Approximately 4408 officers and men of the Combined Fleet had been killed or drowned and 2545 wounded. Against this total the British casualties were remarkably small—449 officers and men killed and 1214 wounded.

THE *PICKLE* HAD BEEN sent home with the news of the great battle. In the *Victory*, Nelson's body had been put in a large cask—called a leaguer—which had been filled with brandy. The crew of the *Victory* were worried that the *Euryalus* would have the honour of returning home with Nelson's body. But as Marine James Bagley later wrote home to his sister: "They have behaved very well to us, for they wanted to take Lord Nelson from us, but we told Captain as we brought him out we would bring him home; so it was so...."

The *Victory*, however, was far from being safe. On the night of the battle Captain Hardy had set the crew to work getting tackles fitted to secure the fore- and mainmasts, and this work continued through October 22. The mainsail having been shot to pieces, an old foresail was brought up and set in its place. All the next day, as the crew tried to get the wreck of the mizzenmast clear, heavy seas threatened to roll what remained of the masts out of the ship. Just before dawn of October 24, the weather eased up, and at eleven a.m. Captain Redmill was able to bring the *Polyphemus* close enough to pass a hawser to the *Victory*. In fresh winds the two ships made their way towards Gibraltar.

The gale returned the next day, October 25, and at evening the towing hawser suddenly parted. "We shipped three heavy seas which filled the deck," wrote Midshipman Rivers. "Turned all hands to the pumps . . . and kept her from foundering."

Almost helpless in the gale, the former flagship had to be pumped the whole night. Dawn on October 26 brought little encouragement. Across the great grey and swirling waves to the northeast, her crew could see the *Royal Sovereign* flying a distress signal. Hardy, disregarding the *Victory*'s danger, sent the *Polyphemus* to her aid. Later that day the wind dropped slightly, and Thomas Fremantle brought the *Neptune* down to take the *Victory* in tow. On the evening of October 28, Captain Hardy's journal noted: "At 7, anchored in Rosia Bay, Gibraltar."

On November 3, having been partially refitted, the *Victory* sailed for England. A month and a day later she anchored at St. Helens, where Nelson had boarded her to sail for his last battle. On December 22 she was heading up the Thames, where she was met by the yacht *Chatham*, sent by the Board of Admiralty to receive Nelson's body and take it to Greenwich.

The body was taken from the cask in front of "all the officers in the ship, and several of his Lordship's friends," according to Beatty. After being dressed in a shirt, stockings and uniform, it was placed in the coffin which Captain Hallowell had had made from the *L'Orient*'s mast, which in turn was placed inside a leaden coffin and sealed. As the yard tackle lifted it from the deck of the *Victory* onto the *Chatham*, Nelson's flag at the fore was struck for the last time and hoisted at half-mast aboard the *Chatham*.

On January 9, 1806, Nelson was buried under the great dome of St. Paul's Cathedral. Among those watching the funeral procession were Vice Admiral Villeneuve and Captain Magendie, who had been given permission to come up from Hampshire, where they were living on parole.

EPILOGUE

IN APRIL 1806, HAVING been a prisoner for just over five months, Villeneuve was freed in exchange for four British post captains and sent back to France. Settling himself in at a hotel in Morlaix, Brittany, he wrote to Admiral Decrès, reporting his arrival. What were the minister's instructions? He would now go on to Rennes and there await the minister's orders. In Rennes, Villeneuve discovered that Lucas and Infernet, who were already in Paris, had been promoted to rear admiral.

But no reply came from Decrès; there was no summons from the Emperor bidding him to St.-Cloud. And as the days passed, Villeneuve grew more and more agitated. Finally, on the morning of April 22, he was found lying dead in his bed, an ordinary table knife driven up to its hilt in his chest. A letter addressed to his wife, saying that his life was a disgrace and asking her forgiveness for his suicide, has never been proved to be authentic. Whether Villeneuve did in fact commit suicide or, as rumour had it, he was murdered on Napoleon's orders will never be known for certain.

TRAFALGAR WAS ONE of the most decisive battles ever fought by the Royal Navy, and its effects are still felt in Britain today. Yet the day before Nelson defeated Napoleon at sea, the Emperor had won an apparently crushing victory on land against the Austrians at Ulm. When this news reached England—seven days before Lapenotière arrived with Collingwood's Trafalgar dispatch—the nation despaired. Pitt's masterly plan to bring the power of Russia and Austria to bear against Napoleon had failed even before it was properly launched. And even with the news of Trafalgar, the nation mourned the death of Nelson instead of celebrating the victory; they were far too close to the event to see exactly what it had achieved.

In the war with France, which was to last another ten years, there seemed at the time no hope for Britain. Yet the tide *had* turned. After Trafalgar, Napoleon had no fleet to use in the Mediterranean. Sicily was in British hands and Napoleon's door to Egypt was shut, and with it, his dreams of an eastern empire.

Forced into a purely continental strategy, Napoleon took the first steps on the course which led him inexorably to defeat on the snow-covered plains of Russia and, eventually, to the decks of the *Bellerophon* and exile on the island of St. Helena. And with the fleet of France destroyed as a challenger, Britain was given more than a hundred years in which to build an empire, a century in which the Royal Navy guaranteed that the sea-lanes were kept open—not only for Britain but for every other law-abiding nation.

It was a woman, Lady Londonderry, stepmother of Lord Castlereagh, who wrote perhaps the wisest words about Trafalgar and the death of Nelson:

> Never was there indeed an event so mournfully and so triumphantly important to England as the Battle of Trafalgar. The sentiment of the lamenting the individual more than rejoicing in the victory, shows the humanity and affection of the people of England; but their good sense and reflection will dwell only on the conquest, because no death, at a future moment, could have been more glorious.
>
> Had I been his wife, or his mother, I would rather have wept him dead than seen him languish on a less splendid day. In such a death there is no sting, and in such a grave everlasting victory.

THE GREAT WHITE WHALE
from MOBY DICK
by Herman Melville

THE GREAT WHITE WHALE

from
MOBY DICK
by
HERMAN MELVILLE

ILLUSTRATED
BY BARRON STOREY

When the man called Ishmael
signed aboard the *Pequod* for a whaling
cruise, he wanted only to escape the
dreariness of his life ashore, but
he soon found himself caught up in
an adventure far more strange
and sinister than any he had
imagined. The ship's skipper, Ahab,
wanted the death of only one
whale, the great white monster
known as Moby Dick which, on
a previous voyage, had mauled
him and made him a peg-legged
cripple. Ahab's lust for revenge
now drove him to risk his crew, his
ship and himself until eventually,
after long journeying in far seas, he
found the beast itself—or had
the beast found him?

HERMAN MELVILLE
(1819–1891) was the
son of a merchant who
died bankrupt and left him
to fend for himself
from an early age. After
working as clerk,
farmhand and teacher, he
shipped aboard a vessel as
cabin boy and made the
first of many adventurous
voyages. Underestimated
during his lifetime, he is
now counted among
the greatest of
American authors.

I. LOOMINGS

CALL ME ISHMAEL. Some years ago—never mind how long precisely—having little or no money in my purse and nothing particular to interest me onshore, I thought I would sail about a little and see the watery part of the world. It is a way I have of driving off spleen and regulating circulation. Whenever I find myself growing grim about the mouth, whenever it is a damp, drizzly November in my soul, whenever I find myself bringing up the rear of every funeral I meet—then I account it high time to get to sea as soon as I can. There is nothing surprising in this. Almost all men, sometime or other, cherish very nearly the same feelings toward the ocean.

I do not mean that I go to sea as a passenger. I go as a simple sailor, right before the mast, because they make a point of paying me for my trouble, whereas they never pay passengers a single penny that I ever heard of. True, they order me about some and make me jump from spar to spar, like a grasshopper in a May meadow. And at first this sort of thing is unpleasant enough. It touches one's sense of honor, particularly if you come of an old established family and if, just previous to putting your hand into the tarpot, you have been lording it as a country schoolmaster, making the tallest boys stand in awe of you. The transition is a keen one, I assure you, from a schoolmaster to a sailor. But even this wears off in time.

Finally, I always go to sea as a sailor because of the wholesome exercise and pure air of the forecastle deck. Wherefore was it that after having repeatedly smelled the sea as a merchant sailor, I should now take it into my head to go on a whaling voyage? The invisible police officer of the Fates, who influences me in some unaccountable way, can better answer this than anyone else. Doubtless, my going on this whaling voyage formed part of some grand program of Providence. Yet I think I can see a little into the motives which, being cunningly presented to me under various disguises, induced me to set about performing the part I did.

Chief among these motives was the overwhelming idea of the great whale himself. Such a portentous and mysterious monster roused all my curiosity. Then there were the wild and distant seas where he rolled his island bulk, the undeliverable, nameless perils of the whale. These, with all the attending marvels of a thousand Patagonian sights and sounds, helped to sway me to my wish. I am tormented with an everlasting itch for things remote. I love to sail forbidden seas, and land on barbarous coasts. Not ignoring what is good, I am quick to perceive a horror, and could still be social with it.

By reason of these things, then, the whaling voyage was welcome. The great floodgates of the wonderworld of dreams swung open, and in the wild conceits that swayed me to my purpose, two and two there floated into my inmost soul endless processions of the whale, and midmost of them all, one grand hooded phantom, like a snow hill in the air.

With a shirt or two in my old carpetbag, I quit the good city of New York, and arrived in New Bedford on a Saturday night in December. Much was I disappointed to learn that the packet for Nantucket had already sailed and that there was no way of reaching that place till Monday. For my mind was made up to sail in no other than a Nantucket craft, because there was a fine, boisterous something connected with that famous old island, which amazingly pleased me.

Now, having a night, a day, and still another night before me in New Bedford, it became a matter of concern where I was to eat and sleep. It was a very dark and dismal night, bitingly cold and cheerless. With anxious grapnels I had sounded my pocket and only brought up a few pieces of silver. So, wherever you go, Ishmael, said I to myself, be sure to inquire the price, and don't be too particular.

With halting steps I paced the streets, and passed the sign of The Crossed Harpoons, but it looked too expensive and jolly there. So on I went, by instinct following the streets that took me waterward. Such dreary streets! Blocks of blackness, not houses, on either hand, and here and there a candle, like a candle moving about in a tomb. At this hour of the night, of the last day of the week, that quarter of the town proved all but deserted. But presently I came to a dim light not far from the docks, and heard a forlorn creaking in the air. Looking up, I saw a swinging sign with a white painting upon it, faintly representing a tall straight jet of misty spray, and these words underneath: THE SPOUTER INN—PETER COFFIN.

Coffin? Spouter? Rather ominous in that particular connection, thought I. But it is a common name in Nantucket, they say, and I suppose this Peter comes from there. The place, for the time, looked quiet enough, the very spot for cheap lodgings.

Entering, I found myself in a wide, low, straggling entry with old-fashioned wainscots. On one side hung a very large oil painting, thoroughly besmoked. It represented a Cape Horner in a great hurricane, the half-foundered ship weltering, its three masts alone visible. An enormous, exasperated whale, purposing to spring clean over the craft, was in the act of impaling himself upon the three mastheads. The opposite wall of this dusky entry was hung all over with a heathenish array of monstrous clubs and spears. Mixed with these were rusty old whaling lances and harpoons all broken and deformed.

Through yon low-arched doorway you enter the public room. A still duskier place is this, with low ponderous beams above and old wrinkled planks beneath. Projecting from the farther angle of the room stands a dark-looking den—the bar—a rude attempt at a whale's head. There stands the vast arched bone of the whale's jaw, so wide, a coach might almost drive beneath it. Within are shabby shelves, ranged around with old decanters, bottles, flasks.

Upon entering the place I found a number of young seamen gathered about a table, examining specimens of *skrimshander*—ingenious little contrivances carved out of, or on, whale teeth. I sought the landlord, and telling him I desired to be accommodated with a room, received for answer that his house was full, not a bed unoccupied. "But avast," he added, "you hain't no objections to sharing a harpooner's blanket, have ye? It's a nice bed. Sal and me slept in that ere bed the night we were spliced. There's plenty room for two to kick about. It's almighty big. I s'pose you are goin' a-whalin', so you'd better get used to that sort of thing." I told him that I never liked to sleep two in a bed, but that rather than wander further about a strange town on so bitter a night, I would put up with the half of any decent man's blanket.

"I thought so. All right, take a seat. Supper? You want supper? Supper'll be ready directly."

I sat down on an old wooden settle, carved all over. At one end a ruminating tar was still further adorning it with his jackknife. At last some four or five of us were summoned to our meal in an adjoining room. It was cold as Iceland, no fire at all, nothing but two dismal tallow candles. We were fain to button up our monkey jackets and hold to our lips cups of scalding tea with our half-frozen fingers. But the fare was of the most substantial kind, not only meat and potatoes, but dumplings.

Supper over, the company went back to the barroom, where I spent the rest of the evening as a looker-on. But though the other boarders kept coming in by ones, twos, and threes, and going to bed, yet no sign of my harpooner bedfellow.

"Landlord," said I, "what sort of a chap is he—does he always keep such late hours?" It was now hard upon twelve o'clock.

The landlord chuckled. "No," he answered, "generally he's airley to bed and airley to rise. But tonight he went out a-peddling, you see, and I don't see what on airth keeps him so late, unless maybe he can't sell his head."

"Can't sell his head? What sort of a bamboozingly story is this? Do you pretend to say that this harpooner is actually engaged this blessed Saturday night in peddling his head around this town?"

"That's precisely it," said the landlord, "and I told him he couldn't sell it here, the market's overstocked."

"With what?" shouted I.

"With heads to be sure; ain't there too many heads in the world?"

"You'd better stop spinning that yarn to me, landlord," said I, now flying into a passion. "I'm not green."

"Wall," said the landlord, fetching a long breath, "be easy, be easy, this here harpooner has just arrived from the South Seas, where he bought up a lot of 'balmed New Zealand heads—great curios, you know—and he's sold 'em all but one, and that one he's trying to sell tonight, 'cause tomorrow's Sunday and it would not do to be sellin'

human heads about the streets when folks is goin' to churches. He
wanted to last Sunday, but I stopped him just as he was goin' out
the door with four heads strung on a string, for all the airth like
a string of onions."

This account cleared up the mystery, but at the same time what
could I think of a harpooner who engaged in such a cannibal business as selling the heads of dead idolaters? "Depend upon it, landlord, that harpooner is a dangerous man."

"He pays reg'lar," was the rejoinder. "But come, it's getting
dreadful late, you had better be turning flukes." So saying, he lighted
a candle and held it toward me, offering to lead the way. But I stood
irresolute. Then, looking at a clock in the corner, he said, "I vow
it's Sunday—you won't see that harpooner tonight. He's come to
anchor somewhere—come along then."

Upstairs we went, and I was ushered into a small room, cold as
a clam, and furnished, sure enough, with a prodigious bed.

"There," said the landlord, placing the candle on a crazy old sea
chest that did double duty as a washstand and center table, "there,
make yourself comfortable now, and good night." I turned from
eyeing the bed, but he had disappeared. I then glanced around
the room, and besides the bed and table could see no other furniture.
In one corner there was a hammock lashed up and thrown on the
floor, also a large seaman's bag containing no doubt the harpooner's
wardrobe. Likewise, there was a parcel of outlandish bone fishhooks
on the shelf over the fireplace, and a tall harpoon standing at the
head of the bed. I took off my coat, jumped out of my pantaloons
and boots, and then, blowing out the light, tumbled into bed and
commended myself to the care of heaven. But I could not sleep for
a long time. I had slid off into a light doze when I heard a heavy
footfall in the passage, and saw a glimmer of light come into the
room from under the door. Lord save me, thinks I, that must be the
harpooner, the infernal head peddler. But I lay still, and resolved
not to say a word till spoken to.

Holding a candle in one hand and the shrunken New Zealand
head in the other, the stranger entered. Without looking toward
the bed, he placed his candle on the floor, and then began working
away at the knotted cords of the large bag in the corner. I was all
eagerness to see his face, and when he turned around—good heavens,

what a sight! Such a face! It was of a dark, purplish yellow color, here and there stuck over with blackish-looking squares. Yes, it's just as I thought, he's a terrible bedfellow; he's been in a fight, got cut, and here he is, just from the surgeon. But at that moment he chanced to turn his face toward the light, and I plainly saw they could not be sticking plasters at all, those black squares on his cheeks. They were stains of some sort. Having opened his bag, he commenced fumbling in it, and presently pulled out a sort of tomahawk. Placing this on the old chest in the middle of the room, he then took the New Zealand head and crammed it down into the bag. He now took off the beaver hat he had been wearing, and I came nigh singing out with fresh surprise. There was no hair on his head, nothing but a small scalpknot twisted up on his forehead. His bald purplish head looked for all the world like a mildewed skull.

He continued undressing, and at last showed his chest and arms. As I live, these parts of him were checkered with the same squares as his face. Still more, his very legs were marked, as if a parcel of dark green frogs were running up the trunks of young palms. It was now quite plain that he must be some abominable savage shipped aboard of a whaler in the South Seas, and so landed in this Christian country. A peddler of heads, too, perhaps the heads of his own brothers. He might take a fancy to mine—heavens, look at that tomahawk!

Now the savage picked up his heavy jacket, fumbled in the pockets, and produced a curious little deformed image that glistened like polished ebony. I concluded that it must be a wooden idol, which indeed it proved to be. For now the savage goes up to the empty fireplace and sets up this little image between the andirons. Next he takes a handful of shavings out of his jacket pocket and kindles them into a sacrificial blaze. He then began praying in a guttural singsong, during which his face twitched in the most unnatural manner. At last extinguishing the fire, he took the idol up very unceremoniously and bagged it again in his jacket.

I am no coward, but what to make of this head-peddling idol-worshipping, purple rascal passed my comprehension. I confess I was now as much afraid of him as if it were the devil himself who had broken into my room.

He took up his tomahawk, examined the head of it, and then, holding it to the candle, with his mouth at the handle, he puffed out great clouds of tobacco smoke. The next moment the light was extinguished, and this wild cannibal, tomahawk between his teeth, sprang into bed with me. I sang out in sudden fright, and he, giving a grunt of astonishment, began feeling me. Stammering out something, I knew not what, I rolled away from him against the wall, and then conjured him, whoever he might be, to keep quiet and let me get up and light the candle again. But his guttural responses showed that he but ill comprehended my meaning.

"Who-ee debel you?" he said. "You no speak-ee, dam-me, I kill-ee." And so saying, he began flourishing the tomahawk in the dark, the hot tobacco ashes scattering about me till I thought my linen would get on fire.

"Landlord, for God's sake, Peter Coffin!" shouted I. "Landlord! Coffin! Angels, save me!"

Thank heaven, the landlord came into the room, light in hand, and leaping from the bed, I ran to him.

"Don't be afraid now," said he, grinning. "Queequeg here wouldn't harm a hair of your head. Queequeg, look here—you sabbee me, I sabbee you—this man sleepee you—you sabbee?"

"Me sabbee plenty," grunted Queequeg, puffing at his pipe and sitting up in bed. "You gettee in," he added, motioning to me and throwing the clothes to one side. He did this in not only a civil but a really kind and charitable way. I stood looking at him a moment. For all his tattooings, he was on the whole a clean, comely-looking cannibal. Thought I to myself, The man's a human being just as I am. He has just as much reason to fear me as I have to be afraid of him. Better sleep with a sober cannibal than a drunken Christian.

"Landlord," said I, "tell him to stop smoking and I will turn in with him. I don't fancy having a man smoking in bed with me. It's dangerous. Besides, I ain't insured."

This being told to Queequeg, he at once complied, and rolling over to one side, again politely motioned me to get into bed.

I turned in, and never slept better in my life.

UPON WAKING NEXT morning about daylight, I found Queequeg's tattooed arm thrown over me in the most loving and affectionate manner. I strove to rouse him, but his only answer was a snore. At length, by dint of much wriggling and loud expostulations, I succeeded in extracting a grunt, and presently he drew back his arm, shook himself all over like a Newfoundland dog just from the water, and sat up in bed, rubbing his eyes.

Then he jumped out upon the floor and commenced dressing by donning his beaver hat, a very tall one, then his boots. At that time in the morning any Christian would have washed his face, but Queequeg restricted his ablutions to his chest, arms, and hands. Taking up a piece of hard soap on the washstand—center table, he dipped it into water and commenced lathering his face. I was watching to see where he kept his razor, when lo and behold, he takes his harpoon from the bed corner, slips out the long wooden stock, unsheathes the head, whets it a little on his boot, and striding up to the bit of mirror against the wall, begins a vigorous scraping, or rather harpooning, of his cheeks. I wondered the less at this operation when I came to know of what fine steel the head of a harpoon is made, and how exceedingly sharp the long straight edges are always kept. He then donned trousers, waistcoat, and jacket, and proudly marched out of the room, sporting his harpoon like a marshal's baton.

I quickly followed suit, and descending into the barroom, found Queequeg at his breakfast among a shaggy set of whalemen, all wearing monkey jackets. He sat there, at the head of the table, it so chanced, as cool as an icicle. To be sure, I cannot say much for his breeding. His greatest admirer could not have justified his bringing his harpoon in to breakfast and, using it without ceremony, reaching over the table with it, to the imminent jeopardy of many heads, and grappling the beefsteaks toward him. But it was certainly very coolly done, and everyone knows that to do anything coolly is to do it genteelly.

When breakfast was over, we withdrew like the rest into the public room. Queequeg, producing his pouch and tomahawk pipe, quietly offered me a puff. And then we sat exchanging puffs from that wild pipe of his, while we went to jabbering as best we could about the sights to be seen in this famous town. If there yet lurked any ice of indifference toward me in the pagan's breast, this genial smoke we had soon thawed it out, and left us cronies. He seemed to take to me quite as naturally as I to him, and when our smoke was over, he pressed his forehead against mine and said that henceforth we were bosom friends.

I asked him what might be his immediate purpose. He answered, to go to sea again. Upon this, I told him that whaling was my own design, and informed him of my intention to sail out of Nantucket. He at once resolved to accompany me and ship aboard the same vessel. To this I joyously assented. Queequeg was an experienced harpooner, and could not fail to be of great usefulness to one who, like me, was wholly ignorant of the mysteries of whaling.

On Monday, after disposing of the embalmed head to a barber, for a wig block, we took the packet to Nantucket, and after finding lodgings, we concocted our plans. To my surprise, however, Queequeg now gave me to understand that he had been consulting Yojo—his little black god or idol—and Yojo had told him that the selection of our ship among the whaling fleet in harbor should rest wholly with me, inasmuch as Yojo purposed befriending us and, in order to do so, had already pitched upon a vessel which, if left to myself, I, Ishmael, should infallibly light upon, for all the world as though it had turned out by chance.

Now this plan I did not like at all. Queequeg had sailed on whaling ships for many years, and was an expert harpooner, and I had relied upon his sagacity to point out the whaler best fitted to carry us and our fortunes securely. But, as all my remonstrances produced no effect upon Queequeg, I was obliged to acquiesce. Next morning early, leaving him in our bedroom, I sallied out among the shipping. After much sauntering and many inquiries, I learned that there were three ships up for three-year voyages. I peered and pried about all three, and, finally, going on board one called the *Pequod*, decided that this was the very ship for us.

You never saw such a rare old craft. She was a ship of the old school, rather small if anything, with an old-fashioned claw-footed look about her. Long seasoned in the typhoons and calms of all the oceans, her old hull's complexion was darkened like a French grenadier's who has fought in Egypt. Her venerable bows looked bearded. Her masts, cut on the coast of Japan, where her original ones were lost overboard in a gale, stood stiffly up like the spines of the three old kings of Cologne. Her ancient decks were worn and wrinkled. All around, her bulwarks were garnished like one continuous jaw, with the long sharp teeth of the sperm whale, inserted there for pins, to fasten her hempen tendons to. Instead of a turnstile wheel at her helm, she sported there a tiller, curiously carved from the long narrow lower jaw of her hereditary foe, the sperm whale. The helmsman who steered by that tiller in a tempest felt like the Tartar when he holds back his fiery steed by clutching its jaw. A noble craft, but somehow a most melancholy! All noble things are touched with that.

Now when I looked about the quarterdeck for someone having authority, in order to propose myself as a candidate for the voyage, I at length found an elderly man, brown and brawny, seated on an old-fashioned oaken chair. "Is this the captain of the *Pequod?*" said I, advancing to him.

"Supposing it be the captain of the *Pequod*, what dost thou want of him?" he demanded.

"I was thinking of shipping."

"Thou wast, wast thou? I see thou are no Nantucketer. Ever been in a stove boat?"

"No, sir, I never have."

"Dost know nothing at all about whaling?"

"Nothing, sir, but I've been several voyages in the merchant service, and I think—"

"Merchant service be damned. Talk not that lingo to me. What takes thee a-whaling? I want to know that before I think of shipping ye. Looks a little suspicious. Hast not been a pirate, hast thou?"

"No, sir. I just want to see what whaling is. I want to see the world."

"Want to see what whaling is, eh? Have ye clapped eye on Captain Ahab?"

"Who is Captain Ahab, sir?"

"Aye, aye, I thought so. Ahab is the captain of this ship. Thou art speaking to Captain Peleg, young man, a part owner. If thou wantest to know what whaling is, I can put ye in a way of finding it out before ye bind yourself to it, past backing out. Clap eye on Captain Ahab, young man, and thou wilt find that he has only one leg."

"What do you mean, sir? Was the other one lost by a whale?"

"Lost by a whale! Young man, it was devoured, chewed up, crunched by the monstrousest parmacety that ever chipped a boat!"

I was a little alarmed by this, but remained calm.

"Look ye now, young man, *sure* ye've been to sea before now? Sure of that?"

"Sir," said I, "I told you that I had been on voyages in the merchant—"

"Hard down out of that! Mind what I said about the merchant service—don't aggravate me—I won't have it. But let us understand each other. I have given thee a hint about what whaling is, do ye yet feel inclined for it?"

"I do, sir."

"Art thou the man to pitch a harpoon down a live whale's throat, and then jump after it? Answer quick!"

"I am, sir, if it should be positively indispensable to do so."

Seeing me so determined, he finally expressed his willingness to ship me. "Thou mayest as well sign the papers right off. Come along with ye." And so saying, he led the way belowdecks into the cabin.

There he threw open a chest, and drawing forth the ship's articles, placed pen and ink beside them on a little table. I was already aware that in the whaling business they paid no wages. All hands, including the captain, received certain shares of the profits, called lays, which were proportioned to one's degree of importance in the ship's company. I was also aware that being a green hand at whaling, my own lay would not be very large. It was settled that my lay should be the three hundredth, that is, the three-hundredth part of the clear net proceeds of the voyage, whatever that might eventually amount to.

"I have a friend with me who wants to ship, too. Killed more whales than I can count," said I. "Shall I bring him down tomorrow?"

"To be sure," said Peleg. "We'll look at him."

After signing the papers, off I went, nothing doubting but that I had done a good morning's work and that the *Pequod* was the identical ship that Yojo had provided to carry Queequeg and me around Cape Horn.

But I had not proceeded far when I began to bethink me that the captain with whom I was to sail yet remained unseen by me. Turning back, I accosted my elderly friend, inquiring where Captain Ahab was to be found.

"And what dost thou want of Captain Ahab? It's all right enough. Thou art shipped."

"Yes, but I should like to see him."

"But I don't think thou wilt be able to at present. I don't know exactly what's the matter with him, but he keeps close inside the house. Anyhow, young man, he won't always see me, so I don't suppose he will thee. He's a queer man, Captain Ahab—so some think—but a good one. Not a pious good man, but a swearing good man. Aye, I know that on the last passage home he was a little out of his mind for a spell, but that was from the pains in his bleeding stump. And, aye, ever since he lost his leg last voyage by that accursed whale, he's been moody—savage sometimes—but that will all pass off. And let me assure thee, young man, it's better to sail with a moody good captain than a laughing bad one. So wrong not Captain Ahab. Thou'lt like him well enough, no fear. Besides, my boy, he has a wife—not three voyages wedded—a sweet, resigned girl. Think of it; and by that sweet girl that old man has a child. Hold ye then there can be any harm in Ahab? No, no, my lad. Stricken, blasted, if he be, Ahab has his humanities!"

As I walked away, I was full of thoughtfulness. What had been incidentally revealed to me of Captain Ahab filled me with a certain strange awe of him, which I cannot describe. However, my thoughts were at length carried in other directions, so that for the present, dark Ahab slipped my mind.

THE NEXT DAY I took Queequeg down to the *Pequod*. When Captain Peleg asked about his experience as a harpooner, Queequeg, without saying a word, jumped upon the bulwarks, from thence leaped into the bows of one of the whaleboats hanging to one side, and then braced his left knee. Poising his harpoon, he cried out, "Cap'ain, you see him small drop tar on water dere? Well, s'pose him one whale eye, well, den!" Taking sharp aim, he darted the iron clean across the ship's decks and struck the glistening tar spot out of sight. Quietly hauling in the line, Queequeg said, "S'pose him whale eye. Why, dat whale dead!" He was signed on immediately and given a ninetieth lay.

A day or two passed, and there was great activity aboard the *Pequod*. The old sails were being mended, and new sails and coils of rigging were coming on board. In short, everything betokened that the ship's preparations were hurrying to a close.

During these preparations, Queequeg and I often visited the craft, and as often I asked about how Captain Ahab was and when he was going to come on board. They would answer that he was better and was expected aboard every day. If I had been honest with myself, I would have seen in my heart that I did not fancy being committed this way to so long a voyage without once laying my eyes on the man who was to be the absolute dictator of it. But I said nothing and tried to think nothing.

At last it was given out that sometime next day the ship would certainly sail. So next morning, which happened to be Christmas, Queequeg and I took a very early start. It was still only gray misty dawn when we drew nigh the wharf and went aboard. Captain Ahab, we were told, had come aboard during the night, and was now invisibly enshrined within his cabin. Toward noon the ship's riggers were dismissed, and the *Pequod* was hauled out from the wharf. Then the anchor was up, the sails were set, and off we glided, with two pilots aboard to guide us. It was a short, cold Christmas, and as day merged into night, we found ourselves almost broad upon the wintry ocean, whose freezing spray cased us in ice, as in polished armor. The long rows of teeth on the bulwarks glistened in the moonlight and, like the ivory tusks of some huge elephant, vast curving icicles depended from the bows.

When we gained such an offing that the two pilots were needed no longer, the stout sailboat that had accompanied us began ranging alongside. Both pilots went over the side and dropped into the boat. Ship and boat diverged, the cold, damp night breeze blew between, and a screaming gull flew overhead. We gave three heavy-hearted cheers and blindly plunged like Fate into the lone Atlantic.

II. THE VOYAGE OUT

FOR SEVERAL DAYS after leaving Nantucket, nothing above hatches was seen of Captain Ahab. The mates regularly relieved each other at the watches and seemed to be the only commanders of the ship. Sometimes, however, they issued from the cabin with orders so sudden and peremptory that after all it was plain they commanded vicariously.

The chief mate of the *Pequod* was Starbuck, a native of Nantucket. He was a long, lean, earnest man of about thirty. His pure tight skin was an excellent fit; and closely wrapped up in it, and embalmed with inner health and strength, this Starbuck seemed to have a vitality warranted to do well in all climates. A steadfast man, uncommonly conscientious for a seaman, he was endued with a deep natural reverence. Outward portents and inward presentiments were his. And if at times these things bent the welded iron of his soul, his faraway domestic memories of his young wife and child tended to bend him still more from the original ruggedness of his nature. "I will have no man in my boat," said Starbuck, "who is not afraid of a whale." By this he meant that the most reliable and useful courage was that which arises from the fair estimation of the encountered peril, and that an utterly fearless man is a far more dangerous comrade than a coward. Starbuck had no fancy for lowering for whales after sundown, nor for persisting in fighting a fish that too much persisted in fighting him. I am here in this ocean to kill whales for my living, thought Starbuck, and not to be killed by them for theirs. And that hundreds of men had been so killed, Starbuck well knew. What doom was his own father's? Where, in the bottomless deeps, could he find the torn limbs of his brother? With memories like these, and given to a certain superstitiousness, the courage of this Starbuck, which could still flourish, must indeed have been extreme.

Stubb, a native of Cape Cod, was the second mate. Happy-go-lucky, good-humored, neither craven nor valiant, he took perils with an indifferent air, and presided over his whaleboat as if the most deadly encounter were but a dinner and his crew invited guests. When close to the whale, in the very death lock of the fight, he handled his lance coolly, offhandedly, as a whistling tinker his hammer. What he thought of death, there is no telling. Whether he ever thought of it at all might be a question. Like his nose, his short, black little pipe was one of the regular features of his face. He kept a whole row of pipes ready loaded by his bunk, stuck in a rack. When he dressed, instead of first putting his legs into his trousers, he put his pipe into his mouth.

The third mate was Flask, a native of Tisbury, on Martha's Vineyard. A short, stout, ruddy young fellow, very pugnacious concerning whales, he seemed to think that the great leviathans had personally affronted him, and it was therefore a point of honor with him to destroy them whenever encountered. So lost was he to all sense of reverence for their majestic bulk and mystic ways, so dead to any apprehension of danger, that in his opinion the wondrous whale was but a species of magnified mouse or water rat, requiring only a little time and trouble to kill and boil. This made him a little waggish in the matter of whales. He followed these fish for the fun of it.

Now these three mates—Starbuck, Stubb, and Flask—were momentous men. They commanded three of the *Pequod's* whaleboats as headsmen. In that grand order of battle in which Captain Ahab would marshal his forces to descend on the whales, these three were as captains of companies. And since each headsman is accompanied, like a knight of old, by his boatsteerer or harpooner, who in certain conjunctures provides him with a fresh lance, and as there generally subsists between the two a close intimacy, it is but meet that we set down who the harpooners were, and to what headsman each of them belonged.

First of all was Queequeg, whom Starbuck, the chief mate, had selected for his squire. Next was Tashtego, an unmixed Indian from Gay Head, on Martha's Vineyard. Tashtego's long sable hair, his high cheekbones and black, glittering eyes, the tawny brawn of his lithe limbs—all this sufficiently proclaimed him an inheritor of the blood of those proud warrior hunters who had scoured, bow in hand, the aboriginal forests of the main. Tashtego was squire to Stubb, the second mate. Third was Daggoo, a gigantic, coal-black Negro with a lionlike tread. Suspended from his ears were two golden hoops so large that the sailors called them ringbolts. In his youth Daggoo had voluntarily shipped on board of a whaler lying in a lonely bay on his native coast of Africa. He retained all his barbaric virtues and, erect as a giraffe, moved about the decks in all the pomp of six feet five in his socks. Daggoo was the squire of little Flask, who looked like a chessman beside him.

Captain Ahab, too, would head a boat, but for it he had brought aboard his own crew—five men, all Asians. Four were tiger yellow in hue. The fifth, a tall, swart old man named Fedallah, was the harpooner. He was a Parsee, and wore wide trousers of funereal black cotton and a rumpled jacket of the same stuff. Crowning his ebony face was the turbanlike arrangement of his own white hair, coiled and braided around the top of his head. One white tooth evilly protruded from his lips.

IT BEING CHRISTMAS when the ship shot from out her harbor, for a space we had biting polar weather, though all the time running away from it to southward. By every degree of latitude we gradually left that merciless winter behind us. I waited meanwhile for my first glimpse of the captain, and every time I ascended to the deck from below, I gazed aft to mark if any strange face were visible.

It was on one of those gray mornings of the transition, when with a fair wind the ship was almost leaping through the water, that as I mounted to the deck and leveled my glance toward the taffrail, foreboding shivers ran over me. Reality outran apprehension; Captain Ahab stood upon his quarterdeck.

There seemed no sign of common bodily illness about him, nor of the recovery from any. His whole high, broad form seemed made of solid bronze and shaped in an unalterable mold. From among his gray hairs, threading its way right down one side of his tawny scorched face and neck till it disappeared in his clothing, you saw a slender mark, lividly whitish. It resembled that perpendicular seam sometimes made in the trunk of a great tree, when the lightning darts down it and grooves out the bark from top to bottom, leaving the tree still greenly alive but branded. Whether it was born with him or was the scar left by some desperate wound, no one could certainly say. By some tacit consent, throughout the voyage little or no allusion was made to it.

So powerfully did the whole grim aspect of Ahab affect me that for the first few moments I hardly noted that not a little of this overbearing grimness was owing to the barbaric ivory leg upon which he partly stood. It had been fashioned at sea from the polished bone of a sperm whale's jaw. Now I was struck with the singular posture he maintained. Upon each side of the *Pequod's* quarterdeck, there was an auger hole, bored about half an inch or so into the plank. His bone leg steadied in that hole, one arm elevated and holding by a shroud, he stood erect, looking straight out beyond the ship's everpitching prow. Not a word he spoke, nor did his officers say aught to him, though by their expressions they plainly showed the uneasy consciousness of being under a master eye.

Ere long, from his first visit in the air, he withdrew into his cabin. But after that morning he was every day visible to the crew, standing in his pivot hole or seated upon a stool or heavily walking the deck.

As the sky grew less gloomy, he became still less a recluse. By and by it came to pass that he was almost continually in the air, and the pleasant weather seemed gradually to charm him from his mood. More than once he put forth the faint blossom of a look, which in any other man would have soon flowered out in a smile.

So some days elapsed and, ice and icebergs all astern, the *Pequod* now went rolling through the bright equatorial spring. The warmly cool, clear, ringing, overflowing days were as crystal goblets of Persian sherbet, heaped up with rosewater snow. The starred and stately nights seemed haughty dames in jeweled velvets. For sleeping man, 'twas hard to choose between such winsome days and such seducing nights. And all the witcheries of that unwaning weather lent new spells and potencies to the outward world. Inward they turned upon the soul, especially when the still, mild hours of eve came on.

One morning shortly after breakfast, Ahab ascended the cabin gangway to the deck. Soon his steady, ivory stride was heard, as to and fro he paced upon planks so familiar to his tread that they were all over dented with the mark of his walk. So full of thought was he that at every turn, now at the mainmast and now at the binnacle, you could almost see that thought turn in him as he turned, and pace in him as he paced.

"D'ye mark him, Flask?" whispered Stubb. "The chick that's in him pecks the shell. 'Twill soon be out."

The hours wore on—Ahab now shut up within his cabin; anon, pacing the deck. It drew near the close of day. Suddenly, Ahab came to a halt by the bulwarks, and inserting his bone leg into the auger hole, and with one hand grasping a shroud, he ordered Starbuck to send everybody aft.

"Sir!" said the mate, astonished at an order seldom or never given on shipboard, except in some extraordinary case.

"Send everybody aft," repeated Ahab. "Masthead standers, there! Come down!"

When the entire ship's company were assembled and with curious faces were eyeing him, Ahab resumed his heavy turns upon the deck. With bent head and half-slouched hat he continued to pace, unmindful of the wondering whispering among the men. But this did not last long. Vehemently pausing, he cried, "What do ye do when ye see a whale, men?"

"Sing out for him!" was the impulsive rejoinder from a score of voices.

"Good!" cried Ahab. "And what do ye next, men?"

"Lower away, and after him!"

"And what tune is it ye pull to, men?"

"A dead whale or a stove boat!"

More and more fiercely approving grew Ahab's countenance at every shout. The mariners began to gaze curiously at each other, as if marveling how it was that they themselves became so excited at such seemingly purposeless questions. And now the old man, half-revolving in his pivot hole, addressed them again.

"All ye masteaders, d'ye see this Spanish ounce of gold?"—holding up a broad bright coin to the sun. "It is a sixteen-dollar piece, men. D'ye see it? Mr. Starbuck, hand me yon top maul."

Receiving the top maul from Starbuck, Ahab advanced toward the mainmast with the hammer uplifted in one hand, exhibiting the gold with the other, and with a high raised voice exclaimed, "Whosoever of ye raises me a white-headed whale with a wrinkled brow and a crooked jaw, with three holes punctured in his starboard fluke— look ye, whosoever of ye raises me that same white whale, he shall have this gold ounce, my boys!"

"Huzzah! Huzzah!" cried the seamen, as the gold was nailed onto the mast.

"It's a white whale," resumed Ahab, as he threw down the top maul. "Skin your eyes for him, men. Look sharp for white water. If ye see but a bubble, sing out."

All this while, Tashtego, Daggoo, and Queequeg had looked on with even more intense interest than the rest. At the mention of the wrinkled brow and crooked jaw they had started as if touched by some specific recollection.

"Captain Ahab," said Tashtego, "that white whale must be the same that some call Moby Dick."

"Moby Dick?" shouted Ahab. "Do ye know the White Whale then, Tash?"

"Does he fantail a little curious, sir, before he goes down?"

"And has he a curious spout, too," said Daggoo, "very bushy, Captain Ahab?"

"And he have one, two, tree—oh, many iron in him hide, too,

Captain!" cried Queequeg. "All twiske-tee betwisk, like him"—
faltering for a word and screwing his hand around—"him—"

"Corkscrew!" cried Ahab. "Aye, Queequeg, the harpoons lie all
twisted and wrenched in him. Aye, Daggoo, his spout is a big one,
and white as Nantucket wool. Aye, Tashtego, and he fantails like a
split jib in a squall. Death and devils, men! It is Moby Dick ye have
seen—Moby Dick—Moby Dick!"

"Captain Ahab," said Starbuck, who had been eyeing his superior
with increasing surprise. "Captain Ahab, was it not Moby Dick that
took off thy leg?"

"Who told thee that?" cried Ahab. Then, after pausing, "Aye, Starbuck; aye, my hearties. It was Moby Dick that dismasted me; Moby
Dick that brought me to this dead stump I stand on now. Then, with
a terrific, loud animal sob he shouted, "Aye, aye! It was that accursed
White Whale that razeed me, made of me a poor pegging lubber!
Aye, aye! And I'll chase him round Good Hope, and round the Horn,
and round perdition's flames before I give him up. And this is what
ye have shipped for, men, to chase that White Whale over all sides of
earth, till he spouts black blood and rolls fin out! What say ye, men,
will ye splice hands on it now? I think ye do look brave."

"Aye, aye!" shouted the harpooners and seamen, running closer to
the excited old man. "A sharp eye for the White Whale, a sharp
lance for Moby Dick!"

"God bless ye." Ahab seemed to half sob, half shout. "God bless ye,
men. Steward, go draw the great measure of grog. But what's this
long face about, Mr. Starbuck; wilt thou not chase the White Whale?
Art not game for Moby Dick?"

"I am game for his crooked jaw, Captain Ahab, and for the jaws
of death, too, if it fairly comes in the way of the business we follow.
But I came here to hunt whales, not my commander's vengeance.
How many barrels will thy vengeance yield thee, even if thou gettest
it, Captain Ahab? It will not fetch thee much in our Nantucket
market."

"Nantucket market! Starbuck, let me tell thee that my vengeance
will fetch a great premium *here!*" And he smote his chest.

"Vengeance on a dumb brute," cried Starbuck, "that simply struck
thee from blind instinct! Madness! To be enraged with a dumb
thing, Captain Ahab, seems blasphemous."

"Hark ye yet again," shouted Ahab. "The White Whale tasks me. I see in him outrageous strength, with an inscrutable malice sinewing it. That inscrutable thing is chiefly what I hate, and I will wreak that hate upon him. Talk not to me of blasphemy, man. I'd strike the sun if it insulted me! Look ye, Starbuck, I meant not to incense thee. Let it go. Look! See the crew, man, the crew! Are they not one and all with Ahab in this matter of the whale? And what is it? Reckon it. 'Tis but to help strike a fin, no wondrous feat for Starbuck. From this one poor hunt the best lance out of all Nantucket surely will not hang back!"

"God keep me! Keep us all!" murmured Starbuck.

"The measure! The measure!" cried Ahab.

Receiving the brimming pewter, and turning to the harpooners, he ordered them to produce their weapons. Then he ranged them before him with their harpoons in their hands, while his three mates stood at his side with their lances, and the rest of the ship's company formed a circle around the group. For an instant he stood searchingly eyeing every man of his crew.

"Drink and pass!" he cried, handing the heavy flagon to the nearest seaman. "Round with it, round! Short drafts, long swallows, men; 'tis hot as Satan's hoof. Well done, almost drained. Steward, refill! Now, my brave mates, flank me with your lances, that I may revive a noble custom of my fisherman fathers. Cross your lances! Well done! Let me touch the axis."

With extended arm he grasped the three radiating lances at their crossed center, and suddenly twitched them, meanwhile glancing intently at the three mates. The men quailed before his strong, sustained, and mystic aspect. Stubb and Flask looked sideways. The honest eye of Starbuck fell.

"Down lances!" cried Ahab. "And now, my valiant harpooners, cut your seizings and draw the poles!" Silently obeying the order, each of the three harpooners stood with the detached iron part of his harpoon, some three feet long, held before him, barbs up. "So, now advance. Hold them while I fill the sockets!" Slowly going from one man to the other, Ahab brimmed the harpoon sockets with fiery waters from the pewter. "Now, commend the murderous chalices! Drink, ye harpooners! Drink and swear, ye men—death to Moby Dick! God hunt us all, if we do not hunt Moby Dick to his death!"

The iron goblets were lifted, and to cries and maledictions against the White Whale, the spirits were quaffed. Once more the replenished pewter went the rounds among the frantic crew. Then, waving his free hand to them, Ahab retired within his cabin.

III. MOBY DICK

I, ISHMAEL, WAS ONE of that crew. My shouts had gone up with the rest, my oath had been welded with theirs. A wild, mystical feeling was in me, and Ahab's quenchless feud seemed mine. With greedy ears I learned the history of that murderous monster against whom we had taken our oaths of revenge.

For some time past the White Whale had haunted those seas mostly frequented by the sperm-whale fishermen. But only a few of them, comparatively, had knowingly seen him, while the number who had knowingly given battle to him was small indeed. In the beginning everyone sighting him had boldly lowered, as for any other whale. But such calamities ensued—everything from sprained wrists, broken limbs, and devouring amputations to deaths—that the fortitude of many brave hunters was badly shaken. In time, few were willing to encounter the perils of his jaw. No wonder, then, that the outblown rumors of the White Whale did in the end incorporate all manner of morbid hints, and suggestions of supernatural terrors. It was said by some superstitious whalemen that Moby Dick could be encountered in opposite latitudes at one and the same instant of time, that he was immortal, that though groves of spears should be planted in his flanks, he would still swim away unharmed. And it was said that if indeed he should ever be made to spout thick blood, such a sight would be but a ghastly deception—for again, hundreds of leagues away, his unsullied jet would once more be seen.

But even stripped of these supernatural surmisings, there was enough in the earthly make of the monster to strike the imagination with unwonted power. His uncommon bulk distinguished him from other sperm whales, as did his peculiar snow-white wrinkled forehead and high, pyramidical white hump. And his whole body was so streaked and marbled with the same shrouded hue that, in the end, he had gained his appellation of the White Whale, a name indeed justified by his vivid aspect when seen gliding at high noon through a dark blue sea, leaving a milky-way wake of creamy foam, all spangled with golden gleamings. Nor was it so much his magnitude, nor his remarkable hue, that invested him with natural terror, as that intelligent malignity which he had over and over again evinced in his assaults. More than all, his treacherous retreats struck dismay. For, when swimming before his exulting pursuers, with every apparent symptom of alarm, he had several times been known to turn around suddenly, either staving their boats to splinters or driving them back in consternation to their ship.

This, I had heard, is what happened to Captain Ahab. Inflamed, impelled to distracted fury, with three boats stove around him, oars and torn comrades whirling in the eddies, he had seized a line knife with only a six-inch blade and had dashed at the whale, blindly seeking to reach its life. Then it was that Moby Dick, suddenly sweeping his sickle-shaped lower jaw beneath him, had reaped away Ahab's leg, as a mower a blade of grass in the field. Small wonder that ever since that almost fatal encounter, Ahab had cherished a wild vindictiveness against the whale, all the more intense because, in his morbidness, he at last came to identify with Moby Dick not only all his bodily woes but all his intellectual and spiritual exasperations.

For long months on the journey home from that voyage, Ahab and anguish lay stretched together. Then it was that his torn body and gashed soul bled into one another and, so interfusing, made him mad. At intervals during the passage he was a raving lunatic, so that his mates were forced to lace him fast in his hammock.

At last, to all appearances, the old man's delirium seemed left behind, and he came forth from his dark den into the blessed light and air. He issued his calm orders once again, and his mates thanked God the direful madness was now gone. Even then, however, Ahab, in his hidden self, raved on. Human madness is oftentimes a cunning and most feline thing. When you think it fled, it may have but become transfigured into some still subtler form. Now the White Whale swam before him as the incarnation of all those malicious agencies which some deep men feel eating in them, till they are left living on with but half a heart. To crazy Ahab, all that most maddens and torments, all evil, were visibly personified in Moby Dick.

Nevertheless, so well did Ahab succeed in dissembling, that when with ivory leg he stepped ashore at last, no Nantucketer thought him otherwise than but naturally grieved with the terrible casualty which had overtaken him. Then, with the mad secret of his rage bolted up in him, Ahab had sailed upon the present voyage with the object of *first* hunting the White Whale. Only afterward would he proceed with the regular business of whaling. Had any one of his old acquaintances onshore dreamed of this, how soon would they have wrenched the ship from him! They were bent on profitable cruises counted down in dollars. He was intent on an audacious revenge.

IN HIS CABIN on the night succeeding that wild scene with his crew, Ahab took from his locker a large roll of sea charts, spread them before him, and intently studied the various lines and shadings. While the heavy pewter lamp suspended over his head continually rocked with the motion of the ship, he traced with slow but steady pencil additional courses over spaces that before were blank. At intervals he referred to piles of old logbooks, wherein were set down the seasons and places in which, on the voyages of various ships, sperm whales had been captured or seen. Knowing the sets of all tides and currents, calculating the driftings of the sperm whale's food and the regular seasons for hunting him in particular latitudes, Ahab was threading an ocean maze in order to make more certain the accomplishment of the monomaniac thought of his soul. Almost every night thereafter the charts were brought out, some pencil marks were effaced, and others substituted.

Days, weeks passed, and under easy sail the ivory *Pequod* had slowly swept across four cruising grounds. It was while gliding through the waters of the Carrol Ground, south of St. Helena, one serene and moonlit night when the waves rolled by like scrolls of silver, that a solitary jet was seen far in advance of the bow. Lit by the moon, it seemed some plumed god uprising from the sea.

Fedallah, the Parsee, first descried this jet. On nights it was his wont to mount the mainmast and stand a lookout, as if it had been day, even though not one whaleman in a hundred would venture a lowering by night. After spending several successive nights there without uttering a single sound, his unearthly voice was heard announcing the silvery jet, and every reclining mariner started to his feet. "There she blows!" Had the trump of judgment blown, the crew could not have quivered more. Yet so impressive was the cry, and so deliriously exciting, that almost every soul on board instinctively desired a lowering.

Walking the deck with quick, side-lunging strides, Ahab commanded every sail spread. The best man in the ship must take the helm. Then, with every masthead manned, the piled-up craft rolled before the wind, rushed along as if two antagonistic influences were struggling in her—one to mount direct to heaven, the other to drive yawingly to some horizontal goal. And Ahab's face also showed two different things warring. While his one good leg made lively echoes along the deck, every stroke of his dead limb sounded like a coffin tap. On life and death this old man walked. But though the ship so swiftly sped, and though from every eye, like arrows, the eager glances shot, yet the silvery jet was no more seen that night. Every sailor swore he saw it once, but not a second time.

This midnight spout had almost been forgotten when, some days after, lo, at the same silent hour it was again announced! Again it was descried by all, but upon making sail to overtake it, once more it disappeared. And so it served us, night after night, till no one heeded it but to wonder. Mysteriously, this solitary jet seemed forever alluring us on. Nor were there wanting some of the seamen who swore that whenever and wherever descried, the unnearable spout was cast by one selfsame whale, and that whale, Moby Dick. For a time there reigned a sense of peculiar dread at this flitting apparition, as if the monster might turn around upon us and rend us at last in the remotest and most savage seas.

For days and days we voyaged along, through seas so blue and mild that all space seemed vacating itself of life. But, at last, when turning to the eastward around the Cape of Good Hope, the winds began howling, and we rose and fell upon long, troubled seas. The *Pequod* bowed sharply and gored the dark waves in her madness, till, like showers of silver chips, the foam flakes flew over her bulwarks. Ahab assumed for the time the almost continual command of the drenched and dangerous deck. With his ivory leg inserted into its accustomed hole, and with one hand firmly grasping a shroud, his hat slouched over his face, he stood up to the blast, gazing dead to windward, while rain or sleet or snow all but congealed his very eyelashes together.

IT WAS SOME MONTHS later, when the *Pequod* was drawing nigh to Formosa and the Bashee Isles, between which lies one of the tropical outlets from the China waters into the South Sea—the Pacific—that my bosom friend, Queequeg, caught a terrible chill, which lapsed into a fever, and at last, after some days' suffering, laid him in his hammock, close to the very door of death.

How he wasted and wasted away, till there seemed little left of him but his frame and tattooing. But, as his cheekbones grew sharper, his eyes seemed to grow fuller and fuller, with a strange softness of luster. Like circles on the water, which expand as they grow fainter, so his eyes seemed rounding and rounding, like the rings of eternity. Not a man of the crew but gave him up. As for Queequeg himself, what he thought of his case was forcibly shown by a curious favor he asked. He called a crewman to him in the gray morning watch and, taking his hand, said that he shuddered at the thought of being buried in his hammock and—according to the usual sea custom—tossed to the death-devouring sharks. He desired a real canoelike coffin in which he might float away to the starry archipelagoes.

When this strange circumstance was made known aft, the ship's carpenter was at once commanded to do Queequeg's bidding. There was some coffin-colored old lumber aboard, which, upon a previous voyage, had been cut from the aboriginal groves of the Lackaday Islands, and from these dark planks the coffin was made.

When the last nail was driven and the lid duly fitted, Queequeg commanded that the thing should be instantly brought to him. He then called for his harpoon and had the iron part placed in the coffin along with one of the paddles of his boat. By his request, also, biscuits were ranged around the sides within, a flask of water was placed at the head, and a piece of sailcloth was rolled up for a pillow. Queequeg now entreated to be lifted into his final bed, that he might make trial of its comforts. He lay without moving a few minutes, then told a crewman to go to his bag and bring out his little god, Yojo. Crossing his arms on his breast, with Yojo between, he called for the coffin lid (hatch, he called it) to be placed over him. The head part turned over with a leather hinge, and there lay Queequeg in his coffin with little but his composed countenance in view. "*Rarmai*"—"It will do"—he murmured at last, and signed to be replaced in his hammock.

Now that he had apparently made every preparation for death, now that his coffin was proved a good fit, Queequeg rallied. He said that he had just recalled a little duty ashore which he was leaving undone, and therefore had changed his mind about dying. Some asked him, then, whether to live or die was a matter of his own sovereign will. He answered yes. It was Queequeg's conceit that if a man made up his mind to live, mere sickness could not kill him: nothing but a whale or a gale or some ungovernable destroyer of that sort. After sitting on the windlass for a few indolent days, he suddenly leaped to his feet, gave himself a good stretching, yawned a little, and then, poising a harpoon, pronounced himself fit for a fight. With a wild whimsiness, he now used his coffin for a sea chest. Emptying into it his canvas bag of clothes, he set them in order.

The coffin did not remain a sea chest for long, however. One day soon after, when gliding by the Bashee Isles, we emerged at last upon the great South Sea. Now the long supplication of my youth was answered—that serene ocean, my dear Pacific, rolled eastward from me a thousand leagues of blue. Just at sunrise a man went from his hammock to the masthead at the fore, and whether it was that he was not yet waked from his sleep (for sailors sometimes go aloft in a transition state) there is now no telling, but he had not been long at his perch when a cry was heard. Looking up, the men on deck saw a falling phantom in the air. Looking down, they saw a little tossed heap of bubbles in the blue of the sea. The life buoy—a long slender cask—was dropped from the stern, where it always hung obedient to a cunning spring. But no hand rose to seize it. The sun having long beat upon this cask, it had shrunk, so that it slowly filled and followed the sailor to the bottom, as if to yield him his pillow, though a hard one. And thus the first man of the *Pequod* that mounted the mast to look out for the White Whale, on the White Whale's own ground, that man was swallowed up in the deep.

The lost life buoy was now to be replaced. Starbuck was directed to see to it, but as no cask of sufficient lightness could be found, they were going to leave the ship's stern without a buoy, when by certain strange signs Queequeg made a hint concerning his coffin.

"A life buoy of a coffin!" cried Starbuck, starting.

"It will make a good enough one," said Flask. "The carpenter here can arrange it easily."

"Bring it up; there's nothing else for it," said Starbuck. "Rig it, carpenter. Do not look at me so— The coffin, I mean. Dost thou hear me? Rig it."

"And shall I nail down the lid, sir?"

"Aye. Now, away! Make a life buoy of the coffin, and no more."

THERE IS, ONE knows not what sweet mystery about the sea, whose gently awful stirrings seem to speak of some hidden soul beneath. Here, millions of mixed shades and shadows, drowned dreams, somnambulisms, reveries—all that we call lives and souls—lie dreaming still, tossing like slumberers in their beds, the ever-rolling waves made so by their restlessness.

The ship's old blacksmith, begrimed, with matted beard, and swathed in a bristling sharkskin apron, now availed himself of the mild weather. With his portable forge lashed to ringbolts by the foremast, he was incessantly asked by the headsmen, harpooners, and bowsmen to do some little job for them, altering or repairing their various weapons or boat furniture. Often he would be surrounded by an eager circle, all holding pike heads, harpoons, and lances, and jealously watching his every sooty movement.

One day, when the blacksmith was less busy than usual, Captain Ahab came along, carrying in his hand a small leather bag. "Look ye here!" he said, jingling the bag as if it were full of gold coins. "I want a harpoon made; one that a thousand fiends could not part; something that will stick in a whale like his own fin bone." He flung the bag upon the anvil. "There's the stuff. These are the gathered nail stubs of the steel shoes of racing horses."

"Horseshoe stubs, sir? Why, Captain Ahab, thou hast here the best and stubbornest stuff we blacksmiths ever work."

"I know it, old man. Quick! Forge me the harpoon. First, twelve rods for its shank. Then wind and twist and hammer these twelve together like the yarns and strands of a towline. Quick! I'll blow the fire."

When at last the twelve rods were made and welded into one, the shank, in one complete rod, received its final heat.

"Now for the barbs! Thou must make them thyself, blacksmith. Here are my razors, the best of steel. Make the barbs sharp as the needle sleet of the icy sea."

Fashioned at last into an arrowy shape and welded to the shank, the steel soon pointed the end of the iron. As the blacksmith was about to give the barbs their final heat, prior to tempering them, he asked Ahab to place the water cask near.

"No, no water for that. I want it of the true death temper. Ahoy, there! Tashtego, Queequeg, Daggoo! What say ye, pagans! Will ye give me as much blood as will cover this barb?" Dark nods replied. Three punctures were made in the heathen flesh, and the barbs were then tempered.

"Ego non baptizo te in nomino patris, sed in nomine diaboli!" ["I baptize thee, not in the name of the father, but in the name of the devil!"] howled Ahab, as the malignant iron scorchingly devoured the baptismal blood.

Mustering the spare poles from below and selecting one of hickory, Ahab fitted the end to the socket of the iron. A coil of new towline was then unwound. At one extremity the rope was unstranded, and the separate spread yarns were all braided and woven around the socket of the harpoon. The pole was then driven hard up into the socket, and from the lower end the rope was traced halfway along the pole's length and secured with twine. This done, Ahab moodily stalked away with the weapon, the sounds of his ivory leg and hickory pole both hollowly ringing on every plank.

Some weeks after Ahab's harpoon had been welded, the *Pequod* encountered another Nantucket ship, the *Bachelor*, which had just wedged in her last cask of oil and bolted down her bursting hatches. Now, in glad holiday apparel, she was joyously sailing around among the widely separated ships on the fishing ground, previous to pointing her prow for home.

The three men at her masthead wore long streamers of narrow red bunting at their hats. From the stern a whaleboat was suspended, bottom down, and hanging captive from the bowsprit was seen the long lower jaw of the last whale they had slain. Signals, ensigns, and jacks of all colors were flying from her rigging on every side. Sideways lashed in each of her three basketed tops were two barrels of sperm oil. Nailed to her truck was a brazen lamp.

As this glad ship bore down upon the moody *Pequod*, the barbarian sound of enormous drums came from her forecastle. A crowd of her men were seen standing around her huge try-pots, which, covered with the parchmentlike poke, or stomach skin, of the blackfish, gave forth a loud roar to every stroke of the clenched hands of the crew. On the quarterdeck the mates and harpooners were dancing with the olive-hued girls who had eloped with them from the Polynesian Isles, while suspended in a boat, firmly secured aloft between the foremast and mainmast, three Negroes with glittering fiddle bows of whale ivory were presiding over the hilarious jig.

Meanwhile, others were tumultuously busy at the masonry of the tryworks, from which the huge pots had been removed. You would have almost thought they were pulling down the cursed Bastille, such wild cries they raised as the now useless brick and mortar were being hurled into the sea. Lord and master over all this scene, the captain stood erect on the ship's elevated quarterdeck.

Ahab, too, was standing on his quarterdeck, shaggy and black, with a stubborn gloom. As the two ships crossed each other's wakes—one all jubilations for things passed, the other all forebodings as to things to come—the *Bachelor*'s commander, lifting a glass and a bottle, cried, "Come aboard, come aboard!"

"Hast seen the White Whale?" gritted Ahab in reply.

"No, only heard of him, but don't believe in him at all," said the other good-humoredly. "We're a full ship and homeward bound. Come aboard!"

"How wondrous familiar is a fool!" muttered Ahab. Then aloud he said, "Thou art a full ship and homeward bound, thou sayest? Well, then, call me an empty ship and outward bound. So go thy ways, and I will mine. Forward there! Set all sail and keep her to the wind."

While the one ship went cheerily before the breeze, the other stubbornly fought against it. So the two vessels parted, the crew of the *Pequod* looking with grave, lingering glances toward the receding *Bachelor*. Ahab, leaning over the taffrail, eyed the homeward-bound craft. Then he took from his pocket a small vial of sand and looked from the ship to the vial. It was filled with Nantucket soundings.

But warmest climes often nurse the cruelest fangs. So it is that in these resplendent seas the mariner encounters the direst of all storms, the typhoon. It will sometimes burst from out that cloudless sky like an exploding bomb upon a sleepy town.

Toward evening one day the *Pequod*, struck by one of these storms, was torn of her canvas and left to fight, bare-poled. When darkness came on, sky and sea roared and split with the thunder, and blazed with the lightning that showed the disabled masts fluttering here and there with the rags which the first fury of the tempest had left.

Holding by a shroud, Starbuck was standing on the quarterdeck, at every flash of the lightning glancing aloft to see what additional disaster might have befallen. In one of the intervals of profound darkness following the flashes, he heard a voice at his side, and almost at the same instant, thunder rolled overhead.

"Who's there?"

"Old Thunder!" said Ahab, groping his way to his pivot hole, then finding his path made plain to him by elbowed lances of fire.

"Look aloft!" cried Starbuck suddenly. "The corposants! The corposants!"

All the yardarms were tipped with a pallid fire, each tripointed lightning-rod end touched with three tapering white flames. Each of the three tall masts was silently burning in that sulfurous air, like three gigantic wax tapers before an altar.

The enchanted crew, in one thick cluster, stood silently on the forecastle, all their eyes gleaming in that pale phosphorescence, like a constellation of stars. Relieved against the ghostly light, the gigantic Negro, Daggoo, loomed up to thrice his stature. The parted mouth of Tashtego revealed his shark-white teeth, strangely gleaming. Lit up by the preternatural light, Queequeg's tattooing burned like satanic blue flames on his body.

"The corposants have mercy on us all," someone cried.

Nearby, from the overhanging rigging, a number of the seamen hung pendulous, like a knot of wasps from an orchard twig. In various enchanted attitudes others remained rooted to the deck, but all their eyes upcast.

"Aye, aye, men!" cried Ahab. "Look up at it; mark it well; the white flame but lights the way to the White Whale!"

Suddenly there were repeated flashes of lightning. "The boat!" cried Starbuck. "Look at thy boat, old man!"

Ahab's harpoon was firmly lashed in the whaleboat, so that it projected beyond the bow, but the wind had caused the leather sheath to drop off. Now from the keen steel barb there came a leveled flame of pale, forked fire. As the silent harpoon burned there like a serpent's tongue, Starbuck grasped Ahab by the arm. "God is against thee,

old man, forbear! 'Tis an ill voyage! Let me square the yards while we may, old man, and make a fair wind of it homeward, to go on a better voyage than this."

Overhearing Starbuck, the panic-stricken crew instantly raised a half-mutinous cry. But snatching the burning harpoon, Ahab waved it like a torch among them, swearing to transfix with it the first sailor that but cast loose a rope's end. Petrified by his aspect, and still more shrinking from his fiery harpoon, the men fell back in dismay. At last Ahab spoke. "All your oaths to hunt the White Whale are as binding as mine, and old Ahab is bound heart, soul, and body, lungs and life. And that ye may know to what tune this heart beats, look ye here— Thus I blow out the last fear!" And with one blast of his breath he extinguished the flame.

Next morning the not-yet-subsided sea rolled in long, slow billows of mighty bulk, and striving in the *Pequod*'s gurgling track, pushed her on like giants' palms outspread. The strong, unstaggering breeze abounded so, that sky and air seemed vast, outbellying sails. The whole world boomed before the wind.

Maintaining an enchanted silence, Ahab stood apart, and every time the teetering ship pitched down her bowsprit he turned to eye the sun's rays produced ahead. When she settled by the stern, he turned behind and saw how the same yellow rays were blending with his undeviating wake. Suddenly he hurried toward the helm, huskily demanding how the ship was heading.

"East-sou'east, sir," said the frightened steersman.

"Thou liest!"—smiting him with his clenched fist. "Heading east at this hour in the morning, and the sun astern?"

Thrusting his head halfway into the binnacle, Ahab caught one glimpse of the compasses. His uplifted arm slowly fell, and for a moment he seemed almost to stagger. Standing behind him Starbuck looked, and lo, the two compasses pointed east, but the *Pequod* was as infallibly going west!

But ere the first wild alarm could get out among the crew, the old man with a rigid laugh exclaimed, "I have it! It has happened before. Mr. Starbuck, last night's thunder turned our compasses, that's all. Thou hast before now heard of such a thing, I take it?"

"Aye; but never before has it happened to me, sir," said the mate gloomily.

Standing before the binnacle and eyeing the transpointed compasses, the old man, with the sharp of his extended hand, now took the precise bearing of the sun. Satisfied that the needles were exactly inverted, he shouted out his orders for the ship's course to be changed accordingly. The yards were hard up, and once more the *Pequod* thrust her undaunted bows into the opposing wind.

For a space the old man walked the deck in rolling reveries. Then he called, "Mr. Starbuck, a lance without a pole, a top maul, and the smallest of the sailmaker's needles. Quick!"

Accessory, perhaps, to the impulse dictating the thing he was now about to do, were certain prudential motives. The old man well knew that to steer by transpointed needles, though clumsily practicable, was not a thing to be passed over by superstitious sailors without some shudderings and evil portents.

"Men," said Ahab, turning upon the crew as the mate handed him the things he had demanded, "the thunder turned old Ahab's needles, but out of this bit of steel Ahab can make one of his own that will point as true as any."

Abashed glances of servile wonder were exchanged by the sailors as this was said. With fascinated eyes they awaited whatever magic might follow.

With a blow from the top maul Ahab knocked off the steel head of the lance, and then, handing to the mate the long iron rod remaining, bade him hold it upright without its touching the deck. Then, after repeatedly smiting the upper end of this rod with the maul, he placed the blunted needle endwise on the top of it and hammered that several times, less strongly, the mate still holding the rod as before. Going through some strange motions—whether necessary or merely intended to awe the crew is uncertain—he called for linen thread. Moving to the binnacle, he slipped out the two reversed needles and suspended the sail needle by its middle, horizontally, over one of the compass cards. At first the needle went around and around, quivering and vibrating, but at last it settled to its place. Ahab, who had been intently watching for this result, stepped back from the binnacle, and pointing toward it, exclaimed, "Look ye, for yourselves, if Ahab be not lord of the level lodestone! The sun is east, and that compass swears it!"

One after another they peered in, for nothing but their own eyes could persuade such ignorance as theirs, and one after another they slunk away. In his fiery eyes of scorn and triumph, you then saw Ahab in all his fatal pride.

STEERING NOW SOUTHEASTWARD, the *Pequod* held on her path toward the equator, making a long passage through unfrequented waters and over waves monotonously mild.

At last a large ship, the *Rachel*, was descried, bearing directly down upon the *Pequod*, all her spars clustering with men. The *Pequod* was making good speed, but as the broad-winged stranger shot nigh to her, the boastful sails fell together as burst bladders, and all life fled from the hull.

"Bad news, she brings bad news," muttered an old seaman. But ere her commander, with trumpet to mouth, could hail, Ahab's voice was heard.

"Hast seen the White Whale?"

"Aye, yesterday. Have ye seen a whaleboat adrift?"

Throttling his joy, Ahab negatively answered this unexpected question, and would then have fain boarded the stranger, when the stranger captain himself, having stopped his vessel's way, was seen descending her side. A few keen pulls, and his boat hook clinched the *Pequod*'s main chains, and he sprang to the deck. Immediately he was recognized by Ahab for a Nantucketer he knew. But no formal salutation was exchanged.

"Where was he? Not killed! Not killed!" cried Ahab, closely advancing. "How was it?"

It seemed that late on the afternoon of the day previous, while three of the stranger's boats were engaged with a shoal of whales, which had led them some four or five miles from the ship, the white hump and head of Moby Dick had suddenly loomed up out of the blue water, not far to leeward. The fourth rigged boat—a reserved one—had then been lowered in chase. After a keen sail before the wind, this fourth boat seemed to have succeeded in fastening a harpoon into the whale—at least, as well as the man at the masthead could tell. In the distance he saw the diminished boat, and then a swift gleam of bubbling white water, and after that nothing more. It was concluded that the stricken whale must have run away with his pursuers, as often happens. The recall signals were placed in the rigging, then darkness came on. Forced to pick up her three wind-ward boats first, the ship had had to leave the fourth boat to its fate till near midnight and to increase her distance from it. The rest of her crew at last being safe aboard, she crowded all sail after the miss-ing boat, kindling a fire in her try-pots for a beacon, and with every other man aloft on the lookout. But though she had thus continued till daylight, pausing again and again to lower her spare boats, yet not the least glimpse of the missing keel had been seen.

The story told, the stranger captain revealed his object in board-ing the *Pequod*. He desired the ship to unite with his own in the search, by sailing over the sea some four or five miles apart, on par-allel lines, and so sweeping a double horizon, as it were.

"I will wager," whispered Stubb to Flask, "that someone in that missing boat wore off that captain's best coat—mayhap his watch—he's so cursed anxious to get it back. Whoever heard of two pious whaleships cruising after one missing whaleboat in the height of the whaling season? See, Flask, only see how pale he looks—look—it wasn't the coat—it must have been the—"

"My boy, my own boy is among them," exclaimed the stranger cap-tain to Ahab. "For God's sake—I beg, I conjure you! For eight and forty hours let me charter your ship—I will gladly pay for it, and roundly pay for it—for eight and forty hours only—only that—you must, oh, you *shall* do this thing."

"His son!" cried Stubb. "Oh, it's his son he's lost! What says Ahab? We must save that boy."

Now, as it shortly turned out, what made this incident of the *Rachel's* the more melancholy was that not only was one of the captain's sons among the number of the missing boat's crew; but among the number of the other boats' crews, separated from the ship during the dark vicissitudes of the chase, there had been still another son. So that for a time, the wretched father was plunged to the bottom of the cruelest perplexity, which was only solved for him by his chief mate's instinctively adopting the ordinary proce-dure of a whaleship, that is, when placed between jeopardized but divided boats, always to pick up the majority first. But the captain had refrained from mentioning all this, and not till forced to it by Ahab's iciness did he allude to his one yet missing boy, a little lad but twelve years old, whose father, with the earnest but unmisgiving hardihood of a Nantucketer's paternal love, had thus early sought to initiate him in the perils and wonders of a vocation almost immemorially the destiny of his race.

"I will not go," said the stranger, beseeching Ahab, "till you say aye to me. Do to me as you would have me do to you in the like case. For *you*, too, have a boy, Captain Ahab—though but a child and nestling safely at home now—a child of your old age, too. Yes, yes, you will; I see it— Run, run, men, now, and stand by to square in the yards."

"Avast," cried Ahab in a voice that prolongingly molded every word, "touch not a rope yarn. Captain, I will not do it. Even now I lose time. Good-by, good-by. God bless ye, man, and may I forgive myself, but I must go. Mr. Starbuck, look at the binnacle watch, and in three minutes from this present instant, warn off all strangers; then forward again, and let the ship sail as before."

Hurriedly turning, with averted face, he descended into his cabin, leaving the other captain transfixed at this unconditional rejection of his earnest suit. But starting from his enchantment, the stranger hurried to the side, more fell than stepped into his boat, and returned to his ship.

Soon the two ships diverged, and as long as the strange vessel was in view, she was seen to yaw hither and thither at every dark spot, however small, on the sea. This way and that her yards were swung, starboard and larboard she continued to tack, her masts and yards thickly clustered with men.

But by her halting course and winding, woeful way, you plainly saw that this ship that so wept with spray still remained without comfort. She was Rachel, weeping for her children, because they were not.

IV. THE CHASE

Now THAT AHAB seemed to have chased his foe into an ocean fold to slay him more securely, there lurked something in the old man's eyes which it was hardly sufferable for feeble souls to see. His purpose now fixedly gleamed down upon the constant midnight of the gloomy crew. All humor, forced or natural, vanished. Stubb no more strove to raise a smile, Starbuck no more strove to check one. Joy and sorrow, hope and fear, seemed ground to finest dust, powdered in the clamped mortar of Ahab's iron soul. Like machines, the crew dumbly moved about the deck, ever conscious that the old man's despot eye was on them.

At no time now, by day or night, could the mariners step up on the deck without seeing Ahab before them, either standing in his pivot hole or pacing the planks between two undeviating limits, the mainmast and the mizzen. The clothes that the night had wet, the next day's sunshine dried upon him. He ate in the open air, taking only two meals—breakfast and dinner. Whatever he wanted from the cabin, he sent for. And so, day after day, night after night, he went no more below.

But when three or four days had passed after meeting the *Rachel*, and no spout had yet been seen, the monomaniac old man seemed distrustful of his crew's fidelity. Or so his actions seemed to hint.

"I will have the first sight of the whale myself," he said. "Aye! Ahab must have the doubloon!" With his own hands he rigged a nest of bowlines. Then, sending a man aloft with a block to secure to the main masthead, he received the two ends of the down-reeved rope and attached one to his basket. Settling his eye on the chief mate, he said, "Take the rope, sir— I give it into thy hands, Starbuck." Arranging himself in the basket, he gave the word to hoist him to his perch. Thus, with one arm clinging around the royal mast, Ahab gazed upon the sea for miles and miles—ahead, astern, this side, and that. After ten minutes, satisfied with his preparations, he had himself lowered.

Then came a night, in the midwatch, when the old man—as was his wont at intervals—stepped forth from the scuttle in which he sometimes rested and went to his pivot hole. Suddenly he thrust out his face fiercely, snuffing up the sea air as a ship's dog will in drawing nigh to some barbarous isle. He declared that a whale must be near. Soon that peculiar odor, sometimes given forth by the living sperm whale to a great distance, was palpable to all the watch. Nor was any mariner surprised when, after inspecting the compass and then ascertaining the precise bearing of the odor as nearly as possible, Ahab rapidly ordered the ship's course to be slightly altered and the sail to be shortened.

The policy dictating these movements was vindicated at daybreak by the sight of a long, almost metallic sleek on the sea directly ahead, smooth as oil, and resembling, in the pleated, watery wrinkles bordering it, some swift riptide.

"Man the mastheads! Call all hands!"

Thundering with the butts of two handspikes on the forecastle deck, Daggoo roused sleepers. Instantaneously they appeared, carrying their clothes.

"What d'ye see?" cried Ahab, flattening his face to the sky.

"Nothing, nothing, sir!" was the sound hailing down in reply.

"T'gallant sails! Stunsails! On both sides!"

All sail being set, Ahab now cast loose the special line he had rigged to sway him to the main masthead, and in a few moments they were hoisting him thither. But two-thirds of the way aloft, and while peering ahead, he raised a gull-like cry. "There she blows! A hump like a snow hill! It is Moby Dick!"

Fired by the cry, which seemed simultaneously taken up by the three lookouts, the men on deck rushed to the rigging to behold the whale they had so long been pursuing. Ahab had now gained his final perch, some feet above the other lookouts, Tashtego standing just beneath him. From this height the whale was now seen some mile or so ahead, at every roll of the sea revealing his high sparkling hump, and regularly jetting his silent spout into the air. To the mariners it seemed the same silent spout they had so long ago beheld in the moonlit Atlantic.

"And did none of ye see it before?" cried Ahab, hailing the men around him.

"I saw him almost that same instant, sir, that Captain Ahab did," said Tashtego.

"Not the same instant, not the same. No, the doubloon is mine, Fate reserved it for me. *I* only. None of ye could have raised the White Whale first. There she blows! There she blows! There again!" he cried in long-drawn, lingering tones. "He's going to sound! Stand by three boats. Mr. Starbuck, stay on board and keep the ship. Helm there! Luff, luff a point! Steady, man! All ready the boats there? Lower me, Mr. Starbuck, quick!" And he slid through the air to the deck. "Stand by the braces! Hard down the helm! Boats, boats!"

Soon all the boats but Starbuck's were dropped, all the boat sails set, all the paddles plying—with rippling swiftness, shooting to lee-ward—and Ahab heading the onset. A pale death glimmer lit up Fedallah's sunken eyes, a hideous motion gnawed his mouth.

Like noiseless nautilus shells the light prows sped through the sea. As slowly they neared the foe, the ocean grew still more smooth, seemed a noon meadow, so serenely it spread. At length the breath-less Ahab came so nigh his prey that the entire dazzling hump was distinctly visible, sliding along the sea in a revolving ring of finest, fleecy, greenish foam. The vast, involved wrinkles of the slightly pro-jecting head were just beyond. Before it went the glistening shadow of his broad, milky forehead, a musical rippling accompanying it. Behind, the blue waters interchangeably flowed over into the moving valley of his wake, and on either hand bright bubbles danced by his side. But these were broken again by the light toes of hundreds of gay fowl softly feathering the sea. And, like a flagstaff rising from the painted hull of an argosy, the tall but shattered pole of a recent lance projected from the White Whale's back. At intervals one of the cloud of fowls, hovering and skimming like a canopy over the fish, silently perched and rocked on this pole, the long tail feathers streaming like pennons.

A gentle joyousness, a mighty mildness of repose in swiftness, in-vested the gliding whale. Thus, through the serene tropical sea, Moby Dick moved on, still withholding from sight the full terrors of his submerged trunk, entirely hiding the wrenched hideousness of his jaw. But soon the forepart of him slowly rose from the water. For an instant his whole marbleized body formed an inverted arch, and warningly waving his bannered flukes in the air, the grand god re-vealed himself. Then he sounded, and went out of sight. Hovering, halting, dipping on the wing, the white seafowls longingly lingered over the agitated pool that he left.

With oars apeak and sails adrift, the three boats now floated still, awaiting Moby Dick's reappearance.

"An hour," said Ahab, standing in his boat's stern, and he gazed beyond the whale's place toward the dim blue vacancies. But in an instant the breeze freshened, the sea began to swell.

"The birds! The birds!" cried Tashtego.

In long file, as when herons take wing, the white birds were now all flying toward Ahab's boat, and when within a few yards began fluttering over the water there, wheeling around with expectant cries. Suddenly, as Ahab peered down into the sea, he profoundly saw a white spot no bigger than a weasel, with wonderful celerity uprising and magnifying as it rose, till it turned, and then there were plainly revealed two long, crooked rows of glistening teeth floating up from the undiscoverable bottom. It was Moby Dick's open mouth and scrolled jaw, his shadowed bulk still half blending with the blue of the sea. The glittering mouth yawned beneath the boat like an open-doored marble tomb. Ahab, giving one sidelong sweep with his steering oar, whirled his craft aside from this tremendous apparition. Quickly calling upon Fedallah to change places with him, he went forward to the bows, and seizing his harpoon, commanded his crew to grasp oars and stand by.

Now, by reason of this timely spinning of the boat on its axis, its bow was made to face the whale's head while yet underwater. But, as if perceiving this stratagem, Moby Dick, with that malicious intelligence ascribed to him, sidelingly transplanted himself, as it were, shooting his pleated head lengthwise beneath the boat.

Through every plank and rib the boat thrilled for an instant, the whale obliquely lying on his back in the manner of a biting shark. Slowly and feelingly he took the bows full within his mouth, so that the long, narrow lower jaw curled high up into the open air. The bluish pearl white of the inside of the jaw was within six inches of Ahab's head, and reached higher than that. In this attitude the White Whale now shook the boat, as a mildly cruel cat would shake a mouse. With unastonished eyes Fedallah gazed, and crossed his arms, while the tiger-yellow crew were tumbling over each other's heads to gain the uttermost stern.

And now both elastic gunwales were springing in and out as the whale dallied with the doomed craft; and since his body was submerged beneath the boat, he could not be harpooned from the bows, for the bows were almost inside of him, as it were. While the other boats involuntarily paused before this impossible crisis, then it was that Ahab, frenzied, furious at being helpless in the very jaws he hated, seized the long bone of the jaw with his naked hands and wildly strove to wrench it from its grip. As he thus vainly strove, the jaw slipped from him, the frail gunwales bent in, collapsed, and snapped, as both jaws, like enormous shears, bit the craft in twain

and locked themselves again in the sea, midway between the two floating wrecks. The crew in the stern wreck clung to the gunwales, striving to hold fast to the oars to lash them across; and Ahab, spilled out of the bow wreck, fell flat-faced upon the sea.

Ripplingly withdrawing from his prey, Moby Dick now lay at a little distance, thrusting his oblong white head up and down in the billows. But soon he began to swim swiftly around and around the wrecked crew, churning the water in his wake, as if lashing himself up to still another assault. The sight of the splintered boat seemed to madden him. Meanwhile, half smothered in the foam of the whale's insolent tail, helpless Ahab's head was seen, like a tossed bubble which the least chance shock might burst. The clinging crew in the broken stern could not succor him. For so appalling was the whale's aspect, so swift the ever-contracting circles he made, that he seemed to be swooping upon them. The other boats, though unharmed, dared not pull into the eddy to strike, lest that should be the signal for the instant destruction of the jeopardized castaways, Ahab and all. With straining eyes they remained on the edge of the direful zone, whose center had now become the old man's head.

Meantime, all this had been descried from the ship's mastheads, and squaring her yards, she had borne down upon the scene. She was now so near that Ahab in the water hailed her. "Sail on the whale!" he shouted. "Drive him off!"

The *Pequod*'s prows were pointed, and breaking into the charmed circle, she parted the White Whale from his victim. As he sullenly swam off, the other boats flew to the rescue. Dragged into Stubb's boat with bloodshot, blinded eyes, the white brine caking in his wrinkles, Ahab's bodily strength cracked, and he lay all crushed in the bottom. Nameless wails came from him, as desolate sounds from out ravines, far inland.

Soon Ahab halfway rose, leaning on one bended arm. "The harpoon," he said, "is it safe?"

"Aye, sir," said Stubb, showing it.

"Any missing men?"

"One, two, three, four, five—all are here."

"That's good. Help me. I wish to stand. I see him! There! Going to leeward still! Hands off from me! The sap runs up in Ahab's bones again! Set the sail—out oars—the helm!"

It is often the case that when a boat is stove, its crew, picked up by another boat, helps to work it, and the chase is continued with double-banked oars. It was thus now. But the added power of the boat did not equal the added power of the whale, for he seemed to have treble-banked his every fin. He was swimming with a velocity which plainly showed that the chase would prove indefinitely prolonged, if not hopeless. The ship itself offered the most promising intermediate means of overtaking him. Accordingly, the boats now made for her, and were swayed up to their cranes, the two parts of the wrecked boat having been previously secured. Hoisting everything to her side and stacking her canvas high, the *Pequod* bore down in the wake of Moby Dick.

At intervals the whale's glittering spout was announced from the mastheads, and when he would be reported as just gone down, Ahab would note the time, binnacle watch in hand, and so soon as the last second of the allotted hour expired, his voice was heard: "Whose is the doubloon now? D'ye see him?" If the reply was "No, sir!" straightway he commanded them to lift him to his perch. In this way the day wore on, Ahab now aloft; anon, pacing the planks.

The day was nearly done when a lookout's voice cried from the air, "Can't see the spout now, sir, too dark."

"How heading when last seen?"

"As before, sir, straight to leeward."

"Good! He will travel slower now 'tis night. Down royals, Mr. Starbuck. We must not run over him before morning. Aloft! Come down! Mr. Stubb, send a fresh hand to the fore masthead, and see it manned till morning." Then, advancing toward the doubloon on the mainmast, he said, "Men, this gold is mine, for I earned it. But I shall let it abide here till the White Whale is dead, and then, whosoever of ye first raises him, upon the day he shall be killed, this gold is that man's. And if on that day I shall again raise him, then ten times its sum shall be divided among all of ye!"

And so saying, he placed himself halfway within the scuttle, and slouching his hat, stood there till dawn.

AT DAYBREAK THE three mastheads were punctually manned afresh.

"D'ye see him?" cried Ahab, after allowing a little space for the light to spread.

"See nothing, sir."

"Turn up all hands and make sail! He travels faster than I thought."

This pertinacious pursuit of one particular whale, continued through day into night and through night into day, was by no means unprecedented in the South Sea fishery. Such is the wonderful skill acquired by some Nantucket commanders that, from observation of a whale through several hours of daylight, they will, under certain circumstances, pretty accurately foretell the direction in which he will swim while out of sight, as well as his probable rate of progression during that period. Now the ship tore on, leaving such a furrow in the sea as when a cannonball, missent, becomes a plowshare and turns up the level field.

"By salt and hemp!" cried Stubb. "This swift motion of the deck creeps upon one's legs and tingles at the heart. This ship and I are two brave fellows! By live oaks! Ha, ha! We go the gait that leaves no dust behind!"

"There she blows—she blows! She blows! Right ahead!" was now the masthead cry.

"Aye, aye!" cried Stubb. "I knew it—ye can't escape—blow on and split your spout, O whale, the mad fiend himself is after ye!"

The frenzies of the chase had by this time worked the crew bubblingly up, like old wine worked anew. Whatever pale fears and forebodings some of them might have felt before, these were now kept out of sight through the growing awe of Ahab. The hand of Fate had snatched all their souls. By the stirring perils of the previous day, the past night's suspense, the reckless way their wild craft went plunging forward, all their hearts were bowled along. They were one man, not thirty. As the one ship that held them all was put together of contrasting things—oak, maple, pinewood, iron, pitch, hemp—yet all ran into each other in the one hull, balanced and directed by the long central keel; even so, all the individualities of the crew, this man's valor, that man's fear, all varieties were welded into oneness. All were directed to that fatal goal which Ahab, their one lord and keel, did point to.

The rigging lived. The mastheads, like the tops of tall palms, were outspreadingly tufted with arms and legs. Clinging to a spar with one hand, some reached forth the other with impatient wavings.

Others, shading their eyes from the vivid sunlight, sat far out on the rocking yards. Ready and ripe for their fate, ah, how they strove through that infinite blueness to seek out the thing that might destroy them.

Then suddenly, like the combined discharge of many rifles, the triumphant halloo of thirty lungs was heard as Moby Dick bodily burst into view! Not by any calm spoutings from that mystic fountain in his head did the White Whale now reveal his vicinity, but by the far more wondrous phenomenon of breaching. Rising with utmost velocity from the farthest depths, the sperm whale thus booms his entire bulk into the pure element of air, and piling up a mountain of dazzling foam, shows his place to the distance of seven miles and more.

"There she breaches! There she breaches!" was the cry as the White Whale tossed himself salmonlike to heaven. So suddenly seen in the blue plain of the sea, relieved against the still bluer margin of the sky, the spray that he raised for the moment intolerably glittered and glared like a glacier, then gradually faded from its first sparkling intensity to a dim mist.

"Aye, breach your last to the sun, Moby Dick!" cried Ahab. "Thy hour and thy harpoon are at hand! The boats! Stand by!" Unmindful of the tedious rope ladders of the shrouds, using the isolated backstays and halyards, the men, like shooting stars, slid to the deck.

So soon as Ahab had reached his boat, a spare one rigged the previous afternoon, he cried, "Lower away! Mr. Starbuck, the ship is thine—keep away from the boats, but keep near them. Lower, all!"

As if to strike quick terror into them, Moby Dick had turned, and was now coming for the three crews. Ahab's boat was central, and cheering his men, he told them he would take the whale head and head, that is, pull straight up to his forehead. This was not uncommon, for within a certain limit such an approach hides the coming onset from the whale's sidelong vision.

But ere that close limit was gained, the White Whale, churning himself into furious speed, rushed among the boats with open jaws and lashing tail, offering appalling battle on every side, heedless of the harpoons darted fast in him from every boat, seemingly intent on annihilating each separate plank of which those boats were made. Skillfully maneuvered, wheeling like trained chargers in the field, the boats for a while eluded him, though at times by a plank's breadth.

But at last in his untraceable evolutions the White Whale so crossed and recrossed, and in a thousand ways entangled the slack of the three lines, that they foreshortened and warped the boats toward him. Now for a moment the whale drew aside a little, as if to rally for a more tremendous charge. Seizing that opportunity, Ahab paid out more line; and at that instant the whale made a sudden rush, and by so doing irresistibly dragged the boats of Stubb and Flask toward his flukes, dashing them together. Then, diving down into the sea, he disappeared in a boiling maelstrom, in which the cedar chips of the wrecks danced around and around, like grated nutmeg in a swiftly stirred bowl of punch.

While the two crews were struggling in the water, Ahab's boat seemed suddenly drawn up toward heaven by invisible wires. Shooting perpendicularly from the sea, the White Whale had dashed his broad forehead against its bottom and sent it, turning over and over, into the air. It fell, gunwale downward, and Ahab and his men fought from under it like seals from a seaside cave.

The momentum of the whale had launched him along the surface, and he now lay for a moment slowly feeling with his flukes from side to side. Whenever a stray oar, a bit of plank, or the least chip or crumb of the boats touched his skin, his tail swiftly drew back, and sideways smote the sea. But soon, as if satisfied that his work for that time was done, he pushed his pleated forehead through the ocean, and trailing after him the intertangled lines, continued his leeward way at a methodic pace.

As before, the ship again came bearing down to the rescue, and dropping a boat, picked up the floating mariners and landed them on her decks. There were some sprained shoulders, wrists, and ankles, and livid contusions, but no fatal ill seemed to have befallen anyone. Ahab was found grimly clinging to his boat's broken half, nor did it so exhaust him as the previous day's mishap.

But when he was helped to the deck, all eyes were fastened upon him. Instead of standing by himself, he hung upon the shoulder of Starbuck. His ivory leg had been snapped off, leaving but one short sharp splinter.

"Aye, aye, Starbuck, 'tis sweet to lean sometimes; and would old Ahab had leaned oftener than he has."

"No bones broken, sir, I hope," said Stubb with true concern.

"Aye, Stubb! D'ye see it? But even with a broken bone, old Ahab is untouched. Aloft there! Which way?"

"Dead to leeward, sir."

"Up helm, then. Pile on the sail again. Shipkeepers, down the rest of the spare boats and rig them. Mr. Starbuck, away, and muster the boat crews."

"Let me first help thee toward the bulwarks, sir."

"Oh, oh, oh! How this splinter gores me now! Accursed Fate! Give me something for a cane— There, that shivered lance will do. Muster the men. I have not seen *him* yet. By heaven, it cannot be! Fedallah missing? Quick! Call them all."

The old man's thought was true. Upon mustering the company, the Parsee was not there.

"The Parsee!" cried Stubb. "He must have been caught in . . ."

"The black vomit wrench thee! Run, all of ye, above, alow—find him—not gone—not gone!"

But quickly they returned with the tidings that the Parsee was nowhere to be found.

"Aye, sir," said Stubb, "caught among the tangles of your line—I thought I saw him dragging under."

"*My* line! *My* line? Gone? Gone? What means that little word? What death knell rings in it, that old Ahab shakes as if he were the belfry? Quick! All hands to the rigging of the boats. I'll ten times girdle the unmeasured globe, and dive straight through it, but I'll slay Moby Dick yet!"

"Great God!" cried Starbuck. "Never, never wilt thou kill him, old man! No more of this, that's worse than devil's madness. Two days chased—twice stove to splinters—thy very leg snatched from under thee—thy evil shadow gone—all good angels mobbing thee with warnings. What more wouldst thou have? Shall we keep chasing this murderous fish till he swamps the last man? Shall we be dragged by him to the bottom of the sea? Shall we be towed by him to the infernal world? Oh, oh, impiety and blasphemy to hunt him more!"

"Starbuck, of late I've felt strangely moved to thee. But in this matter of the whale, Ahab is forever Ahab. This whole act's immutably decreed. 'Twas rehearsed by thee and me a billion years before this ocean rolled. I am the Fates' lieutenant; I act under orders. Look that thou obeyest mine. Stand round me, men. Believe ye in omens? Then laugh aloud! For drowning things will twice rise to the surface, then rise again, to sink forevermore. So with Moby Dick. Two days he's floated—tomorrow will be the third. Aye, men, he'll rise once more—but only to spout his last!"

When dusk descended, the whale was still in sight to leeward. So once more the sail was shortened, and everything passed nearly as on the previous night. The sound of hammers and the hum of the grindstone was heard till nearly daylight, as the men toiled by lanterns, rigging the spare boats and sharpening fresh weapons. Meantime, of the broken keel of Ahab's wrecked craft the carpenter made him another leg. As on the night before, slouched Ahab stood fixed within his scuttle, his glance set due eastward for the earliest sun.

THE MORNING OF the third day dawned fair and fresh, and once more the daylight lookouts dotted every mast. "D'ye see him?" cried Ahab; but the whale was not yet in sight.

"What a lovely day again," Ahab said. "Were it a new-made world, a fairer day could not dawn. Here's food for thought, had Ahab time to think. But Ahab only feels, feels, feels. Thinking is, or ought to be, a coolness and a calmness, and our poor hearts throb and our poor brains beat too much for that."

After some hours had passed, he called again, "Aloft there! What d'ye see?"

"Nothing, sir."

"Nothing! And noon at hand! The doubloon goes a-begging! I've oversailed him. Aye, he's chasing *me* now, not I *him*—that's bad. Aye, aye, I have run him by last night. About! About! Come down, all of ye but the regular lookouts! Man the braces!"

Steering as she had done, the wind had been somewhat on the *Pequod*'s quarter, so that now, being pointed in the reverse direction, the braced ship sailed hard upon the breeze as she rechurned the cream in her own white wake.

"Against the wind he now steers for the open jaw," murmured Starbuck to himself, as he coiled the main brace upon the rail. "God keep us, but already my bones feel damp within me."

"Stand by to sway me up!" cried Ahab, advancing to his hempen basket. "We should meet him soon."

"Aye, aye, sir," and straightway Starbuck did Ahab's bidding, and once more Ahab swung on high.

A whole hour now passed, gold-beaten out to ages. Time itself held long breaths with suspense. But at last, three points off the weather bow, Ahab descried the spout again, and from the mastheads three shrieks went up.

"Forehead to forehead I meet thee this third time, Moby Dick! On deck there, brace sharper up! He's too far off to lower yet, Mr. Starbuck. So, so; he travels fast, and I must down. But let me have one more good look aloft here at the sea, there's time for that. An old, old sight, and yet somehow so young. Aye, and not changed a wink since I first saw it, a boy, from the sand hills of Nantucket! Good-by, masthead—keep a good eye upon the whale while I'm gone."

He gave the word, and still gazing around, descended through the blue air to the deck.

In due time the boats were lowered, but as Ahab, standing in his shallop's stern, was just on the point of descent, he waved to the mate—who held one of the tackle ropes on deck—and bade him pause. "Starbuck!"

"Sir?"

"For the third time, Starbuck, my soul's ship starts upon this voyage."

"Aye, sir, thou wilt have it so."

"Some ships sail from their ports and ever afterward are missing, Starbuck!"

"Truth, sir; saddest truth."

"Some men die at ebb tide, some at low water, some at the full of the flood. I feel now like a billow that's all one crested comb, Starbuck. I am old. Shake hands with me, man."

Their hands met; their eyes fastened, Starbuck's tears the glue.

"Oh, my captain, noble heart, go not! See, it's a brave man that weeps; how great the agony of the persuasion then!"

"Lower away!" cried Ahab, tossing the mate's arm from him. "Stand by the crew!"

In an instant the boat was pulling around close under the stern. "The sharks! The sharks!" cried a voice from the low cabin window there. "Oh, master, my master, come back!"

But Ahab heard nothing, for his own voice was lifted high then, and the boat leaped on. Scarce had it pushed from the ship when numbers of sharks, seemingly rising from out the dark waters beneath the hull, maliciously snapped at the blades of the oars every time they dipped in the water, and in this way accompanied the boat with their bites. It is a thing that not uncommonly happens to whaleboats in those swarming seas—the sharks at times apparently following them in the same way that vultures hover over the banners of marching regiments. But these were the first sharks that had been observed by the *Pequod* since the White Whale had been first descried. Whether it was that Ahab's crew were all such tiger-yellow barbarians, and therefore their flesh more musky to the senses of the sharks—a matter sometimes well known to affect them—however it was, they seemed to follow that one boat without molesting the others.

"Heart of wrought steel!" murmured Starbuck, gazing over the side at the receding boat. "Lowering thy keel among ravening sharks, and followed by them, and this the critical third day? Oh, my God! What is this that shoots through me and leaves me so deadly calm, yet expectant, fixed at the top of a shudder! Mary, girl! Thou fadest in pale glories behind me. Boy! I seem to see but thy eyes grown wondrous blue. Is my journey's end coming? My legs feel faint. Stir thyself, Starbuck! Stave it off! Move! Speak! Masthead there! Aloft! Keep thy keenest eye upon the boats, mark well the whale!"

The boats had not gone very far when—by a signal from the mastheads, a downward pointed arm—Ahab knew that the whale had sounded. Intending to be near him at the next rising, he held on his way a little sideways from the vessel, the becharmed crew maintaining the profoundest silence.

Suddenly the waters around them slowly swelled in broad circles, then quickly upheaved, as if sideways sliding from a rising berg of ice. A low rumbling sound was heard, a subterraneous hum. Then, bedraggled with trailing ropes and harpoons and lances, a vast form shot lengthwise but obliquely from the sea. Shrouded in a thin drooping veil of mist, it hovered for a moment in the rainbowed air, and then fell swamping back into the deep. Crushed thirty feet upward, the waters flashed like heaps of fountains, then brokenly sank in a shower of flakes, leaving the surface creamed like new milk around the marble trunk of the whale.

"Give way!" cried Ahab to the oarsmen, and the boats darted forward to the attack. But maddened by yesterday's fresh irons that corroded in him, Moby Dick seemed possessed by all the angels that fell from heaven. Head-on, he came churning his tail among the boats and once more flailed them apart, spilling out the irons from the two mates' boats and dashing in one side of the upper part of their bows, but leaving Ahab's almost without a scar.

"Away, mates, to the ship!" shouted Ahab. "Those boats are useless now; repair them if ye can, and return to me!"

While Daggoo and Queequeg were stopping the strained planks, the whale shot by them again, showing one entire flank. At that moment a quick cry went up. Lashed around and around to the fish's back, pinioned in the turns upon turns in which, during the past night, the whale had reeled the involutions of the lines around him, the half-torn body of the Parsee was seen, his sable raiment frayed to shreds, his eyes distended.

As if bent upon escaping with the corpse he bore, Moby Dick was now again steadily swimming forward with his utmost velocity, and had almost passed the ship.

"Oh, Ahab," cried Starbuck, "not too late is it, even now, the third day, to desist! See! Moby Dick seeks thee not. It is thou, thou, that madly seekest him!"

Setting sail to the rising wind, Ahab's boat was swiftly impelled to leeward by both oars and canvas. At last, when he was sliding by the vessel, so near as plainly to distinguish Starbuck's face as he leaned over the rail, Ahab hailed him to turn the vessel about and follow him, at an interval. Glancing upward, he saw Tashtego, Queequeg, and Daggoo eagerly mounting to the three mastheads, while the oarsmen in the two staved boats which had but just been hoisted to the side were busily at work repairing them. As he sped, he also caught flying glimpses of Stubb and Flask busying themselves on deck with new irons and lances.

The White Whale, whether fagged by the three days' running chase or because of some latent malice, now began to abate his speed. And still, as Ahab glided over the waves, the unpitying sharks accompanied him, and so continually bit at the plying oars that the blades became jagged and crunched, and left small splinters in the sea.

"Heed them not! Pull on!"

"But at every bite, sir, the blades grow smaller!"

"They will last long enough! Pull on! But who can tell," he muttered, "whether these sharks swim to feast on the whale or on Ahab? But pull on! Aye, all alive, now—we near him. The helm! Take the helm; let me pass." Two of the oarsmen helped him forward to the bows, as the still flying boat rapidly neared the whale.

At length, the craft ran ranging along the White Whale's flank, within the smoky mist thrown off from the spout. Then Ahab, with body arched back and both arms lengthwise high-lifted to the poise, darted his fierce iron and his far fiercer curse into the great hump of the hated whale. As both steel and curse sank to the socket, Moby Dick writhed sideways. Spasmodically, he rolled his nigh flank against the boat's bow and canted it over. Had it not been for the elevated part of the gunwale to which he clung, Ahab would once more have been tossed into the sea. As it was, three of the oarsmen were flung out, but two of them clutched the gunwale again, and rising to its level on a wave, hurled themselves bodily inboard. The third man helplessly floated astern.

Almost simultaneously, with a mighty, instantaneous swiftness, the White Whale darted through the weltering sea. Ahab cried out to the steersman to take new turns with the line and hold it, but the moment the treacherous line felt that double strain, it snapped in the empty air!

Hearing the rush of the sea-crashing boat, the whale wheeled around to present his blank forehead at bay, and in that evolution he caught sight of the nearing black hull of the *Pequod*. Seemingly seeing in it the source of all his persecutions, perhaps bethinking it a larger and nobler foe, of a sudden smiting his jaws amid fiery showers of foam, he bore down upon its advancing prow.

Ahab staggered; his hand smote his forehead. "I grow blind. Hands, stretch out before me! Is't night?"

"The whale! The ship!" cried the cringing oarsmen.

"Oars! Oars! The ship! The ship! Dash on, my men! Will ye not save my ship?"

But as the oarsmen violently forced their boat through the seas, two planks of the whale-smitten bow ends burst through, and almost in an instant the temporarily disabled boat lay nearly level with the waves, its half-wading, splashing crew trying hard to stop the gap and bail out the pouring water.

Meantime, standing upon the *Pequod*'s deck, Starbuck caught sight of the downcoming monster.

"The whale, the whale! Up helm, up helm! Oh, all ye sweet powers of air, now hug me close! Oh, Ahab, Ahab, lo, thy work. Steady, helmsman, steady! Nay! Up helm again! He turns to meet us! My God, stand by me now!"

Strangely vibrating his head from side to side, Moby Dick sent a broad band of overspreading semicircular foam before him as he rushed. Vengeance and eternal malice were in his whole aspect, and in spite of all that mortal man could do, the solid white buttress of his forehead smote the ship's starboard bow, till men and timbers reeled. Some fell flat upon their faces. Aloft, the heads of the harpooners shook on their bull-like necks. Through the breach in the ship's bow they heard the waters pouring in, as mountain torrents down a flume.

Diving beneath the settling ship, the whale ran quivering along its keel. Turning underwater, it swiftly shot to the surface again, far off the other bow, where it lay quiescent within a few yards of Ahab's boat.

"Oh, thou death-glorious ship! Must ye then perish, and without me? Am I cut off from the last fond pride of shipwrecked captains? Oh, lonely death on lonely life! Toward thee I roll, thou all-destroying but unconquering whale. To the last I grapple with thee! From hell's heart I stab at thee, for hate's sake I spit my last breath at thee. Let me then be towed to pieces while still chasing thee, though tied to thee, thou damned whale! *Thus*, I give up the spear!"

The harpoon was darted. The stricken whale flew forward. With igniting velocity the line ran through the groove—ran foul. As Ahab stooped to clear it, the flying turn caught him around the neck. Voicelessly, as Turkish mutes bowstring their victim, he was shot out of the boat, ere the crew knew he was gone. Next instant, the heavy eye splice in the rope's end flew out of the empty rope tub, knocked down an oarsman, and smiting the sea, disappeared in its depths.

For an instant, the tranced boat's crew stood still, then turned. "The ship? Great God, where is the ship?"

Through dim, bewildered eyes they saw the *Pequod*'s sidelong fading phantom, only the uppermost masts out of water. Then concentric circles seized the lone whaleboat itself, and all its crew and each floating oar, and spinning all around and around in one vortex, carried the smallest chip of the *Pequod* out of sight.

Now small fowls flew screaming over the yet yawning gulf; a sullen white surf beat against its steep sides; then all collapsed, and the great shroud of the sea rolled on as it rolled five thousand years ago.

EPILOGUE

And I only am escaped alone to tell thee.
Job

THE DRAMA'S DONE. Why then here does anyone step forth? Because one did survive the wreck.

It so chanced that after the Parsee's disappearance I was he whom the Fates ordained to take the place of Ahab's bowsman, when that bowsman assumed the vacant post; the same who, when on the last day the three men were tossed from out the rocking boat, was dropped astern. So, floating on the margin of the ensuing scene and in full sight of it, when the half-spent suction of the sunk ship reached me, I was then, but slowly, drawn toward the closing vortex.

When I reached it, it had subsided to a creamy pool. Around and around I revolved, ever contracting toward the black bubble at the axis of that slowly wheeling circle. As I neared that vital center, the black bubble upward burst. Now liberated by reason of its cunning spring, and owing to its great buoyancy, rising with great force, the coffin life buoy shot lengthwise from the sea, fell over, and floated by my side.

Buoyed up by that coffin for almost one whole day and night, I floated on a soft and dirgelike main. The unharming sharks, they glided by as if with padlocks on their mouths; the savage sea hawks sailed with sheathed beaks. On the second day a sail drew near, nearer, and picked me up at last. It was the devious-cruising *Rachel*, that in her retracing search after her missing children, only found another orphan.

YOUTH
by Joseph Conrad

A
CONDENSATION
OF
Youth
BY
JOSEPH CONRAD

Judea, London. Her name was on the stern and below it some sort of a coat of arms with the motto "Do or Die" underneath. She was a rusty old freighter, and the voyage was ill-fated from the start—equipment breakdowns, then a violent storm, and finally a smouldering fire in the cargo hold. Young Marlow, however, was just twenty—this was his first berth as second mate and, from his point of view, the old ship was bearing him over enchanted seas to the exotic East. Yet even the unquenchable optimism of youth would be taxed by the nightmare that lay ahead.

JOSEPH CONRAD (1857–1924) was born in Poland and brought up in Russia. He travelled the world as a sailor, obtaining his master mariner's certificate in 1886, the same year that he became a naturalized British subject. Although he did not speak a word of English until he was nineteen, he is now hailed as a master stylist of the language.

THIS COULD HAVE occurred nowhere but in England, where men and sea interpenetrate, so to speak—the sea entering into the life of most men, and the men knowing something or everything about the sea, in the way of amusement, of travel, or of breadwinning.

We were sitting round a mahogany table that reflected the bottle, the claret glasses, and our faces as we leaned on our elbows. There was a director of companies, an accountant, a lawyer, Marlow, and myself. The director had been a *Conway* boy, the accountant had served four years at sea, the lawyer—a fine crusted Tory, High Churchman—had been chief officer in the P & O service in the good old days when mail boats were square-rigged and used to come down the China Sea before a fair monsoon with stunsails set alow and aloft. We all began life in the merchant service. Between the five of us there was the strong bond of the sea, and also the fellowship of the craft, which no amount of enthusiasm for yachting, cruising, and so on can give, since one is only the amusement of life and the other is life itself.

Marlow told the story, or rather the chronicle, of a voyage:

"Yes, I have seen a little of the Eastern seas; but what I remember best is my first voyage there. You fellows know there are those voyages that seem ordered for the illustration of life, that might stand for a symbol of existence. You fight, work, sweat, nearly kill yourself, sometimes do kill yourself, trying to accomplish something—and you can't. Not from any fault of yours. You simply can do nothing—not even marry an old maid, or get a wretched six-hundred-ton cargo of coal to its port of destination.

"It was my first voyage to the East, and my first voyage as second mate; it was also my skipper's first command. You'll admit it was time. He was sixty if a day; a little man, with a broad, not very straight back, with bowed shoulders and one leg more bandy than the other. He had a nutcracker face—chin and nose trying to come together over a sunken mouth—and it was framed in iron-gray fluffy hair that looked like a chin strap of cotton wool sprinkled with coal dust. And he had blue eyes in that old face of his, which were amazingly like a boy's, with that candid expression some quite common men preserve to the end of their days by a rare internal gift of simplicity of heart and rectitude of soul. What induced him to accept me was a wonder. I had come out of a crack Australian clipper, where I had been third officer, and he seemed to have a prejudice against crack clippers as aristocratic and high-toned. He said to me, 'You know, in this ship you will have to work.' I said I had to work in every ship I had ever been in. 'Ah, but this is different, and you gentlemen out of them big ships . . . but there! I daresay you will do. Join tomorrow.'

"I joined tomorrow. It was twenty-two years ago; and I was just twenty. How time passes! It was one of the happiest days of my life. Fancy! Second mate for the first time—a really responsible officer! I wouldn't have thrown up my new billet for a fortune. The mate looked me over carefully. He was also an old chap, but of another stamp. He had a Roman nose, a snow-white, long beard, and his name was Mahon, but he insisted that it should be pronounced Mann. He was well connected; yet there was something wrong with his luck, and he had never got on.

"As to the captain, he had been for years in coasters, then in the Mediterranean, and last in the West Indian trade. He had never been round the Capes. Both were thorough good seamen, of course, and between those two old chaps I felt like a small boy between two grandfathers.

"The ship also was old. Her name was the *Judea*. Queer name, isn't it? She belonged to a man Wilmer, Wilcox—some name like that; but he has been bankrupt and dead these twenty years or more, and his name don't matter. She had been laid up in Shadwell basin for ever so long. You can imagine her state. She was all rust, dust, grime—soot aloft, dirt on deck. To me it was like coming out of a palace into a ruined cottage. She was about four hundred tons, had a primitive windlass, wooden latches on the doors, not a bit of brass about her, and a big square stern. There was on it, below her name in big letters, a lot of scrollwork, with the gilt off, and some sort of a coat of arms, with the motto 'Do or Die' underneath.

"We left London in ballast—sand ballast—to load a cargo of coal in a northern port for Bankok. We worked out of the Thames under canvas, with a North Sea pilot on board; and we were a week working up as far as Yarmouth Roads. Then we got into a gale. It was wind, lightning, sleet, snow, and a terrific sea. We were flying light, and you may imagine how bad it was when I tell you we had smashed bulwarks and a flooded deck. On the second night she shifted her ballast into the lee bow, and by that time we had been blown off somewhere on the Dogger Bank. There was nothing for it but go below with shovels and try to right her, and there we were in that vast hold, gloomy like a cavern, the tallow dips stuck and flickering on the beams, the gale howling above, the ship tossing about like mad on her side; there we all were, the pilot, the captain, everyone, trying to toss shovelfuls of wet sand up to windward. At every tumble of the ship you could see vaguely in the dim light men falling down with a great flourish of shovels.

"On the third day the gale died out, and by and by a North Country tug picked us up. We took sixteen days in all to get from London to the Tyne! When we got into dock we had lost our turn for loading, and they hauled us off to a pier where we remained for a month. Mrs. Beard (the captain's name was Beard) came from Colchester to see the old man, and lived on board. The crew of runners had left and there remained only the officers, one boy, and the steward, a mulatto who answered to the name of Abraham. Mrs. Beard was an old woman, with a face all wrinkled and ruddy like a winter apple, and the figure of a young girl. She caught sight of me once, sewing on a button, and insisted on having my shirts to repair. This was something different from the captains' wives I had known on board crack clippers. When I brought her the shirts, she said: 'And the socks? They want mending, I am sure, and Captain Beard's things are all in order now. I would be glad of something to do.' Bless the old woman.

"They loaded us at last. We shipped a crew. Eight able seamen and two boys. We hauled off one evening to the buoys at the dock gates, ready to go out, and with a fair prospect of beginning the voyage next day. Mrs. Beard was to start for home by a late train. When the ship was fast we went to tea. We sat rather silent through the meal—Mahon, the old couple, and I. I finished first, and slipped away for a smoke, my cabin being in a deckhouse just against the poop. It was high water, blowing fresh with a drizzle; the double dock gates were opened, and the steam colliers were going in and out in the darkness. I watched the procession of headlights gliding high and of green lights gliding low in the night, when suddenly a red gleam flashed at me, vanished, came into view again, and remained. The fore end of a steamer loomed up close.

"I shouted down the cabin, 'Come up, quick!' and then heard a startled voice saying afar in the dark, 'Stop her, sir.' A bell jingled. Another voice cried warningly, 'We are going right into that bark, sir.' The answer to this was a gruff 'All right,' and the next thing was a heavy crash as the steamer struck a glancing blow with the bluff of her bow about our forerigging. There was a moment of confusion, yelling, and running about. Steam roared. Then somebody was heard saying, 'All clear, sir.' . . . 'Are you all right?' asked the gruff voice. I had jumped forward to see the damage, and hailed back, 'I think so.' 'Easy astern,' said the gruff voice. A bell jingled. 'What steamer is that?' screamed Mahon. By that time she was no more to us than a bulky shadow maneuvering a little way off. They shouted at us some name—a woman's name, *Miranda* or *Melissa*—or some such thing. 'This means another month in this beastly hole,' said Mahon to me, as we peered with lamps about the splintered bulwarks and broken braces. 'But where's the captain?'

"We had not heard or seen anything of him all that time. We went aft to look. A doleful voice arose, hailing somewhere in the middle of the dock, '*Judea*, ahoy!' . . . How the devil did he get there? 'Hallo!' we shouted. 'I am adrift in our boat without oars,' he cried. A belated waterman offered his services, and Mahon struck a bargain with him for half-a-crown to tow our skipper alongside; but it was Mrs. Beard that came up the ladder first. They had been floating about the dock in that mizzly cold rain for nearly an hour. I was never so surprised in my life.

"It appears that when he heard my shout 'Come up,' he understood at once what was the matter, caught up his wife, ran on deck, and across, and down into our boat, which was fast to the ladder. Not bad for a sixty-year-old. Just imagine that old fellow saving heroically in his arms that old woman—the woman of his life. He set her down on a thwart, and was ready to climb back on board when the painter came loose somehow, and away they went together. Of course in the confusion we did not hear him shouting. He looked abashed. She said cheerfully, 'I suppose it does not matter my losing the train now?' 'No, Jenny—you go below and get warm,' he growled. Then to us: 'A sailor has no business with a wife—I say. There I was, out of the ship. Well, no harm done this time. Let's go and look at what that fool of a steamer smashed.'

"It wasn't much, but it delayed us three weeks. At the end of that time, the captain being engaged with his agents, I carried Mrs. Beard's bag to the railway station and put her all comfy into a third-class carriage. She lowered the window to say, 'You are a good young man. If you see John—Captain Beard—without his muffler at night, just remind him from me to keep his throat well wrapped up.' 'Certainly, Mrs. Beard,' I said. The train pulled out suddenly; I took my cap off to the old woman: I never saw her again. . . . Pass the bottle.

"We went to sea next day. When we made that start for Bankok we had been already three months out of London. We had expected to be a fortnight or so—at the outside.

"It was January, and the weather was beautiful. It lasted all down the North Sea, all down Channel; and it lasted till we were three hundred miles or so to the westward of the Lizards; then the wind went round to the sou'west and began to pipe up. In two days it blew a gale. The *Judea*, hove to, wallowed on the Atlantic like an old candlebox. It blew day after day: it blew with spite, without interval, without mercy, without rest. The world was nothing but an immensity of great foaming waves rushing at us, under a sky low enough to touch with the hand and dirty like a smoked ceiling. Day after day there was nothing round the ship but the howl of the wind, the tumult of the sea, the noise of water pouring over her deck. She tossed, she pitched, she stood on her head, she sat on her tail, and we had to hold on while on deck and cling to our bunks when below, in a constant effort of body and worry of mind.

"One night Mahon spoke through the small window of my berth. It opened right into my very bed, and I was lying there sleepless, in my boots. He said excitedly:

" 'You got the sounding rod in here, Marlow? I can't get the pumps to suck. By God! it's no child's play.'

"I gave him the sounding rod and lay down again, trying to think of various things—but I thought only of the pumps. When I came on deck they were still at it, and my watch relieved at the pumps. We pumped all night, all day, all the week—watch and watch. She was working herself loose, and leaked badly—not enough to drown us at once, but enough to kill us with the work at the pumps. And while we pumped, the ship was going from us piecemeal: the bulwarks went, the stanchions were torn out, the ventilators smashed, the cabin door burst in. The longboat changed, as if by magic, into matchwood where she stood in her gripes. And we pumped. And there was no break in the weather.

"We pumped watch and watch, for dear life; and it seemed to last for months, for years, for all eternity, as though we had been dead and gone to a hell for sailors. The sails blew away, the ship lay broadside on under a weather cloth, the ocean poured over her, and we did not care. We turned those handles, and had the eyes of idiots. As soon as we had crawled on deck I used to take a round turn with a rope about the men, the pumps, and the mainmast, and we turned, we turned incessantly, with the water to our waists, to our necks, over our heads. We had forgotten how it felt to be dry.

"And there was somewhere in me the thought: By Jove! this is the deuce of an adventure—something you read about; and it is my first voyage as second mate—and I am only twenty—and here I am lasting it out as well as any of these men, and keeping my chaps up to the mark. I was pleased. I would not have given up the experience for worlds. I had moments of exultation. Whenever the old dismantled craft pitched heavily with her counter high in the air, she seemed to me to throw up, like an appeal, like a defiance, like a cry to the clouds without mercy, the words written on her stern: '*Judea*, London. Do or Die.'

"O youth! The strength of it, the faith of it, the imagination of it! To me she was not an old rattletrap carting about the world a lot of coal for a freight—she was the endeavor, the test, the trial of life. I think of her with pleasure, with affection, with regret—as you would think of someone dead you have loved. I shall never forget her. . . . Pass the bottle.

"One night when tied to the mast, we were pumping on, and a heavy sea crashed aboard and swept clean over us. As soon as I got my breath I shouted, as in duty bound, 'Keep on, boys!' when suddenly I felt something hard floating on deck strike the calf of my leg. I made a grab at it and missed. It was so dark we could not see each other's faces within a foot—you understand.

"After that thump the ship kept quiet for a while, and the thing, whatever it was, struck my leg again. This time I caught it—and it was a saucepan. At first, being stupid with fatigue, I did not understand what I had in my hand. Suddenly it dawned upon me, and I shouted, 'Boys, the house on deck is gone. Leave this, and let's look for the cook.'

"There was a deckhouse forward, which contained the galley, the cook's berth, and the quarters of the crew. As we had expected for days to see it swept away, the hands had been ordered to sleep in the cabin—the only safe place in the ship. The steward, Abraham, however, persisted in clinging to his berth—from sheer fright I believe. So we went to look for him. It was chancing death, since once out of our lashings we were as exposed as if on a raft. But we went. The house was shattered; most of it had gone overboard. Only two posts, holding a portion of the bulkhead to which Abraham's bunk was attached, remained as if by a miracle. We groped in the ruins and came upon this, and there he was, sitting in his bunk, surrounded by foam and wreckage, jabbering cheerfully to himself. He was out of his mind; completely and forever mad. One would think that the sole purpose of that fiendish gale had been to make a lunatic of that poor mulatto. We snatched him up, lugged him aft, and pitched him headfirst down the cabin companion. You understand there was no time to carry him down with infinite precautions and wait to see how he got on. Those below would pick him up at the bottom of the stairs all right. We were in a hurry to go back to the pumps. That business could not wait.

"Next day the sky cleared, and as the sea went down the leak took up. The crew demanded to put back—and really there was nothing else to do. Boats gone, decks swept clean, cabin gutted, men without a stitch but what they stood in, stores spoiled, ship strained. We put her head for home, and—would you believe it? The wind came east right in our teeth. It blew fresh, it blew continuously. We had to beat up every inch of the way, but she did not leak so badly. Two hours' pumping in every four is no joke—but it kept her afloat as far as Falmouth.

"The good people there live on casualties of the sea, and no doubt were glad to see us. A hungry crowd of shipwrights sharpened their chisels at the sight of that carcass of a ship. And, by Jove! they had pretty pickings off us before they were done. I fancy the owner was already in a tight place. There were delays. Then it was decided to take part of the cargo out and caulk her topsides. When this was done, the owner came down for a day, and said she was as right as a little fiddle. Poor old Captain Beard looked like a ghost—through the worry and humiliation of it. Remember he was sixty, and it was his first command. Mahon said it was a foolish business, and would end badly. I loved the ship more than ever, and wanted awfully to get to Bankok. To Bankok! Magic name. Remember I was twenty, and it was my first second mate's billet, and the East was waiting for me.

"We went out and anchored in the outer roads with a fresh crew. She leaked worse than ever. It was as if those confounded shipwrights had actually made a hole in her. This time we didn't even go outside. The crew simply refused to man the windlass.

"They towed us back to the inner harbor, and we became a fixture, a feature, an institution of the place. People pointed us out to visitors. On holidays small boys pulling about in boats would hail, 'Judea, ahoy!' and if a head showed above the rail shouted, 'Where you bound to?—Bankok?' and jeered. We were only three on board. The poor old skipper mooned in the cabin. Mahon undertook the cooking, and I looked languidly after the rigging. We became citizens of Falmouth. Every shopkeeper knew us. At the barber's or tobacconist's they asked familiarly, 'Do you think you will ever get to Bankok?' Meantime the owner, the underwriters, and the charterers squabbled amongst themselves in London, and our pay went on. . . . Pass the bottle.

"It was horrid. Morally it was worse than pumping for life. It seemed that, as if bewitched, we would have to live forever in that inner harbor. I obtained three months' pay and a five days' leave, and made a rush for London. It took me a day to get there and pretty well another to come back—but three months' pay went all the same. I don't know what I did with it. I went to a music hall, I believe, lunched, dined, and supped in a swell place in Regent Street, and was back in time, with nothing but a complete set of Byron's works and a new railway rug to show for three months' work. The boatman who pulled me off the ship said, 'Hallo! I thought you had left the old thing. *She* will never get to Bankok.' 'That's all *you* know about it,' I said scornfully—but I didn't like that prophecy at all.

"Suddenly a man, some kind of agent to somebody, appeared with full powers. He had grog blossoms all over his face, an indomitable energy, and was a jolly soul. We leaped into life again. A hulk came alongside, took our cargo, and then we went into dry dock to get our copper stripped. No wonder she leaked. The poor thing, strained beyond endurance by the gale, had, as if in disgust, spat out all the oakum of her lower seams. She was recaulked, new coppered, and made as tight as a bottle. We went back to the hulk and reshipped our cargo.

"Then on a fine moonlight night, all the rats left the ship.

"We had been infested with them. They had destroyed our sails, consumed more stores than the crew, and now, when the ship was made seaworthy, concluded to clear out. I called Mahon to enjoy the spectacle. Rat after rat appeared on our rail, took a last look over his shoulder, and leaped with a hollow thud into the empty hulk. Mahon said, 'Well, well! don't talk to me about the intelligence of rats. They ought to have left before, when we had that narrow squeak from foundering. There you have the proof how silly is the superstition about them. They leave a good ship for an old rotten hulk. . . . I don't believe they know what is safe or what is good for them, any more than you or I.'

"And after some more talk we agreed that the wisdom of rats had been grossly overrated, being in fact no greater than that of men.

"The story of the ship was known, by this, all up the Channel from Land's End to the Forelands, and we could get no crew on the south coast. They sent us one all complete from Liverpool, and we left once more—for Bankok.

"We had fair breezes, smooth water right into the tropics, and the old *Judea* lumbered along in the sunshine at the rate of three miles an hour. What could you expect? She was tired—that old ship. Her youth was where mine is—where yours is—you fellows who listen to this yarn; and what friend would throw your years and your weariness in your face? We didn't grumble at her. It seemed as though we had been born in her, reared in her, had never known any other ship. I would just as soon have abused the old village church at home for not being a cathedral.

"And for me there was also my youth to make me patient. There was all the East before me, and all life, and the thought that I had been tried in that ship and had come out pretty well. And I thought of men of old who, centuries ago, went that road in ships that sailed no better, to the land of palms, and spices, and yellow sands, and of brown nations ruled by kings more cruel than Nero the Roman and more splendid than Solomon the Jew. The old bark lumbered on, heavy with her age and the burden of her cargo, while I lived the life of youth in ignorance and hope. She lumbered on through an interminable procession of days; and the fresh gilding flashed back at the setting sun seemed to cry out over the darkening sea the words painted on her stern, '*Judea*, London. Do or Die.'

"Then we entered the Indian Ocean and steered northerly for Java Head. The winds were light. Weeks slipped by. She crawled on, do or die, and people at home began to think of us as overdue.

"One Saturday evening, I being off duty, the men asked me to give them an extra bucket of water or so—for washing clothes. I went forward whistling, and with a key in my hand to unlock the fore-peak scuttle, intending to serve the water out of a spare tank we kept there. The smell down below was as unexpected as it was frightful. One would have thought hundreds of paraffin lamps had been flaring and smoking in that hole for days. I was glad to get out. The man with me coughed and said, 'Funny smell, sir.' I answered negligently, 'It's good for the health, they say,' and walked aft.

"I put my head down the square of the midship ventilator, and as I lifted the lid a visible breath, something like a thin fog, rose from the opening. The ascending air was hot, and had a heavy,

sooty, paraffiny smell. I put down the lid gently. It was no use choking myself. The cargo was on fire.

"Next day she began to smoke in earnest. You see it was to be
expected, for though the coal was of a safe kind, that cargo had been
so broken up with handling that it looked more like smithy coal than
anything else. Then it had been wetted—more than once. It rained
all the time we were taking it back from the hulk, and now with this
long passage it got heated, and there was another case of spontaneous
combustion.

"The captain called us into the cabin. He had a chart spread on
the table, and looked unhappy. He said, 'The coast of West Australia is near, but I mean to proceed to our destination. No more
putting back anywhere, if we all get roasted. We will try first to stifle
this 'ere damned combustion by want of air.'

"We tried. We battened down everything, and still she smoked.
The smoke kept coming out through imperceptible crevices; it
forced itself through bulkheads and covers; it oozed here and there
and everywhere in slender threads. It made its way into the cabin,
into the forecastle; it poisoned the sheltered places on the deck, it
could be sniffed as high as the main yard. It was clear that if the
smoke came out, the air came in. This was disheartening. This combustion refused to be stifled.

"We resolved to try water, and took the hatches off. Enormous
volumes of smoke, whitish, yellowish, thick, greasy, misty, choking,
ascended. All hands cleared out aft. Then the poisonous cloud blew
away, and we went back to work in a smoke no thicker now than
that of an ordinary factory chimney. We rigged the force pump, got
the hose along, and by and by it burst. Then we pumped with the
feeble head pump, drew water with buckets, and managed in time
to pour lots of Indian Ocean into the main hatch. The bright stream
flashed in sunshine, fell into a layer of white crawling smoke, and
vanished on the black surface of coal. Steam ascended mingling with
the smoke. We poured salt water as into a barrel without a bottom.
It was our fate to pump in that ship; and after pumping water out
of her to save ourselves from being drowned, we frantically pumped
water into her to save ourselves from being burned.

"And she crawled on, do or die, in the serene weather. The sky
was a miracle of purity. The sea was sparkling blue, like a precious

stone, extending on all sides, all round to the horizon—as if the whole terrestrial globe had been one jewel, one colossal sapphire. And on the luster of the great calm waters the *Judea* glided imperceptibly, enveloped in a lazy and unclean cloud that drifted to leeward, defiling the splendor of sea and sky.

"All this time of course we saw no fire. The cargo smoldered at the bottom somewhere. Once Mahon, as we were working side by side, said to me with a queer smile, 'Now, if she only would spring a tidy leak—like that time when we first left the Channel—it would put a stopper on this fire. Wouldn't it?' I remarked irrelevantly, 'Do you remember the rats?'

"We fought the fire and sailed the ship too as carefully as though nothing had been the matter. Everyone took his turn, captain included. There was equality, and a deal of good feeling. Sometimes a man, as he dashed a bucketful of water down the hatchway, would yell out, 'Hurrah for Bankok!' and the rest laughed. But generally we were taciturn and serious—and thirsty. Oh! how thirsty! And we had to be careful with the water. Strict allowance. The ship smoked, the sun blazed. . . . Pass the bottle.

"We tried everything. We even made an attempt to dig down to the fire. No good, of course. No man could remain more than a minute below. Mahon, who went first, fainted there, and the man who went to fetch him out did likewise. We lugged them out on deck. Then I leaped down to show how easily it could be done. They had learned wisdom by that time, and contented themselves by fishing for me with a chain hook tied to a broom handle, I believe. I did not offer to go and fetch up my shovel, which was left down below.

"Things began to look bad. We put the longboat into the water. The second boat was ready to swing out. We had also another, a fourteen-foot thing, on davits aft, where it was quite safe. Then behold, the smoke suddenly decreased. We redoubled our efforts to flood the bottom of the ship. In two days there was no smoke at all. Everybody was on the broad grin. This was on a Friday. On Saturday the men washed their clothes and their faces for the first time in a fortnight, and had a special dinner given them. But a beastly smell of burning hung about the ship. Captain Beard had hollow eyes and sunken cheeks. He and Mahon prowled soberly about hatches and ventilators, sniffing. It struck me suddenly poor Mahon was a very, very old chap. As to me, I was as pleased and proud as though I had helped to win a great naval battle. O! Youth!

"The night was fine. In the morning a homeward-bound ship passed us hull down—the first we had seen for months; but we were nearing the land at last, Java Head being about a hundred and ninety miles off, and nearly due north.

"Next day it was my watch on deck from eight to twelve. At breakfast the captain observed, 'It's wonderful how that smell hangs about the cabin.' About ten, the mate being on the poop, I stepped down on the main deck for a moment. The carpenter's bench stood abaft the mainmast; I leaned against it sucking at my pipe, and the carpenter, a young chap, came to talk to me. He remarked, 'I think we have done very well, haven't we?' and then I perceived with annoyance the fool was trying to tilt the bench. I said curtly, 'Don't, Chips,' and immediately became aware of a queer sensation, of an absurd delusion—I seemed somehow to be in the air, and felt a dull concussion which made my ribs ache. No doubt about it—I was in the air, and my body was describing a short parabola. But short as it was, I had the time to think several thoughts in, as far as I can remember, the following order: This can't be the carpenter—What is it?—Submarine volcano?—Coals, gas!—By Jove! we are being blown up—Everybody's dead—I am falling into the afterhatch—I see fire in it.

"The coal dust suspended in the air of the hold had glowed dull red at the moment of the explosion. In an infinitesimal fraction of a second since the first tilt of the bench, I was sprawling full length on the cargo. I picked myself up and scrambled out. The deck was a wilderness of smashed timber; an immense curtain of soiled rags waved gently before me—it was the mainsail blown to strips. I thought, The masts will be toppling over directly; and to get out of the way bolted on all fours toward the poop ladder. The first person I saw was Mahon, with eyes like saucers, and the long white hair standing straight on end round his head like a silver halo. He was just about to go down when the sight of the main deck stirring, heaving up, and changing into splinters before his eyes, petrified him on the top step. He stared at me with a queer kind of shocked curiosity. I did not know that I had no hair, no eyebrows, no eyelashes, that my young mustache was burned off, that my face was black, one cheek laid open, my nose cut, and my chin bleeding. I had lost my cap, one of my slippers, and my shirt was torn to rags. Of all this I was not aware. I was amazed to see the ship still afloat, the poop deck whole—and, most of all, to see anybody alive. Also the peace of the sky and the serenity of the sea were distinctly surprising. . . . Pass the bottle.

"Presently I saw the captain—and he was mad. He asked me eagerly, 'Where's the cabin table?' and to hear such a question was a frightful shock. I had just been blown up, you understand, and vibrated with that experience—I wasn't quite sure whether I was alive. Mahon began to stamp with both feet and yelled at him, 'Good God! don't you see the deck's blown out of her?' I found my voice, and stammered out as if conscious of some gross neglect of duty, 'I don't know where the cabin table is.' It was like an absurd dream.

"Do you know what he wanted next? Well, he wanted to trim the yards. The old chap, it seems, was in his own berth, winding up the chronometers, when the shock sent him spinning. Immediately it occurred to him—as he said afterward—that the ship had struck something, and he ran out into the cabin. There, he saw, the cabin table had vanished somewhere. The deck being blown up, it had fallen down into the lazaret of course. Where we had our breakfast that morning he saw only a great hole in the floor. This appeared to him so awfully mysterious that what he saw and heard after he got on deck were mere trifles in comparison. And, mark, he noticed directly the wheel deserted and his bark off her course—and his only thought was to get that miserable, stripped, undecked, smoldering shell of a ship back again with her head pointing at her port of destination. Bankok! That's what he was after. I tell you this quiet, bowed, bandy-legged, almost deformed little man was immense in the singleness of his idea and in his placid ignorance of our agitation. He motioned us forward with a commanding gesture, and went to take the wheel himself.

"Yes; that was the first thing we did—trim the yards of that wreck! No one was killed, or even disabled, but everyone was more or less hurt. You should have seen them! Some were in rags, with black faces, like coal heavers, like sweeps, and had bulletheads that seemed closely cropped, but were in fact singed to the skin. Others, of the watch below, awakened by being shot out from their collapsing bunks, shivered incessantly, and kept on groaning even as we went about our work. But they all worked. That crew of Liverpool hard cases had in them the right stuff. It's my experience they always have. It is the sea that gives it—the vastness, the loneliness surrounding their dark stolid souls. Ah! Well! we stumbled, we crept, we fell, we barked our shins on the wreckage, we hauled. It was nearly calm, but a long swell ran from the west and made her roll. The masts stood, but we did not know how much they might be charred down below. They might go at any moment. We looked at them with apprehension. One could not foresee which way they would fall.

"Then we retreated aft and looked about us. The deck was a tangle of planks on edge, of planks on end, of splinters, of ruined woodwork. The masts rose from that chaos like big trees above a matted undergrowth. The interstices of that mass of wreckage were full of something whitish, sluggish, stirring—like a greasy fog. The smoke of the invisible fire was coming up again, was trailing, like a poisonous thick mist in some valley choked with deadwood. Here and there a piece of timber, stuck upright, resembled a post. Half of a fife rail had been shot through the foresail, and the sky made a patch of glorious blue in the ignobly soiled canvas. A portion of several boards holding together had fallen across the rail, and one end protruded overboard, like a gangway leading over the deep sea, leading to death—as if inviting us to walk the plank at once and be done with our ridiculous troubles.

"The captain had surrendered the wheel to the helmsman, and elbow on rail and chin in hand, gazed at the sea wistfully. We asked ourselves, What next? I thought, This is great. I wonder what will happen. O youth!

"Suddenly Mahon sighted a steamer far astern. Captain Beard said, 'We may do something with her yet.' We hoisted two flags, which said in the international language of the sea, 'On fire. Want immediate assistance.' The steamer grew bigger rapidly, and by and by spoke with two flags on her foremast, 'I am coming to your assistance.'

"In half an hour she was abreast, to windward, within hail, and rolling slightly, with her engines stopped. We lost our composure, and yelled all together with excitement, 'We've been blown up.' A man in a white helmet, on the bridge, cried, 'Yes! All right! all right!' and he nodded his head, and smiled, and made soothing motions with his hand as though at a lot of frightened children. One of the boats dropped in the water, and walked toward us upon the sea with her long oars. Four Calashes pulled a swinging stroke. This was my first sight of Malay seamen, and what struck me then was their unconcern: they came alongside, and even the bowman standing up and holding to our main chains with the boat hook did not deign to lift his head for a glance. I thought people who had been blown up deserved more attention.

"A little man, dry like a chip and agile like a monkey, clambered up. It was the mate of the steamer. He gave one look, and cried, 'O boys—you had better quit.'

"He talked apart with the captain for a time—seemed to argue with him. Then they went away together to the steamer. When our skipper came back we learned that the steamer was the *Sommerville*, Captain Nash, from West Australia to Singapore via Batavia with mails, and that she would tow us to Batavia, where we could extinguish the fire by scuttling, and then proceed on our voyage—to Bankok! The old man seemed excited. 'We will do it yet,' he said to Mahon, fiercely. He shook his fist at the sky. Nobody else said a word.

"At noon the steamer began to tow, and what was left of the *Judea* followed at the end of seventy fathom of towrope—followed her swiftly like a cloud of smoke with mastheads protruding above. We went aloft to furl the sails. We coughed on the yards, and were careful about the bunts. Do you see the lot of us there, putting a neat furl on the sails of that ship doomed to arrive nowhere? There was not a man who didn't think that at any moment the masts would topple over. And, mind, these were men without the drilled-in habit of obedience. To an onlooker they would be a lot of profane scallywags without a redeeming point. What made them do it—what made them obey me when I made them drop the bunt of the foresail twice to try to do it better? What? They had no professional reputation—no example, no praise. It wasn't a sense of duty; they all knew well enough how to shirk when they had a mind to it. Was it the two pounds ten a month that sent them there? They didn't think their pay half good enough. No; it was something in them, something inborn and subtle. I don't say that the crew of a French or German merchantman wouldn't have done it, but I doubt whether it would have been done in the same way. There was a completeness in it, something solid like a principle, and masterful like an instinct—a disclosure of something secret—of that hidden something that makes racial difference, that shapes the fate of nations.

"It was that night at ten that, for the first time since we had been fighting it, we saw the fire. The speed of the towing had fanned the smoldering destruction. A blue gleam appeared forward, shining below the wreck of the deck. It wavered in patches, it seemed to stir and creep like the light of a glowworm. I saw it first, and told Mahon. 'Then the game's up,' he said. 'We had better stop this towing, or she will burst out suddenly fore and aft before we can clear out.' We set up a yell; rang bells to attract their attention; they towed on. At last Mahon and I had to crawl forward and cut the rope with an axe. There was no time to cast off the lashings. Red tongues could be seen licking the wilderness of splinters under our feet as we made our way back to the poop.

"Of course they very soon found out in the steamer that the rope was gone. She gave a loud blast of her whistle, her lights were seen sweeping in a wide circle, she came up ranging close alongside, and stopped. We were all in a tight group on the poop looking at her. Every man had saved a little bundle or a bag. Suddenly a conical flame with a twisted top shot up forward and threw upon the black sea a circle of light, with the two vessels side by side and heaving gently in its center. Captain Beard had been sitting on the gratings still and mute for hours, but now he rose slowly and advanced in front of us, to the mizzen shrouds. Captain Nash hailed: 'Come along! Look sharp. I have mailbags on board. I will take you and your boats to Singapore.'

" 'No!' said our skipper. 'We must see the last of the ship.'

" 'I can't wait any longer,' shouted the other. 'Mails—you know.'

" 'Ay! ay! We are all right.'

" 'Very well! I'll report you in Singapore. . . . Good-by!'

"He waved his hand. Our men dropped their bundles quietly. The steamer moved ahead, and passing out of the circle of light, vanished at once from our sight, dazzled by the fire which burned fiercely. And then I knew that I would see the East first as commander of a small boat. I thought it fine; and the fidelity to the old ship was fine. We should see the last of her. Oh, the glamour of youth! Oh, the fire of it, more dazzling than the flames of the burning ship, throwing a magic light on the wide earth, leaping to the sky, presently to be quenched by time, more cruel, more pitiless, more bitter than the sea—and like the flames of the burning ship surrounded by an impenetrable night."

"THE OLD MAN warned us in his gentle and inflexible way that it was part of our duty to save for the underwriters as much as we could of the ship's gear. Accordingly we went to work aft, while she blazed forward to give us plenty of light. We lugged out a lot of rubbish. What didn't we save? An old barometer fixed with an absurd quantity of screws nearly cost me my life: a sudden rush of smoke came upon me, and I just got away in time. There were various stores, bolts of canvas, coils of rope; the poop looked like a marine bazaar, and the boats were lumbered to the gunwales. The old man was very, very quiet, but off his balance evidently. Would you believe it? He wanted to take a length of old stream cable and a kedge anchor with him in the longboat. We said, 'Ay, ay, sir,' deferentially, and on the quiet let the thing slip overboard. The heavy medicine chest went that way, two bags of green coffee, tins of paint—fancy, paint!—a whole lot of things. Then I was ordered with two hands into the boats to make a stowage and get them ready against the time it would be proper for us to leave the ship.

"We put everything straight, stepped the longboat's mast for our skipper, who was to take charge of her. I was not sorry to sit down for a moment. My face felt raw and every limb ached as if broken. The boats, fast astern, lay in a deep shadow, and all around I could see the circle of the sea lighted by the fire. A gigantic flame arose forward straight and clear. It flared fierce, with noises like the whir of wings, with rumbles as of thunder. There were cracks, detonations, and from the cone of flame the sparks flew upward, as man is born to trouble.

"What bothered me was that the ship, lying broadside to the swell and to such wind as there was, the boats would not keep astern where they were safe, but persisted in getting under the counter and then swinging alongside. They were knocking about dangerously and coming near the flame, while the ship rolled on them, and, of course, there was always the danger of the masts going over the side at any moment. I and my two boatkeepers kept them off as best we could with oars and boat hooks; but to be constantly at it became exasperating, since there was no reason why we should not leave at once. I had not only my share of the work, but also had to keep at it two men who showed a constant inclination to lay themselves down and let things slide.

"At last I hailed 'On deck there,' and someone looked over. 'We're ready here,' I said. The head disappeared, and very soon popped up again. 'The captain says, All right, sir, and to keep the boats well clear of the ship.'

"Half an hour passed. Suddenly there was a frightful racket, rattle, clanking of chain, hiss of water, and millions of sparks flew up into the shivering column of smoke that stood leaning slightly above the ship. The catheads had burned away, and the two red-hot anchors had gone to the bottom, tearing out after them two hundred fathom of red-hot chain. The ship trembled, the mass of flame swayed as if ready to collapse, and the fore topgallant mast fell. It darted down like an arrow of fire, shot under, and instantly leaping up within an oar's length of the boats, floated quietly, very black on the luminous sea. I hailed the deck again. After some time a man in an unexpectedly cheerful tone informed me, 'Coming directly, sir,' and vanished. For a long time I heard nothing but the whir and roar of the fire. I couldn't stand it any longer, and swarming up a rope, clambered aboard over the stern.

"It was as bright as day. Coming up like this, the sheet of fire facing me was a terrifying sight, and the heat seemed hardly bearable at first. On a settee cushion dragged out of the cabin Captain Beard, with his legs drawn up and one arm under his head, slept with the light playing on him. Do you know what the rest were busy about? They were sitting on deck, round an open case, eating bread and cheese and drinking bottled stout.

"On the background of flames twisting in fierce tongues above their heads they seemed at home like salamanders, and looked like a band of desperate pirates. The fire sparkled in the whites of their eyes, gleamed on patches of white skin seen through the torn shirts. Each had the marks as of a battle about him—bandaged heads, tied-up arms, a strip of dirty rag round a knee—and each man had a bottle between his legs and a chunk of cheese in his hand. Mahon got up. With his handsome and disreputable head, his hooked profile, his long white beard, and with an uncorked bottle in his hand, he resembled one of those reckless sea robbers of old making merry amidst violence and disaster. 'The last meal on board,' he explained solemnly. 'We had nothing to eat all day, and it was no use leaving all this.' He flourished the bottle and indicated the sleeping skipper. 'He said he couldn't swallow anything, so I got him to lie down,' he went on. 'The man has had no sleep to speak of for days—and there will be dam' little sleep in the boats.' 'There will be no boats by and by if you fool about much longer,' I said, indignantly. I walked up to the skipper and shook him by the shoulder. At last he opened his eyes, but did not move. 'Time to leave her, sir,' I said, quietly.

"He got up painfully, looked at the flames, at the sea sparkling round the ship, and black, black as ink farther away; he looked at the stars shining dim through a thin veil of smoke in a sky black, black as Erebus.

" 'Youngest first,' he said.

"And the ordinary seaman, wiping his mouth with the back of his hand, got up, clambered over the taffrail, and vanished. Others followed. One, on the point of going over, stopped short to drain his bottle, and with a great swing of his arm flung it at the fire. 'Take this!' he cried.

"The skipper lingered disconsolately, and we left him to commune alone for a while with his first command. Then I went up again and brought him away at last. It was time. The ironwork on the poop was hot to the touch.

"Then the painter of the longboat was cut, and the three boats, tied together, drifted clear of the ship. It was just sixteen hours after the explosion when we abandoned her. Mahon had charge of the second boat, and I had the smallest—the fourteen-foot thing. The longboat would have taken the lot of us; but the skipper said we must save as much property as we could—for the underwriters—and so I got my first command. I had two men with me, a bag of biscuits, a few tins of meat, and a breaker of water. I was ordered to keep close to the longboat, that in case of bad weather we might be taken into her.

"And do you know what I thought? I thought I would part company as soon as I could. I wanted to have my first command all to myself. I wasn't going to sail in a squadron if there were a chance for independent cruising. I would make land by myself. I would beat the other boats. Youth! All youth! The silly, charming, beautiful youth.

"But we did not make a start at once. We must see the last of the ship. And so the boats drifted about that night, heaving and setting on the swell. The men dozed, waked, sighed, groaned. I looked at the burning ship.

"Between the darkness of earth and heaven she was burning fiercely upon a disk of purple sea shot by the blood-red play of gleams. A high, clear flame ascended from the ocean, and from its summit the black smoke poured continuously at the sky. She burned furiously, mournful and imposing like a funeral pile kindled in the night, surrounded by the sea, watched over by the stars. A magnificent death had come like a gift, like a reward to that old ship at the end of her laborious days. The surrender of her weary ghost to the keeping of stars and sea was stirring like the sight of a glorious triumph. The masts fell just before daybreak, and for a moment there was a burst and turmoil of sparks that seemed to fill with flying fire the night patient and watchful, the vast night lying silent upon the sea. At daylight she was only a charred shell, floating still under a cloud of smoke and bearing a glowing mass of coal within.

"Then the oars were got out, and the boats forming in a line moved round her remains as if in procession—the longboat leading. As we pulled across her stern a slim dart of fire shot out viciously at us, and suddenly she went down, headfirst, in a great hiss of steam. The unconsumed stern was the last to sink; but the paint had peeled off, and there were no letters, there was no word, no stubborn device that was like her soul, to flash at the rising sun her creed and her name.

"We made our way north. A breeze sprang up, and about noon all the boats came together for the last time. I had no mast or sail in mine, but I made a mast out of a spare oar and hoisted a boat awning for a sail, with a boat hook for a yard. She was certainly overmasted, but I had the satisfaction of knowing that with the wind aft I could beat the other two. I had to wait for them. Then we all had a look at the captain's chart, and, after a sociable meal of hard bread and water, got our last instructions. These were simple: steer north, and keep together as much as possible. 'Be careful with that jury rig, Marlow,' said the captain; and Mahon, as I sailed proudly past his boat, wrinkled his curved nose and hailed, 'You will sail that ship of yours underwater, if you don't look out, young fellow.' He was a malicious old man—and may the deep sea where he sleeps now rock him gently, rock him tenderly to the end of time!

"Before sunset a thick rainsquall passed over the two boats, which were far astern, and that was the last I saw of them for a time. The next day I sat steering my cockleshell—my first command—with nothing but water and sky around me. I did sight in the afternoon the upper sails of a ship far away, but I said nothing, and my men did not notice her. You see I was afraid she might be homeward bound, and I had no mind to turn back from the portals of the East. I was steering for Java—another blessed name—like Bankok, you know. And I steered many days.

"I need not tell you what it is to be knocking about in an open boat. I remember nights and days of calm when we pulled, we pulled, and the boat seemed to stand still, as if bewitched within the circle of the sea horizon. I remember the heat, the deluge of rainsqualls that kept us baling for dear life (but filled our water cask), and I remember sixteen hours on end with a mouth dry as a cinder and a steering oar over the stern to keep my first command head-on to a breaking sea. I did not know how good a man I was till then. I remember the drawn faces, the dejected figures of my two men, and I remember my youth and the feeling that will never come back anymore—the feeling that I could last forever, outlast the sea, the earth, and all men; the deceitful feeling that lures us on to joys, to perils, to love, to vain effort—to death; the triumphant conviction of strength, the glow in the heart that with every year grows dim, grows cold, grows small, and expires—and expires, too soon, too soon—before life itself.

"And this is how I see the East. I have seen its secret places and have looked into its very soul; but now I see it always from a small boat, a high outline of mountains, blue and afar in the morning; like faint mist at noon; a jagged wall of purple at sunset. I have the feel of the oar in my hand, the vision of a scorching blue sea in my eyes. And I see a bay, a wide bay, smooth as glass and polished like ice, shimmering in the dark. A red light burns far off upon the gloom of the land, and the night is soft and warm. We drag at the oars with aching arms, and suddenly a puff of wind, a puff faint and tepid and laden with strange odors of blossoms, of aromatic wood, comes out of the still night—the first sigh of the East on my face. That I can never forget. It was impalpable and enslaving, like a charm, like a whispered promise of mysterious delight.

"We had been pulling this finishing spell for eleven hours. Two pulled, and he whose turn it was to rest sat at the tiller. We had made out the red light in that bay and steered for it, guessing it must mark some small coasting port. We passed two vessels, sleeping at anchor, and, approaching the light, now very dim, ran the boat's nose against the end of a jutting wharf. We were blind with fatigue. My men dropped the oars and fell off the thwarts as if dead. I made fast to a pile. The scented obscurity of the shore was grouped into vast masses, a density of colossal clumps of vegetation, probably. And at their foot the semicircle of a beach gleamed faintly. There was not a light, not a stir, not a sound. The mysterious East faced me, perfumed like a flower, silent like death, dark like a grave.

"And I sat weary beyond expression, exulting like a conqueror.

"A splashing of oars made me jump up. A boat, a European boat, was coming in. I invoked the name of the dead; I hailed: '*Judea*, ahoy!' A thin shout answered.

"It was the captain. I had beaten the flagship by three hours, and I was glad to hear the old man's voice again, tremulous and tired. 'Is it you, Marlow?' 'Mind the end of that jetty, sir,' I cried.

"He approached cautiously, and brought up with the deep sea lead line which we had saved—for the underwriters. I eased my painter and fell alongside. He sat, a broken figure at the stern, his hands clasped in his lap. His men were asleep already. 'I had a terrible time of it,' he murmured. 'Mahon is behind—not very far.' We conversed in whispers.

"Looking around as we talked, I saw away at sea a bright light traveling in the night. 'There's a steamer passing the bay,' I said. She was not passing, she was entering, and she even came close and anchored. 'I wish,' said the old man, 'you would find out whether she is English. Perhaps they could give us a passage somewhere.' So by dint of punching and kicking I started one of my men into a state of somnambulism, and giving him an oar, took another and pulled toward the lights of the steamer.

"There was a murmur of voices in her, metallic hollow clangs of the engine room, footsteps on the deck. Her ports shone, round like dilated eyes. Shapes moved about, and there was a shadowy man high up on the bridge. He heard my oars.

"And then, before I could open my lips, a torrent of words was poured into the enigmatical, the fateful silence; outlandish, angry words, mixed with words and even whole sentences of good English. The voice swore and cursed violently. It began by calling me Pig, and from that went crescendo into unmentionable adjectives—in English. The man up there raged aloud, and with a sincerity in his fury that almost convinced me I had, in some way, sinned against the harmony of the universe.

"Suddenly he ceased, and I said:

" 'What steamer is this, pray?'

" 'Eh? What's this? And who are you?'

" 'Castaway crew of an English bark burned at sea. I am the second mate. The captain is in the longboat, and wishes to know if you would give us a passage somewhere.'

" 'Oh, my goodness! I say. . . . This is the *Celestial* from Singapore on her return trip. I'll arrange with your captain in the morning . . . and . . . I say . . . did you hear me just now?'

" 'I should think the whole bay heard you.'

" 'I thought you were a shore boat. Now, look here—this infernal lazy scoundrel of a caretaker has gone to sleep again—curse him. The light is out, and I nearly ran foul of the end of this damned jetty. This is the third time he plays me this trick. Now, I ask you, can anybody stand this kind of thing? I'll get the assistant resident to give him the sack, by . . . See—there's no light. It's out, isn't it? I take you to witness the light's out. There should be a light, you know. A red light on the—'

" 'There was a light,' I said, mildly.

" 'But it's out, man! What's the use of talking like this? You can see for yourself it's out—don't you? If you had to take a valuable steamer along this godforsaken coast, you would want a light too. I'll kick him from end to end of his miserable wharf. You'll see—'

" 'So I may tell my captain you'll take us?' I broke in.

" 'Yes, I'll take you. Good night,' he said, brusquely.

"I pulled back, made fast again to the jetty, and then went to sleep at last. I had faced the silence of the East. When I opened my eyes again the silence was as complete as though it had never been broken. I was lying in a flood of light, and the sky had never looked so far, so high, before. I lay without moving.

"And then I saw the men of the East—they were looking at me. The whole length of the jetty was full of people. I saw brown, bronze, yellow faces, the black eyes, the glitter, the color of an Eastern crowd. And all these beings stared without a murmur, without a sigh, without a movement. They stared down at the boats, at the sleeping men who at night had come to them from the sea. Nothing moved. The fronds of palms stood still against the sky. Not a branch stirred along the shore, and the brown roofs of hidden houses peeped through the green foliage, through the big leaves that hung shining and still like leaves forged of heavy metal. This was the East of the ancient navigators, so old, so mysterious, resplendent and somber, living and unchanged, full of danger and promise. And these were the men. I sat up suddenly. A wave of movement passed through the crowd from end to end, passed along the heads, swayed the bodies, like a breath of wind on a field—and all was still again. I see it now—the wide sweep of the bay, the glittering sands, the wealth of green infinite and varied, the sea blue like the sea of a dream, the crowd of attentive faces, the blaze of vivid color—the water reflecting it all, the curve of the shore, the jetty, and the three boats with tired men from the West sleeping, unconscious of the land and the people and of the violence of sunshine. They slept thrown across the thwarts, curled on bottom boards, in the careless attitudes of death. The head of the old skipper, leaning back in the stern of the longboat, had fallen on his breast, and he looked as though he would never wake. Farther out old Mahon's face was upturned to the sky, with the long white beard spread out, as though he had been shot where he sat at the tiller; and a man, all in a heap in the bows of the boat, slept with both arms embracing the stemhead and with his cheek laid on the gunwale. The East looked at them without a sound.

"I have known its fascinations since: I have seen the mysterious shores, the still water, the lands of brown nations, where a stealthy Nemesis lies in wait, pursues, overtakes so many of the conquering race, who are proud of their wisdom, of their knowledge, of their strength. But for me all the East is contained in that vision of my youth. It is all in that moment when I opened my young eyes on it. I came upon it from a tussle with the sea—and I was young—and I saw it looking at me. And this is all that is left of it! Only a moment; a moment of strength, of romance, of glamour—of youth! . . . A flick of sunshine upon a strange shore, the time to remember, the time for a sigh, and—good-by!—Night—Good-by . . . !"

He drank.

"Ah! The good old time—the good old time. Youth and the sea. Glamour and the sea! The good, strong sea, the salt, bitter sea, that could whisper to you and roar at you and knock your breath out of you."

He drank again.

"By all that's wonderful, it is the sea, I believe, the sea itself—or is it youth alone? Who can tell? But you here—you all had something out of life: money, love—whatever one gets onshore—and, tell me, wasn't that the best time, that time when we were young at sea; young and had nothing, on the sea that gives nothing, except hard knocks—and sometimes a chance to feel your strength—that only— what you all regret?"

And we all nodded at him: the man of finance, the man of accounts, the man of law, we all nodded at him over the polished table that like a still sheet of brown water reflected our faces, lined, wrinkled; our faces marked by toil, by deceptions, by success, by love; our weary eyes looking still, looking always, looking anxiously for something out of life, that while it is expected is already gone—has passed unseen, in a sigh, in a flash—together with the youth, with the strength, with the romance of illusions.

HMS ULYSSES
by Alistair MacLean

HMS
ULYSSES

A condensation of
the book by
**ALISTAIR
MACLEAN**

Illustrated by
Ivan Lapper

The crew of HMS *Ulysses* was at the end of its endurance. For months on end the cruiser had been escorting convoys on the infamous run to Murmansk. Cold, hunger, danger, plain lack of sleep had already driven some of the men beyond breaking point. The recent unpleasant incident at Scapa Flow when seamen and stokers had refused to obey orders was already classified by the Admiralty as mutiny. Nevertheless, their lordships were determined that *Ulysses* should once again put to sea and face the hazards of the hostile Arctic. The story of the terrible voyage that ensued has become one of the great classics of World War II literature.

ALISTAIR MACLEAN served as a torpedo-man in the Royal Navy's East Coast convoy escorts, and later aboard a cruiser. After the war, he graduated from Glasgow University and became a teacher, writing in his spare time. *HMS Ulysses* (250,000 hardback copies sold in six months) launched his spectacular career as a best-selling novelist.

PRELUDE: SUNDAY AFTERNOON

Slowly, deliberately, Vice Admiral Vincent Starr, Assistant Director of Naval Operations, crushed out the butt of his cigarette. Captain Vallery knew what was coming next, but for a moment he was too tired really to care.

"I'm sorry, gentlemen, genuinely sorry." Starr smiled thinly and proffered his platinum cigarette case to the four senior officers from HMS *Ulysses* sitting with him round the cabin table. At the four mute headshakes the smile flickered again. He selected a cigarette, lit it and slid the case back into the breast pocket of his double-breasted charcoal grey suit. Then he sat back in his chair the smile quite gone.

"When I flew here to Scapa Flow from London this morning," he continued, "—let us be perfectly frank, gentlemen—I expected full co-operation from you in settling this unpleasant business with all speed. And yet what do I find?" His glance travelled slowly round the table. "Commissioned officers in His Majesty's Navy sympathizing with—if not actually condoning—a lower-deck mutiny!"

He's overstating it, Vallery thought dully. He's provoking us. The words were a challenge inviting reply.

There was none. The four men seemed apathetic, indifferent, their faces heavy and deeply lined, their eyes tired.

"You are not convinced, gentlemen?" he went on softly. "You find my choice of words a trifle—ah—disagreeable? Mutiny—you would call it something else, perhaps?" He smoothed out a signal sheet.

" 'Returned from strike on Lofotens, 1545,' " he read out: " '1630—provisions, stores lighters alongside, mixed seaman–stoker party detailed unload lubricating drums. 1650—reported to captain stokers refused to obey CPO Hartley, then successively Chief Stoker Hendry and Commander (E) Dodson: ringleaders apparently Stokers Riley and Petersen. 1715—seaman branch stopped work, apparently in sympathy: no violence offered. 1725—broadcast by captain, warned of consequences: ordered to return to work: order disobeyed. 1730—signal to C-in-C *Duke of Cumberland* for assistance. 1830—Marine boarding party from *Cumberland*: attempted to arrest suspected ring-leaders: strong resistance by stokers and seamen, heavy fighting: no firearms used, but one marine dead, six stokers and seamen seriously injured, thirty-five to forty minor casualties.' " Starr crumpled the paper. "You know, gentlemen, I believe you have a point after all. 'Mutiny' is hardly the term. Nearly fifty dead and injured: 'pitched battle' would be much nearer the mark."

The four men still sat motionless. Admiral Starr's face hardened. "The ringleaders must be punished—heavily punished." The voice had a biting edge to it. "Meantime the 14th Aircraft Carrier Squadron will rendezvous with Convoy FR 77 at Denmark Strait as arranged, at 1030 Wednesday instead of Tuesday—we radioed Halifax and held up the sailing. You will proceed to sea at 0600 tomorrow." He looked across at Rear Admiral Tyndall, the squadron commander in whose day-cabin on board HMS *Ulysses* he had ordered this meeting. "You will please advise all ships under your command at once, Admiral."

Rear Admiral Giles Tyndall—universally known throughout the Fleet as Farmer Giles—said nothing. His ruddy features, usually so cheerful, were set and grim.

"I don't really think there's more to say, gentlemen," Starr went on smoothly. "I won't pretend you're in for an easy trip—you know yourselves what happened to the last three major convoys. I'm afraid we haven't yet found the answer to acoustic torpedoes and glider bombs. Further, our intelligence in Bremen and Kiel report that the latest U-boat policy is to get the escorts first. . . . Maybe the weather will save you."

You vindictive old devil, Tyndall thought dispassionately. Starr pushed back his chair. "We may say that the *Ulysses* is being given the opportunity of—ah—redeeming herself. After that, gentlemen, the Med. But first—FR 77 to Murmansk, come hell or high water!" His voice became strident. "The *Ulysses* must be made to realize that the Navy will never tolerate disobedience of orders, dereliction of duty, organized revolt and sedition!"

"Rubbish!"

Starr jerked back in his chair. His glance whipped round and settled on Surgeon Commander John Brooks, on the unusually vivid blue eyes so hostile now under that magnificent silver mane. Tyndall moaned softly to himself. He knew the signs too well—old Socrates was about to blow his Irish top.

"What did you say, Commander?"

"Rubbish," repeated Brooks distinctly. "Rubbish. That's what I said. 'Let's be perfectly frank,' you say. Well, sir, I'm being frank. 'Dereliction of duty, organized revolt and sedition' my foot!" He sat in silence for a few seconds, his hand running through the heavy silver hair, then looked up abruptly. "I'm a naval doctor, Admiral Starr—I've been a doctor for over thirty years now." He smiled. "I believe I can claim to know a great deal about human nature, about how the mind works, about the wonderfully intricate interaction of mind and body. . . . The Russian convoys, sir, are something entirely new and quite unique in the experience of mankind."

He gazed out through the scuttle at the sleet slanting heavily across the grey waters and hills of the Scapa anchorage. No one spoke.

"Mankind, of course, can and does adapt itself to new conditions." Brooks spoke quietly, almost to himself. "But, the saturation capacity for adaptation is soon reached. Push men beyond that limit and anything can happen. And this I do know, Admiral Starr—the crew of the *Ulysses* has been pushed to the limit—and clear beyond."

"Very interesting, Commander." Starr's voice was sceptical. "And most instructive. Unfortunately, your theory—and it's only that, of course—is quite untenable. The vast gulf you claim to lie between the convoys to Russia and normal operational work at sea just doesn't exist."

"You will not be unaware, however, that after the last two trips we shipped nineteen men to sanatoria—mental sanatoria?" Brooks was on his feet now, his broad, strong fingers splayed over the polished

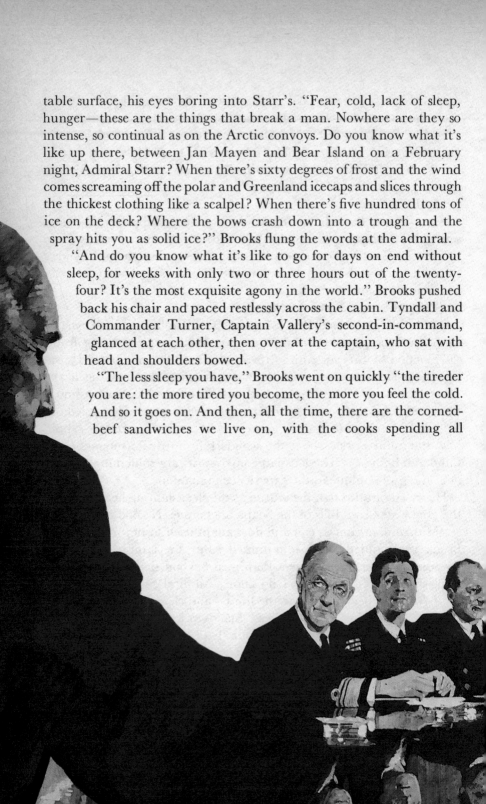

table surface, his eyes boring into Starr's. "Fear, cold, lack of sleep, hunger—these are the things that break a man. Nowhere are they so intense, so continual as on the Arctic convoys. Do you know what it's like up there, between Jan Mayen and Bear Island on a February night, Admiral Starr? When there's sixty degrees of frost and the wind comes screaming off the polar and Greenland icecaps and slices through the thickest clothing like a scalpel? When there's five hundred tons of ice on the deck? Where the bows crash down into a trough and the spray hits you as solid ice?" Brooks flung the words at the admiral.

"And do you know what it's like to go for days on end without sleep, for weeks with only two or three hours out of the twenty-four? It's the most exquisite agony in the world." Brooks pushed back his chair and paced restlessly across the cabin. Tyndall and Commander Turner, Captain Vallery's second-in-command, glanced at each other, then over at the captain, who sat with head and shoulders bowed.

"The less sleep you have," Brooks went on quickly "the tireder you are: the more tired you become, the more you feel the cold. And so it goes on. And then, all the time, there are the corned-beef sandwiches we live on, with the cooks spending all their time in the magazines. . . . I saw the break-up coming months ago. I warned the Fleet surgeon several times. I wrote to the Admiralty twice. They were sympathetic—and that's all. Shortage of ships, shortage of men. . . .

"The last hundred days did it, sir—on top of the previous months. A hundred days of pure bloody hell and not a single hour's shore leave. In port only twice—for ammunitioning: all oil and provisions from the carriers at sea. And every day an eternity of cold and hunger and danger and suffering. In the name of God," Brooks cried, "we're not machines!"

He walked over to Starr, hands thrust deep in his pockets. "I hate to say this in front of the captain, but every officer in the ship—except Captain Vallery—knows that the men would have mutinied, as you call it, long ago, but for one thing—Captain Vallery. The intense loyalty and devotion of the crew to the captain are quite unique in my experience, Admiral Starr."

Tyndall and Turner murmured approval.

"But there was a limit even to that. It had to come. And now you talk of punishing these men." Brooks shook his head in despair.

"They just couldn't help it. They can't think straight. They just want a rest, a few days' blessed quiet. Can't you see that, Admiral Starr? Can't you?"

For perhaps thirty seconds there was silence, then Starr was on his feet. "Have my barge alongside, Captain Vallery. At once, please." Starr was detached, quite emotionless. "Complete oiling, provisioning and ammunitioning as soon as possible. Admiral Tyndall, I wish you and your squadron a successful voyage. As for you, Commander Brooks, I quite see the point of your argument—at least, as far as you are concerned." His lips parted in a bleak, wintry smile. "You are quite obviously overwrought, badly in need of some leave. Your relief will be aboard before midnight. If you will come with me, Captain. . . ."

Vallery's voice stopped him at the door. "One moment, sir, if you please. Surgeon Commander Brooks," he said precisely, "is a quite exceptional officer. I wish to retain his services."

"I've made my decision, Captain," Starr snapped. "And it's final."

Vallery was unmoved. "I repeat, however, that we cannot afford to lose an officer of Brooks's calibre. As for his views on punishing hopelessly tired men, they are my own exactly."

Brooks stepped forward, distressed, but before he could speak, Turner cut in smoothly. "I feel it's time I said something. I also unreservedly endorse old Brooks's remarks—every word of them."

Starr looked at Tyndall.

"And you, Admiral?" he said.

Tyndall looked up quizzically, more like a West Country Farmer Giles than ever. He supposed wryly that his career was at stake; funny, he thought, how suddenly unimportant a career could become. "As officer commanding, maximum squadron efficiency is my sole concern. Some people *are* irreplaceable. Captain Vallery suggests Brooks is one of these. I agree. I also agree that, in the circumstances, the disturbance on board should be overlooked."

"I see, gentlemen, I see," Starr said heavily. Two spots of colour burned on his cheekbones. "The convoy has sailed from Halifax, and my hands are tied. But you make a great mistake, gentlemen, a great mistake, in pointing pistols at the head of the Admiralty. We have long memories in Whitehall. We shall—ah—discuss the matter at length on your return. Good day, gentlemen."

SHIVERING IN THE SUDDEN CHILL, Surgeon Commander Brooks clumped down to the upper deck and turned for'ard past the galley into the sick-bay. Johnson, the leading sick-bay attendant, looked out from the dispensary.

"How are our sick and suffering, Johnson?" Brooks inquired. "Bearing up manfully?"

Johnson surveyed the eight beds and their occupants morosely. "Just a lot of bloody chancers, sir. Half of them are a damned sight fitter than I am. Look at Stoker Riley there—him with the broken finger and whacking great pile of *Reader's Digest*. Going through all the medical articles, he is, and roaring out for sulph., penicillin and all the latest antibiotics. Can't pronounce half of them. Thinks he's dying."

"A grievous loss," the surgeon commander murmured. He shook his head. "What Engineer Commander Dodson sees in him I don't know. . . . What's the latest from hospital?"

The expression drained out of Johnson's face.

"They're just off the blower, sir," he said woodenly. "Five minutes ago. Ordinary Seaman Ralston died at three o'clock."

Brooks nodded heavily. "Don't feel too good about that."

"Eighteen, sir. Exactly eighteen." Johnson's voice was bitter. "I've just been talking to Burgess—that's him in the next bed. Says Ralston steps out across the bathroom coaming, a towel over his arm. A mob rushes past, then this bloody great ape of a marine comes tearing up and bashes him over the skull with his rifle. Never knew what hit him, sir—and he never knew why."

Brooks smiled faintly. "That's what they call—ah—seditious talk, Johnson." Brooks paused. Ralston had an older brother on board. "How's the other boy going to take the news?"

"Can't say, sir. He's already received bad news this week. Croydon was pasted. The boys' mother and three sisters live there—lived there. It was a land-mine, sir—there was nothing left."

Brooks turned and pushed his way through the surgery curtains. Johnny Nicholls, acting surgeon lieutenant, rose quickly to his feet.

"Hello, sir. Have a pew."

Brooks climbed into the dentist's chair and sank back with a groan, fiddling with the neck-rest. "If you'll just adjust the foot-rest, my boy . . . so. Ah—thank you." He leaned back luxuriously, eyes closed, head far back on the rest, and groaned again. "I'm an old man, Johnny, my boy, just an ancient has-been."

"Nonsense, sir," Nicholls said briskly. "Just a slight malaise. Now, if you'll let me prescribe a suitable tonic. . . ."

He turned to a cupboard, fished out two tooth-glasses and a dark-green, ribbed bottle marked "Poison". He filled the glasses and handed one to Brooks. "First-class stuff—produce of the Island of Coll. My personal recommendation."

The surgeon looked at the amber liquid, then at Nicholls. "You're an admirable feller, Johnny."

"Good health, Commander. . . . How did things go up top, sir?"

"Bloody awful. His nibs threatened to string us all from the yard-arm. Actually he's a brilliant bloke. Master strategist and all that. . . ."

"And the upshot of it all?"

"Murmansk again. Sailing at 0600 tomorrow."

"What! Again? This bunch of walking zombies?" Nicholls was openly incredulous. "Why, they can't do that, sir! They—they just can't!"

"They're doing it anyway, my boy. The *Ulysses* must—ah—redeem itself." Brooks opened his eyes. "Gad, the very thought appalls me. If there's any of that poison left, my boy. . . ."

CAP IN HAND, Leading Torpedo Operator Ralston sat down opposite the captain. Vallery looked at him, wondering what to say, how best to say it.

Richard Vallery hated war. Not because it interfered with his life-long passion for music and literature, but because he was a deeply religious man, and he saw war all too clearly as the wild and insensate folly it was.

But some things he had to do, and Vallery had clearly seen that this war had to be his. And so he had come back to the service, and had grown older as the bitter years passed, older and frailer, and more kindly and tolerant and understanding. He sighed. It troubled him just what he ought to say to Ralston. But it was Ralston who spoke first. "It's all right, sir. I know. The torpedo officer told me."

Vallery cleared his throat.

"Words are useless, Ralston. Your young brother—and your family at home. All gone. I'm sorry, my boy, terribly sorry about it all." He looked into the expressionless face and smiled wryly. "Or maybe you think that these are all words—just a formula."

Suddenly, surprisingly, Ralston smiled. "No, sir, I don't. I can appreciate how you feel, sir. You see, my father—well, he's a captain too. He tells me he feels the same way."

"Your father, Ralston? Did you say—"

"Yes, sir." Vallery could have sworn to a flicker of amusement in the blue eyes, so quiet, so self-possessed, across the table. "In the Merchant Navy, sir—a tanker captain—sixteen hundred tons."

Ralston went on quietly: "And about Billy, sir—my young brother. It's nobody's fault but mine—I asked to have him aboard here. I'm to blame, sir—only me." His lean brown hands were round the brim of his hat, twisting it, crushing it.

"Look, my boy, I think you need a few days' rest, time to think things over. PRO is making out your travelling warrant just now. You will start fourteen days' leave as from tonight."

"Where is the warrant made out for, sir? Croydon?"

"Of course. Where else—" Vallery stopped dead. "Forgive me, my boy. What a damnably stupid thing to say!"

"Don't send me away, sir," Ralston pleaded quietly. "The truth is I've nowhere to go. I belong here—on the *Ulysses*. I can do things all the time—I'm busy—working, sleeping—I don't have to talk about things—I can do things . . ." The self-possession was only the thinnest veneer, taut, with the quiet desperation immediately below.

"I can get a chance to help pay 'em back," Ralston hurried on. "Oh, I don't know. I can't find the words, sir."

Vallery sighed. "Of course you shall remain, Ralston. Go down to the police office and tell them to tear up your warrant. If I can be any help to you at any time—"

"I understand, sir. Thank you very much. Good night, sir."

MONDAY

"CLOSE ALL watertight doors and scuttles. Hands to stations for leaving harbour." Impersonally the metallic voice of the broadcast system reached into every corner of the ship.

And from every corner men came in answer to the call. They were cold men, shivering in the icy north wind. They were tired men, for fuelling, provisioning and ammunitioning had gone on far into the middle watch. And they were still angry, hostile men. Orders were obeyed, to be sure; but obedience was surly, and insolence lay close beneath the surface. But divisional officers and NCOs handled the men with velvet gloves: Vallery had been emphatic about that.

At 0600, to the minute, the *Ulysses* slipped her moorings and steamed slowly towards the boom under leaden clouds, and sudden, heavy flurries of snow.

The *Ulysses* had become a legend in her own brief lifetime. She was known and cherished by the men who sailed the bitter seas of the north, from St. John's to Archangel, from the Shetlands to Jan Mayen, from Greenland to far reaches of Spitzbergen, remote on the edge of the world, for, a young ship, she had grown old in the Russian convoys and on the Arctic patrols. She had been there from the beginning, and had known no other life. At first operating alone, now she never moved without her squadron, the 14th Escort Carrier group.

Technically, the *Ulysses* was a light cruiser, a modification of the famous *Dido* type. Five hundred and ten feet long, narrow in her fifty-foot beam with a raked stem and square cruiser stern, she was lean, fast and compact. Quadruple screws powered by four great Parsons single-reduction geared turbines—two in the for'ard, two in the after engine room—developed an unbelievable horsepower that many a battleship, by no means obsolete, could not match. Officially, she was rated at 33.5 knots. Off Arran, in her full-power trials, she had covered the measured mile at an incredible 39.2 knots—the nautical equivalent of 45 mph.

She was well equipped for destruction. Her radar, with a 40–45 mile operating range, had once located a Condor, subsequently destroyed by a Blenheim, at a range of eighty-five miles. She had four twin gun-turrets, two for'ard, two aft, 5.25 quick-firing and dual-purpose. These were her main armament. There were also batteries of multiple pom-poms, isolated clusters of twin Oerlikons, and depth-charges and torpedoes. Her 21-inch torpedoes, sleek and menacing in the triple tubes on the main deck, had not yet been blooded.

This, then, was the *Ulysses*, the perfect fighting machine—but only so long as it was manned by a smoothly-functioning team. And the crew of the *Ulysses* was disintegrating; the lid was clamped on the volcano, but the rumblings never ceased. In fact the first signs of further trouble came within three hours of clearing harbour. As always, minesweepers swept the channel ahead of them, but Vallery left nothing to chance, and at 0620 he streamed paravanes—the torpedo-shaped bodies angled out from the bows and designed to deflect the wires connecting mines to the sea floor.

At 0900, Vallery ordered the paravanes to be recovered. The *Ulysses* slowed down. Lieutenant Commander Carrington went to the fo'c'sle to supervise operations: seamen, winch drivers, and the sub-lieutenants in charge of either side closed up to their respective stations.

Quickly, the recovery booms were swung out and rigged with re-covery wires. Immediately, the three-ton winches on "B" gun-deck took the strain, the paravanes cleared the water.

Then it happened, and it was AB Ferry's fault. It was just ill-luck that the port winch was suspect, operating on a power circuit with a defective breaker, just ill-luck that Ralston was the winch-driver, a taciturn, bitter-mouthed Ralston to whom, just then, nothing mattered a damn. But it was Carslake's responsibility that the affair developed into what it did.

Son of a rear admiral, rtd., who had practically forced him into the Navy, Sub Lieutenant Carslake had a long, narrow face, with prominent pale blue eyes and protruding upper teeth. Vain, superior, uncouth and ill-educated, he was a complete ass.

Now, striving to maintain balance, feet dramatically braced at a wide angle, he shouted unceasing, unnecessary commands at his men. CPO Hartley groaned aloud, but kept otherwise silent in the interests of discipline. But AB Ferry felt himself under no such restraints.

"'Ark at his Lordship," he murmured to Ralston. "All for the skipper's benefit." Vallery was leaning over the bridge, twenty feet above Carslake's head.

"Just you forget about Carslake and keep your eyes on that wire," Ralston advised. "And take those damned great gloves off. One of these days—"

"Yes, yes, I know," Ferry jeered. "The wire's going to snag 'em and wrap me round the drum." He fed in the hawser expertly. "Don't you worry, chum, it's never going to happen to me."

But it did. Ralston, watching the swinging paravane closely, flicked a glance inboard. He saw the broken strand only inches away from Ferry, saw it hook viciously into the gloved hand and drag him towards the spinning drum before Ferry had a chance to cry out.

Ralston's reaction was immediate. The foot-brake was only six inches away—but that was too far. Savagely he spun the control wheel, full ahead to full reverse in a split second. Simultaneously with Ferry's cry of pain as his forearm crushed against the lip of the drum came a muffled explosion and clouds of acrid smoke from the winch as £500 worth of electric motor burnt out in a searing flash.

Immediately the wire began to run out again, accelerating under the weight of the plunging paravane. Ferry went with it. Twenty feet from the winch the wire passed through a snatch-block on the deck: if Ferry was lucky, he might lose only his hand.

He was less than four feet away when Ralston's foot stamped viciously on the brake. The racing drum screamed to a shuddering stop, the wire snapped, the paravane crashed down into the sea and the wire, weightless now, swung idly to the rolling of the ship. In the nick of time Ferry had been spared a fate far worse than his present state of shock.

Carslake's sallow face suffused with anger. He strode up to Ralston. "You bloody fool! You've lost us that paravane. By God, LTO, you'd better explain yourself! Who the hell gave you orders to do anything?"

Ralston's mouth tightened, but he spoke civilly enough. "Sorry, sir. Couldn't help it—it had to be done. Ferry's arm—"

"Too hell with Ferry's arm!" Carslake was almost screaming with rage. "I'm in charge here—and I give the orders. Look! Look!" He pointed to the swinging wire. "Your work, Ralston, you—you blundering idiot! It's gone!"

Ralston looked over the side with an air of large surprise. "Well, now, so it is." He patted the winch. "And don't forget this—it's gone too, and it costs a ruddy sight more than any paravane."

"I don't want any of your damn impertinence!" Carslake shouted. "What you need is to have some discipline knocked into you and, by God, I'm going to see you get it, you insolent young bastard!"

Ralston flushed darkly. He took a step forward, his fist balled, then relaxed as CPO Hartley caught his arm. But the damage was done now. There was nothing for it but the bridge.

Vallery listened calmly as Carslake made his outraged report. "Is this true, Ralston?" he asked quietly. "You disobeyed orders, swore at the lieutenant and insulted him?"

"No, sir. It's not true." Ralston looked at Carslake, his face expressionless. "I didn't disobey orders—there were none. And I didn't swear at him. There are plenty of witnesses that Sub Lieutenant Carslake swore at me—several times. And if I insulted him—" he smiled faintly "—it was pure self-defence."

"This is no place for levity, Ralston." Vallery's voice was cold. "As it happens, I saw the entire incident. Your promptness, your resource, saved that rating's arm, possibly even his life—and against that a lost paravane and wrecked winch are nothing." Carslake whitened at the implied rebuke. "I'm grateful for that—thank you. As for the rest, Commander's Defaulters tomorrow morning. Carry on, Ralston."

Ralston saluted abruptly and left the bridge.

"Carslake, we'll discuss it later." Vallery made no attempt to conceal the dislike in his voice. "You may carry on, Lieutenant. Hartley—a word with you."

Hartley stepped forward. Forty-four years old, CPO Hartley was the Royal Navy at its best. Very tough, very kindly and very competent, he enjoyed the admiration of all, ranging from the vast awe of the youngest ordinary seaman to the warm respect of the captain himself. They had been together from the beginning.

"Well, Chief, let's have it. Between ourselves."

"Nothing to it really, sir." Hartley shrugged. "Ralston did a fine job. Sub Lieutenant Carslake lost his head. Maybe Ralston *was* a bit sassy, but he was provoked. He's only a kid, but he's a professional." Hartley paused and looked up at the sky. "And he doesn't like being pushed around by amateurs."

Vallery smothered a smile. "Could that be interpreted as—er—a criticism, Chief?"

"I suppose so, sir." He nodded forward. "A few ruffled feathers on the lower deck, sir. Men are pretty sore about this. Shall I—?"

"Thanks, Chief. Play it down as much as possible."

When Hartley had gone, Vallery turned to Admiral Tyndall.

"Well, you heard it, sir? Another straw in the wind."

"A straw?" Tyndall was acid. "Hundreds of straws. More like a bloody great cornstack. . . . Wonder what old Socrates thinks of it all, now? May be only a pill-roller, but the wisest head we've got . . . Well, speak of the devil!"

The gate to the bridge swung open, and a burly, unhappy-looking figure, duffel-coated, oilskinned and wearing a Russian beaver-skin helmet—the total effect was of an elderly grizzly bear caught in a thunderstorm—shuffled across the duckboards of the bridge. He brought up facing the Kent screen—an inset, circular sheet of glass which revolved at high speed and offered a clear view in all weather conditions—rain, hail, snow. For half a minute he peered miserably through this and obviously didn't like what he saw.

"Some more trouble, Captain." Brooks was serious. "Couldn't tell it over the phone."

"Trouble?" Vallery broke off, coughed harshly into his handkerchief. "Sorry," he apologized. "Trouble? There's nothing else."

"Young Nicholls was doing some path. work late last night in the dispensary. Lights out in the bay, and the patients either didn't know or had forgotten he was there. Heard Stoker Riley—a real trouble-maker, that Riley—and the others planning a sit-down strike in the boiler room when they return to duty. A strike in a boiler room. Good lord, it's fantastic! Anyway, Nicholls let it slide—pretended he hadn't heard."

"What!" Vallery's voice was sharp. "And Nicholls didn't report it to me?" He reached out for the bridge phone.

Brooks laid a gauntleted hand on Vallery's arm.

"I wouldn't do that, sir. Nicholls is a smart boy—very smart indeed. He knew that if he let the men know they had been overheard, they would know that he must report it to you. And then you'd have been bound to take action—and open provocation of trouble is the last thing you want. You said so yourself in the wardroom last night."

Vallery hesitated. "Yes, yes, of course I said that. But this could be a focal point for spreading the idea to—"

"I told you, sir," Brooks interrupted. "Johnny Nicholls is a very smart boy. He's got a big notice, in huge red letters, outside the sick-bay door: 'Keep clear: Suspected scarlet fever infection'. Kills me to watch 'em. Everybody avoids the place like the plague. Not a hope of communicating with their pals in the stokers' mess."

Tyndall guffawed, and even Vallery smiled slightly.

"Sounds fine, Doc. Still, I should have been told last night."

"Why should you be woken up and told every little thing in the middle of the night?" Brooks's voice was brusque. "Sheer selfishness on my part. When things get bad, you damn well carry this ship on your back—and when we've all got to depend on you, we'd prefer you as fit as possible. Agreed, Admiral?"

Tyndall nodded solemnly. "Agreed, O Socrates. A very complicated way of saying that you wish the captain to have a good night's sleep. But agreed."

Brooks grinned amiably. "Well, that's all, gentlemen." He cocked a jaundiced eye over his shoulder, into the thickening snow. "Won't the Med. be wonderful?" The gate clanged shut behind him.

Vallery turned to the admiral, his face grave. "Looks as if you were right about that cornstack, sir."

Tyndall grunted, non-committally. "Maybe. Trouble is, the men have nothing to do right now except brood and curse and feel bitter about everything. Later on it'll be all right—perhaps."

"When we get—ah—busier, you mean?"

"Mmm. When you're fighting for your life—well, you haven't much time for plots and pondering over the injustices of fate. Self-preservation is still the first law of nature. . . . Speaking to the men tonight, Captain?"

"Usual routine broadcast, yes. In the first dog watch, when we're all closed up to dusk action stations." Vallery smiled briefly. "Make sure they're all awake."

"Good. Lay it on, thick and heavy. Give 'em plenty to think about—and, if I'm any judge of Admiral Starr's hints, we're going to *have* plenty to think about on this trip. It'll keep 'em occupied."

Vallery laughed, the laugh transforming his thin sensitive face. "Things are bad indeed, when only the enemy can save us."

ALL DAY LONG the wind blew steadily out of the nor'-nor'-west, and slowly, stealthily, it was lifting a swell. Men like Lieutenant Commander Carrington, who knew every sea and port in the world, like Vallery and Hartley, looked at it and were troubled.

The mercury crept down and the snow lay where it fell. The tripods and yardarms were glistening great Christmas trees, festooned with woolly stays and halyards. All day long the snow fell, steadily and persistently, and the *Ulysses* slid on silently through the swell.

But not alone in her world. She had the company of the 14th Aircraft Squadron, a tough, experienced and battle-hardened escort group. The *Ulysses* was in her usual position—the position dictated by her role as squadron flagship—as nearly as possible in the centre of the thirteen warships. Dead ahead steamed the cruiser *Stirling*. An old Cardiff-class cruiser, many years older and many knots slower than the *Ulysses*, adequately armed but hardly built to hammer her way through Arctic gales, her primary role was squadron defence: her secondary, to take over the squadron if the flagship were crippled or sunk.

The carriers—*Defender, Invader, Wrestler* and *Blue Ranger*—were in position to port and starboard. They were converted merchantmen, American-built, with flight decks above the open fo'c'sle, and flew off about thirty fighters, or twenty light bombers. They were odd craft, awkward, ungainly and singularly unwarlike; yet their record of kills, above, on, and below the water was impressive and frequently disbelieved by the Admiralty.

The destroyer screen was a weird hodge-podge. One, the *Nairn*, was a River-class frigate of 1,500 tons: another, the *Eager*, was a Fleet minesweeper, and a third, the *Gannet*, was a rather elderly and very tired Kingfisher corvette, supposedly restricted to coastal duties only. Two more, the *Vectra* and the *Viking* were twin-screwed, modified "V" and "W" destroyers, in the superannuated class now, lacking in speed and fire-power, but tough and durable. Yet another, the *Baliol*, was a diminutive Hunt-class destroyer which had no business in the great waters of the north, while the seventh, the *Portpatrick*, a lean four-stacker, was one of the fifty lend-lease World War I destroyers from the United States.

These seven escorts kept their screening stations all day—the frigate and minesweeper ahead, the destroyers at the sides, and the corvette astern. The eighth escort, a fast, modern "S" class destroyer, under the command of the Captain (Destroyers), Commander Orr, prowled restlessly around the fleet. The *Sirus* had an uncanny nose for trouble, an almost magnetic affinity for U-boats lying in ambush.

From the warmth of the *Ulysses*'s wardroom—long, incongruously comfortable, running fifty feet along the starboard side of the fo'c'sle deck—Acting Surgeon Lieutenant Johnny Nicholls gazed out at this raggle-taggle of a squadron. He supposed he ought to feel cynical at the sight of these old and worn-out ships. But, he couldn't. He knew what they could do, what they had done. If he felt anything at all towards them, it was something uncommonly close to admiration—perhaps even pride. Nicholls turned away from the porthole. His gaze fell on the somnolent form of the Kapok Kid, flat on his back in an armchair, an enormous pair of fur-lined flying-boots perched above the electric fire. As always, he was dressed from head to foot in a one-piece overall of heavy, quilted kapok; there was a great, golden "J" embroidered on the right breast pocket: what it stood for was anyone's guess.

The Kapok Kid, Lieutenant the Honourable Andrew Carpenter, RN, navigator of the *Ulysses* and his best friend. The most glorious extrovert Nicholls had ever known, the Kapok Kid was equally at home anywhere—on a dance floor or in the cockpit of a racing yacht at Cowes, at a garden party, on a tennis court or at the wheel of his big crimson Bugatti, windscreen down and the loose ends of a seven-foot scarf streaming out behind him. But appearances were deceptive. For the Royal Navy was the Kapok Kid's whole life, and he lived for that alone. Behind that slightly inane façade lay, besides a first-class brain, a deeply romantic streak, an almost Elizabethan love for sea and ships which he sought, successfully, he imagined, to conceal from all his fellow-officers. It was so patently obvious that no one ever thought it worth mentioning.

Theirs was a curious friendship, Nicholls mused. An attraction of opposites, if ever there was one. For Carpenter's ebullience, his own natural reserve and reticence were the perfect foil: over against his friend's near-idolatry of all things naval stood his own thorough-going detestation of them. Three years ago the war had snatched him from the wards of a great Glasgow hospital, his first year's internship barely completed. A highland Scot, Nicholls objected strongly to the thousand and one pin-pricks of discipline, authority and bureaucratic naval stupidity which were a constant affront to his intelligence and self-respect. But, in spite of this antipathy—or perhaps because of it and the curse of a Calvinistic conscience—Nicholls had become a first-class officer. But it still disturbed him vaguely to discover in himself something akin to pride in the ships of his squadron.

He sighed as the loudspeaker in the corner of the wardroom crackled into life. "Do you hear there? Do you hear there?" The Kapok Kid slept on in magnificent oblivion. "The captain will broadcast to the ship's company at 1730 tonight. Repeat. The captain will broadcast to the ship's company at 1730 tonight. That is all."

Nicholls prodded the Kapok Kid with a heavy toe. "On your feet, Andy. It's lovely up top now—sea rising, temperature falling and a young blizzard blowing. Just what you were born for!"

The Kapok Kid struggled to a sitting position. "Know where I was, Johnny?" he asked. "Back on the Thames, at the Grey Goose, just up from Henley. It was summer, Johnny. Dressed all in green, she was—"

"Indigestion," Nicholls cut in briskly. "Too much easy living. . . . It's four thirty, and the old man's speaking in an hour's time. Dusk stations at any time—we'd better eat."

Carpenter stood up and stretched. He glanced out through the porthole, then shuddered. "Wonder what's the topic for tonight?"

"No idea. The situation is somewhat delicate, to say the least. Not to mention the fact that the crew don't know that they're off to Murmansk again—although they must have a pretty good idea."

"Mmm." The Kapok Kid nodded absently. "Don't suppose the old man'll try to play it down—the hazards of the trip, I mean."

"Never." Nicholls shook his head decisively. "Not the skipper." He stared into the fire for a long time, then looked up quietly. "The skipper's a very sick man, Andy—very sick indeed."

"What! . . . Good lord, you're joking!"

"I'm not," Nicholls interrupted flatly, his voice low. "Old Socrates says he's pretty far through—and he knows," Nicholls continued. "Vallery phoned him to come to his cabin last night. Place was covered in blood and he was coughing his lungs up. Brooks has suspected these attacks for a long time, but the captain would never let him examine him. Brooks says a few more days of this will kill him." He broke off. "I talk too much," he said abruptly. "Shouldn't have told you, I suppose—violation of professional confidence and all that. All this under your hat, Andy."

"Of course, of course." There was a long pause. "What you mean is, Johnny—he's dying."

"Just that. Come on, Andy—char."

TWENTY MINUTES LATER, Nicholls made his way down to the sick-bay. The light was beginning to fail and the *Ulysses* was pitching heavily. Commander Brooks was in the surgery.

"Evening, sir. Dusk action stations any minute now. Mind if I stay in the bay tonight? I want to observe the reactions of Stoker Riley and his—ah—confederates when the skipper makes his speech. Might be most instructive."

"Sherlock Nicholls, eh? Right-o, Johnny. By rights you should be aft for action stations. Phone the Damage Control Officer. Tell him you're tied up."

When the bugle blared for dusk action stations, Nicholls was sitting in the dispensary. The lights were out, the curtains almost drawn. He could see into every corner of the brightly lit sick-bay. Five of the men were asleep. The others—Petersen, the giant, half-Norwegian stoker, and Burgess, the dark little cockney—were sitting up in bed, talking softly. A swarthy, heavily-built patient lay between them. Stoker Riley was holding court.

Alfred O'Hara Riley had, at a very early age indeed, decided upon a career of crime. Life had never really given him a chance. Born of a drunken, illiterate mother in a filthy, overcrowded and fever-ridden Liverpool slum, he was an outcast from the beginning: allied to that, his hairy, ape-like figure, the heavy under-slung jaw, the twisted mouth, and cunning black eyes squinting out beneath the negligible clearance between hairline and eyebrows, suited all too well what was to become his chosen vocation. Robbery—preferably robbery with violence. He had been in prison six times, the last time for two years.

Following his induction into the Navy, Riley had gone through the bomb-shattered "G" and "H" blocks of the Royal Naval Barracks, Portsmouth, like a high wind through a field of corn, leaving behind him a trail of slashed suitcases and empty wallets. He had been apprehended without much difficulty, done sixty days' cells, then been drafted to the *Ulysses* as a stoker.

His career of crime aboard the *Ulysses* had been brief and painful. He had been caught red-handed by Colour Sergeant Evans and Sergeant MacIntosh rifling a locker in the marine sergeants' mess. They preferred no charges against him, but Riley spent the next three days in the sick-bay. He claimed to have tripped on a ladder and fallen twenty feet to the boiler-room floor. But the actual facts of the case were common knowledge, and Turner had recommended his discharge. To everyone's astonishment, Engineer Commander Dodson had insisted he be given a last chance, and Riley had been reprieved.

Since that date, four months previously, he had confined his activities to stirring up trouble. He had precipitated the mutiny which had led to the death of Ralston, the stoker, and the marine—mysteriously dead from a broken neck. Nicholls wondered what new devilment was hatching behind those lowering, corrugated brows, wondered also how on earth it was that the same Riley could continually be in trouble for bringing aboard the *Ulysses* and devotedly tending every stray kitten, every broken-winged bird he found.

The loudspeaker crackled, cutting through Nicholl's thoughts, stilling the low voices in the sick-bay.

"This is the captain speaking. Good evening." The voice was calm, without sign of strain or exhaustion. "As you all know, it is my custom at the beginning of every voyage to inform you as soon as possible of what lies in store for you. I feel that you have a right to know, and that it is my duty. It's not always a pleasant duty—it never has been during recent months. This time, however, I'm almost glad." He paused. "This is our last operation as a unit of the Home Fleet. In a month's time, God willing, we will be in the Med."

Good for you, thought Nicholls. Sweeten the pill.

"But first, gentlemen, the job on hand. It's the mixture as before—Murmansk again. We rendezvous at 1030 Wednesday, north of Iceland, with a convoy from Halifax. There are eighteen ships in this convoy—big and fast—all fifteen knots and above. Our third Fast-Russian convoy, gentlemen—FR 77. These ships are carrying tanks, planes, aviation spirit and oil—" He broke off short, and the sound of his harsh, muffled coughing echoed weirdly through the silent ship.

He went on slowly. "There are enough fighter planes and petrol in this convoy to alter the whole character of the Russian war. The Nazis will stop at nothing—I repeat, nothing—to stop this convoy from going through to Russia. . . . I have never tried to mislead you. I will not now. In our favour we have, firstly, our speed, and secondly—I hope—the element of surprise. We shall try to break through direct for the North Cape. But the signs are not good.

"There are four major factors against us. The steady worsening weather . . . it almost certainly means that the carriers will be unable to fly off fighter cover. Secondly, we are taking no rescue ships on this convoy. There will be no time to stop. Thirdly, two—possibly three—U-boat packs are known to be strung out along latitude seventy degrees and our northern Norway agents report a heavy mustering of German bombers of all types in their area.

"Finally, we have reason to believe that the *Tirpitz* is preparing to move out." Again he paused, as if he knew the tremendous shock carried in these few words. "I need not tell you what that means. The Germans may risk her to stop the convoy. The Admiralty hope they will. During the latter part of the voyage, capital units of the Home Fleet will parallel our course at twelve hours' steaming distance. They have been waiting a long time, and we are the bait to spring the trap . . . .

"It is possible that things may go wrong. But this convoy must still get through. If the carriers cannot fly off cover, the *Ulysses* must cover the withdrawal of FR 77. You will know what that means. I hope this is all perfectly clear."

There was another long bout of coughing, another long pause, and when he spoke again he was very quiet.

"I know what I am asking of you. I know how tired, how hopeless, how sick at heart you all feel. I know—no one knows better—what you have been through, how much you need, how much you deserve a rest. Rest you shall have. The entire ship's company goes on ten days' leave from Portsmouth on the eighteenth, then for refit in Alexandria. But before that—well, I know it seems cruel to ask you to go through it again, perhaps worse than before. But I can't help it—no one can."

Every sentence, now was punctuated by long silences.

"No one has any right to ask you to do it, I least of all. But I know you *will* do it. I know you will not let me down. I know you will take the *Ulysses* through. Good luck. Good luck and God bless you. Good night."

The loudspeakers clicked off. With a heavy sigh—it seemed ages since he had breathed last—Nicholls pulled to the sliding door behind the curtains and switched on the light. He looked round at Brooks.

"Well, Johnny?" The commander's voice was soft, almost bantering.

"I just don't know, sir, I don't know at all." Nicholls's voice trailed off and he shook his head.

"It was beautifully done, Johnny." Brooks insisted. "Don't you see? As black a picture as man could paint: no silver lining, no promises and yet the appeal was tremendous. . . ."

"I don't know." Nicholls lifted his head abruptly. "Maybe there *was* no appeal. Listen." Noiselessly, he slid the door back, flicked off the lights. The rumble of Riley's harsh voice was unmistakable.

"—just a lot of bloody clap-trap. Alex.? The Med.? Not on your life, mate. You'll never see it. You'll never even see Scapa again. Captain Richard Vallery. DSO! Know what that old bastard wants, boys? Another bar to his DSO. . . ." He paused a moment, then rushed on. "The *Tirpitz*! Christ Almighty! The *Tirpitz*! We're going to stop it—us? This bloody toy ship?" His voice rose. "I tell you, mates, nobody gives a damn about us. They're throwing us to the bloody wolves! And that old bastard up top—"

"*Shaddap!*" Petersen's whisper was fierce. His hand stretched out, and Brooks and Nicholls in the surgery winced as they heard Riley's wrist-bones crack under the tremendous pressure of the giant's hand. "Often I've wondered about you, Riley," Peterson went on slowly. "But not now, not any more. You make me sick!" He flung Riley's hand down and turned away.

Riley rubbed his wrist and turned to Burgess. "For God's sake, what's the matter with him? What the hell . . ." He broke off as Burgess eased himself down in bed, pulled the blankets up to his neck and deliberately turned his back on him.

Brooks rose quickly to his feet, closed the door and pressed the light switch.

"That scarlet fever notice of yours, Johnny. I don't think we'll be needing it any more."

Nicholls grinned. "No sir," he said. "I don't think we will."

SOON AFTER the captain's broadcast, radar reported a contact, closing. But no one paid the slightest attention to the report, other than Admiral Tyndall's order for a 45° course alteration. This was as routine as dusk action stations. It was their old reconnaissance friend Charlie, coming to pay his respects again.

"Charlie"—usually a four-engine Focke-Wulf Condor—was an institution on the Russian convoys. In the early days, before the advent of escort carriers, Charlie frequently spent the entire day, from first light to last, circling a convoy and radioing to base pin-point reports of its position. Latterly, however, he had grown circumspect, rarely appearing except at dusk. His usual practice was to make a single circle of the convoy at a prudent distance, report its course and strength, and then disappear into the darkness. That night was no exception. And Tyndall had little hope that his change of course would fool German Intelligence—especially since they certainly knew of the convoy's departure from Halifax.

No attempt was made to fly off Seafires—the only plane with a chance of overhauling the Condor. To locate the carrier again in almost total darkness, even on a radio beam, was difficult: to land at night, extremely dangerous; and to land, in the snow on a pitching deck, a suicidal impossibility.

Back on course again, the *Ulysses* pushed blindly into the gathering storm. Hands fell out from action stations, and resumed normal defence stations—watch and watch, four on, four off. Step by step, mercury and barograph crept down in a deadly dualism. The waves were higher now, and the bone-chilling wind lashed the snow into a blinding curtain. A bad night, a sleepless night, both above deck and below, on watch and off.

At ten minutes to midnight Commander Turner, and Marshall, the Canadian torpedo officer, made their way to the bridge. Even at this late hour and in the wicked weather, the commander was his usual self, imperturbable and cheerful, lean and piratical, a throwback to the Elizabethan buccaneers, if ever there was one. He stood for a minute accustoming his eyes to the dark, located the first lieutenant and thumped him resoundingly on the back.

"Well, watchman, and what of the night?" he boomed cheerfully. "Situation completely out of control as usual, I suppose? Where are all our chickens this lovely evening?" He peered out into the snow. "All gone to hell and beyond, I suppose."

"Not too bad," Carrington grinned. An RNR officer and an ex-Merchant Navy captain in whom Vallery reposed complete confidence, Lieutenant Commander Carrington was normally a taciturn man, grave and unsmiling. But a particular bond lay between him and Turner, the professional bond of respect which two exceptional seamen have for each other. "We can see the carriers now and then. Anyway, Bowden and his radar boys have 'em all pinned to an inch. At least, that's what they say."

"Better not let old Bowden hear you say that," Marshall advised. "Thinks radar is the only step forward the human race has taken since the first man came down from the trees." He shivered and turned his back on the driving wind. "Anyway, I wish to God I had his job," he added feelingly. "This is worse than winter in Alberta!"

"Nonsense, my boy, stuff and nonsense!" the commander roared. "Decadent, that's the trouble with you youngsters nowadays. This is the only life for a self-respecting human being." He sniffed the icy air appreciatively and turned to Carrington. "Who's on with you tonight, Number One?"

A dark figure detached itself from the binnacle and approached.

"Ah, there you are. Well, well, 'pon my soul, if it isn't our navigating officer, the Honourable Mr. Carpenter, lost as usual and dressed to kill in his natty gent's suiting."

"Ha!" The Kapok Kid patted his quilted chest affectionately. "Just wait till we're all down there in the drink together, everybody else dragged down or frozen to death, me drifting by warm and dry and comfortable, maybe smoking the odd cigarette—"

"Enough. Be off. Course, Number One?"

"Three-twenty, sir. Fifteen knots."

"And the captain?"

"In the shelter." Carrington jerked his head towards the reinforced steel circular casing at the after end of the bridge. This supported the director tower, the control circuits to which ran through a central shaft in the casing. A sea bunk was kept there for the captain's use. "Sleeping, I hope," he added, "but I very much doubt it. Gave orders to be called at midnight."

"Cancel the order," Turner said briefly. "Captain's got to learn to obey orders like anybody else—especially doctor's orders. I'll take full responsibility. Good night, Number One."

The gate clanged shut. Silence fell again. The snow was lifting now, but the wind still strengthening. It howled eerily through masts and rigging. Half-past twelve came, one o'clock, then half-past one. Turner's thought turned fondly towards coffee and cocoa. Coffee or cocoa? Cocoa, he decided, a steaming potent brew, thick with melted chocolate and sugar. He turned to Chrysler, the bridge messenger, young brother of the leading Asdic operator.

"WT—Bridge. WT—Bridge." The loudspeaker above the Asdic cabinet crackled urgently. Turner jumped for the hand transmitter, barked an acknowledgement.

"Signal from *Sirrus*. Echoes, port bow, 300, strong, closing. Repeat, echoes, port bow, strong, closing."

Turner's hand cut down on the gleaming phosphorescence of the emergency action stations switch. Inside two minutes, the *Ulysses* was closed up to action stations.

The modern destroyer, *Sirrus*, two miles away to port, remained in contact for half an hour. The aged *Viking* was detached to help her, and below-deck in the *Ulysses* the peculiar, tinny clanging of depth-charging was clearly heard at irregular intervals. Finally, the *Sirrus* reported. "No success: contact lost: trust you have not been disturbed." The two destroyers were recalled, and the bugle blew the stand-down.

Commander Turner sent for his long overdue cocoa. He retired to the chart room on the port side, just aft of the compass platform, and closed the black-out door. Relaxed in his chair, he put his mug on the chart table and his feet beside it, drew the first deep inhalation of cigarette smoke into his lungs. Then he was on his feet, cursing: the crackle of the WT loudspeaker was unmistakable. Again he reached for the EAS switch.

The commander was to have no cocoa that night. Three times more during the hours of darkness all hands closed up to action stations, and only minutes, it seemed, after the last stand-down, the bugle went for dawn stations.

TUESDAY

As the men dragged themselves wearily back to their action stations there was a vague, almost imperceptible lightening in the sky, a bleak, chill greyness. Vallery, as always, was on the bridge. Courteous, kind and considerate as ever, he looked ghastly. His face was haggard, the colour of putty, his bloodshot eyes deep-sunk in hollowed sockets, his lips bloodless.

In the half-light, the squadron came gradually into view. Miraculously, most of them were still in position. The frigate and mine-sweeper were together and far ahead of the fleet—during the night they had been understandably reluctant to have their tails tramped on by a heavy cruiser or a carrier. The aircraft-carrier *Invader* had lost position during the night, and lay outside the screen on the port quarter.

She received a testy signal, and came steaming up to resume station, corkscrewing violently in the heavy cross seas.

Stand-down came at 0800. At 0810 the port watch was below, making tea, washing, queueing up at the galley for breakfast trays, when a muffled explosion shook the *Ulysses*. Towels, soap, cups, plates and trays went flying: blasphemous and bitter, the men were on their way before Vallery's hand closed on the Emergency switch.

Less than half a mile away the *Invader* was slewing round in a violent half-circle, her flight-deck tilted over at a crazy angle, great gouts of black oily smoke belching up for'ard of her bridge. Even as they watched, she came to rest, wallowing dangerously in the troughs between the great waves.

"The fools!" Tyndall was bitter. "This is what happens, Captain, when a ship loses station! Make a signal please: 'Estimate of damage —please inform.' That damned U-boat must have trailed her from first light, waiting for a line-up."

"Going to investigate, sir?" Vallery inquired.

Tyndall hesitated. "Yes, I think we'd better do it ourselves. Order squadron to proceed, same speed, same course. Signal the destroyers *Baliol* and *Nairn* to stand by the *Invader*."

Vallery, watching the flags fluttering to the yardarm, was aware of someone at his elbow.

"That was no U-boat, sir." The Kapok Kid was very sure of himself. "She can't have been torpedoed."

Tyndall swung round in his chair. "What the devil do you know about it, sir?"

"Well, sir, in the first place the *Sirrus* is covering the *Invader*'s port side, though well ahead, ever since your recall signal. She's been quartering that area for some time. I'm sure Commander Orr would have picked up a submarine. Also, it's far too rough for any sub to maintain periscope depth, far less line up a firing track. . . . No sir," Carpenter persisted. "I can't swear to it—" he had his binoculars to his eyes "—but I'm almost sure the *Invader* is going astern. Could only be because her bows—below the waterline, that is—have been damaged or blown off. Must have been a drifting mine, sir, probably acoustic. Or an old acoustic torpedo—spent German torpedoes don't always sink."

A light winked on the *Invader*. The signalman acknowledged, then tore a sheet off his signal pad and handed it to Vallery. " '*Invader* to Admiral,' " the captain read. " 'Am badly holed, starboard side for'ard, very deep. Suspect drifting mine. Am investigating extent of damage. Will report soon.' "

Tyndall took the signal from him and read it slowly. Then he looked at Carpenter and smiled faintly. "It seems you were dead right, my boy."

The *Invader* had lost most of her bows and twenty minutes later, with *Baliol* and *Nairn* as escorts, was heading back to base.

In another ten minutes, watchers on the *Ulysses* had lost sight of them buried in a flurrying snow squall. Three gone and eleven left behind; but it was the eleven who now felt strangely alone.

THE *INVADER* and her troubles were soon forgotten. All too soon, the 14th Aircraft Carrier Squadron had enough, and more than enough, to worry about on its own account.

The wind was fairly steady, and the snow had stopped. A temporary cessation only—far ahead to the northwest the sky was a peculiarly livid colour, faintly luminous and menacing.

The sea had been building up steadily all morning and the cold was now intense. As well as the snow on the decks, ice was forming everywhere, a deadly menace in the slippery surface it presented. But the real danger of the ice lay in its weight. There were over three hundred tons of it already on the decks of the *Ulysses*, and more accumulating every minute.

Conditions aboard the destroyers were even worse. The tremendous weight of the ice was pushing the little ships down by their heads; they buried their noses deeper in the sea with each successive plunge, and each time, more and more sluggishly, they staggered laboriously up from the depths.

Two hours passed in which the temperature fell steadily beyond zero, two hours in which the barometer tumbled crazily after it. Curiously the snow still held off, the livid sky to the northwest was as far away as ever, and the sky to the south and east had cleared completely. The squadron presented a fantastic picture now, little toy-boats of sugar-icing, sparkling in the pale, winter sunshine, pitching crazily through the grey and green Norwegian Sea, pushing on towards that purply glowing horizon. It was an incredibly lovely spectacle.

Rear Admiral Tyndall saw nothing beautiful about it. A man who was wont to claim that he never worried, he was seriously troubled now. Ceaselessly his gaze circled the fleet; constantly he twisted in his chair. Finally he climbed down, passed through the gate, and went into the captain's shelter.

It was in semi-darkness. Vallery lay on his settee, a couple of blankets over him. In the half-light, his face looked ghastly. His right hand clutched a stained handkerchief. With a painful effort, he swung his legs down and pulled forward a chair. Tyndall choked off his protest, sank gratefully into the seat.

"The weather's really piling up against us, Dick . . . What on earth ever induced me to become a squadron commander?"

Vallery grinned sympathetically, then broke down into a bout of harsh, dry coughing. When it was done he looked up. "I don't particularly envy you, sir. How far to go, exactly?"

"Young Carpenter makes it a hundred and seventy miles, more or less."

"One hundred and seventy." Vallery looked at his watch. "Twenty hours—in these conditions. We *must* make it!"

Tyndall nodded heavily. "Eighteen ships sitting out there . . . ."

He broke off as a hand rapped on the door and Signalman Bentley looked in.

"Two signals, Captain, sir."

"Just read them out, Bentley, will you?"

"First is from the destroyer *Portpatrick*: 'Sprung bow-plates: making water fast: pumps coping: fear further damage: please advise.'"

Tyndall swore. Vallery said calmly: "And the other?"

"From the corvette *Gannet*, sir. 'Breaking up.'"

"Ha! One of those taciturn characters," Tyndall growled. "Wait a minute, Bentley, will you?" He sank back in his chair, hand rasping his chin, forcing his tired mind to think.

"Troubled waters, sir," Vallery murmured. "Perhaps the carriers—"

Tyndall slapped his knee. "Two minds with but a single thought. Bentley, make two signals. One to all screen vessels—tell 'em to take position—close astern—of the carriers. Other to the carriers. Oil hose, one each through port and starboard loading ports, about—ah—how much would you say, Captain?"

"Twenty gallons a minute, sir?"

"Twenty gallons it is. Understand, Chief? Right-o, get 'em off at once. And Chief—tell the navigator to bring his chart here." Bentley left, and Tyndall turned to Vallery. "We've all got to come alongside the carriers to fuel sooner or later, but we can't do it here. . . . Ah! Here you are, Pilot. Let's see where we are. How's the wind, by the way?"

"Force Ten, sir." Bracing himself against the wild lurching of the *Ulysses*, the Kapok Kid smoothed out the chart on the captain's bunk. "Backing slightly."

"Northwest, would you say, Pilot?" Tyndall rubbed his hands. "Looks as if this might be the last chance of shelter this side of Murmansk. Excellent. Now, my boy, our position?"

"It's 12.40 West. 66.15 North," said the Kapok Kid without consulting the chart. "Course 310, sir."

"Now, if it were necessary for us to seek shelter for fuelling—"

"Course exactly 290, sir. I've pencilled it in—there. Four and a half hours' steaming, approximately."

"How the devil—" Tyndall exploded. "Who told you to—to—"

"I worked it out five minutes ago, sir. It—er—seemed inevitable. 290 would take us a few miles inside the Langanes peninsula. There should be plenty of shelter there."

"Seemed inevitable!" Tyndall roared. "Would you listen to him, Captain Vallery? Inevitable! And it's only just occurred to me! Of all the . . . Get out! Take yourself and that damned comic-opera fancy dress elsewhere!"

With an air of injured innocence the Kapok Kid gathered up his charts and left. Tyndall's voice halted him at the door.

"Pilot! The screen vessels are taking up a new position. As soon as they're done tell Bentley to send them the new course."

"Yes, sir. Certainly." He hesitated, and Tyndall chuckled. "All right, all right," he said resignedly. "I admit it—I'm just a crusty old curmudgeon . . . Now shut that damned door! We're freezing in here."

The wind was rising now and the wave troughs were deepening rapidly, but the effect of the long oil-slicks trailing behind the carriers was almost miraculous. Although the destroyers were still plunging, the surface tension of the fuel held the water and spray from breaking aboard.

Towards half-past four in the afternoon, with shelter still a good fifteen miles away, there was a whole gale blowing and Tyndall had to signal for a reduction in speed.

From deck level, the seas were gigantic, frightening. Nicholls stood with the Kapok Kid, off watch now, sheltering in the lee of the fo'c'sle deck. Clinging to a davit to steady himself, he looked over to where the aircraft carrier *Defender*, with two destroyers tailing behind, was pitching grotesquely, under a serene blue sky. The blue sky above, the tremendous seas below—a macabre contrast.

"They never told me anything about this in the medical school," Nicholls observed at last. "My God, Andy," he added in awe, "have you ever seen anything like this?"

"Number One says this is damn all compared to what's coming tonight—and he knows. God I wish I was back in Henley!"

Nicholls looked at him curiously.

"Can't say I know Lieutenant Commander Carrington well. Not a very approachable customer, is he? But everyone talks of him with bated breath. What's so extra special about him?"

"He's just the greatest seaman you'll ever see. Holds two master's-tickets—square-rigged and steam. He was going round the Horn in Finnish barques when we were still in our prams. Commander Turner could tell you enough stories about him to fill a book."

The Kapok Kid paused then went on quietly: "He really is one of the few great seamen of today. Old Turner is no slouch himself, but he'll tell anyone that he can't hold a candle to Jimmy Carrington . . . I'm no hero-worshipper, Johnny. You know that. But you can say about Carrington what they used to say about Shackleton—when there's nothing left and all hope is gone, get down on your knees and pray for him. Believe me, Johnny, I'm damned glad he's here."

Surprise held Nicholls silent. For the Kapok Kid seriousness was a crime and anything that smacked of adulation bordered on blasphemy. Nicholls wondered what manner of man Carrington must be.

The cold was vicious. The wind was tearing great gouts of water off the wave-tops, driving the atomized spray at bullet speed against fo'c'sle and sides. It was impossible to breathe without turning one's back, without wrapping layers of wool round mouth and nose.

"God Almighty!" Nicholls's voice was stunned. He was staring out at the aircraft carrier *Defender*. She was climbing up the lee side of a wave that staggered the imagination. Reaching the crest, she hesitated, crazily tilted up her stern till screw and rudder were entirely clear of the water, then crashed down, down, down. . . .

Even at two cable-lengths' distance in that high wind, the smash of the plummeting bows came like a thunder-clap. An aeon ticked by, and still the *Defender* seemed to keep on going under, completely buried now, right back to the bridge island, in a sea of foaming white. How long she remained like that, arrowed down into the depths of the Arctic, no one could afterwards say: then slowly, incredibly, great rivers of water cascaded off her bows, she broke surface again, to present a grim spectacle. The upthrusting pressure of thousands of tons of water had torn the open flight-deck completely off its mountings and bent it backwards, in a great, sweeping "U", almost as far as the bridge. It was a sight to leave men speechless—all, that is, except the Kapok Kid. He rose magnificently to the occasion.

"My word!" he murmured thoughtfully. "That *is* unusual."

ANOTHER SUCH WAVE, and it would have been the end for the *Defender*. But there were no more such freaks and shortly before six o'clock, the squadron hove-to under the shelter of Langanes, on the northeast tip of Iceland, less than two miles offshore. At once the cruisers and the screen vessels—except the *Portpatrick* and the *Gannet*—moved alongside the carriers, took oil hoses aboard. Tyndall reluctantly had decided that the *Portpatrick* and *Gannet* were a potential liability: they were to escort the crippled *Defender* back to Scapa.

Six gone now, only eight left of the carrier force.

FOR A BRIEF MOMENT that evening, white-hot anger ran through the *Ulysses* like a flame. It all happened simply enough. During routine evening tests, it was discovered that the fighting lights on the lower yardarm were not working. Ice was at once suspected as being the cause.

The lower yardarm, heavily coated with snow and ice, paralleled the deck, sixty feet above it. The fighting lights were suspended below the outer tip: to work on these, a man had either to sit on the yardarm or in a bosun's chair suspended from the yardarm. It was a difficult enough task at any time: tonight, it had to be done with maximum speed, because the repairs would interrupt radio transmission—the heavy steel transmission aerial was bolted to the yard-arm's upper length and the 3000-volt "Safe-to-Transmit" boards (which carried the current) were always withdrawn to break the circuit, and left in the keeping of the officer of the watch during the repair. The job was more than ordinarily difficult—it was highly dangerous.

Marshall asked for volunteers, and from them picked Ralston.

The task took half an hour—twenty minutes to climb the mast, edge out to the yardarm tip, fit the bosun's chair and lifeline, and ten minutes for the actual repair. Long before he was finished, a hundred, two hundred tired men, had come on deck to watch.

Ralston swung in a great arc across the darkening sky, the gale plucking viciously at his duffel and hood. Twice, wind and wave flung him out parallel to the yardarm, forcing him to hang on for his life. On the second occasion he lost his gauntlets—he must have had them in his lap, while making some delicate adjustment: they dropped down over the side.

A few minutes later, while Vallery and Turner were standing amidships examining a damaged motor-boat, a short, stocky figure came out of the after screen door. It was Hastings, the master-at-arms.

"What's the matter, Hastings?" Vallery asked curtly. He disliked the master-at-arms, disliked him for his unnecessary harshness.

"Trouble on the bridge, sir," Hastings jerked out breathlessly. "Don't know exactly what—I think you'd better come, sir."

They found only three people on the bridge: Etherton, the gunnery officer, still clutching a phone; Ralston, his hands hanging by his sides, the palms raw and torn, his face ghastly, its chin with the dead pallor of frostbite, its forehead masked in furrowed, frozen blood; and, lying in a corner, Sub Lieutenant Carslake, moaning in agony and fingering his smashed mouth.

"Good God!" Vallery ejaculated. He swung round on the gunnery officer. "What the devil's happened here, Etherton?"

"Ralston hit him, sir."

"We can see that. Why?"

"A WT messenger came up for the 'Safe-to-Transmit' boards. Carslake gave them to him—about ten minutes ago, I—I think."

"You think! Where were you, Etherton, and why did you permit it?"

"I was down below, sir." Etherton was looking at the deck. "Just —just for a moment, sir."

"I see. You were down below." Vallery's eyes held an expression that promised ill for Etherton. He looked round at Turner. "Is he badly hurt, Commander?"

"He'll survive," said Turner briefly. He had Carslake on his feet now still moaning.

For the first time, the captain looked at Ralston. "Well?"

"Yes, sir. I did it. I hit him—the treacherous bastard!"

"Ralston!" Hastings's voice was a whiplash.

Suddenly Ralston sagged. "I'm sorry. I forgot. He's got a stripe on his arm—only ratings are bastards. But he—"

"You've got frostbite. Rub your chin, man!" Turner interrupted sharply.

Mechanically, Ralston did as he was told. He used the back of his hand. Vallery winced as he saw the palm of the hand, raw and mutilated. The agony of that bare-handed descent from the yard-arm. . . .

"He tried to murder me, sir. He returned the boards five minutes before I left the yardarm. It was a miracle that the WT didn't start transmitting until just after I reached the mast, coming down."

"Nonsense, Ralston. How dare you—"

"He's right, sir." Etherton was replacing the receiver. "I've just checked."

Ralston took two quick steps forward. "I gave him these boards, sir, when I came to the bridge. I asked for the officer of the watch and he said *he* was—I didn't know the gunnery officer was on duty, sir. When I told him the boards were to be returned only to me, he said: 'I don't want any of your damned insolence, Ralston. I know my job—you stick to yours. Just you get up there and perform your heroics.' He *knew*, sir."

Carslake appealed wildly to the captain, his words slurred. "That's a lie, sir! It's a damned, filthy lie!"

"Commander Turner." Vallery's voice was expressionless. "Please phone for a couple of our marines. Have Lieutenant Carslake taken down to his cabin and ask Brooks to have a look at him. Master-at-arms?"

"Sir?"

"Take this rating to the sick-bay, let him have any necessary treatment. Then put him in cells. With an armed guard. Understand?"

"I understand, sir." There was no mistaking the satisfaction in Hastings's voice.

Vallery, Turner and the gunnery officer stood in silence as Ralston and the master-at-arms left, and two burly marines helped Carslake below. Vallery moved after them.

"Sir?" It was Etherton. Vallery turned back, impatiently. "I'm not concerned with excusing myself, sir. But I was standing at the Asdic door when Ralston handed the boards to Carslake. I overheard them—every word they said . . . Ralston told the exact truth."

Vallery turned heavily away. Old Socrates had told him a hundred times that he carried the ship on his back. He could feel the weight of it now, the crushing burden of every last ounce of it.

VALLERY WAS AT DINNER with Tyndall, in the admiral's day-cabin, when the message from the convoy commander arrived.

"On course. On time. Sea moderate, wind freshening. Expect rendezvous as planned. Commodore 77."

The admiral laid the signal down. "Good God! Seas moderate, fresh wind! Do you reckon he's in the same damned ocean as us?" He turned to the messenger.

"Make a signal. 'You are running into severe storm. Rendezvous unchanged. You may be delayed. Will remain at rendezvous until your arrival. Radio silence. Admiral, 14th Aircraft Carrier Squadron.' Get it off at once, will you? Then tell WT to shut down themselves."

The door shut softly. Tyndall poured himself some coffee, looked across at Vallery. "What are you going to do about Ralston, Dick? A heinous offence, we all know, to clout one of HM commissioned officers. But if Etherton's story is true, my only regret is that Ralston didn't make a really large-scale job of replanning that young swine's face."

"It's true, I'm afraid," said Vallery soberly. "What it amounts to is that naval discipline—oh, how Admiral Starr would love this—compels me to punish the near victim of positively criminal careless-ness!" He broke off in a paroxysm of coughing, and Tyndall looked away in distress. "A victim," Vallery went on at last, "who has already lost his mother, brother and three sisters . . . I believe he has a father at sea somewhere."

"And Carslake?"

"I shall see him tomorrow. I should like you to be there, sir. I will tell him that he will remain an officer of this ship till we return to Scapa, then resign his commission".

Tyndall nodded. "Still he'll bear watching ... Oh, damn! I wish the ship would stay still. Half my coffee on the tablecloth...."

AT 2020 ALL SHIPS had completed oiling. Hove to, they had had the utmost difficulty in keeping position in that great wind; but they were infinitely safer than in the open sea. They were given orders to proceed when the weather moderated, the *Defender* and escorts to Scapa, the squadron to a position one hundred miles ENE of rendezvous. Radio silence was to be strictly observed.

At 2030 the *Ulysses* got under way to the east. The biggest, most seaworthy warship there, she would try to make the original rendezvous alone. And at 2100, she moved out into the Denmark Strait—into the worst storm of the war.

At 2230, with all doors and hatches battened shut, all traffic prohibited on the upper deck, all crews withdrawn from gun turrets and magazines and all normal deck watchkeeping stopped for the first time since her commissioning, the *Ulysses* crossed the Arctic Circle. It was then that the monster struck. How the *Ulysses* ever survived the fury of that first attack, God only knew. The wind caught her on the bow and flung her round in a 45° arc and pressed her far over on her side as she fell forty heart-stopping feet down the precipitous walls of a giant trough. She crashed into the valley with a tremendous concussion that jarred every Clyde-built rivet in her hull. Miraculously she held, but lay far over on her starboard side, the gunwales dipping: half a mile away, towering high above the mast-top, a great wall of water was roaring down on the helpless ship.

The "Dude" saved the day. The "Dude", officially known as Engineer Commander Dodson, immaculately clad as usual in overalls of dazzling white, had been at his control position in the engine room when that tremendous gust had struck. He had no means of knowing what had happened, that the ship was momentarily not under command, that no one on the bridge had recovered from that first shattering impact, but he did know that the *Ulysses* was listing crazily, almost broadside on, and he suspected the cause.

His shouts on the bridge tube brought no reply. He pointed to the port engine controls, roared "Slow" in the ear of the engineer WO— then leapt quickly for the starboard controls.

Fifteen seconds later and it would have been too late. As it was, the accelerating starboard screw brought her round just far enough to take the roaring mountain of water under her bows, to dig her stern into the level of the depth-charge rails, till forty feet of her keel lay poised above the abyss below. When she plunged down again, the fo'c'sle disappeared. But she was bows on again. At once the Dude signalled his WO for more revolutions, cut back the starboard engine.

Below decks, everything was an unspeakable shambles. On the mess-decks, steel lockers in their scores had broken adrift, been thrown in a dozen different directions, bursting hasps, spilling their contents everywhere. Hammocks had been catapulted from their racks, books, papers, teapots, kettles and crockery were scattered in insane profusion. And amidst this jumbled, sliding wreckage, hundreds of frightened and exhausted men struggled to their feet.

Surgeon Commander Brooks and Lieutenant Nicholls, with Winthrop, the untiring padre as good as a third doctor, were worked off their feet. Riley and his fellows were unceremoniously turfed out to make room for the men brought in to the sick-bay in their dozens all night long as the *Ulysses* fought for her life. Serious injuries were fortunately rare. Among the officers, only the Kapok Kid needed major attention, with a deep, ugly gash on his forehead.

Time and again that night, hove to with the wind fine off her starboard bow, as her bows crashed into and under the far shoulder of a trough, it seemed that the *Ulysses* could never shake free from the great press of water. But time and again she did just that, shuddering, quivering under the fantastic strain.

At the height of the storm a series of heavy explosions almost lifted her stern out of the water. Panic spread in the after mess-decks: practically every light abaft the after engine room smashed or failed. In the darkness, cries of "Torpedoed!" "Mined!" "She's breaking up!" galvanized exhausted men into frantic stampeding towards doors and hatches. Conditions were ripe for disaster when Ralston's voice cut cleanly through the bedlam. He had been released on the captain's orders: the cells were in the very forepeak of the ship, and conditions there were impossible in a head sea: even so, Hastings had freed him only with the worst possible grace.

"It's our own depth charges! Do you hear me, you fools—it's our own depth charges! They must have been washed over the side!"

He was right. The entire contents of a rack had broken adrift, lifted from their cradles by some freak wave, and tumbled over the side. Through some oversight, they had been left set at their shallow setting and had gone off almost directly under the ship. The damage, it seemed, was only minor.

For the men below, it was discomfort and danger: for the bare handful of men above, the officers and ratings on the bridge, it was pure undiluted hell. Five minutes at a time was enough for any man, then he had to retire to the captain's shelter. Not that manning the open bridge was more than a gesture anyway—it was impossible to look into that terrible wind: the cold would have seared the eyeballs blind. And it was impossible to see through the Kent clear-view windscreens. They still spun at high speed, but uselessly: the ice-laden storm, a gigantic sandblaster, had starred and abraded the plate glass until it was completely opaque.

On his watch below, Lieutenant Nicholls dragged himself reluctantly up from the mist-fogged depths of exhausted sleep. The Kapok Kid, forehead swathed in bandages, was bending over him. He looked disgustingly cheerful.

"Want to come up top, see Carrington do his stuff? He's going to turn the ship round. In this little lot, it should be worth seeing!"

"What! Dammit to hell! Have you woken me just—?"

"Brother, when this ship turns, you would wake up anyway—probably on the deck with a broken neck. But as it so happens, Jimmy requires your assistance. At least, he requires one of these heavy plate-glass squares which I happen to know you have in great numbers in the dispensary. But the dispensary's locked—I tried it," he added shamelessly.

"But what—I mean—plate glass—"

"Come and see for yourself," the Kapok Kid invited.

Above decks it was dawn now, wild and terrible. Trailing bands of misty-white vapour swept by barely at mast-top level, but high above the sky was clear. The seas, still gigantic, were shorter now, and steeper: the *Ulysses* was slowed right down, with barely enough steerage way to keep her head up—and even then, taking severe punishment in the precipitous head seas. The wind had dropped to a steady fifty knots—gale force: even at that, it seared like fire in Nicholls's lungs as he stepped outside, blinded him with ice and cold. Hastily he wrapped scarves over his entire face, clambered up to the bridge by touch and instinct. The Kapok Kid followed with the glass.

Turner and the first lieutenant were alone on the bridge, swathed like mummies. Not even their eyes were visible—they wore goggles.

"Morning, Nicholls," boomed the commander. "It *is* Nicholls, isn't it?" He pulled off his goggles, his back turned to the wind, threw them away in disgust. "Can't see damn all through these bloody things . . . Ah, Number One, our navigator's brought the glass."

Nicholls crouched in the for'ard lee of the compass platform. In one corner the duckboards were littered with goggles, eye-shields and gas-masks. He jerked his head towards them.

"What's this—a clearance sale?"

"We're turning round, Doc." Carrington was as calm and precise as ever. "But we've got to see where we're going, and as the commander says, all those damn things there are useless—mist up immediately they're put on—it's too cold. If you'll just hold the glass—so—and if you would wipe it, Andy?"

Nicholls looked back at the great seas. He shuddered. "Excuse my ignorance, but why turn round at all?"

"Because we have a rendezvous. And we'll never make it without calmer water," Carrington answered briefly. Then he chuckled. "This is going to make me the most unpopular man on the ship. We've just broadcast a warning. Ready, sir?"

"Stand by, engine room: stand by, wheelhouse. Ready, Number One."

For a whole minute, Carrington stared steadily, unblinkingly through the glass while the Kapok Kid rubbed it industriously. Then: "Half-ahead, port engine! Starboard 20 on the wheel!"

Nicholls risked a glance forward. In the split second before his eyes blinded, he saw a huge wave bearing down on them, the bows already swinging diagonally away from it. Good God! Why hadn't Carrington waited until that was past?

It flung the bows up, pushed the *Ulysses* far over to starboard, then passed under. The *Ulysses* staggered over the top, corkscrewed wickedly down the other side, her great gleaming masts heavy with ice, swinging in a great arc as she rolled over, burying her port rails in the rising shoulder of the next sea.

"Full ahead port! Starboard 30!"

The next sea, passing beneath, merely straightened the *Ulysses* up. And then, at last, Nicholls understood. Incredibly, because it had been impossible to see so far ahead, Carrington had known that two opposing wave systems were due to interlock in an area of comparative calm: how he had sensed it, no one knew, not even Carrington himself: but he was a great seaman, and he *had* known. For fifteen, twenty seconds, the sea was a seething white mass of violently disturbed, conflicting waves, and the *Ulysses* curved gratefully through. And then another great sea, towering almost to bridge height, caught her, striking broadside against the entire length of the *Ulysses*—for the first time that night—with tremendous weight. It threw her far over on her side, the lee rails vanishing. Nicholls was flung off his feet, crashed heavily into the side of the bridge. He could have sworn he heard Carrington laughing. He clawed his way back to the middle of the compass platform.

And still the great wave had not passed. It towered high above the trough into which the *Ulysses*, now heeled far over to 40°, had been flung, bore down remorselessly from above and sought with an almost animistic savagery to press her under. The inclinometer swung relentlessly—45°, 50°, 53°—and hung there an eternity, while men stood on the side of the ship, braced with their hands on the deck. This was the end. The *Ulysses* could never come back.

A lifetime ticked agonizingly by. Tilted at that crazy angle, the bridge was sheltered from the wind, Carrington's voice, calm, conversational, carried with amazing clarity.

"She'd go to 65° and still come back," he said matter-of-factly. "Hang on to your hats, gentlemen. This is going to be interesting."

Just as he finished, the *Ulysses* shuddered, then slowly, then with vicious speed lurched back and whipped through an arc of 90° and back again. Once more Nicholls found himself in the corner of the bridge. But the *Ulysses* was almost round.

The Kapok Kid, grinning with relief, picked himself up and tapped Carrington on the shoulder. "Don't look now, sir, but we have lost our mainmast."

It was a slight exaggeration, but the top fifteen feet, which had carried the after radar scanner, were undoubtedly gone. That wicked, double whiplash, with the weight of the ice, had been too much.

"Slow ahead both! Midships!"

"Slow ahead both! Midships!"

"Steady as she goes!"

The *Ulysses* was round.

The Kapok Kid caught Nicholls's eye, nodded at the first lieutenant. "See what I mean, Johnny?"

"Yes." Nicholls was very quiet. "Yes, I do see what you mean."

Running straight before the heavy stern sea, the *Ulysses* was amazingly steady. The wind, too, was dead astern now, the bridge in magical shelter. The scudding mist overhead had thinned out. Far away to the southeast a dazzling white sun climbed up above a cloudless horizon. The long night was over.

An hour later, with the wind down to thirty knots, radar reported contacts to the west. At 1030, in position, on time, the *Ulysses* made her rendezvous with the convoy from Halifax.

WEDNESDAY

THE CONVOY CAME steadily up from the west, a magnificent prize for any German wolfpack of submarines. Eighteen ships, fifteen big, modern cargo ships, three 16,000-ton tankers, carrying tanks, planes and petrol.

Aboard the merchant ships, crews lined the decks and looked and wondered as the *Ulysses* steamed up between the port and centre lines. The *Ulysses*, seen from another deck, was a strange sight: broken-masted, stripped of her rafts, with her boat falls hauled taut over empty cradles, she glistened like crystal in the morning light: the great wind had blown away all snow, had abraded and rubbed and polished the ice to a satin-smooth, transparent gloss: but on either side of the bows and before the bridge were huge patches of crimson, where the hurricane blast of that long night had stripped off camouflage and base coats, exposing the red lead below.

The American convoy escort was small—a heavy cruiser, two destroyers and two near-frigates of the coast-guard type. They sailed in company, east-north-east, freighters, American warships and the

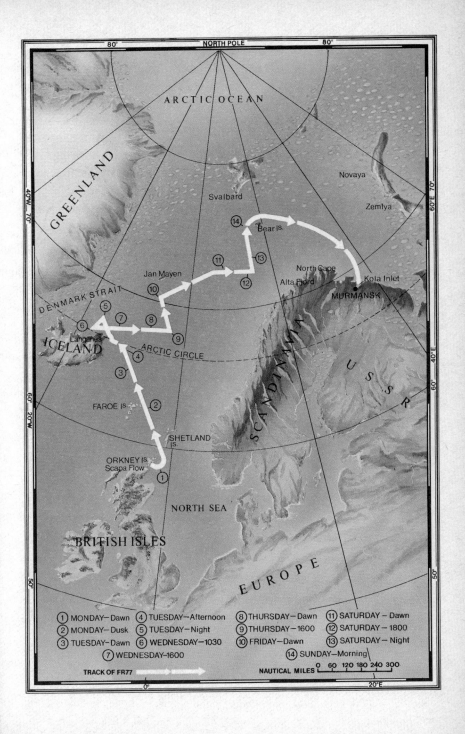

80°   NORTH POLE   80°

ARCTIC OCEAN

GREENLAND

Novaya

Svalbard

Zemlya

Jan Mayen

⑭

Bear Is.

⑪

⑬

North Cape

⑩

⑫

Alta Fjord

Kola Inlet

DENMARK STRAIT

MURMANSK

⑤

⑦

⑧

Langanes

⑨

ICELAND

ARCTIC CIRCLE

SCANDINAVIA

U.S.S.R.

④

③

FAROE IS.

②

SHETLAND
IS.

ORKNEY IS.
Scapa Flow

①

NORTH SEA

BRITISH ISLES

EUROPE

① MONDAY—Dawn   ④ TUESDAY—Afternoon   ⑧ THURSDAY—Dawn   ⑪ SATURDAY—Dawn

② MONDAY—Dusk   ⑤ TUESDAY—Night   ⑨ THURSDAY—1600   ⑫ SATURDAY—1800

③ TUESDAY—Dawn   ⑥ WEDNESDAY—1030   ⑩ FRIDAY—Dawn   ⑬ SATURDAY—Night

⑦ WEDNESDAY—1600   ⑭ SUNDAY—Morning

TRACK OF FR77   NAUTICAL MILES   0 60 120 180 240 300

Ulysses, until late in the afternoon the silhouettes of the British escort carriers climbed slowly over the horizon ahead. Half an hour later, at 1600, the American escorts dropped astern and turned, winking farewell messages of good luck.

The 14th Aircraft Carrier Squadron—or what was left of it—was only two miles away now. Tyndall, coming to the bridge, swore fluently as he saw that a carrier and minesweeper were missing. An angry signal went out to the escort's acting commander, asking why orders had been disobeyed, where the missing ships were.

An Aldis flickered back its reply. The carrier *Wrestler* had gone aground on the Vejle bank behind Langanes and was still there, her steering gear fractured, with the minesweeper *Eager* in attendance, when the squadron had sailed shortly after dawn.

Later, refloated but damaged, she would return to Scapa, *Eager* in company.

The *Ulysses* was at dawn action stations when at 0702, the aircraft carrier *Blue Ranger* was torpedoed. The *Ulysses* was two cable-lengths away, on her starboard quarter, and felt the physical shock of the twin explosions, as two searing columns of flame fingered skywards, high above the *Blue Ranger*'s bridge and well aft of it. A second later a signalman shouted and pointed forward and down. It was another torpedo, running astern of the carrier.

Vallery was shouting down the voice-pipe, pulling the *Ulysses* round to avoid collision with the slewing carrier. Aldis lamps and the fighting lights were already stuttering out the "maintain position" code signal to ships in the convoy. Gun barrels were depressing, and the destroyer *Sirrus* was already knifing through the convoy, headed for the estimated position of the U-boat.

Within a minute, the signal-lamp of the destroyer *Vectra*, up front with the convoy, started winking. "Contacts, repeat contacts. Green 90, green 90. Closing. . . ."

Tyndall cursed softly. "Acknowledge. Investigate." He turned to Vallery. "Let's join him, Captain. This is it. Wolfpack number one— and in force. No bloody right to be here," he added bitterly, "So much for Admiralty Intelligence!"

The *Ulysses* was round again, heading for the *Vectra*, but the *Blue Ranger*, her squadron fuel tanks on fire, lay almost athwart of the flagship's course.

She was almost gone, heeled far over to starbord, ammunition and petrol tanks going up in a series of crackling reports. Suddenly, a succession of dull, heavy explosions rumbled over the sea: the entire bridge island structure lurched crazily sideways, held. then ponderously toppled into the sea. God only knew how many men perished with it, deep down in the Arctic ocean, trapped in its iron walls. They were the lucky ones.

The *Vectra*, barely two miles ahead now, was pulling round south in a tight circle. Vallery saw her, altered course to intercept. He heard the signalman shouting something from the compass platform, and pointing, and leapt up beside him.

The sea was on fire, a vast carpet of flames, and it was alive with swimming, struggling men.

For a man in the sea, oil on fire is a hellish thing, death by torture, a slow death by drowning, by burning, by asphyxiation. All this Vallery knew.

At the same time, for the *Ulysses* to stop, starkly outlined against the burning carrier, would be suicide. And to come sharply round to starboard would waste invaluable minutes, time and to spare for the U-boats ahead to line up firing-tracks on the convoy; and the *Ulysses*'s first responsibility was to the convoy. Again all this Vallery knew. But, at that moment, what weighed most heavily with him was common humanity. Fine off the port bow, close in to the *Blue Ranger*, the oil was heaviest, the flames fiercest, the swimmers thickest: Vallery looked over his shoulder at the officer of the watch.

"Port 10! Midships! Steady as she goes!"

For fifteen seconds the *Ulysses* held her course, arrowing through the burning sea to the spot where two hundred men were knotted together in a writhing mass.

"Starboard 30!" Vallery's voice was low, but it carried clearly through the shocked silence on the bridge.

"Starboard 30, sir."

For the third time in ten minutes, the *Ulysses* slewed crazily round in a racing turn. Her side, still at an acute angle, caught the edge of the group on the port bow: almost on the instant, the entire length of the swinging hull smashed into the heart of the fire, into the thickest press of dying men.

For most of them, it was extinction, swift and merciful. . . . But on board the *Ulysses*, men cursed and wept as pitiful, charred faces, turned up towards the *Ulysses* and alight with joy and hope, petrified into horror as she trampled them under.

Suddenly, mercifully, the sea was empty. The air was strangely still and quiet, heavy with the sickening stench of charred flesh and burning diesel. The *Ulysses*'s stern was swinging wildly almost under the black pall overhanging the *Blue Ranger* amidships, when the shells struck her.

The shells—three 3.7s ignited by the heat—came from the *Blue Ranger*. The first exploded harmlessly against the armour-plating: the second wrecked the bosun's store, fortunately empty: the third penetrated No. 3 low power room via the deck. There were nine men in there—an officer and eight ratings. In that confined space, death was instantaneous.

Only seconds later a heavy rumbling explosion blew out a great hole along the waterline of the *Blue Ranger* and she fell over on her starboard side, her flight-deck vertical to the water.

On the bridge, Vallery still stood on the yeoman's platform, leaning over the windscreen. He was retching blood desperately. Tyndall stood helplessly beside him till he was brushed unceremoniously aside by the surgeon commander, whom he had sent for and who pushed a towel to Vallery's mouth and led him gently below.

Carrington straightened the *Ulysses* out on course, while he waited for Turner to move up from the after director tower to take over the bridge. In three minutes the cruiser was up with the *Vectra*, methodically quartering for a lost contact. Twice the ships regained contact, twice they dropped heavy patterns. A heavy oil slick rose to the surface: possibly a kill, probably a ruse, but in any event, neither ship could remain to investigate further. The convoy was two miles ahead now, and only the destroyers *Stirling* and *Viking* were there for its protection —a wholly inadequate cover and powerless to save the convoy from any determined attack.

It was the *Blue Ranger* that saved the convoy. A light westerly wind carried the heavy black smoke from the blazing carrier along the southern flank of the ships, at sea level, the perfect smoke-screen from the wolfpack lying to the south, dense, impenetrable. Within an hour, the convoy had left the wolfpack far behind.

Aboard the flagship, the WT transmitter was chattering out a coded signal to London. There was little point in maintaining radio silence, Tyndall had decided, now that the enemy knew their position.

"Admiral, 14 ACS: To DNC, London. Made rendezvous FR 77 1030 yesterday. Weather conditions extreme. Severe damage to carriers: *Defender, Wrestler* unserviceable, returning base under escort: *Blue Ranger* torpedoed 0702, sunk 0730 today: Convoy escorts now *Ulysses, Stirling, Sirrus, Vectra, Viking*: no minesweepers—*Eager* to base: Urgently require air support. Can you detach carrier battle squadron? Please advise immediately."

The wording of the message, Tyndall pondered, could have been improved. Besides, he knew well that for almost two years now it had been Admiralty policy not to break up the Home Fleet squadrons by detaching capital ships or carriers; the official strategy was based on keeping the Home Fleet intact, containing the German Grand Fleet— and risking the convoys. . . . Tyndall took a last look round, sighed, then clumped his way heavily down the bridge ladders and into the captain's cabin. Vallery, partly undressed, was lying in his bunk. From one corner of his mouth blood trickled down a parchment cheek. As Tyndall shut the door, he lifted a hand, all ivory knuckles and blue veins, in feeble greeting.

Tyndall made no attempt to disguise his concern. "Thank God for old Socrates!" he said feelingly. "Only man in the ship who can make you see even a modicum of sense." He parked himself on the edge of the bed. "How do you feel, Dick?"

Vallery grinned crookedly. "All depends what you mean, sir. Physically or mentally? I feel a bit worn out—not really ill, you know. Doc says he can fix me up—temporarily anyway. He's going to give me a plasma transfusion—says I've lost too much blood." He paused, wiped some froth off his lips, and smiled again, as mirthlessly as before. "It's not really a doctor I need, Giles, it's a padre—and forgiveness." His voice trailed into silence.

Tyndall shifted uncomfortably. "Forgiveness? What on earth do you mean, Dick?"

"You know damn well what I mean. You were with me on the bridge this morning."

He broke into a fresh paroxysm of coughing. Tyndall felt a quick stab of fear. But Vallery spoke again, his eyes closed.

"The boys in the water. I hadn't the right—I mean, perhaps some of them would ...." Again his voice was lost for a moment, then he went on strongly: "Captain Richard Vallery, DSO—judge, jury and executioner. Tell me, Giles, what am I going to say when *my* turn comes?"

Tyndall hesitated, heard the authoritative rap on the cabin door thankfully.

Brooks walked in, and pulled a chair up to the captain's bunk. Vallery's wrist between his fingers, he looked coldly across at Tyndall. The pulse was very fast, irregular.

"You've been upsetting him," Brooks accused.

"Me? Good God, no!" Tyndall was injured. "So help me, Doc, I never said—"

"Not guilty, Doc." Vallery's voice was stronger now. "He never said a word. *I'm* the guilty man—guilty as hell."

Brooks looked at him for a long moment. Then he smiled understandingly. "Forgiveness, sir. That's it, isn't it?"

Vallery opened his eyes. "Socrates!" he murmured. "You would know."

"Forgiveness," Brooks mused. "Forgiveness. From whom—the living, the dead—or the judge?"

"From all three, Doc. A tall order, I'm afraid."

"From the dead, sir, there would be only their blessing, for there is nothing to forgive. I'm a doctor, don't forget—I saw those boys in the water ... you sent them home the easy way. As for the judge—mercy and charity, sir. You know it's so ...."

Vallery propped himself up on his pillow. "You make good medicine, Doctor. It's a pity you can't speak for the living also."

"Oh, can't I?" Brooks laughed softly in sudden recollection. "Just fifteen minutes ago a bunch of sympathetic stokers deposited in the sick-bay the extremely unconscious form of one of their shipmates. Guess who? None other than our resident nihilist, our old friend Riley. Slight concussion and assorted facial injuries, but he should be restored to the bosom of his mess-deck by nightfall. Anyway, he insists on it—claims his kittens need him."

Vallery looked up, amused, curious. "Fallen down the stokehold again, I presume?"

"Exactly the question I put, sir—although it looked more as if he had fallen into a concrete mixer. 'No, sir,' says one of the stretcher-bearers. 'Poor old Riley just came all over queer—took a weak turn, 'e did. I 'ope 'e ain't 'urt 'isself?' He sounded quite anxious."

"What had really happened?" Tyndall queried.

"I let it go at that. Young Nicholls took two of them aside, promised no action and had it out of them in a minute flat. Seems that Riley saw in this morning's affair a magnificent opportunity for provoking trouble. Cursed you for an inhuman, cold-blooded murderer. And all of this, mind you, where he thought he was safe— among his own friends. His friends half-killed him. . . . You know, sir, I envy you. . . ." He broke off. "Now, sir, if you'll just lie down and roll up your sleeve . . . Oh, damn!"

"Come in." Tyndall answered the knock. "Ah, for me, young Chrysler. From London, I see. Thank you." He opened the signal.

" 'DNO to Admiral commanding 14 ACS,' " he read slowly. " '*Tirpitz* reported preparing to move out. Impossible detach Fleet carrier: FR 77 vital: proceed Murmansk all speed: good luck: Starr.' " Tyndall paused. "Good luck! He might have spared us that!"

The three men looked at each other. Characteristically, it was Brooks who broke the silence.

"Speaking of forgiveness," he murmured quietly, "what I want to know is—who on earth is ever going to forgive that unrelenting old bastard?"

THURSDAY

I T WAS STILL ONLY afternoon, but the grey Arctic twilight was already thickening over the sea as the *Ulysses* dropped slowly astern. The wind had died away; again the snow was falling; visibility was down to a cable length; it was bitterly cold.

In groups of three and four, officers and men made their way aft to the starboard side of the poop-deck, exhausted and bone-chilled, to range themselves behind the captain or in a line inboard and aft of a long row of snow-covered hummocks.

The captain was flanked by three of his officers—Carslake, Etherton and the surgeon commander. Carslake was by the guard rail, the lower half of his face swathed in bandages. For the second time in twenty-four hours he had waylaid Vallery, begging in vain for him to reconsider the decision to deprive him of his commission. Now he stared unseeingly into the gloom, his eyes heavy with hate.

Etherton stood just behind Vallery, pale-faced and shivering uncontrollably. In complete contrast Surgeon Commander Brooks was red of face and wrathful. Vallery, as he had told him, had no bloody right to be there, was all sorts of a damned fool for leaving his bunk. But, as Vallery had mildly pointed out, somebody had to conduct a funeral service, and that was the captain's duty if the padre couldn't do it. And this day the padre couldn't do it, for the padre, among others, lay dead at his feet.

The padre had died four hours ago, just after Charlie and three others of his kind had flown over the convoy: the barrage from merchant ships and escorts was intense, and the bombing attack was pressed home with a marked lack of enthusiasm. Almost at once the Condors had broken off the attack and disappeared to the east, impressed—but apparently unharmed—by the warmth of their reception.

In the circumstances, the attack was highly suspicious, and almost certainly diversionary, the main danger lying elsewhere. The watch over and under the sea had been intensified.

Fifteen minutes passed and nothing happened. Radar and Asdic screens remained obstinately clear. Tyndall had finally decided that there was no justification for keeping the entire ship's company, so desperately in need of rest, at action stations, and ordered the stand-down to be sounded, and normal defence stations to be resumed.

Brooks and Nicholls had their patients to attend to: the navigator returned to the chart-house: Marshall, the torpedo officer, resumed his interrupted routine rounds: and the gunnery officer, Lieutenant Etherton, nervous, anxious to redeem himself for his share in the Carslake-Ralston episode, remained huddled and watchful in the cold, lonely eyrie of the director tower.

The sharp call from the deck outside brought Marshall from No. 2 electrical shop out through the screen door and peering over the side following the gesticulating finger of an excited marine.

"There, sir! Look! Out there—no, a bit more to your right! It's a sub, sir, a U-boat!"

"What? What's that? A U-boat?" Winthrop, the padre, squeezed to the rail beside Marshall. "Where? Show me, show me!"

"Straight ahead, padre. I can see it now—but it's a damned funny shape for a U-boat—if you'll excuse the language," Marshall added hastily. The strange squat shape had now drifted almost abreast of them.

High up in the tower, Etherton had already seen it. He immediately thought it was a U-boat caught surfacing—the thought that Asdic or radar would certainly have picked it up never occurred to him. Time, speed—that was the essence. Unthinkingly, he grapped the phone to the for'ard multiple pom-pom.

"Director—pom-pom!" he barked urgently. "U-boat, port 60. Range 100 yards, moving aft. Repeat, port 60. Can you see it? . . . Oh, good, good! Commence tracking."

"On target, sir," the receiver crackled in his ear.

"Open fire—continuous!"

"Sir—but, sir—Kingston's not here. He went—"

"Never mind Kingston!" Etherton shouted furiously. Kingston, he knew, was captain of the gun. "Open fire, you fools—now! I'll take full responsibility." He thrust the phone back on the rest, moved across to the observation panel . . . Then realization, sickening, shocking, seared through his mind and he lunged desperately for the phone.

"Belay the last order!" he shouted wildly. "Cease fire! Cease fire! Oh, my God, my God, my God!" Through the receiver came the staccato, angry bark of the two-pounder. It was too late.

He had committed the cardinal sin—he had forgotten to order the removal of the muzzle-covers—the metal plates that sealed off the flash-covers of the guns when not in use. And the shells were fused to explode on contact. . . .

The first shell exploded inside its barrel, killing the trainer: the other three smashed through their flimsy covers and exploded within a second of each other, a few feet from the faces of the watchers on the fo'c'sle deck.

All four were miraculously untouched by the flying metal, but the blast of the explosion was backwards. The padre and the marine died instantly, hurled backwards by the blast, the back of their heads smashing to pulp against the bulkhead. The blood seeped darkly into the snow, was obliterated in a moment.

Marshall was lucky, fantastically so. The explosion—he said afterwards that it was like getting in the way of the driving piston of the Coronation Scot—flung him through the open door behind him, ripped off the heels of both shoes as they caught on the stormsill: he slithered along the passage and smashed squarely into the trunking of "B" turret, his back framed by the four big spikes of the butterfly nuts securing an inspection hatch. By the laws of chance Lieutenant Marshall had no right to be alive. As it was, he was now sitting up in the sick-bay, strapped, broken ribs making breathing painful, but otherwise unharmed.

Meanwhile the upturned lifeboat, mute token of some earlier tragedy on the Russian convoys, had long since vanished into the white twilight. . . .

Captain Vallery stepped back, closing the Prayer Book, and the bugle echoed briefly over the poop. Men stood silent as, one by one, the bodies of the three men, together with those of the officer and eight ratings killed the previous day, all shrouded in weighted canvas, slid down the tipped plank, down from under the Union Flag, splashed heavily into the Arctic and were gone. For long moments, no one moved, not even when Etherton, his eyes dull, crumpled down quietly in the snow. Then suddenly the spell was shattered: the strident scream of the emergency stations whistle seared through the gathering gloom.

It took Vallery about three minutes to reach the bridge, Brooks half-carrying him through the gate.

"Contact closing, closing: steady on course, interception course: speed unchanged." The calm precise tones of Lieutenant Bowden were unmistakable, though the radar loudspeaker was muffled.

"Good, good! We'll fox him yet!" Tyndall's face lit up. The prospect of action always delighted him. "Trouble, I'm afraid, Captain. Radar reports a surface vessel approaching, big, fast, more or less on interception course for us."

"And not ours, of course? By jove, sir, it couldn't be—?"

"The *Tirpitz*?" Tyndall shook his head. "My first thought, too, but no. Admiralty and Air Force are watching her like lynxes. If she moves a foot, we'll know. . . . Probably some heavy cruiser."

"Closing. Closing. Course unaltered." Bowden's voice, clipped, easy, was vaguely reminiscent of a cricket commentator's. "Estimated speed 24, repeat 24 knots."

Tyndall had sent a signal ordering the convoy to alter course to NNW. It was now six and a half miles ahead.

"Far enough away, Captain," Tyndall said. "He'll never pick 'em up. Bowden says he hasn't even picked us up yet, that the intersection of courses must be pure coincidence. I gather Lieutenant Bowden has a poor opinion of German radar."

"I hope he's right." Vallery gazed to the south, his binoculars to his eyes: there was only the sea, the thinning snow.

"Five miles," the loudspeaker cut in. "Repeat, five miles. Course, speed, constant."

"Five miles," Tyndall repeated in relief. "Time to trail our coats a little, Captain. We'll soon be in what Bowden reckons is his radar range. Due east, I think—it'll look as if we're covering the tail of the convoy and heading for the North Cape."

"Starboard 10," Vallery ordered. The cruiser came gradually round on her new course.

Five minutes passed, then the loudspeaker blared again. "Radar bridge. Constant distance, altering on interception course."

"Excellent! Really excellent!" The admiral was almost purring. "We have him, gentlemen. He's missed the convoy. Commence firing by radar!"

The *Ulysses* shuddered to the whiplike crash of "X" turret as the 5.25 shells screamed away into the twilight. Seconds later, the ship shook again as "Y" turret joined in. Thereafter the guns fired alternately, one shell at a time, the barest minimum to distract the enemy, every half-minute until Vallery ordered "X" turret to cease fire, to load with star-shell.

Abruptly, the snow was gone and the enemy was there, big and menacing, a black featureless silhouette with the sudden flush of sunset striking incongruous golden gleams from the water creaming high at her bows.

"Starboard 30!" Vallery snapped. "Full ahead. Smoke-screen!" Tyndall nodded compliance. It was no part of his plan to become embroiled with a German heavy cruiser or pocket battleship ... especially at an almost point-blank range of four miles.

On the bridge, half a dozen pairs of binoculars peered aft, trying to identify the enemy. Suddenly, as they watched, gouts of flame lanced out from the heart of the silhouette: simultaneously, their own star-shells burst high up in the air, directly above the enemy, bathing him in an intense white glare.

Everyone ducked in reflex instinct, as the shells whistled just over their heads and plunged into the sea ahead. Everyone, that is, except the Kapok Kid. He bent an impassive eye on the admiral as the latter slowly straightened up.

"Hipper class, sir," he announced. "Ten-thousand tons, 8-inch guns, carries aircraft."

Tyndall looked at him suspiciously. Then he caught sight of the German cruiser's turrets belching smoke. Shells hissed into the sea through the *Ulysses*'s boiling wake, about 150 feet astern. "Bracketed in the first two salvoes," he exclaimed. "Damned good shooting."

The *Ulysses* was still heeling round, the black smoke beginning to pour from the after funnel. Vallery clapped his binoculars to his eyes, saw heavy clouds of smoke were mushrooming from the enemy's starboard deck, just for'ard of the bridge.

"Oh, well done!" he burst out. "Well done indeed!"

"Well done indeed!" Tyndall echoed. "A beauty! Still, I don't think we'll stop to argue the point with them. . . ." The stern of the *Ulysses*, swinging round now almost to the north, disappeared from sight as a salvo crashed into the sea, dead astern. "Ah! Just in time, gentlemen! Gad, that was close!"

The next salvo—obviously the hit on the enemy cruiser hadn't affected her fire-power—fell a cable length's astern. The German was now firing blind. Engineer Commander Dodson was making smoke with a vengeance, the oily, black smoke flattening down on the surface of the sea, rolling, thick, impenetrable. Vallery doubled back on course, then headed east at high speed.

For the next two hours, in the dusk and darkness, they played cat and mouse with the Hipper-class cruiser. All the time, radar was their eyes and their ears and never played them false. Finally, satisfied that all danger to the convoy was gone, Tyndall laid smoke in a great curving "U", and vanished to the southwest.

Ninety minutes later, at the end of a giant half-circle to port, the *Ulysses* was sitting far to the north, while Bowden and his radar men tracked the progress of the enemy. He was reported as moving steadily east, then, just before contact was lost, as altering course to the southeast.

Tyndall climbed down from his chair, numbed and stiff. He stretched himself luxuriantly.

"Not a bad night's work, Captain, not bad at all. What do you bet our friend spends the night circling to the south and east at high speed, hoping to come up ahead of the convoy in the morning?" Tyndall felt almost jubilant, in spite of his exhaustion. "And by that time FR 77 should be two hundred miles to the north of him. . . . Oh, damn! Not more trouble, I hope?"

The communication rating behind the compass platform picked up the jangling phone, listened briefly.

"For you, sir," he said to Vallery. "The surgeon lieutenant."

Vallery lifted the receiver, listened to Nicholls. Lieutenant Etherton had shot himself in his cabin, five minutes ago.

FRIDAY

At four o'clock in the morning, in heavy snow, but in a calm sea, *Ulysses* rejoined the convoy.

By mid-morning, a bare six hours later, Admiral Tyndall had become an old man, haunted by remorse and bitter self-criticism. He had done what he thought right, what any commander would have done in his place. But when, to protect it from the German cruiser, he re-routed the convoy far to the north, ignoring official orders to break straight for the North Cape, it was on that latitude of 70°N that FR 77, in the cold, clear windless dawn, had blundered straight into the heart of the heaviest concentration of U-boats encountered in the Arctic during the entire course of the war—exactly where their Lordships had told him they would be.

The wolfpack had struck at its favourite hour—dawn—and from its favourite position—the northeast, with the dawn in its eyes. It struck cruelly, skilfully and with a calculated ferocity. The *Cochella*, third tanker in the port line, was the first to go. She carried over three million gallons of 100-octane petrol, and was hit by at least three torpedoes: the first two broke her almost in half, the third triggered off a stupendous detonation that literally blew her out of existence. A storm of lethal metal swept over the fleet.

Two ships took the full force of the explosion. A huge mass of metal —it might have been a winch—passed clear through the superstructure of the destroyer *Sirrus*, a cable-length away on the starboard: it completely wrecked the radar office. What happened to the merchant ship immediately astern, the *Tennessee Adventurer*, was not clear, but almost certainly her wheelhouse and bridge were severely damaged: she lost steering control, was not under command.

Tragically, this was not at first understood. Tyndall, recovering fast from the sheer physical shock of the explosion, broke out the signal for the convoy to turn to port. The wolfpack, obviously, lay on the port hand, and the only action to minimize further losses was to head straight towards them. He had adopted this tactic several times in the past with success. It cut the U-boats' target to an impossible tenth, forcing on them the alternative of diving or the risk of being trampled under.

With the immaculate precision and co-ordination of Olympic equestrians, the convoy slewed majestically round. Too late, it was seen that the *Tennessee Adventurer* was not under command. With dismaying speed, she came round to the east, angling directly for another merchantman, the *Tobacco Planter*. Frantically, the *Planter*'s helm went hard over in an attempt to clear the other astern, but the wildly swinging *Adventurer*, completely out of control, struck the *Planter* with sickening violence just for'ard of the bridge. The *Adventurer*'s bows, crumpling as they went, bit deeply into her side, a chaos of tearing, rending metal: the stopping power of 10,000 tons deadweight travelling at 15 knots is fantastic. The wound was mortal, and the *Planter*'s own momentum, carrying her past, wrenched her free from the lethal bows, opening the wound to the sea and hastening her own end. Almost at once she began to fill, to list heavily to starboard. The *Adventurer*, her engine stopped, lay almost motionless alongside the sinking ship, slightly down by the head.

The rest of the convoy cleared the drifting vessels, steadied west by north. Far out on the starboard hand, Commander Orr, in the *Sirrus*, clawed his damaged destroyer round in a violent turn, headed back towards the crippled freighters. He was recalled by the flagship. Tyndall was under no illusions. The *Adventurer*, he knew, might remain there all day—it was obvious that the *Planter* would be gone in a matter of minutes—but the enemy would be there, waiting to the last possible second before dark in the hope that some rescue destroyer would heave to alongside the *Adventurer*.

In that respect, Tyndall was right. The *Adventurer* was torpedoed just before sunset. Three-quarters of the ship's company escaped in lifeboats, along with twenty survivors picked up from the *Planter*. A month later the frigate *Esher* found them, in three lifeboats tied line ahead, off the bitter, iron coast of Bear Island, heading steadily north. The captain was still upright, sitting in the stern-sheets, empty eye-sockets searching for some lost horizon, a withered claw locked to the tiller. The rest were sitting or lying about the boats, one actually standing, his arm cradled around the mast, and all with shrunken sun-blackened lips drawn back in hideous mirth. The log book lay beside the captain, empty: all had frozen to death on that first night.

But in the major respect, that of anticipating enemy disposition, the admiral was utterly wrong. The tactic of swinging an entire convoy into the face of a torpedo attack was well known to the enemy. The submarine that had torpedoed the *Cochella* had been the last, not the first, of the pack. The others had lain well to the west of the track of FR 77—clear beyond the reach of Asdic. And when the convoy wheeled to the west, the U-boats lined up leisurely firing tracks as the ships steamed up to cross their bows at right angles. The sea was as calm as a millpond, the snow-squalls of the night had passed away. Far to the southeast a brilliant sun was shouldering itself clear of the horizon, its level rays striking a great band of silver across the Arctic, high-lighting the ships, shrouded white in snow, against the darker sea and sky beyond. The conditions were ideal for a massacre.

And a massacre there must inevitably have been but for the warning that came almost too late. A warning given neither by radar nor Asdic, but simply by the keen eyes of an eighteen-year-old ordinary seaman.

"Captain, sir! Captain, sir!" Young Chrysler was shouting in wild excitement, his eyes glued to the powerful binoculars clamped on the port searchlight control position. "There's something flashing to the south, sir! It flashed twice—there it goes again! Port 50, sir—no, port 60. . . ."

Every pair of glasses on the bridge swung round on the given bearing. There was nothing to be seen. Tyndall shrugged his shoulders.

"There they go again!" Chrysler screamed. "Two flashes—no, *three* flashes!"

Tyndall gazed at Chrysler and abruptly made up his mind. "Hard aport, Captain. Bentley—the signal!"

Slowly, on the unsupported word of an eighteen-year-old, FR 77 came round to the south, slowly, just too slowly. Suddenly, the sea was alive with running torpedoes—Vallery counted thirty in as many seconds. They were running shallow and their bubbling trails rose swiftly to the surface and lay there milkily on the glassy sea. Parallel in the centre, they fanned out to the east and west to embrace the entire convoy.

It was a fantastic sight. In a moment the confusion was complete. There was no time for signals. It was every ship for itself, but escape for all was impossible: the torpedoes were far too closely bunched. The cruiser *Stirling* was the first casualty. Just when she seemed to have cleared all danger, she lurched under some unseen hammerblow, slewed round crazily and steamed away to the east, smoke hanging heavily over her poop. The *Ulysses*, brilliantly handled, heeled over on maximum rudder and slid down an impossibly narrow lane between four torpedoes, two of them racing by a bare boat's length from either side: she was still a lucky ship. The destroyers, fast, highly man-oeuvrable, impeccably handled, weaved their way to safety and headed south under maximum power.

The merchant ships, big, clumsy, relatively slow, were less fortunate. Two ships in the port line, a tanker and a freighter, were struck: miraculously, both kept on coming. Not so the big freighter im-mediately behind them, her holds and decks crammed with tanks. She was torpedoed three times: ripped from stern to stem, she sank quickly, dragged down by the sheer weight of metal. No one below decks had the slightest chance of escaping.

A merchantman in the centre line, the *Belle Isle*, was torpedoed amidships. There were two separate explosions and she was instantly on fire. Within seconds, the list to port was pronounced: gradually her rails dipped under, the outslung lifeboats almost touching the sur-face of the sea. Men were seen sliding down the sheering decks to-wards the nearest lifeboat. Desperately they hacked at securing ropes, piled in, seized the oars and pulled frantically away.

Half a dozen powerful strokes had them clear beyond their ship's counter: two more took them straight under the swinging bows of the *Walter A. Baddeley*, her companion tank-carrier in the starboard line. The little boat splintered like a matchwood toy, catapulting screaming men into the icy sea. They were still struggling, almost abreast the poop, when the torpedoes struck the *Baddeley*, close together and simul-taneously, just for'ard of the rudder.

The *Walter A. Baddeley*'s stern was almost completely blown off. Then, in quick succession from deep inside the hull, came a muffled explosion, the frightening roar of escaping high-pressure steam and the thunderous crash of massive boilers rending away from their stools as the ship upended. Almost immediately the shattered stern plunged under the sea, the bows rearing high against the blue of the sky, buoyed up by half a million cubic feet of trapped air. Two 30-ton tanks, broken loose from their foredeck lashings, smashed down on the bridge structure, awash in the sea. She and the *Belle Isle* were both gone inside a minute.

Less than two miles away, the destroyers, *Sirrus*, *Vectra* and *Viking*, dazzling white in the morning sun, were weaving an intricate pattern over the sea, depth-charges cascading from either side of their poop-decks. The cruiser *Stirling*, more than a mile astern, was coming round fast, her speed at least twenty knots. She was under control now, and on emergency steering.

The *Ulysses* found nothing to the north. The U-boat that had sunk the *Cochella* had wisely decamped. While they were quartering the area, they heard the sound of gunfire, saw the smoke erupting from the *Sirrus*'s 4.7s. The *Vectra* and *Viking* had damaged, probably destroyed a U-boat, and *Sirrus* had sunk a surfaced boat.

"Carrington!" Tyndall was curt, impatient.

"Sir!" the first lieutenant was his invariable self, freshly shaven, alert, unshadowed by fatigue. He hadn't slept for three days.

"What do you make of that?" Tyndall pointed to the northwest. Woolly grey clouds were blotting out the horizon; before them the sea dusked to indigo under wandering catspaws from the north.

"It's fog, sir."

"Fair enough." Tyndall grunted. "Let's get the hell out of it. Bentley —signal the destroyers: 'Break off engagement. Rejoin convoy.' "

Within the hour, merchant ships and escorts were on station again, on a northeast course at first to clear any further packs on latitude 70. To the southeast, the sun was still bright: but the first writhing tendrils of the mist were already swirling round the convoy. Speed had been reduced to six knots. All ships were streaming fog-buoys.

Tyndall climbed stiffly from his chair as the stand-down sounded. He passed through the gate, stopped in the passage outside. He laid a gloved hand on Chrysler's shoulder.

"Just wanted a squint at these eyes of yours, laddie," he smiled. "We owe them a lot. Thank you very much—we will not forget." He looked a long time into the young embarrassed face.

"How old are you, Chrysler?" he asked abruptly.

"Eighteen, sir . . . in two days' time." The soft West Country voice was almost defiant.

"He'll be eighteen—in two days' time!" Tyndall repeated slowly to himself. He walked wearily aft to the captain's shelter, and sagged down in a chair. "Ten green bottles, hanging on a wall," he murmured.

"I beg your pardon, sir?" Vallery propped himself up on the settee. The plasma transfusion seemed to have helped him.

"Thirty-two ships in all," Tyndall said softly. "And now there are seventeen—and three of those damaged. I'm counting the *Tennessee Adventurer* as a dead duck." He swore savagely. "Rear Admiral Tyndall, master strategist . . . alters convoy course to run smack into a heavy cruiser, alters it again to run straight into the biggest wolfpack I've ever known—and just where the Admiralty said they would be."

He rose heavily to his feet. The light of the single lamp caught his face. Vallery was shocked at the change.

"Where to, now, sir?" he asked.

"The bridge. No, no, stay where you are, Dick." He tried to smile. "Leave me in peace while I ponder my next miscalculation."

He stopped dead as he heard the unmistakable whistle of shells close above, heard the emergency action stations signal screaming. He turned his head slowly. "It looks as if I've already made it."

THE FOG, TYNDALL SAW, was all around them now. He hurried through the gate, Vallery close behind him.

"What is it, Commander Turner?" the admiral demanded. "Who fired? Where did it come from?"

"I don't know, sir. Shells came from astern. But I've a damned good idea who it is. Our friend of last night is back again."

Tyndall swore and jumped for the radar handset. "Bowden, what the devil are you doing down there? Asleep, or what? We are being attacked, Lieutenant Bowden. By a surface craft." He ducked as another salvo screamed overhead and crashed into the water less than half a mile ahead, then straightened quickly. "He's got our range, and got it accurately. In God's name, Bowden, where is he?"

"Sorry, sir." Bowden was cool, unruffled. "We can't seem to pick him up. We still have the *Adventurer* on our screens, and there appears to be a very slight distortion on his bearing, sir . . . I suggest the enemy ship is screened by the *Adventurer*, or if she's closer, is on the *Adventurer*'s direct bearing."

Tyndall turned to Vallery. "Does Bowden really expect me to believe that yarn?" he asked angrily. "A million to one coincidence like that—an enemy ship accidentally choosing the only possible course to screen her from our radar? Fantastic!"

Vallery answered quietly. "The U-pack would have radioed her, given our bearing and course. The rest was easy."

"He's firing by radar, sir," Bowden went on. "He must be. He's also tracking by radar, which is why he's keeping himself in line with our bearing on the *Adventurer*. And he's extremely accurate . . . I'm afraid, Admiral, that his radar is at least as good as ours." The speaker clicked off.

Radar! Of course, that was it! Tyndall shook his head in an attempt to clear a woolly, exhausted mind. Hell, a six-year-old could have seen that. . . . Radar—and as good as the *Ulysses*'s. It was now painfully clear. And everybody had believed that the *Ulysses* was the only efficient radar ship in the world.

Last night, for instance, when the *Ulysses* had been laying a false trail to the east, the German cruiser had obligingly tagged behind, firing wildly each time the *Ulysses* disappeared behind a smoke-screen. Had done so to conceal the efficiency of her radar, to conceal the fact that, during the first half-hour at least, she must have been tracking the escaping convoy as it disappeared to the NNW—a process made all the easier because he, Tyndall, had expressly forbidden the use of the zigzag.

And then, when the *Ulysses* had so brilliantly circled, first to the south and then to the north again, the enemy must have had her constantly on his screen. And later, after his faked withdrawal to the southeast, he too had circled to the north again, picked up the British cruiser on the edge of his screen, worked out her intersection course as a cross check on the convoy's, and radioed ahead to the wolfpack, positioning them almost to the foot.

And now, finally, the enemy had opened fire at extreme range, but with extreme accuracy—an insulting give-away, now that it no longer mattered, to the fact that the firing was radar-controlled. Tyndall pounded his fist on the edge of the windscreen. God, what a fool he'd been.

"Captain Vallery?" His voice was a husky whisper. "Captain, this enemy cruiser must be destroyed. I propose to detach the escorts—including ourselves—and nail him. We—the *Stirling* and ourselves—will take him from the south, soak up his fire and radar. Orr and his death-or-glory boys will approach from the north."

"All the escorts," Vallery said blankly. "You propose to detach *all* the escorts? But—but—perhaps that's exactly what he wants. To pull us off, to leave the convoy uncovered."

"Well, what of it?" Tyndall demanded. "Who's going to find them in this lot?" He waved an arm at the rolling, twisting fog-banks. He felt desperately tired and confused. "Perhaps he's hoping to panic us into altering course—to the north, of course—where a U-pack *may* very well be."

"Possible, possible," Vallery conceded. "On the other hand, he may have gone a step farther. Maybe he wants us to be too clever for our own good. Perhaps he expects us to see the obvious, to avoid it, to continue on our present course—and so do exactly what he wants us to do. . . . He's no fool, sir—we know that now."

Tyndall appreciated dimly that he was at the limit. That aching, muzzy forehead where to think was to be a blind man wading through a sea of molasses. "It's no good guessing, Dick," he said heavily. "And we've got to do something. We'll leave the *Vectra* as a sop to our consciences. No more." He smiled wanly. "We must have at least two destroyers for the dirty work. Bentley—take this signal for WT. . . ."

Within ten minutes, the four warships, boring southeast through the impenetrable wall of fog, had halved the distance that lay between them and the enemy. The seconds ticked by, the *Ulysses* knifed her way through icy sea. Suddenly, the loudspeaker called.

"Enemy 180° turn. Heading southeast. Speed 28 knots."

"28 knots? He's on the run!" Tyndall seemed to have gained a fresh lease on life. "Captain, commence firing by radar. We have him, we have him. He's waited too long! We have him, Captain!"

Vallery shook his head doubtfully. "I don't know at all. Why did he wait so long? Why didn't he turn and run the minute we left the convoy?"

Tyndall growled and lapsed into silence as the *Ulysses* shuddered from the recoil of "A" turret. For a moment, the billowing fog on the fo'c'sle cleared, and they caught a glimpse of the *Sirrus*, dead on the beam, scything to the southeast at something better than 34 knots. The *Stirling* and *Viking* were still lost in the fog astern.

The twin 5.25s of "B" turret roared in deafening unison, flame and smoke lancing out through the fog. Simultaneously, a tremendous crash and explosion heaved up the duckboards beneath the feet of the men in the bridge, catapulting them all ways.

Gradually the smoke cleared away. Tyndall pulled himself to his feet: the explosion had blown him clean out of his chair into the centre of the compass platform. He shook his head, dazed, uncomprehending. . . . Suddenly he saw Carpenter rise up before him: the bandages were blown off his face, the gash received on the night of the great storm gaping wide again, his forehead masked with blood.

"What is it, Pilot?" Tyndall's voice was hoarse. "In God's name, what's happened? A breech explosion in 'B' turret?"

"No, sir." Carpenter drew his forearm across his eyes: the kapok sleeve came away covered in blood. "A direct hit, sir—smack in the superstructure."

"He's right, sir." Carrington was peering down over the windscreen. "And a heavy one. It's wrecked the for'ard pom-pom and there's a hole the size of a door just below us."

Tyndall scarcely heard the last words. He was kneeling over Vallery, who lay crumpled against the gate, barely conscious.

"Get Brooks up here, Chrysler—the surgeon commander, I mean!" Tyndall shouted. "At once!"

"WT—bridge. WT—bridge. Please acknowledge. Please acknowledge." The loudspeaker's voice was hurried, anxious even in its metallic anonymity. "We have been hit aft. Damage control reports coding room destroyed. Number 6 and 7 radar offices destroyed. Canteen wrecked. After control tower severely damaged."

Tyndall swore, pulled off his gloves. Carefully he pillowed Vallery's head on the gloves, rose to his feet, and made for the after end of the bridge at a stumbling run. At first he could see nothing, not even the after funnel and mainmast. The fog was too dense. Then, suddenly, an icy catspaw cleared away the mist.

The after superstructure had disappeared. In its place was a crazy mass of jumbled twisted steel, with "X" turret, normally invisible from the bridge, showing up clearly beyond, apparently unharmed. But the rest was gone—radar offices, coding room, police office, canteen, probably most of the after galley. Nobody could have survived there. Miraculously, the truncated mainmast still stood, but immediately aft of it, perched crazily on top of this devil's scrap-heap, the after tower, lay over at a grotesque angle, its rangefinder gone. . . . A lucky ship, they called the *Ulysses*. Twenty months on the worst run and in the worst waters in the world and virtually unscathed. . . . But Tyndall had always known that some time, some place, her luck would run out.

He heard hurried steps clattering up the steel laddder. It was Leading Signalman Davies, from the flag deck. "The fighter direction room, sir!" His eyes were dark with horror. "The shell exploded in there. It's—it's just gone, sir. And the plot above . . . They—well, they never had a chance."

He stopped abruptly as the high-pitched scream and impact explosion of high explosive shells blurred into shattering cacophony, appallingly close.

"My God!" Tyndall whispered. His voice choked off in an agonized grunt, arms flailing wildly, as Davies was suddenly catapulted into him with irresistible force.

He surfaced slowly from unconsciousness.

"Are you all right, sir? Don't move. We'll soon have you out of this!" The voice, deep, authoritative, boomed directly above the admiral's head. His eyelids flickered and were open. Barely a foot above him were the lean, piratical features of the commander, who was kneeling anxiously at his side.

"Turner!" Tyndall clutched gratefully at the reassuring solidity of the commander's arm. "Thank God! . . . What in the name of heaven is that?"

Close above Turner's head, angling for'ard and upward to port, a great white tree-trunk stretched as far as he could see in either direction.

"The foremast, sir," Turner explained. "It was sheared clean off by that last shell, just above the lower yardarm. The back blast flung it onto the bridge. Took most of the AA tower with it, I'm afraid—and caved in the main tower. . . . Davies saw it coming—"

"Davies!" Tyndall's dazed mind had forgotten all about him. "Of course!" He saw a huddled figure at his feet, the great weight of the mast lying across its back. "For God's sake, Commander, get him out of that!"

"Just lie down, sir, till Brooks gets here. Davies is all right." Turner's voice was surprisingly gentle. "Really he is, sir. He's all right. Davies doesn't feel a thing. Not any more."

The admiral closed his eyes in shock.

His eyes were still shut when Brooks appeared, doubly welcome in his confidence and competence. Within seconds, almost, the admiral was on his feet, shocked, badly bruised, but otherwise unharmed. Doggedly, and in open defiance of Brooks, Tyndall demanded that he be assisted back to the bridge. His eyes lit up momentarily as he saw Vallery standing shakily on his feet, a white towel to his mouth. But he said nothing. His head bowed, he hoisted himself painfully into his chair.

Vallery glanced at the silent admiral, then turned to gaze vaguely at the wrecked shambles of his bridge. What damnably accurate gunnery! He wondered if the *Ulysses* had registered any hits. Probably not. And now, of course, the *Ulysses*, still racing southeast through the fog, was completely blind, both radar eyes gone, victims to the weather and the German guns. Worse still, all the fire control towers were damaged beyond repair. If this goes on, he thought wryly, all we'll need is a set of grappling irons and a supply of cutlasses. In terms of modern naval gunnery, even although her main armament was intact, the *Ulysses* was hopelessly crippled.

"WT—bridge. WT—bridge." Everyone on the bridge jumped, swung round in nerve-jangled startlement. "Signal from *Vectra*. Signal reads: 'Contacts, contacts, 5, repeat 5. Heavy concentration of U-boats ahead and abeam of convoy. Am in close contact. Depth-charging. Depth-charging. One vessel torpedoed, sinking. Tanker torpedoed, damaged, still afloat, under command. Please advise. Please assist. Urgent! Urgent!' "

Every eye on the bridge swung back to Tyndall. His, they knew, had been the responsibility, his the decision—taken alone, against the advice of his senior officer—to leave the convoy almost unguarded. Impersonally, Vallery admired the baiting and springing of the trap. How would poor Giles react to this, the culmination of a series of disastrous miscalculations—miscalculations for which, in all fairness, he could not justly be blamed. . . . But for which he would be held accountable.

Tyndall climbed down from his chair. His movements were stiff, he limped heavily. But there was about him a sort of dignity.

"I am not well," he said. "I am going below."

Chrysler held open the gate, caught Tyndall as he stumbled on the step. He glanced back over his shoulder, a quick, pleading look, caught and understood Vallery's compassionate nod. Side by side, the old and the young, they moved slowly aft.

The shattered bridge curiously empty now, Vallery felt strangely alone. Giles, the cheerful, indestructible Giles was gone. He turned to Bentley. "Three signals, Chief. First to *Vectra*. 'Steer 360°. Do not disperse. Repeat, do not disperse. Am coming to your assistance.'" He paused, then went on: "Sign it, 'Admiral, 14 ACS.' Got it? . . . Right. No time to code it. Plain language.

"Second: To *Stirling*, *Sirrus* and *Viking*. 'Abandon pursuit immediate. Course northeast. Maximum speed.' Plain language also." He turned to the Kapok Kid. "How's your forehead, Pilot? Can you carry on?"

"Of course, sir."

"Thank you, boy. You heard me? Convoy re-routed north—say in a few minutes' time, at 1015, six knots. Give me an intersection course as soon as possible."

"Third signal, Bentley: To *Stirling, Sirrus* and *Viking*: 'Radar out of action. Cannot pick you up on screen. Stream fog-buoys. Siren at two-minute intervals.' Have that message coded. All acknowledgments to the bridge at once. Commander!"

"Sir?" Turner was at his elbow.

"It's my guess the pack will have gone before we get there. Hands to defence stations. Who'll be off watch?"

"Lord only knows," said Turner frankly. "Let's call it port."

Vallery smiled faintly. "Port it is. Organize two parties. First of port to clear away all loose wreckage. Second of port as burial party. Nicholls in charge. All bodies recovered to be laid out in the canteen when it's clear . . . Perhaps you could give me a full report of casualties and damage inside the hour?"

"Long before that, sir. . . . Could I have a word with you in private?"

They walked aft. Turner unbuttoned his coat, his hand struggling

into the depths of a hip-pocket. He dragged out a flat half-bottle, held it up to the light. "Thank the Lord for that!" he said piously. "I was afraid it got smashed when I fell . . . Rum, sir. Neat. I know you hate the stuff, but never mind, come on, you need this!"

Vallery's brows came down in a straight line.

"Rum. Look here, Commander, do you—"

"To hell with regulations, sir!" Turner interrupted rudely. "Take it —you need it badly! You've been hurt, you've lost a lot more blood and you're almost frozen to death." He thrust the bottle into Vallery's hands. "Face facts. We need you—more than ever now—and you're almost dead on your feet—and I mean dead on your feet," he added brutally. "This might keep you going a few more hours."

"You put things so nicely," Vallery murmured. "Very well. Against my better judgment. . . ." He paused. "And you give me an idea, Commander. Have the bosun break out the rum. Pipe 'Up spirits'. Double ration to each man. They, too, are going to need it." He swallowed, and grimaced. "Especially," he added soberly, "the burial party."

THE LIGHT CLICKED on in the darkening surgery. Nicholls woke with a start. Four o'clock! Had it been that long since the burial party? God, it was bitterly cold!

Brooks was standing by the door, fumbling with a packet of cigarettes. "Hello, there, Johnny! Sorry to waken you, but the skipper wants you. Plenty of time, though." He lit his cigarette. "Have you any of that poison left? . . . I am referring to that bottle of bootleg hooch from the Isle of Mull."

"Coll," Nicholls corrected, and duly crossed to the poison cupboard, and unscrewed the top off the appropriate bottle.

Brooks sighed in bliss as he felt the grateful warmth sinking down inside him. "Thank you, my boy. Thank you. You have the makings of a first-class doctor."

"You think so, sir? I don't. Not any longer. Not after today." He winced, remembering. "Forty-four of them, sir, over the side in ten minutes, one after the other, like—like so many sacks of rubbish . . . I'd better screen that porthole."

He walked across the surgery. Low on the horizon, through the thinly-falling snow, he caught intermittent sight of an evening star. That meant that the fog was gone—the fog that had saved the convoy, had hidden them from the U-boats when the convoy had turned so sharply to the north. He could see the destroyer *Vectra*, her depth-charge racks empty and nothing to show for it. He could see the *Vytura*, the damaged tanker, close by, almost awash in the water, hanging grimly on to the convoy. . . . He slammed the scuttle, then swung round abruptly.

"Why the hell don't we turn back?" he burst out. "Who does the old man think he's kidding—us or the Germans? No air cover, no radar, not the faintest chance of help! The Germans have us pinned down to an inch now—and it'll be easier still for them as we go on. And there's a thousand miles to go!" His voice rose. "This is just murder —or suicide." He broke off, face white and strained.

Brooks coughed, looked meaningfully at the "poison" bottle. Nicholls filled the glasses, brought them back. Brooks lifted his glass, inspected the contents lovingly. "To our enemies, Johnny: their downfall and confusion." He drained the glass at a gulp, set it down, looked at Nicholls for a long moment.

"I think you should hear why Vallery doesn't turn back." He smiled wryly. "It's not because there are as many of these damned U-boats behind us as there are in front—which there undoubtedly are." He lit a fresh cigarette, went on quietly: "The captain radioed London. Gave it as his considered opinion that FR 77 would be a goner— 'annihilated' was the word he used—long before it reached the North Cape. He asked at least to be allowed to go north about, instead of east for the Cape. . . . The answer took four hours to come through." Brooks shrugged. "There's something big, something on a huge scale brewing up somewhere. It can only be some major invasion—this under your hat, Johnny?"

"Of course, sir!"

"What it is I haven't a clue. Maybe even the long-awaited Second Front. Anyway, the support of the Home Fleet seems to be regarded as vital to success. But the Home Fleet is tied up—by the *Tirpitz*. And so the orders have gone out—get the *Tirpitz*. Get it at all costs." Brooks smiled, and his face was very cold. "We're big fish, Johnny, we're important people. We're bait offered up for the biggest, juiciest prize in the world today. . . . The signal came from the First Sea Lord. The decision was taken at Cabinet level. We go on. We go east. . . ."

As the clamour of the dusk action stations' bugle died away, he added, "The skipper wants you. On the bridge, ten minutes after stations begin."

"What? On the bridge? What the hell for?"

"Your language is unbecoming to a junior officer," said Brooks solemnly. "Anyway," he continued briskly, "get up there. Captain's going to make a tour of the ship."

Nicholls was astounded. "During action stations? Leave the bridge? But he'll kill himself!"

"That's what I said," Brooks agreed wryly. "Anyway, I talked him into taking you with him. . . . Better not keep him waiting."

For Lieutenant Nicholls, the next two hours were purgatory. Two hours the captain took for his inspection, two hours of constant walking, of climbing over storm-sills and tangled wreckage of steel, of squeezing and twisting through impossibly narrow apertures, of climbing and descending a hundred ladders, two hours of exhausting torture in the bitter, heart-sapping cold of a sub-zero temperature. But it was a memory that was to stay with him always, that was never to return without filling him with warmth, with a strange and wonderful gratitude.

They started on the poop—Vallery, Nicholls and Chief Petty Officer Hartley—and wherever they went, Vallery left the men the better for his coming. In personal contact, he had some strange indefinable power that lifted men above themselves, that brought out in them something they had never known to exist. To see dull apathy and hopelessness slowly give way to resolution, albeit a kind of numbed and desperate resolve, was to see something that baffled the understanding. Physically and mentally, Nicholls knew, these men had long since passed the point of no return.

They came in due course to the engine and boiler rooms. In "A" boiler room, Nicholls insisted on Vallery's resting for some minutes. He was grey with pain and weakness, his breathing very distressed.

Then Nicholls caught sight of a burly, swarthy stoker, with bruised cheeks and the remnants of a black eye, stalking across the floor. He carried a canvas chair, set it down with a thump behind Vallery.

"A seat, sir," he growled.

"Thank you." Vallery lowered himself gratefully, then looked up in surprise. "Riley?" he murmured, then switched his glance to Hendry, the chief stoker. "Doing his duty with a minimum of grace, eh?"

Hendry stirred uncomfortably.

"He did it off his own bat, sir."

"I'm sorry," Vallery said sincerely. "Forgive me, Riley. Thank you very much." He leaned against the canvas back and closed his eyes in exhaustion. Nicholls bent over him.

"Look, sir," he urged quietly, "why not give it up? Frankly, sir, you're killing yourself. Can't we finish this some other time?"

"I'm afraid not, my boy. 'Some other time' will be too late." He rose painfully to his feet. "Ready, Hartley?" He stopped short, seeing a giant duffel-coated figure waiting at the foot of the ladder, the face below the hood dark and sombre. "Who's that?" he queried.

"It's Petersen, sir," Hartley said softly. "Riley's—er—lieutenant in the Scapa business. . . . Surgeon Commander's orders, sir. Petersen's going to give us a hand."

"Us? Me, you mean." There was no resentment in Vallery's voice. "Hartley, take my advice—never let yourself get into the hands of the doctors. . . . You think he's safe?" he added half-humorously.

"He'd probably kill the man who looked sideways at you," Hartley stated matter-of-factly. "He's a good man, sir. Simple, easily led—but good."

At the foot of the ladder, Vallery stopped, looked up at the giant towering six inches above him, into the grave, blue eyes below the flaxen hair.

"Hello, Petersen! Hartley tells me you're coming with us. Do you really want to? You don't have to, you know."

"Please, Captain." The speech was slow, the face curiously dignified in unhappiness. "I am very sorry for what has happened—"

"No, no!" Vallery was instantly contrite. "You misunderstand. It's a bitter night up top. But I would like it very much if you would come. Will you?"

Petersen's face brightened with pleasure. As the captain set foot on the first step, the giant arm came round him. From there they visited the torpedo room, then the boat-deck gun-sites.

Their tour finished at the capstan flat. They walked slowly round the heavy machinery in the middle for'ard past the battery room and sailmaker's shop, past the electrical workshop and cells to the locked door of the painter's shop, the most for'ard compartment in the ship.

Passing the cell door, Vallery casually flicked open the inspection port and glanced in. "What in the name of—Ralston! What on earth are you doing here?" he shouted. "In the cells—and at this time! Speak up, man!"

"I was locked up here, sir."

"When?"

"At 1030 this morning, sir."

"And by whom, may I inquire?"

"By the master-at-arms, sir."

"On what authority?" Vallery demanded furiously.

"On yours, sir."

"Mine?" Vallery was incredulous. "I didn't tell him to lock you up again!"

"You never told him not to," said Ralston evenly. Vallery winced: the oversight was his, and that hurt him badly.

"Where's your night action station?" he asked sharply.

"Port tubes, sir." That, Vallery realized, explained why only the starboard crew had been closed up.

"And why—why have you been left here during action stations? Don't you know it's forbidden, against all regulations?"

"Yes, sir. But does the master-at-arms know?" Ralston paused. "Or maybe he just forgot."

"Hartley! The master-at-arms here, immediately. See that he brings his keys!" He broke into a harsh bout of coughing, spat blood into his towel, looked at Ralston again.

"I'm sorry about this, my boy," he said. "Genuinely sorry—"

He stopped abruptly as a muffled roar crashed through the night, the pressure blast listing the *Ulysses* sharply to starboard. Vallery staggered and would have fallen but for Petersen's arm. He braced himself, looked at Nicholls in dismay. The sound was all too familiar.

Nicholls nodded slowly. "Afraid you're right, sir. Torpedo. Somebody's stopped a packet."

"Do you hear there!" The capstan flat speaker was hurried, loud. "Do you hear there! Captain on the bridge: urgent. Captain on the bridge: urgent. . . ."

FROM THE PORT LADDER leading up to the fo'c'sle deck, Captain Vallery saw the silhouette of a tanker deep in the water—and a great column of flame, hundreds of feet in height, streaking upwards from the heart of the dense mushroom of smoke that obscured the bows of the torpedoed ship. Even at the distance of half a mile, the roaring of the flames was almost intolerable. Vallery watched appalled. Behind him he could hear Nicholls swearing, softly, bitterly, continuously.

Vallery felt Petersen's hand on his arm. "Does the Captain wish to go up to the bridge?"

"In a moment, Petersen. Just hang on." His eyes swept the horizon. Funny, he thought, you can hardly see the tanker—the *Vytura*, it must be—she's shielded by that thick pall of smoke, probably; but the other ships in the convoy, white, ghost-like, sharply etched against the indigo blue of the sky, were bathed in that deadly glare. Even the stars had died.

"A tanker, isn't it, sir? Hadn't we better take shelter? Remember what happened to that other one!"

"When tankers go up, they go up, Nicholls." Vallery seemed curiously far away. "If they just burn, they may live where any other ship would sink. Tankers die hard, terribly hard, my boy."

"But—but she must have a hole the size of a house in her side!" Nicholls protested.

"No odds," Vallery replied. He seemed to be watching for something. "Tremendous reserve buoyancy in these ships. Maybe twenty-seven sealed tanks, not to mention coffer-dams, pump rooms, engine rooms . . ." He broke off suddenly, and when he spoke again, the lethargy of the voice was gone.

"I thought so! She's still under way, still under command! Good God, she must still be doing almost 15 knots! The bridge, quick!"

Vallery's feet barely touched the deck again till Petersen set him down carefully on the duckboards in front of the startled commander. Vallery grinned. "It's all right, Commander. This is Stoker Petersen. Over-enthusiastic, maybe a trifle apt to take orders too literally . . . But he was a godsend to me tonight . . . But never mind me." He jerked his thumb towards the tanker, blazing even more whitely now. "How about him?"

"Makes a bloody fine lighthouse for any German ship or plane that happens to be looking for us," Turner growled. "Might as well send a signal to Trondheim giving our lat. and long."

"Exactly," Vallery nodded. "Besides setting up some beautiful targets for the sub that's just got her."

"The *Viking*'s in contact right now, sitting over the top of him. . . . I sent her right away."

"Good man!" Vallery said warmly. He turned to look at the burning tanker, then looked back at Turner, his face set. "She'll have to go, Commander. It *is* the *Vytura*, isn't it?"

"That's her. Same one that caught it this morning."

"Who's the master?"

"Haven't the foggiest," Turner confessed.

"Never mind." Vallery was impatient. "There's no time. Bentley—to the master, *Vytura*: 'Please abandon ship immediately: we are going to sink you.'"

Suddenly Vallery stumbled, caught hold of Turner's arm.

"Sorry," he apologized. "I'm afraid my legs are going. Gone, rather." He smiled up wryly at the anxious faces.

"And no bloody wonder!" Turner swore. "I wouldn't treat a mad dog the way you treat yourself! Come on, sir. Admiral's chair for you—now. If you don't, I'll get Petersen to you."

Vallery meekly allowed himself to be helped into the chair and relaxed, feeling ghastly, his wasted body a sea of pain, and deadly cold. . . . but also proud and grateful—Turner had never even suggested that he go below.

He heard the gate crash behind him, the murmur of voices, then Turner was at his side.

"The master-at-arms, sir. Did you send for him?"

"I certainly did." Vallery twisted in his chair, his face grim. "Come here, Hastings!"

The master-at-arms stood at attention before him.

"Listen carefully." Vallery sighed deeply. "You will release Leading Seaman Ralston immediately. You will then hand over your duties, your papers and your keys to Regulating Petty Officer Perrat. Twice, now, you have overstepped the limits of your authority: that is insolence, but it can be overlooked. But you have also kept a man locked in cells during action stations. The prisoner would have died like a rat in a trap. You are no longer master-at-arms of the *Ulysses*. That is all."

For a couple of seconds Hastings stood rigidly in silence, then the iron discipline snapped. "Relieved of my duties? But, sir, you can't do that! You can't . . ."

He broke off in a gasp of pain as Turner's iron grip closed over his elbow. "Don't say 'can't' to the captain," the commander hissed in his ear. "You heard him? Get off the bridge!"

The gate clicked behind him. Carrington said, conversationally: "Somebody's using his head aboard the *Vytura*—fitted a red filter to his Aldis. Couldn't see it otherwise."

Immediately the tension eased. All eyes were on the winking red light, a hundred feet aft of the flames, and even then barely distinguishable.

"What does he say, Bentley?" Vallery asked quickly.

Bentley coughed apologetically. "Message reads: 'Are you hell. Try it and I will ram you. Engine intact. We can make it.'"

Vallery closed his eyes for a moment. When he looked up again, he had made his decision.

"Signal: 'You are endangering entire convoy. Abandon ship at once. Repeat, at once.'" He turned to the commander. "I take off my hat to him. How would *you* like to sit on top of enough fuel to blow you to kingdom come ... God, how I hate to have to threaten a man like that!"

He peered aft, searched briefly for the torpedo lieutenant. "Where's Marshall?"

"He's in sick-bay, sir," Turner replied. "I'll take over the bridge torpedo control. Used to be the worst torps. officer on the China station.... We'll have to take him from starboard, port control was smashed this morning—"

The WT loudspeaker clicked on. "WT—bridge. WT—bridge. Signal from *Viking*: 'Lost contact. Am continuing search.'"

"Lost contact!" Vallery exclaimed. Lost contact—the worst possible thing that could have happened! A U-boat out there, loose, unmarked, and the whole of FR 77 lit up like a fairground. He wheeled round. "Bentley! No reply from the *Vytura* yet?"

"No, sir." Bentley was as aware as the captain of the desperate need for speed. "Maybe his power's gone—no, no, no, there he is now, sir!"

"Captain, sir."

Vallery looked round. "Yes, Commander, what is it? Not more bad news, I hope?"

"'Fraid so, sir. Starboard tubes won't train—rack and turntable buckled—kaput!"

"Very well, then!" Vallery was impatient. "It'll have to be the port tubes. Fire by local control. After all, that's what torpedo crews are trained for. Get on to the port tubes—I assume the communication line there is still intact—tell them to stand by."

"Yes, sir." He nodded and was gone.

"Well, Bentley? What does he say?"

"Bit confused, sir," Bentley apologized. "Couldn't get it all. Says he's going to leave the convoy, proceed on his own. Something like that, sir."

Proceed on his own! That was no solution, Vallery knew. He might still burn for hours, a dead give-away, even on a different course. But to proceed on his own! An unprotected, crippled, blazing tanker—and a thousand miles to Murmansk, the worst thousand miles in all the world! Vallery closed his eyes. He felt sick to his heart. A man like that, and a ship like that—and he had to destroy them both!

Behind him Turner was shouting angrily into the telephone. "You'll damn well do what you're told, do you hear? Get them out immediately! Yes, I said 'immediately'!"

"What's the matter, Commander?"

"Of all the bloody insolence!" Turner snorted. "Telling *me* what to do!"

"Who?"

"The LTO on the tubes. Your friend Ralston!" said Turner wrathfully.

"Ralston! Of course!" Vallery remembered now. "He told me that was his night action stations. What's wrong?"

"What's wrong? Says he doesn't wish to do it, if you please. Blasted insubordination! I'm going down there to knock some sense into that mutinous young devil!" Turner was angrier than Vallery had ever seen him. "Can you get Carrington to man this phone, sir?"

"Yes, yes, of course!" Vallery himself had caught some of Turner's anger. "Off you go. Going in to attack in three or four minutes." He passed onto the compass platform, and peered over the windscreen. The *Vytura* was falling rapidly astern.

"They're clearing the davits, sir!" the Kapok Kid reported excitedly. "I think—yes, yes, I can see the boat coming down!"

"Thank God for that!" Vallery whispered. He felt as though he had been granted a new lease of life. "WT code signal to *Sirrus*," he ordered quietly. " 'Circle well astern. Pick up survivors from the

Vytura's lifeboat.'" He raised his voice. "Pilot! Slow ahead both!"

"Slow ahead both, sir!"

The *Ulysses* dropped slowly astern of the convoy. Soon, even the last ships in the lines were ahead of her, thrashing their way to the northeast. The snow was falling more thickly now, but still the ships were bathed in that savage glare, frighteningly vulnerable in their helplessness.

At the port torpedoes, Turner brought up short, seething with anger. The tubes were out, their mouths high-lighted by the great flames, pointing out over the rolling swell. Ralston was perched high on the unprotected control position above the central tube.

"Ralston! I want to speak to you!"

Ralston jumped on to the deck, and faced the commander.

"What the hell's the matter with you, Ralston?" Turner ground out. "Refusing to obey orders, is that it?"

"No, sir. That's not true."

"Not true! Then what's all this bloody claptrap about not wanting to man the tubes? Are you thinking of emulating Stoker Riley? Or have you just taken leave of your senses—if any?"

Ralston said nothing. The silence infuriated Turner. He grasped Ralston's duffel coat, and pulled the rating towards him. "I asked a question, Ralston. I haven't had an answer. I'm waiting. What *is* all this?"

"Nothing, sir." Distress in his eyes, perhaps, but no fear. "I—I just don't want to, sir. I hate to do it—to send one of our own ships to the bottom!"

"As it so happens she's endangering the entire convoy!" Turner's face was within inches of Ralston's. "You've got a job to do, orders to obey. Just get up there and obey them! Go on!" he roared, as Ralston hesitated. "Get up there!"

Ralston didn't move. "There are other LTOs, sir! Couldn't *they*—?"

"Let someone else do the dirty work, eh? That's what you mean, isn't it?" Turner was bitingly contemptuous. "Get them to do what you won't do yourself, you—you contemptible young bastard! Communications Number? Give me your set. I'll take over from the bridge." He watched Ralston climb slowly back up and sit hunched forward. "Number One? Commander speaking. All set here. Captain there?"

"Yes, sir. I'll call him."

Up on the bridge Carrington put down the phone, walked through the gate. "Captain, sir. Commander's on the—"

"Just a moment!" The voice stopped him. "Have a look, Number One. What do you think?" Vallery pointed towards the *Vytura*.

The lifeboat, dimly visible through the thickening snow, had slipped her falls while the *Vytura* was still under way. Crammed with men, she was dropping quickly astern under the great twisting column of flame —dropping far too quickly astern as the first lieutenant suddenly realized.

"She's picking up, sir. Under way, under command . . . The captain's stayed on board sir. What are you going to do?"

"God help me, I've no choice. Nothing from the *Viking*, nothing from the *Sirrus*, nothing from our Asdic—and that U-boat's still out there . . . Bentley!"

"Sir?"

"Signal the *Vytura*. 'Abandon ship. Torpedoing you in three minutes. Last signal.' Port 20, Pilot!"

"Port 20 it is, sir."

The *Vytura* was breaking off tangentially, heading north. Slowly, the *Ulysses* came round, almost paralleling her course, now a little astern of her.

"Half-ahead, Pilot!"

Vallery looked across to the *Vytura*. The red Aldis was winking again. He tried to read it, but it was too fast: or his eyes were too tired.

"Signal from the *Vytura*, sir. Message reads: 'Nuts to the Senior Service. Tell him I send all my love.'"

"All my love." Vallery shook his head in silent wonderment. "All my love! He's crazy! He must be. 'All my love', and I'm going to destroy him. . . . Number One!"

"Sir?"

"Tell the commander to stand by!" Vallery said huskily. "Ninety seconds. Pilot—starboard 10." He watched the *Vytura*, 50° off the port bow, drop steadily aft. Even at that distance, the blast of heat was barely tolerable—what in the name of heaven was it like on her bridge?

"Set course, Number One," he called. "Local control."

"Set course, local control." Carrington might have been on a peace-time exercise in the Solent.

Down on the torpedo flat Turner hung up the set, looked round. "You're on your own, Ralston ... Thirty seconds! All lined up?"

"Yes, sir. All lined up." Suddenly, Ralston swung round, in desperate final appeal. "For God's sake, sir! Is there no other—"

"Twenty seconds!" Turner said viciously. "Do you want a thousand lives on your lily-livered conscience? And if you miss ..."

Ralston swung slowly back. For a mere breath of time, his face was caught in the harsh glare of the *Vytura*: with sudden shock Turner saw that the eyes were masked with tears. The left sleeve came up to brush the eyes, then the right hand closed round the grip of "X" firing lever, and suddenly jerked back. Turner heard the click of the tripping lever, the muffled roar in the explosion chamber, the hiss of compressed air, and the torpedo was gone. The tubes shuddered again and the second torpedo was on its way.

For ten seconds Turner watched the arrowing wakes of bubbles vanish in the distance. A total of 1,500 lbs. of Amatol in these warheads—God help any poor bastard still aboard the *Vytura* ... The deck speaker clicked on.

"Do you hear there? Do you hear there? Take cover immediately! Take cover immediately!"

Turner saw that Ralston was still crouched in his seat. "Come down out of there, you young fool!" he shouted. "Want to be riddled when the *Vytura* goes up? Do you hear me? ... Ralston!"

"I'm all right, sir." Ralston's voice was muffled. He did not even trouble to turn his head.

Turner swore, leapt up on the tubes, dragged Ralston down to the deck and into shelter. Ralston offered no resistance: he seemed sunk in a vast apathy, an uncaring indifference.

Both torpedoes struck home. The end was swift, curiously unspectacular. Broken-backed, the *Vytura* simply collapsed in on her stricken mid-ships, lay wearily over on her side and was gone.

Three minutes later, Turner opened the door of the captain's shelter, pushed Ralston in before him.

"Here you are, sir," he said grimly. "Thought you might like to see what a conscientious objector looks like!"

"I certainly do!" Vallery turned a cold eye on the torpedo-man. "A fine job, Ralston, but it doesn't excuse your conduct. Just a minute, Commander." He turned back to the Kapok Kid. "Remember to signal the convoy commander in the morning, ask for the name of the master of the *Vytura*."

"He's dead. . . . You needn't trouble yourself!" said Ralston bitterly.

"You insolent young devil!" Turner was breathing heavily, his eyes dark with anger.

"You misunderstand me, sir." There was no anger. Ralston's voice was a fading murmur, they had to strain to catch his words. "The master of the *Vytura*—I can tell you his name. It's Ralston. Captain Michael Ralston. He was my father."

SATURDAY

DAWN FOUND THE CONVOY some three hundred and fifty miles north of the Arctic Circle, steaming due east along the 72nd parallel of latitude, halfway between Jan Mayen and the North Cape. Roughly six hundred nautical miles to go. Six hundred miles, forty hours, and the convoy—or what was left of it would be in the Kola Inlet, safely steaming up-river to Polyarnoe and Murmansk.

The fourteen remaining ships were scattered over three square miles of sea and rolling heavily in the deepening swell from the NNE: fourteen ships, for another, the *Washington State*, had gone in the night, nobody knew how. A sleepless night of never-ending alarms had emptied the last depth-charge rack in the convoy. There was not a single depth-charge left—not one. The fangs were drawn, the defences were down. It was only a matter of time before the wolfpacks discovered that they could strike at will.

With the dawn, of course, came dawn action stations, or what would have been dawn stations had the men not already been closed up for fifteen endless hours of intense cold and suffering, fifteen hours during which they had been sustained by cocoa and one bully-beef sandwich, thin-sliced and stale, for there had been no time to bake the previous day. But the alarm halfway through dawn stations was the last that morning.

Noon came, and the convoy, closed up in tight formation now, rolled eastwards in the blinding snow. Thirty-six hours to go, now, only thirty-six hours. And if this weather continued, the strong wind and blinding snow that made flying impossible, the near-zero visibility and heavy seas that would blind any periscope . . . there was always that chance. Only thirty-six hours.

Admiral Giles Tyndall died a few minutes after noon. Brooks, who had sat with him all morning, officially entered the cause of death as "shock and exposure". The truth was that Giles had died because he no longer wished to live. His professional reputation was gone: his faith, his confidence in himself were gone, and there was only remorse for the hundreds of men who had died. He died gladly.

He was buried at two o'clock, in the heart of a blizzard. The captain's voice, reading the burial service, was shredded away by snow and wind: the Union Flag on the tilted board was flapping emptily before the men knew his body was gone: the bugle notes were broken and fading: and then the men, two hundred of them at least, turned silently away and trudged back to their frozen mess-decks.

Barely half an hour later, the wind had eased, and though the sky was still dark and heavy with snow, it was clear that the deterioration in the weather had stopped. On the bridge, in the turrets, in the mess-decks, men avoided each other's eyes and said nothing.

Just before 1500, the destroyer *Vectra* picked up an Asdic contact. Vallery ordered her to investigate.

He was too late. The *Vectra* was still winking acknowledgment of the signal when the rumble of a heavy explosion reached the bridge of the *Ulysses*. The *Electra*, leading merchantman in the starboard line, was slowing up, coming to a powerless stop, already settling in the water on an even keel. Almost certainly, she had been holed in the engine room.

The Aldis on the *Sirrus* had begun to flash. Bentley read the message. "Commander Orr requests permission to go alongside, port side, take off survivors."

"Port, is it?" Turner nodded. "The sub's blind side. It's a fair chance, sir—in a calm sea. As it is . . ." He looked over at the *Sirrus*, rolling heavily in the beam sea, and shrugged. "Won't do her paintwork any good."

The *Vectra* was almost a mile distant, rolling one minute, pitching the next as she came round in a tight circle. She had found the killer— and her depth-charge racks were empty.

"Signal the *Sirrus*," Vallery ordered. " 'Go ahead: exercise extreme care.' " Faintly, his ear caught the faraway murmur of underwater explosions, all but inaudible against the wind. "What the devil's the *Vectra* doing?" he demanded. "And what's she using?"

"Scuttling charges—twenty-five pounders," Carrington said briefly.

A scuttling charge has less than a tenth part of the disruptive power of a depth-charge—but one lodged snugly in the conning-tower or exploding alongside a steering plane could be almost as lethal. Carrington had hardly finished speaking when a U-boat—the first the *Ulysses* had seen above water for almost six months—porpoised high above the surface of the sea, hung there for two or three seconds, then crashed down on even keel, wallowing wickedly in the troughs between the waves.

The dramatic abruptness of her appearance—one moment the empty sea, the next a U-boat rolling in full view of the entire convoy—took every ship by surprise, including the *Vectra*. She was caught on the wrong foot, moving away on the outer leg of a figure-of-eight turn. By the time she was round, her main armament coming to bear, the U-boat had disappeared slowly under the surface.

In spite of this, the *Vectra*'s 4.7s opened up, firing into the sea where the U-boat had submerged, but stopping almost immediately when two shells in succession had ricocheted off the water and whistled dangerously through the convoy. She steadied on course, raced over the position of the submerged U-boat and hurled more scuttling charges over the side.

Again the U-boat surfaced, even more violently than before, and this time, she was up to stay. Whatever captain and crew lacked, it wasn't courage. The hatch was open, the men were swarming over the side of the conning-tower to man the gun, in a token gesture of defiance against crushing odds.

The first two men over the side never reached the gun—towering waves washed them over the side and they were gone. But others flung themselves forward to take their place, frantically training their gun to bear on the onrushing bows of the *Vectra*. Incredibly their first shell smashed squarely into the bridge of the *Vectra*. The first shell and the last shell, for the *Vectra* had two Bolton-Paul Defiant night-fighter turrets bolted to her fo'c'sle, and these had opened up simultaneously, firing, between them, something like a fantastic three hundred shells every ten seconds.

It was impossible for a man to live on the exposed deck of that U-boat.

Afterwards, no one aboard the *Ulysses* could say when they first realized that the *Vectra*, pitching steeply through the heavy seas, was going to ram the U-boat. Perhaps her captain never intended to do so, or perhaps he changed his mind at the last second, for the *Vectra*, which had been arrowing in on the conning-tower, suddenly slewed sharply to starboard.

For an instant, it seemed that she might just clear the U-boat's bows, but the hope died the second it was born. Plunging heavily down the sheering side of a trough, the *Vectra*'s forefoot smashed down and through the hull of the submarine, some thirty feet aft of the bows, slicing through the toughened steel of the pressure hull as if it were cardboard. She was still driving down when two shattering explosions completely buried both vessels under a mushroom of boiling water. Some freak of chance must have triggered off the TNT in a warhead in one of the U-boat's tubes: and then the torpedoes in the storage racks behind and possibly the for'ard magazine of the *Vectra* had gone up in sympathetic detonation.

The great clouds of water fell back into the sea, and the *Vectra* and the U-boat came abruptly into view. The U-boat, deep in the water, seemed to end abruptly just for'ards of the gun platform; the *Vectra* looked as if some great knife had sheared her athwartships, just for'ard of the bridge. Her shattered hull lurched into the same trough as the U-boat, rolled heavily over on top of her, bridge and mast crushing the conning-tower of the submarine. And then the water closed over them and they were gone, locked together to the bottom of the sea.

The last ships in the convoy were two miles away now, and in the broken seas it was impossible to see whether there were any survivors. It did not seem likely. . . . The convoy steamed on, beating steadily east. All but two, that is—the *Electra* and the *Sirrus*.

The *Electra* lay beam on to the seas, rolling sluggishly, dead in the water. She now had a list of almost 15° to port. Her decks, fore and aft of the bridge, were lined with men waiting for the *Sirrus*, rolling up behind them, fine on the port quarter. She made two runs past in all —Orr had no intention of stopping alongside, of being trampled under by the 15,000-ton deadweight of a toppling freighter. On his first run he steamed slowly by at five knots, at a distance of twenty feet—the nearest he dared go with the set of the sea rolling both ships towards each other at the same instant.

As the *Sirrus*'s swinging bows slid up past the bridge of the *Electra*, the waiting men began to jump. They jumped as the *Sirrus*'s fo'c'sle reared up level with their deck, they jumped as it plunged down fifteen, twenty feet below. Some crashed onto the ice-coated deck below, fracturing legs and thighs. Some jumped and missed.

It was just then that it happened. Even Commander Orr's skill was helpless against two successive freak waves, twice the size of the others. The first flung the *Sirrus* close in to the *Electra*, then passing under the *Electra*, lurched her steeply to port as the second wave heeled the *Sirrus* far over to starboard. There was a grinding crash. The *Sirrus*'s guard-rails and upper side plates buckled and tore along a 150-foot length. Immediately, the telegraphs jangled, the water boiled whitely at the *Sirrus*'s stern, and then the destroyer was clear, sheering sharply away from the *Electra*.

In five minutes the *Sirrus* was round again. It was typical of Orr's ice-cold nerve and of the luck that never deserted him that he should choose this time to rub the *Sirrus*'s shattered starboard side along the length of the *Electra*—she was too low in the water now to fall on him— and that he should do so in a momentary spell of slack water. Willing hands caught men as they jumped. Thirty seconds and the destroyer was gone again and the decks of the *Electra* were deserted. Two minutes later and a muffled roar shook the sinking ship—her boilers going. She toppled slowly over, bottom and keel gleamed fractionally against the grey of sea and sky, and were gone. For a minute, great gouts of air rushed turbulently to the surface. By and by the bubbles grew smaller and smaller and then there were no more.

The *Sirrus* steadied on course, crowded decks throbbing as she began to pick up speed, to overtake the convoy. Convoy FR 77. The convoy the Royal Navy would always want to forget. Thirty-six ships had left Scapa and St. John's. Now there were twelve. And still almost thirty-two hours to the Kola Inlet.

The *Sirrus* was still a mile astern when her Aldis started flickering. Bentley took the message.

"Signal, sir. 'Have 25–30 injured men aboard. Three very serious cases, perhaps dying. Urgently require doctor.'"

"Acknowledge," Vallery said. He hesitated a moment, then: "My compliments to Surgeon Lieutenant Nicholls. Ask him to come to the bridge." He turned to the commander, grinning faintly. "I somehow don't see Brooks at his athletic best in a breeches buoy on a day like this. It's going to be quite a crossing." The *Sirrus* was rolling and crashing her way up from the west.

"It'll be no picnic," Turner agreed.

The gate creaked. Vallery acknowledged Nicholl's sketchy salute. "The *Sirrus* needs a doctor. How do you fancy it?"

Nicholls steadied himself against the canted bridge. Leave the *Ulysses*—suddenly, he hated the thought, was amazed at himself for his reaction. He, Johnny Nicholls—unique, among the officers anyway, in his thorough-going detestation of all things naval—to feel like that. Must be going soft in the head! And just as suddenly he knew why he wanted to stay. It was not a matter of pride or principle or sentiment: it was just that—well, just that he belonged. He couldn't put it more accurately than that.

"I don't fancy it at all," he said frankly. "But of course I'll go, sir. Right now?"

"As soon as you can get your stuff together."

"That's now. We have an emergency kit packed all the time." He cast a jaundiced eye over the heavy sea again. "What am I supposed to do, sir—jump?"

Turner clapped him on the back. "You haven't a thing to worry about," he boomed cheerfully, "you positively won't feel a thing— these, if I recall rightly, were your exact words to me when you extracted that old molar of mine two or three weeks back." He winced in painful recollection. "Breeches buoy, laddie, breeches buoy! It'll be like a ride in a Rolls! We're going to rig it now. Chrysler—ask Chief Petty Officer Hartley to come up to the bridge."

Chrysler had the top half of his face crushed into the rubber eyepiece of the powerful binoculars on the starboard searchlight control. He suddenly jerked back, his face alive with excitement. "Green one-double-oh!" he shouted. "Green one-double-oh! Aircraft. Just on the horizon!" He fairly flung himself back at his binoculars. "Four, seven —no, *ten!* Ten or more Condors!" he yelled.

"Signal to convoy," Vallery said rapidly. "Code H. Full ahead, Number One. Broadcaster: stand by all guns. Commander?"

"Sir?"

"Independent targets, independent fire all AA guns." Vallery beckoned to Nicholls. "Better get below, young man. Sorry your little trip's been postponed." As Nicholls walked off the bridge, he beckoned to the WT messenger, then turned to the Kapok Kid. "When was our last signal to the Admiralty, Pilot? Have a squint at the log."

"Noon yesterday," said the Kapok Kid readily.

"Thank you." He looked at Turner. "No point in radio silence now, Commander?"

Turner shook his head.

"Take this message," Vallery said quickly. " 'To DNO, London. . . . How are our friends doing, Commander?"

"Circling well to the west, sir. Usual high altitude gambit from the stern, I suppose," he added morosely. "Still," he brightened, "cloud level's barely a thousand feet."

Vallery nodded. " 'FR 77. 1600. 72.20, 13.40. Steady on 090. Force 9, north, heavy swell: Situation desperate. Deeply regret Admiral Tyndall died 1200 today. Tanker *Vytura* torpedoed last night, sunk by self. *Washington State* sunk 0145 today. *Vectra* sunk 1515, collision U-boat. *Electra* sunk 1530. Am being heavily attacked by twelve, minimum twelve, Focke-Wulf 200s. Imperative send help. Air cover essential. Advise immediately.' Get that off at once, will you?"

"Your nose, sir!" Turner said sharply.

"Thank you." Vallery rubbed the frostbite, dead white in the haggard grey and blue of his face, gave up after a few seconds. "My God, it's bitter, Commander!" he murmured quietly.

Shivering, he pulled himself to his feet, swept his glasses over FR 77. Code H was being obeyed. The ships were scattered over the sea apparently at random, broken out from the two lines ahead which would have made things far too simple for bomb-aimers in aircraft attacking from astern. They would have to aim now for individual targets. Vallery swivelled his glasses to the west.

There was no mistaking them now, he thought—they were Condors, all right. Almost dead astern now, massive wing-tips dipping, the big four-engined planes banked ponderously to starboard, then straightened on a 180° overtaking course. And they were climbing.

Two things were suddenly clear to Vallery. They had known where to find FR 77. For a certainty, some submarine had located them earlier on, given their position and course; at any distance at all, their chance of seeing a periscope in that heavy sea had been remote. The Focke-Wulfs were now climbing to gain the low cloud. They would break cover only seconds before it was time to bomb.

Even as he watched, the last of the labouring Condors climbed through the low ceiling, was completely lost to sight. Vallery lowered his binoculars.

"Bentley! Code R. Immediate."

The flags fluttered up. And, like toy marionettes under the hand of a master puppeteer, the bows of every ship in the convoy began to swing round again—those to the port of the *Ulysses* to the north, those to the starboard to the south. When the Condors broke through—two minutes, at the most, Vallery reckoned—they would find beneath them only the empty sea. Empty, that is, except for the *Ulysses* and the *Stirling*, ships admirably equipped to take care of themselves. And then the Condors would find themselves under heavy cross-fire from the merchant ships and destroyers, and too late—at that low altitude—to alter course for fore-and-aft bombing runs on the freighters. As a defensive tactic, it was little enough, but the best he could do in the circumstances.

Two minutes passed, and still no sign of the Condors. "Anybody seen anything?" Vallery asked anxiously. His eyes never left that patch of cloud astern.

Three minutes. Three and a half. Four.

"Eyes skinned, everyone!" Turner boomed. "Fourteen days' leave to the first man to sight a Condor! They're up there, somewhere—"

The thudding of the fo'c'sle Oerlikons had him whirling round and plunging for the broadcast transmitter in one galvanic movement. But even then he was too late. The Condors—the first three in line ahead—were already through the cloud, five hundred feet up and barely half a mile away—dead ahead. *Ahead.* The bombers must have bypassed the convoy as soon as they reached the clouds, then turned back, completely fooling them . . . Six seconds—six seconds is time and to spare for even a heavy bomber to come less than half a mile in a shallow dive. There was barely time for realization, for the first bitter welling of mortification and chagrin when the Condors were on them.

It was almost dusk now. The leading Condor levelled out about three hundred feet, its medium 250-kilo bombs momentarily paralleling its line of flight, then arching down lazily towards the *Ulysses* while the plane pulled up and away.

The bombs missed by about thirty feet, exploding on contact with the water just abaft the bridge. Waterspouts, twenty feet in diameter at their bases, streaked up whitely into the twilight, then collapsed in drenching cascades on the bridge and boat-deck aft, soaking every gunner on the pom-pom and in the open Oerlikon cockpits. The temperature stood at 2° above zero—30° of fros

More dangerously, the blinding sheets of water completely unsighted the gunners. The next Condor pressed home its attack against a minimum of resistance, but the pilot overshot. The bombs fell into the sea directly astern, and the *Ulysses* steamed on, apparently unharmed.

Then, ironically, she brought disaster on herself. Good shooting by her for'ard AA guns sheared away the starboard wing of the third Condor. For a fraction of a second it held on course, then abruptly the nose tipped over and the giant plane screamed down in an almost vertical dive, straight for the deck of the *Ulysses*.

There was no time to take avoiding action—the *Ulysses* was already doing upwards of thirty knots. A cluster of jettisoned bombs crashed into the fo'c'sle, exploding in the flat below, heaving up the deck in a tangled wreckage of broken steel. One second later, with a tremendous roar and in a blinding sheet of petrol flame, the Condor itself, at a speed of upwards of three hundred mph, crashed squarely into the side of "Y" turret.

Incredibly, that was the last attack by the German bombers. "Y" turret was gone, "X" turret, still magically undamaged, was half-buried under the splintered wreckage of the Condor, blinded by the smoke and leaping flame. The boat-deck Oerlikons, too, had fallen silent. The gunners, half-drowned under the deluge of less than a minute ago, were being frantically dragged from their cockpits and rushed below, thrust into the galley passage to thaw, literally to thaw.

The remaining Condors pulled away, unhurt, to the southeast.

Vallery had plenty to worry about. The *Ulysses* was heavily on fire aft—a deck and mess-deck fire, admittedly, but potentially fatal for all that—"X" and "Y" magazines were directly below. Already, dozens of men from the damage control parties were running aft on the rolling ice-covered deck, unwinding the hose drums behind them, or carrying the big, red foam-extinguishers.

Gradually, the deck fire was brought under control—less through the efforts of the firefighters than the fact that there was little inflammable material left after the petrol had burnt off. Hoses and extinguishers were then directed through the great jagged rents in the fo'c'sle to the fires roaring in the mess-deck below, while two asbestos-suited figures struggled through the red-hot, jangled mass of smoking wreckage on the poop. Nicholls was one, Leading Telegraphist Brown, a specialist in rescue work, the other.

Picking his way gingerly, Brown climbed up to the entrance of "Y" turret, and stepped inside. Less than ten seconds later he appeared at the door again, on his knees and clutching desperately at the side for support. He was being violently sick into his oxygen mask.

Nicholls saw this, wasted time neither on "Y" turret nor on the charred skeletons still trapped in the incinerated fuselage of the Condor. He climbed quickly up the vertical steel ladders to "X" gun-deck, moved inside. Every man in the turret was stone dead, all sitting or lying at their stations, apparently unharmed and quite unmarked except for an occasional tiny trickle of blood from ear and mouth, trickles already coagulated in the intense cold—the speed of the *Ulysses* had carried the flames aft, away from the turret. The concussion must have been tremendous, death instantaneous. Heavily, Nicholls called the bridge.

Vallery himself took the message. "That was Nicholls," he said to Turner. Shock and sorrow showed clearly in every deeply-etched line on that pitiably wasted face. "'Y' turret is gone—no survivors. 'X' turret seems intact—but everyone inside is dead. Concussion, he says. Fires in the after mess-deck still not under control. . . ." He turned away. It was beginning to snow again and the darkness was falling all around them.

THE *Ulysses* rolled on through the Arctic twilight, a strange and stricken sight with both masts gone, with all boats and rafts gone, with shattered fore-and-aft superstructure, with a crazily tilted bridge and broken after-turret, half-buried in the skeleton of the Condor's fuselage. But despite all that, she still remained uncannily ghost-like and graceful, a creature of her own element, inevitably at home in the Arctic. And she still had sufficient of her guns—and her great engines.

Five minutes dragged interminably by, five minutes during which the sky grew steadily darker, during which reports from the poop showed that the firefighters were barely holding their own.

A bell shrilled through the silence and the gloom.

Turner took it. It was the after engine room. "It never rains, et cetera," Turner growled, replacing the phone. "Engine running rough, temperature hotting up. Distortion in inner starboard shaft. Dodson himself is in the shaft tunnel right now. Bent like a banana, he says. . . . The bearing will have to be lubricated by hand. Wants engine revs at a minimum or engine shut off altogether. They'll keep us posted."

"And no possibility of repair?" Vallery asked wryly.

"No, sir. None."

"Very well, then. Convoy speed. And Commander!"

"Sir?"

"Hands to stations all night. You needn't tell 'em so—but, well, I think it would be wise. I have a feeling—"

"What's that!" Turner shouted. "Look! What the hell's she doing?"

The last freighter in the starboard line was blazing away at some unseen target, the tracers lancing whitely through the twilight sky. The Condors, without a shadow of doubt. Condors that had outguessed them again, that gliding approach, throttles cut right back, muted roar of the engines drifting downwind, away from the convoy. Their timing, their judgment of distance, had been superb.

The freighter was bracketed twice, directly hit by at least seven bombs. As the bombs plummeted down on the next ship in line, the first freighter was already a broken-backed mass of licking, twisting flames, and was gone before the clamour of the last aero engine had died away in the distance.

Tactical surprise had been complete. One ship gone, a second slewing wildly to an uncontrolled stop, a third heavily damaged but still under command. Not one Condor had been lost.

Turner ordered the cease-fire. Then, as the last Oerlikon fell silent, he heard it again—the drone of the heavy aero engines. The Focke-Wulf, although lost in the low cloud, was making no attempt to conceal its presence. Clearly, it was circling almost directly above.

"What do you make of it, sir?" Turner asked.

"I don't know," Vallery said slowly. "I just don't know at all. No more attacks from the Condors, I'm sure of that. It's just that little bit too dark—and they know they won't catch us again. Tailing us, like as not."

"Tailing us! It'll be black as tar in half an hour!" Turner disagreed. "Psychological warfare, if you ask me."

"God knows," Vallery sighed wearily. "All I know is that I'd give all my chances, here and to come, for a couple of Corsairs, or radar, or fog, or another such night as we had in the Denmark Straits." He laughed shortly, broke down in a fit of coughing. "Did you hear me?" he whispered. "I never thought I'd ask for that again . . . How long since we left Scapa, Commander?"

Turner thought briefly. "Five—six days, sir."

"Six days!" He shook his head unbelievingly. "Six days. And—and thirteen ships—we have thirteen ships now."

"Twelve," Turner corrected quietly. "Another's almost gone. Seven freighters, the tanker and ourselves. Twelve . . . I wish they'd have a go at the old *Stirling* once in a while," he added morosely.

Vallery shivered in a sudden flurry of snow, then bent forward, head bowed against the bitter wind. Turner did what he had never done before. In the near-darkness he bent over the captain, pulled his face round gently and searched it with troubled eyes.

"Do me a favour, sir," he said quietly. "Go below. I can take care of things—and Carrington will be up before long. They're gaining control aft."

"No, not tonight." Vallery was smiling, but there was a curious finality about the voice. "And it's no good dispatching one of your minions to summon old Socrates to the bridge. Please, Commander. I want to stay here—I want to see things through tonight."

"Yes, yes, of course." Suddenly Turner no longer wished to argue. He turned away. "Chrysler! I'll give you just ten minutes to have a gallon of boiling coffee in the captain's shelter. . . . And you're going to go in there for half an hour," he said firmly, turning to Vallery, "and drink the damned stuff, or—or—"

"Delighted!" Vallery murmured. "Laced with your incomparable rum, of course?"

The WT broadcaster clicked on. "WT—bridge. WT—bridge. Signal from London for Captain. Decoding." After a few seconds the speaker boomed again. "'To Officer Commanding, 14 ACS, FR 77. Deeply distressed at news. Imperative maintain 090. Battle squadron steaming SSE at full speed on interception course. Rendezvous approx. 1400 tomorrow. Their Lordships expressly command best wishes Rear Admiral, repeat Rear Admiral Vallery. DNO, London.' ''

The speaker clicked off and there was only the pinging of the Asdic, the throbbing monotony of the prowling Condor's engines, the lingering memory of the gladness in the broadcaster's voice.

"Uncommon civil of their Lordships," murmured the Kapok Kid, rising to the occasion as usual. "Downright decent, one might almost say."

"Bloody long overdue," Turner growled. "Congratulations, sir," he added warmly. "Signs of grace at last along the banks of the Thames." A murmur of pleasure ran round the bridge.

"Thank you, thank you." Vallery was deeply touched. Promise of help at long, long last, a promise which might hold for every member of his crew the difference between life and death—and they could only think to rejoice in his promotion! Dead men's shoes, he thought, and thought of saying it, but dismissed the idea immediately: a rebuff, a graceless affront to such genuine pleasure.

"Thank you very much," he repeated. "But gentlemen, you appear to have missed the only item of news of any real significance—"

"Oh, no, we haven't," Turner growled. "Battle squadron—ha! Too bloody late as usual. Oh, to be sure, they'll be in at the death—or shortly afterwards, anyway." He broke off, looked up sharply into the thin, driving snow. "Hello! Charlie's getting damned nosy, don't you think?"

The roar of the Condor's engines increased every second as the bomber roared directly overhead, then died away to a steady drone as the plane circled round the convoy.

"WT to escorts!" Vallery called quickly. "Let him go—don't touch him! No starshells—nothing. He's trying to draw us out, to have us give away our position.... Oh, God! The fools, the fools! Too late, too late!"

A merchantman in the port line had opened up, firing blind, and the damage was done. With a suddenness that blocked thought, night was transformed into day. High above the *Ulysses* a parachute flare burst into intense life and drifted slowly seawards, towards a sea where every ship, in its glistening sheath of ice and snow, was silhouetted in dazzling whiteness against the inky backdrop of sea and sky.

"Get that flare!" Turner was barking into the transmitter as the Condor's engines faded. "All Oerlikons, all pom-poms, get that flare!" He replaced the transmitter. "Might as well throw empty beer bottles at it with the old girl rolling like this," he muttered. "Lord, gives you a funny feeling, waiting like this!"

"I know," the Kapok Kid supplied. Absently he brushed the snow off the quilted kapok, exposing the embroidered "J" on the breast pocket, while his eyes probed into the circle of darkness outside the pool of light. "I don't like this at all," he complained.

"Neither do I." Vallery was unhappy. "And I don't like Charlie's sudden disappearance either."

"He hasn't disappeared," Turner said grimly. "Listen!"

Less than a minute later the Condor roared overhead again, higher this time, lost in the clouds. Again he released a flare, and this time squarely over the heart of the convoy.

Again the roar of the engines died to a distant murmur, as the Condor overtook the convoy a second time. Glimpsed only momentarily between the scudding clouds, it flew wide, this time far out on the port hand, riding clear above the glare of the sinking flares. And, as it thundered by, more flares exploded into blazing life—four of them, just below cloud level, at four-second intervals. The northern horizon was alive with light that threw every tiny detail into the starkest relief. And to the south there was only the blackness: the rim of light stopped abruptly just beyond the starboard line of ships.

It was Turner who first appreciated the significance of this. He fairly flung himself at the broadcast transmitter.

" 'B' turret!" he roared. "Starshells to the south. Green 90, green 90. Urgent! Urgent! Starshells, green 90. Maximum elevation 10. Close settings. Fire when you are ready!" He looked quickly over his shoulder. "Pilot! Can you see—?"

" 'B' turret training, sir."

"Good, good!" He lifted the transmitter again. "All guns! All guns! Stand by to repel air attack from starboard. Probable bearing green 90. Hostiles probably torpedo-bombers." Even as he spoke, he caught sight of the intermittent flashing of the fighting lights on the lower yardarm: Vallery was sending out an emergency signal to the convoy.

"You're right, Commander," Vallery whispered. "You must be. Every ship silhouetted from the north—and a maximum run-in from the south under cover of darkness." He broke off suddenly as the shells exploded in great overlapping globes of light, two miles to the south. "You *are* right," he said gently. "Here they come."

The torpedo-bombers came from the south, wing-tip to wing-tip, flying in three waves with four or five planes in each wave. And as they dived it became obvious that they were concentrating on two ships—the *Stirling* and the *Ulysses*.

By this time, every gun in the convoy had opened up, the barrage was intense: the torpedo-bombers had to fly through a concentrated lethal curtain of steel and high explosive. The element of surprise was gone: the starshells of the *Ulysses* had gained a priceless twenty seconds.

Five bombers were coming at the *Ulysses* now, running in on firing tracks almost at wave-top height, when one of them straightened up a fraction too late, brushed against a wave-top, then catapulted crazily from wave-top to wave-top before disappearing in a trough.

A second later the leading plane in the middle disintegrated in a searing burst of flame—a direct hit on its torpedo warhead. A third plane sheered off violently to the left to avoid the hurtling debris, and its torpedo ran half a cable length behind the *Ulysses*, to spend itself in the empty sea beyond. The last two bombers came in together, wing-tip to wing-tip. The plane nearer the bows dropped its torpedo less than two hundred yards away. It hit the water obliquely, porpoised high into the air, then crashed back again steeply into the sea and passed under the *Ulysses*.

But seconds before that the last torpedo-bomber had come roaring in less than ten feet above the waves without releasing its torpedo. Suddenly the pilot had begun to climb: it was obvious that the torpedo release mechanism had jammed. The nose of the bomber smashed squarely into the for'ard funnel. There was an instantaneous sheet of petrol flame. A moment later the shattered bomber plunged into the sea a dozen yards away. The water had barely closed over it when a gigantic underwater explosion heeled the *Ulysses* far over to starboard, a vicious hammerblow that flung men off their feet and shattered the lighting system on the port side of the cruiser.

Commander Turner hoisted himself painfully to his feet. The shock of the detonating torpedo had not thrown him to the duckboards— he had hurled himself there five seconds previously as the guns of the other bomber raked the bridge from point-blank range.

His first thought was for Vallery, who was lying on his side, crumpled against the binnacle. Dry-mouthed, Turner turned him gently over. No sign of blood, no gaping wound—thank God for that! The Kapok Kid was standing above him.

"Get Brooks up here, Pilot," he said swiftly. "It's urgent!"

Unsteadily, the Kapok Kid crossed over the bridge. The communication rating was leaning over the gate, telephone in his hand.

"The sick-bay, quickly!" the Kapok Kid ordered. "Here, give me that phone!" Impatiently, he grabbed the telephone, then stiffened in horror as the man slipped gradually backwards over the top of the gate. Carpenter stared down at the dead man at his feet: there was a hole the size of his gloved fist between the shoulder-blades.

He lay alongside the Asdic cabinet, a cabinet now riddled with machine-gun bullets and shells. The Kapok Kid's first thought was the numbing appreciation that the set must be smashed beyond recovery, that their last defence against the U-boats was gone. Hard on the heels of that came the sickening realization that there had been an Asdic operator inside there. . . . He caught sight of Chrysler rising to his feet by the torpedo control. He, too, was staring at the Asdic cabinet, his face drained of expression. Before the Kapok Kid could speak, Chrysler lurched forward, battering frantically at the jammed door of the cabinet. Like a man in a dream, Carpenter heard him sobbing. . . . And then he remembered. The Asdic operator—his name was Chrysler too. The boy's older brother. Sick to his heart, the Kapok Kid lifted the phone again.

Turner pillowed Vallery's head, then moved across to the starboard corner of the compass platform. Bentley was sitting on the deck, his back wedged between two pipes, his head resting peacefully on his chest. Turner gazed down into the sightless eyes, the only recognizable feature of what had once been a human face. He swore, tried to prize the dead fingers locked round the hand-grip of the Aldis, then gave up. The barred beam shone eerily across the darkening bridge.

Turner found three other casualties. Five dead men for a three-second burst—a very fair return, he thought bitterly, as he returned to the compass platform.

The *Stirling*, a mile ahead, was slewing away to starboard, to the southeast, her for'ard superstructure enveloped in a writhing cocoon of white flame. It was learned later that she had been struck twice:

torpedoed in the for'ard boiler room, and seconds later a bomber had crashed into the side of her bridge, her torpedo still slung beneath the belly of her fuselage: almost certainly, in the light of the similar occurrence on the *Ulysses*, severe icing had jammed the release mechanism. Death must have been instantaneous for every man on the bridge and the decks below; among the dead were the captain, the first lieutenant and the navigator.

The last bomber was hardly lost in the darkness when Carrington, down in the poop, replaced the phone and turned to Chief Petty Officer Hartley.

"Think you can manage now, Chief? I'm wanted on the bridge."

"I think so, sir." Hartley, blackened and stained with smoke and extinguisher foam, passed his sleeve wearily across his face. "The worst is over. . . . Where's Lieutenant Carslake. Shouldn't he—?"

"Forget him," Carrington interrupted brusquely. "There's no need for us to beat about the bush, Chief. We're better without him." He walked quickly for'ard along the port alley, the pad of his rubber sea-boots completely soundless. He was passing the shattered canteen when he saw a tall shadowy figure standing in the gap between the snow-covered lip of the outer torpedo tube and the end stanchion of the guard-rails, trying to open a jammed extinguisher valve. A second later, he saw another blurred form detach itself stealthily from the shadows, creep stealthily up behind the man with the extinguisher, a heavy bludgeon of wood or metal held high above his head.

"Look out!" Carrington shouted. "Behind you!"

It was all over in two seconds—the sudden, flailing rush of the attacker, the crash as the intended victim, lightning fast in his reactions, dropped his extinguisher and fell crouched to his knees, the thin piercing scream of anger and terror as the attacker catapulted over the stooping body and through the gap between tubes and rails—the splash and then the silence.

Carrington ran up to the man on the deck, helped him to his feet. It was still light enough to see who it was—Ralston, the LTO. Carrington gripped his arms.

"Are you all right? Did he get you? Good God, who on earth—?"

"Thank you, sir." Ralston was breathing quickly. "That was too close! Thank you very much, sir."

"But who on earth—?" Carrington repeated in wonder.

"Never saw him, sir." Ralston was grim. "But I know who it was—Sub Lieutenant Carslake. He's been following me around all night, never let me out of his sight, not once. Now I know why."

The first lieutenant shook his head in slow disbelief. "I knew there was bad blood! But that it should come to this! What the captain will say to this I just—"

"Why tell him?" Ralston said indifferently. "Why tell anyone? Perhaps Carslake had relations. What good will it do to hurt them?" He laughed shortly. "Let them think he died a hero's death firefighting, fell over the side, anything." He looked down into the dark, rushing water, then shivered. "Let him go, sir, please. He's paid."

For a second Carrington looked at the tall boy before him. Then he clapped his arm, nodded and turned away.

COMMANDER TURNER lowered the binoculars to find Carrington standing on the bridge by his side. Just then Vallery moaned and Carrington looked down quickly.

"My God! The Old Man! Is he hurt badly, sir?"

"I don't know," Number One. But I've sent for the surgeon commander." Turner stooped down, raised the dazed Vallery to a sitting position.

"Are you all right, sir?" he asked anxiously. "Do you—have you been hit?"

Vallery coughed, then shook his head feebly.

"I'm all right," he whispered weakly. "I dived for the deck, but I think the binnacle got in my way. How's the ship, Commander?"

"To hell with the ship!" Turner said roughly. He passed an arm round Vallery, raised him carefully to his feet. "How are things aft, Number One?"

"Under control. Still burning, but under control. I left Hartley in charge." Carrington made no mention of Carslake.

"Good! Take over. Radio *Stirling*, *Sirrus*, see how they are. Come on, sir. Shelter for you!"

Vallery protested feebly, a token protest only, for he was too weak to stand. They passed by Bentley's body stretched outside the gate. The captain paused, stared down at the dead man at his feet, already covered with a thin layer of snow.

"Have that Aldis unplugged, Commander, will you?" he asked.

He moved on again, then stopped at the Asdic cabinet. Chrysler's sobbing figure was crouched into the angle between the shelter and the jammed door of the hut. Vallery laid a hand on the shaking shoulder. "What's the matter, Chrysler?"

"The door, sir!" Chrysler's voice was muffled. "The door—I can't open it."

Vallery had a sudden, horrifying thought of the gashed and mangled operator that must lie behind that door. "Yes," he said quietly. "The door's buckled. There's nothing anyone can do, Chrysler. Come on my boy, there's no need—"

"My brother's in there, sir." The words struck Vallery like a blow. Dear God! He had forgotten. . . . Of course—Leading Asdic Operator Chrysler. "Chrysler?" he murmured. "Go below and get yourself some coffee, man."

"Coffee, sir! But—but—my—my brother—"

"I know," Vallery said gently. "I know. Get yourself some coffee, will you?"

Chrysler stumbled off. When the shelter door closed behind them, Vallery turned to the commander, clicking on the light. "Cue for moralizing on the glories of war," he murmured quietly. "*Dulce et decorum*, and the proud privilege of being the sons of Nelson and Drake. It's not twenty-four hours since Ralston watched his father die . . . And now this boy. Perhaps—"

Turner nodded. "I'll take care of things. Keep him busy out of the way till we open up the cabinet. . . . Sit down, sir. Have a swig of this. . . . Hello! Company."

Brooks stood blinking in the light. His eyes focused on the bottle in Turner's hand. "Ha! Having a bottle party, are we? All contributions gratefully received, I have no doubt." He opened his case on a convenient table, was rummaging inside when someone rapped sharply on the door.

A signalman entered, handed a note to Vallery. "From London, sir. Chief says there may be some reply."

"Thank you. I'll phone down." The door closed behind him. Vallery smiled. "My eyes—they don't seem so good. Perhaps you would read the signal, Commander?"

"And perhaps *you* would like some decent medicine," Brooks boomed. He fished in his bag, produced the bottle of Johnny Nicholls's amber liquid. "With all the resources of modern medicine—well, practically all, anyway—at my disposal, I can find nothing to equal this."

Vallery was stretched out on the settee now, his eyes closed. "Thanks. Let's have the good news, Turner."

"Good news!" The commander's voice fell chilly over the waiting men. "No, sir, it's not good news." With deliberate care he read the message aloud. "'Rear Admiral Vallery, Commanding 14 ACS, FR 77. *Tirpitz*, escorting cruisers, destroyers, reported moving out Alta Fjord sunset. Intense activity Alta Fjord airfield. Fear sortie under air cover. All measures avoid useless sacrifice merchant, naval ships. DNO, London.'"

Vallery was sitting bolt upright on the settee, blind to the blood trickling down crookedly from one corner of his mouth. His face was calm, unworried. "I think I'll have that glass, now, Brooks, if you don't mind," he said. "It seems we've proved a tempting bait after all."

"Sunset. My God!" Turner said sharply, "even allowing for negotiating the fjord they'll be on us in four hours on this course!"

"Exactly," Vallery nodded. "And it's no good running north. They'd overtake us before we're within a hundred miles of our big boys up north."

"Them?" Turner scoffed. "I hate to sound like a gramophone record, but you'll recall my earlier statement about them—too late as usual!"

Vallery drained his glass, lay back exhausted. "We don't seem to have much option. Inform all merchant ships, all escorts. Tell them to break north."

Turner stared at him. "North? Did you say 'north'? But the Admiralty—"

"North, I said," Vallery repeated quietly. He propped himself on an elbow, his mind made up. He smiled at Turner, and his face was almost boyish again. "The Admiralty can do what they like about it. *Avoid useless sacrifice merchant ships*, they said. This way there's a chance—an almost hopeless chance, perhaps, but a fighting chance. For them to go east is suicide." He smiled again. "I don't think I'll have to answer for this. Not now—not ever."

Turner grinned at him, his face lit up. "North, you said."

"Inform C-in-C," Vallery went on. "Ask Pilot for an interception course. Tell the convoy we'll tag along behind, give 'em as much cover as we can, as long as we can. . . . As long as we can. Let us not delude ourselves, One thousand to one at the outside. . . . Nothing else we can do, Commander?"

"Pray," Turner said succinctly.

"And sleep," Brooks added. "Why don't you have half an hour, sir?"

"Sleep!" Vallery seemed genuinely amused. "We'll have all the time in the world to sleep, by and by."

"You have a point," Brooks conceded, but led him to his cabin.

Messages began to pour in to the bridge. From the *Sirrus*: she was making water now to the capacity of the pumps. From merchant ships, asking for confirmation of the *Tirpitz* breakout. From the *Stirling*: although still burning furiously, her superstructure fire was under control and the engine room water-tight bulkheads were holding. . . .

A quarter of an hour later the *Ulysses* was rearing and pitching through the head seas on her new course of 350°, when the gate of the bridge crashed open and a panting, exhausted stoker, clad only in a pair of thin dungarees, stumbled on to the compass platform.

"The transmitting station, sir! It's full of water!"

"The TS?" Turner was appalled. The TS was twenty feet below water level. And above it a series of hatches, deliberately heavy, designed to stay shut in the event of damage. The men in the TS knew this. "Flooded! When did this happen?"

"I'm not sure, sir." He was still gasping for breath. "But there was a bloody awful explosion, sir, just about amid—"

"I know! I know!" Turner interrupted impatiently. "Bomber carried away the funnel. But that was fifteen minutes ago, man! Good God, they would have—"

"TS switchboard's gone, sir." The stoker grasped Turner's duffel without realizing what he was doing. "All the power's gone, sir. And the hatch is jammed! The men can't get out!"

"The hatch-cover jammed?" Turner's eyes narrowed. "What happened?"

"The counter-weight's broken off, sir. A quarter of a bloody ton if it's an ounce, sir. It's on top of the hatch. We can only get it open an inch. You see, sir—"

"Number One!" Turner shouted.

"Here, sir." Carrington was standing just behind him, calm and unruffled. "I heard. . . . Hatch-cover plus pulley—one thousand pounds. We need a special man for a special job."

"Petersen, sir!" The stoker understood immediately. "Petersen!"

"Of course!" Carrington clapped gloved hands together. "We're on our way, sir. Acetylene? No time! Crow-bars, sledges . . . Perhaps if you would ring the engine room for Stoker Petersen, sir?"

But Turner already had the phone in his hand.

AFT ON THE POOP-DECK, the fire was under control, all but in a few odd corners where the flames were fed by a fierce through draught. In the mess-decks, bulkheads, ladders, mess partitions, lockers had been twisted into strange shapes by the intense heat: on deck, petrol-fed flames had cleanly stripped the two and three-quarter inch deck planking and exposed the steel deck-plates, plates that hissed and spat as heavy snowflakes drifted down to sibilant extinction.

On and below decks, toiled Chief Petty Officer Hartley and his crews, freezing one moment, reeling in the blast of heat the next. From the turrets, from the master-at-arm's office, from mess-decks and emergency steering position, they pulled out man after man. As the dead were ranged in the starboard alleyway, a leading seaman was waiting for them. Impassively he picked up one dead man after the other, walked to the guard-rail and dropped his burden over the side. How many times he repeated that brief journey that night, the leading seaman never knew: he lost count after the first twenty or so. The Navy was very strong on decent burial, and this was not decent burial. But the sailmakers were dead and no man could have sewn up these ghastly charred heaps in the weighted and sheeted canvas.

ENGINEER COMMANDER DODSON was huddled in the shaft tunnel. He stirred and moaned, struggling to open his eyes. The blackness around remained impenetrable.

He wondered dully what had happened. Down here in the bowels of the ship, sound did not penetrate: but there had been no mistaking the jarring shock of the 5.25s surging back on their hydraulic recoils. And then—a torpedo perhaps, or a near miss by a bomb. Thank God he'd been sitting facing inboard when the *Ulysses* had lurched.

The side of his head, just below the ear, hurt abominably. Slowly he peeled off his glove, reached up an exploratory hand. It came away wet and sticky: his hair, he realized with mild surprise, was thickly matted with blood. It must be blood—he could feel it trickling slowly down his cheek.

And that deep vibration overlain with an indefinable note of strain that set his engineer's teeth on edge—he could hear it immediately in front of him. His bare hand reached out, recoiled as it touched something smooth and revolving—and burning hot.

The shaft! It was running almost red-hot on dry bearings! They'd discovered fractured lubricating pipes on the port shafts too, so he'd decided to risk keeping this engine turning. Frantically, he pawed around for his emergency lamp and for his pocket torch: both were smashed. Desperate now, he searched blindly for his oil can: it was empty.

No oil, none. Heaven only knew how near that over-stressed metal was to the critical limit. Oil—he would have to get oil. But he was weak from shock and loss of blood, and the tunnel was long and slippery and dangerous—and unlighted. One slip, one stumble against or over that merciless shaft . . . But there was no choice. He swayed dizzily to his feet, his back bent against the arching tunnel.

It was then that he noticed a tiny pinpoint of light advancing steadily in the dark tunnel. Gratefully he sank down again, his feet braced once more against the bearing block.

The man with the light stopped a couple of feet away, hooked the lamp onto an inspection bracket, lowered himself carefully beside Dodson. The rays of the lamp fell full on the dark heavy face, the jagged brows. Dodson stiffened in sudden surprise.

"Riley! Stoker Riley!" His eyes narrowed in suspicion. "What the devil are you doing here?"

"I've brought a two-gallon drum of lubricating oil," Riley growled. He thrust a thermos flask into the engineer commander's hands. "And here's some coffee. I'll tend to this—you drink that. My God! This bloody bearing's red-hot!"

Dodson set down the thermos with a thump.

"Are you deaf?" he asked harshly. "Why are *you* here? Who sent you? Your station's in 'B' boiler room!"

"Lieutenant Grierson sent me," Riley said roughly. His dark face was impassive. "Said he couldn't spare his engine-room men—too bloody valuable. Too much?" The oil, thick, viscous, was pouring slowly onto the overheated bearing.

"Lieutenant Grierson?" Dodson's voice was a whiplash of icy correction. "And that's a damned lie, Riley! Lieutenant Grierson never sent you. I suppose you told *him* that somebody else had sent you?"

"Drink your coffee," Riley advised sourly. "You're wanted in the engine room."

The engineer commander restrained himself with difficulty. "Commander's defaulters in the morning. You'll pay for this, Riley!"

"No, I won't, sir. Oh, you can report me all right. But I won't be at the commander's table tomorrow morning."

"Why not?" Dodson demanded dangerously.

Riley grinned. "'Cos there'll *be* no commander *and* no table to-morrow morning." He clasped his hands luxuriously behind his head. "In fact, there'll be no nothin'. Commander's just finished broadcastin'," he continued. "The *Tirpitz* is out—we have four hours left."

The bald, flat statement left no possible room for doubt. The *Tirpitz* —out. The *Tirpitz*—out. Dodson repeated the phrase to himself. Four hours, just four hours to go. . . .

"Well?" Riley was anxious now, restive. "Are you goin' or aren't you? You don't need no three gold stripes on your sleeve to handle a bloody oil can."

"Possibly not." Dodson braced against a sudden, violent pitch. "Tell me, Riley, what brought you here?"

"That's my bloody business!" Riley answered savagely.

"What brought you here?"

"Oh, for Christ's sake, leave me alone!" Riley shouted. Suddenly he turned round, his mouth twisted bitterly. "You know bloody well why I came."

"To do me in, perhaps?"

Riley looked at him a long second, then turned away, his shoulders hunched, his head low.

"You're the only bastard in this ship that ever gave me a break," he muttered. "The only bastard I've ever *known* who ever gave me a chance," he amended slowly.

Bastard, Dodson supposed, was Riley's accolade of friendship, and he felt suddenly ashamed of his last remark.

"If it wasn't for you," Riley went on, "I'd've been in cells the first time, in a civvy jail the second. Remember, sir?"

Dodson nodded. "You were rather foolish, Riley," he admitted.

"Why did you do it?" The big stoker was intense, worried. "God, everyone knows what I'm like—"

"Do they? I wonder. . . . I thought you had the makings of a better man than you—"

"Don't give me that bull!" Riley scoffed. "*I* know what I'm like. I know what I am. I'm no bloody good! Everybody says I'm no bloody good! And they're right. . . ." He leaned forward. "Do you know somethin'? I'm a Catholic. Four hours from now. . . ." He broke off. "I should be on my knees, shouldn't I? Lookin' for—repentance—what do they call it?"

"Absolution?"

"Aye. That's it. Absolution. And do you know what? I don't give a single, solitary damn!"

"Maybe you don't have to," Dodson murmured. "For the last time, get back to that engine room!"

"No!"

The engineer commander sighed, picked up the thermos.

"In that case, perhaps you would care to join me in a cup of coffee?"

IN THE CAPTAIN'S SHELTER Vallery rolled over on his side, his legs doubled up, his hand automatically reaching for the towel. His emaciated body shook violently, and the sound of the harsh, retching cough beat back at him from the iron walls of his shelter. Funny, he thought, as the attack eased, it doesn't hurt any more.

"You carry this damned ship on your back!" Unbidden, old Socrates's phrase came into his mind and he smiled faintly. Well, if ever they needed him, it was now.

He sat up, sweating with the effort, swung his legs carefully over the side. As his feet touched the deck, the *Ulysses* pitched suddenly, and he fell forward to the floor. It took an eternity to drag himself to his feet again: another effort like that, he knew, would surely kill him.

Somehow he opened the heavy steel door, and suddenly he was outside, gasping as the cruel, sub-zero wind seared down into his wasted lungs.

He looked fore and aft. The fires were dying, the fires on the *Stirling* and on his own poop-deck. Beside him, two men had just finished levering the door off the Asdic cabinet, were flashing a torch inside. But he couldn't bear to look: he staggered with outstretched hands for the gate of the compass platform.

Turner saw him coming, hurried to meet him, helped him slowly to his chair.

"You've no right to be here," he said quietly. He looked at Vallery for a long moment. "How are you feeling, sir?"

"I'm a good deal better, now, thanks," Vallery replied. He smiled and went on: "We rear admirals have our responsibilities, you know, Commander. It's time I began to earn my princely salary."

"Stand back, there!" Carrington was standing by the hatch leading to the low power room and, below that, to the transmitting station. "Into the wheelhouse or up on the ladder—all of you. Let's have a look!"

The great, steel hatch-cover, open no more than an inch, was resting on a tommy-bar. He noticed the heavy counterweight lying against the sill of the wheelhouse. So that's off, he thought. Thank the Lord for that, anyway.

"Have you tried a block and tackle?" he asked abruptly.

"Yes, sir," the man nearest him replied. He pointed to a tangled heap in a corner. "No use, sir. The ladder takes the strain all right, but we can't get the hook under the hatch, except sideways—and then it slips off all the time." He gestured to the hatch. "And every clip's either bent—they were opened by sledges—or at the wrong angle...."

Carrington hooked his fingers under the hatch, took a deep breath. The seaman at one side of the cover—the other side was hard against the after bulkhead—did the same. Together they strained. Carrington felt his face turning crimson with effort, heard the blood pounding in his ears, and relaxed. They were only killing themselves and that damned cover hadn't shifted a fraction. Carrington suspected that the hinges were jammed—or the deck buckled. He sank to his knees, put his mouth to the edge of the hatch.

"Below there!" he called. "Can you hear me?"

"We can hear you." The voice was weak, muffled. "For God's sake get us out of here."

"Is that you, Brierley? Don't worry— we'll get you out. How's the water down there?"

"Water? More bloody oil that water! Three-quarters way up already! We're standing on generators, hanging on to switchboards. One of our boys is gone already—we couldn't hold him." Even muffled by the hatch, the strain, the near-desperation in the voice was all too obvious. "For pity's sake, hurry up!"

"I said we'd get you out!" Carrington's voice was sharp, authoritative, he knew how quickly panic could spread down there. "Can you push from below at all?"

"There's room for only one on the ladder," Brierley shouted. "It's impossible to get any pressure, any leverage upwards."

Carrington heard the clatter of heavy footsteps above him, and straightened up. It was Petersen. In that narrow space, the blond Norwegian stoker looked gigantic, one enormous hand negligently holding three heavy crowbars and a sledgehammer as if they were so many lengths of cane. All at once, Carrington felt oddly confident.

"We can't open this, Petersen. Can you?"

"I will try, sir." He laid down his tools, stooped, caught the end of the tommy-bar projecting beneath the corner of the cover. He straightened quickly, easily: the hatch lifted a fraction, then the bar, putty-like, bent over almost to a right angle.

"I think the hatch is jammed." Petersen wasn't even breathing heavily. "It will be the hinges, sir."

He peered closely, then grunted in satisfaction. Three times the heavy sledge, swung with accuracy and all the power of his great shoulders behind it, smashed squarely into the face of the outer hinge. On the third stroke the sledge handle snapped. Petersen threw away the broken shaft in disgust, picked up a second crowbar much heavier than the first.

Again the bar bent, but again the hatch-cover lifted—an inch this time. Petersen took the two smaller sledges that had been used to open clips, hammered at the hinges till these sledges, too, were broken and useless.

This time he used the last two crowbars together, thrust under the same corner of the hatch. For five, ten seconds he remained bent over them, motionless. The sweat began to pour off his face. Then slowly, incredibly, both crowbars began to bend.

Carrington watched, fascinated. Neither of these bars, he would have sworn, would have bent under less than half a ton of pressure. It was fantastic, but it was happening: and as the giant straightened, they were bending more and more. Then suddenly the hatch sprang open five or six inches and Petersen crashed backwards against the bulkhead, the bars falling into the water below.

Petersen flung himself back at the hatch. Hooking his fingers under the edge, he heaved at the massive hatch-cover, the great muscles of his arms and shoulders locking as he tugged. Three times he heaved, four times, then on the fifth the hatch leaped up with a screech of tortured metal and smashed shudderingly home into the retaining latch of the vertical stand behind.

The hatch was open. Petersen just stood there, his face bathed in sweat, his massive chest rising and falling rapidly as his starved lungs sucked in great draughts of air.

The water level in the low power room was within two feet of the hatch. Quickly, the trapped men were hauled to safety, and taken to the sick-bay. Carrington watched the dripping, shivering men being helped away, then turned to the giant stoker with a smile. "We'll all thank you later, Petersen. We're not finished yet. This hatch must be closed and battened down."

"It will be difficult, sir," Petersen said gravely.

"Difficult or not, it *must* be done," Carrington was emphatic. Regularly, now, the water was spilling over the coaming.

Petersen said nothing. He lifted the retaining latch, pulled the protesting hatch-cover down a foot. Then he braced his shoulder against the ladder, planted his feet on the cover and straightened his back: the cover screeched down to 45°. He paused, his hands taking his weight on the ladder, then pounded his feet again and again on the edge of the cover. Fifteen inches to go.

"We need heavy hammers, sir," Petersen said urgently.

"No time!" Carrington shook his head quickly. "Two more minutes and it'll be impossible to shut the hatch-cover against the water-pressure. Hell!" he said bitterly. "If it were only the other way round—closing from below. Even I could lever it shut!"

Again Petersen said nothing. He squatted down by the side of the hatch, gazed into the darkness beneath his feet.

"I have an idea, sir," he said quickly. "If you would stand on the hatch, push against the ladder. Yes, sir, that way—but you could push harder if you turned your back to me."

Carrington heaved with all his strength. Suddenly he heard a metallic clatter, whirled round just in time to see a crowbar clutched in an enormous hand disappear below the edge of the hatch-cover. There was no sign of Petersen: he'd gone down over the edge of the hatch with hardly a sound.

"Petersen!" Carrington was on his knees by the hatch. "What the devil do you think you're doing? Come out of there, you bloody fool! Do you want to drown?"

There was no reply. Suddenly the quiet was broken by the sound of metal hammering against metal, then by a jarring screech as the hatch dropped six inches. Desperately, the first lieutenant seized a crowbar, thrust it under the hatch-cover: a split second later the great steel cover thudded down on top of it. Carrington had his mouth to the gap now. "In the name of God, Petersen," he shouted. "Are you sane? Open up, open up at once, do you hear?"

"I can't." The voice came and went as the water surged over the stoker's head. "I won't. You said yourself . . . there is no time . . . this was the only way."

"But I never meant—"

"I know. It does not matter . . . it is better this way." It was almost impossible to make out what he was saying. "Tell Captain Vallery that Petersen says he is very sorry."

"Sorry! Sorry for what?" Carrington flung all his strength against the iron bar: the hatch-cover did not even quiver.

"The dead marine in Scapa Flow . . . I did not mean to kill him. I could never kill any man. . . . But he angered me," the big Norwegian said simply. "He killed my friend."

For a second, Carrington stopped straining at the bar. Petersen! Of course—who but Petersen could have snapped a man's neck like that?

"Listen, Petersen," he begged. "I don't give a damn about that. Nobody shall ever know, I promise you. Please, Petersen, just—"

"It is better this way." The muffled voice was strangely content. "It is not good to kill a man . . . it is not good to go on living . . . I know . . . Please, it is important—you will tell my captain—Petersen is sorry and filled with shame . . . I do this for my captain."

Without warning, the crowbar was plucked from Carrington's hand. The cover clanged down in position. For a minute the area rang to a succession of muffled, metallic blows.

Suddenly the clamour ceased.

IT WAS A FAVOURITE device of Vallery's when the need for silence on board was not paramount, to pass the long, dark hours by coupling up the record-player to the broadcast system, and now a girl was singing. It was Deanna Durbin, and she was singing "Beneath the Lights of Home," that most heartbreakingly nostalgic of all songs. Below decks and above, bent over the great engines or huddled by their guns, men listened to the lovely voice as it drifted through the darkened ship and the falling snow, and turned their minds inwards and thought of home, thought of the bitter contrast and the morning that would not come. Suddenly, halfway through, the song stopped.

"Do you hear there?" the speakers boomed. "Do you hear there? This—this is the commander speaking." The voice was deep and grave and hesitant. "I have bad news for you. I am sorry—I . . .." He broke off, then went on more slowly still. "Rear Admiral Vallery died five minutes ago." For a moment the speaker was silent, then crackled again. "He died on the bridge, in his chair. He knew he was dying and I don't think he suffered at all. . . . He insisted—he insisted that I thank you for the way you all stood by him. 'Tell them'—these were his words, as far as I remember—'tell them,' he said, 'that I couldn't have carried on without them, that they are the best crew that God ever gave a captain.' Then he said—it was the last thing he said: 'Give them my apologies. After all they've done for me—well, well, tell them I'm terribly sorry to let them down like this.' That was all he said—just 'Tell them I'm sorry.' And then he died."

SUNDAY

RICHARD VALLERY died grieving at the thought that he was abandoning the crew of the *Ulysses*, leaving them behind. But it was only for a short time. Before the dawn, hundreds more, men in the cruisers, the destroyers and the merchantmen, died also. And they did not die as he had feared under the guns of the *Tirpitz*—the *Tirpitz* in fact had not left Alta Fjord after all. They died, primarily, because the weather changed.

With Richard Vallery's death a great change came over the men of the *Ulysses*. They knew that something wonderful, something that had become an enduring part of their minds, something fine and good, was gone and they would never know it again, and they were mad with grief. Rightly or wrongly, the *Ulysses* never thought to blame the captain's death on any but the enemy. There was only, for them, the sorrow and the blind hate. The *Ulysses* became a ship manned by automatons living only for revenge.

The weather changed just before the end of the middle watch. FR 77 was still butting into the heavy, rolling swell from the north, still piling up fresh sheets of glistening ice on their labouring fo'c'sles. But the wind dropped, and almost at once the snowstorm blew itself out. By four o'clock the sky was completely clear.

There was no moon that night, but the stars were out, keen and sharp as the icy breeze that blew steadily out of the north.

Then, gradually, the sky began to change. At first there was only a bare lightening on the northern rim then, slowly, a pulsating flickering band of light began to broaden and deepen and climb steadily above the horizon, climbing higher to the south. Soon other streamers in the most delicate pastel shades of blue and green and violet, but always predominantly white, grew higher and stronger and brighter: at the climax, a great band of white stretched high above the convoy, extending from horizon to horizon. . . . These were the Northern Lights, at any time a spectacle of beauty and wonder, and this night surpassingly lovely: down below, in ships clearly illuminated against the dark and rolling seas, the men of FR 77 looked up and hated them.

On the bridge of the *Ulysses*, the commander was the first to hear the intermittent throbbing of a Condor approaching from the south. He turned wearily to Carrington.

"It's Charlie, all right," he said grimly. "The bastard's spotted us. He'll already have radioed Alta Fjord and . . . Pilot, how far do you reckon we're from Alta Fjord—in flying time, I mean?"

"For a 200-knot plane, just over an hour," the Kapok Kid said quietly. His ebullience was gone: he had been silent and dejected since Vallery had died two hours previously.

"An hour!" Carrington exclaimed. "And they'll be here. My God, sir," he went on wonderingly, "they're really out to get us. We've never been bombed nor torpedoed at night before. We've never had the *Tirpitz* after us before. We never—"

"The *Tirpitz*," Turner interrupted. "Just where the hell *is* that ship?" He broke off, spoke sharply to the signal petty officer. "Look alive, Preston! That ship's flashing us."

"Sorry, sir." The signalman, swaying on his feet with exhaustion, raised his Aldis, clacked out an acknowledgment. Again the light on the merchantman began to wink furiously.

"'Transverse fracture engine bedplate,'" Preston read out. "'Damage serious: shall have to moderate speed.'"

"Acknowledge," said Turner curtly. "What ship is that, Preston?"

"The *Ohio* freighter, sir."

"The one that stopped a tin fish a couple of days back?"

"That's her, sir."

"Make a signal. 'Essential maintain speed and position.'" Turner swore. "What a time to choose for an engine breakdown ... Pilot, when do we rendezvous with the Fleet?"

"Six hours' time, sir: exactly."

"Six hours." Turner compressed his lips. "Just six hours—perhaps!" he added bitterly.

"Perhaps?" Carrington murmured.

"Perhaps," Turner affirmed. "Depends entirely on the weather. C-in-C won't risk capital ships so near the coast unless he can fly off fighter cover against air attack. And, if you ask me, that's why the *Tirpitz* hasn't turned up yet—some wandering U-boat's tipped her off that our Fleet carriers are steaming south. He'll be waiting on the weather. What's he saying now, Preston?" The *Ohio*'s signal lamp had flashed briefly, then died.

"'Imperative slow down,'" Preston repeated. "'Damage severe. Am slowing down.'"

"He is, too," Carrington said quietly. "He's a goner, sir, a dead duck. He hasn't a chance. Not unless—"

"Unless what?" Turner asked harshly. "Unless we leave him an escort? Leave what escort, Number One? The *Viking*—the only effective unit we've left?" He shook his head. "The greatest good of the greatest number: that's how it has to be. They'll know that. Preston, send 'Regret cannot leave you standby. How long to effect repairs?'"

A flare burst directly over FR 77. It was difficult to estimate the height—probably six to eight thousand feet—but at that altitude it was no more than an incandescent pin-point against the great band of the Northern Lights arching majestically above. But it was falling quickly.

The crackling of the WT speaker broke through the stuttering chatter of the Aldis. "WT—bridge. WT—bridge. Message from *Sirrus*: 'Many survivors now dying from serious wounds. Must repeat request for urgent medical assistance, repeat urgent.'"

"Send for Lieutenant Nicholls," Turner ordered briefly. "Ask him to come up to the bridge at once. We must try again to get him across."

Carrington stared down at the dark broad seas, seas flecked with milky foam: the bows of the *Ulysses* were crashing down heavily, continuously.

"You're going to risk it, sir?"

"I must. You'd do the same, Number One. . . . What does the *Ohio* say, Preston?"

"'I understand. Too busy to look after the Royal Navy anyway. We will make up on you. Au revoir!'"

"'We will make up on you. Au revoir.'" Turner repeated softly. "He lies in his teeth, and he knows it. By God!" he burst out. "If anyone ever tells me the Yankee sailors have no guts I'll push his perishing face in. Preston, send: 'Au revoir. Good luck.' Number One, I feel like a murderer." He rubbed his hand across his forehead, nodded towards the shelter where Vallery lay stretched out, strapped to his settee. "Month in, month out, he'd been taking these decisions. It's no wonder . . ." He broke off as the gate creaked open.

"Is that you, Nicholls? There is work for you, my boy. Can't have you medical types idling around uselessly all day long." He raised his hand. "All right, all right," he chuckled. "How do you feel, laddie?"

"Awful." Nicholls's face was deeply lined, haggard to the point of emaciation.

"You look it," Turner said candidly. "Nicholls—I'm terribly sorry, boy—I want you to go over to the *Sirrus*."

"Yes, sir." Nicholls was past surprise or dismay. "How much kit can I take with me, sir?"

"Just your medical gear. You're not travelling by Pullman, laddie!"

Turner smiled briefly. "Pilot—get through to the WT. Tell the *Sirrus* to come alongside, prepare to receive medical officer by breeches buoy."

The gate creaked again. Turner looked at Brooks's bulky figure stumbling wearily onto the compass platform. The surgeon commander, like every man in the crew, was dead on his feet; but the blue eyes burned as brightly as ever.

"My spies are everywhere," he announced. "What's this about the *Sirrus* shanghaiing young Johnny here?"

"Sorry, old man," Turner apologized. "It seems things are pretty bad on the *Sirrus*."

"I see." Brooks looked upwards at the sinking flare. "Pretty, very pretty," he murmured. "What are the illuminations in aid of?"

"We are expecting company," Turner smiled crookedly. "An old world custom, O Socrates—the light in the window—" He stiffened abruptly. "My mistake. The company has already arrived."

The last words were drowned in the rumbling of a heavy explosion. The *Ohio* had already fallen back a mile distant on the starboard quarter, but clearly visible still under the Northern Lights—the Northern Lights that had betrayed her to a wandering U-boat.

She did not remain visible for long. She was carrying a full cargo of tanks and ammunition. There was a curious dignity about her end—she sank quickly, quietly, without any fuss. She was gone in three minutes.

It was Turner who finally broke the heavy silence on the bridge. "Au revoir," he muttered to no one in particular. "Au revoir. That's what he said, the lying. . . ." He shook his head angrily, touched the Kapok Kid on the arm. "Get through to WT. Tell the *Viking* to sit over the top of that sub till we get clear."

"HAVE YOU A minute to spare, Johnny?" The Kapok Kid's voice was low. "I'd like to speak to you."

"Sure." Nicholls looked at him in surprise. "Sure, I've a minute, ten minutes—until the *Sirrus* comes up. What's wrong, Andy?"

"Just a second." The Kapok Kid crossed to the commander. "Permission to go to the charthouse, sir?"

"Sure you've got your matches?" Turner smiled. "O.K. Off you go."

The Kapok Kid led Nicholls into the charthouse, flicked on the lights and produced his cigarettes.

"Know something, Johnny? I've a feeling I won't be seeing you again." He shivered.

"Ah, nonsense! Indigestion, my boy," Nicholls said briskly.

"Won't wash this time," Carpenter shook his head, half-smiling. "Will you do me a favour, Johnny?"

"Don't be so bloody silly. How the hell do you—?"

"Take this with you." The Kapok Kid pulled out a slip of paper, thrust it into Nicholls's hands. "Can you read it?"

There was a name and address on the paper, a girl's name and an address in Henley. "So that's her name," Nicholls said softly. "Juanita . . . Juanita." He pronounced it in the Spanish fashion. "My favourite song and my favourite name," he murmured.

"Is it?" the Kapok Kid asked eagerly. "Is it indeed? And mine, Johnny." He paused. "If, perhaps—well, if I don't—well, you'll go to see her, Johnny?"

"What are you talking about, man?" Nicholls felt embarrassed. "Why, with that suit on, you could *swim* from here to Murmansk. You've said so yourself, a hundred times."

The Kapok Kid grinned a little crookedly. "Sure, sure, I know—will you go, Johnny?"

"Dammit to hell, yes!" Nicholls snapped. "I'll go—and it's high time I was going somewhere else. Come on!" He snapped off the lights, pulled back the door, stopped with his foot halfway over the sill. Slowly, he stepped back inside. "I'm sorry, Andy, I don't know what made me—" He stretched out his hand. "All the best. And don't worry. I'll see her if—well, I'll see her, I promise you. But if I find *you* there," he went on threateningly, "I'll—"

"Thanks, Johnny. Thanks a lot." The Kapok Kid was almost happy. "Good luck, boy. . . . *Vaya con Dios.* That's what she always said to me, what she said before I came away. '*Vaya con Dios.*'"

Thirty minutes later, Nicholls was operating aboard the *Sirrus*. The time was 0445. It was bitterly cold, with a light wind blowing steadily from the north. The sky was still again, for the Northern Lights were fading. The fifth successive flare was drifting steadily seawards.

It was at 0445 that they heard it on board HMS *Ulysses*—the distant rumble of gunfire far to the south. There could be no doubt what was happening. The *Viking*, still in contact with the U-boat, was being heavily attacked. And the attack must have been short, for the firing ceased soon. Ominously, nothing came through on the WT. No one ever knew what had happened to the *Viking*, for there were no survivors.

The last echo of the *Viking*'s guns had barely died away before they heard the roar of the Condor's engines at maximum throttle in a shallow dive. Behind him, the sky opened up in a flaming coruscation of flares more dazzling than the sun, so blinding that the enemy bombers were through the circle of light and upon them before anyone on *Ulysses* realized what was happening.

They were Heinkel 111s. And the Heinkel 111, Turner knew, carried that weapon he dreaded above all others—the glider bomb.

Every gun on the *Ulysses* opened up. The air filled with smoke, the pungent smell of burning cordite: the din was indescribable. And all at once, Turner felt fiercely happy. To hell with them and their glider bombs, he thought. This was war as he liked to fight it: war out in the open, where he could see the enemy and hate him and love him for fighting as honest men should and do his damnedest to destroy him. And, Turner knew, if it were humanly possible, the crew of the *Ulysses* would destroy him. They had crossed the frontier of fear and found that nothing worse lay beyond it, and they would keep on feeding their guns and squeezing their triggers until the enemy overwhelmed them.

The leading Heinkel was blown out of the sky. The Heinkel behind lifted sharply to avoid the hurtling fragments of fuselage and engines, banked steeply to port, and swung back in on the *Ulysses*, to drop his bomb and slew frantically away as the concentrated fire of the Oerlikons and pom-poms closed in on him. Miraculously, he escaped.

The winged bomb glided forwards and downwards to strike home with a tremendous, deafening explosion that shook the *Ulysses* to her keel and almost shattered the eardrums of those on deck. By a freakish chance it had crashed directly into the port torpedo tubes.

There had been only one torpedo left there—the other two had sent the *Vytura* to the bottom—and normally Amatol, the warhead explosive, is extremely stable: but the bursting bomb had been too close, too powerful: sympathetic detonation had been inevitable.

Damage was extensive and spectacular, but not fatal. The side of the *Ulysses* had been ripped open almost to the water's edge; the tubes had vanished; the decks were holed and splintered; the funnel casing was a shambles, the funnel itself tilting over to port almost to fifteen degrees:

but the greatest energy of the explosion had been directed aft, most of the blast expending itself over the open sea.

Almost before the dust and debris of the explosion had settled, the Heinkels were gone, and there were only the flares, drooping slowly to extinction, lighting up the pall above the *Ulysses*, the clouds of smoke rolling up from the newly damaged *Stirling* and a tanker with its after superstructure now almost gone. But not one of the ships in FR 77 had faltered or stopped; and they had destroyed five Heinkels. A costly victory, Turner mused, if it could be called a victory; but he knew the Heinkels would be back. It was not difficult to imagine the fury of the high command in Norway: as far as Turner knew, no Russian convoy had ever sailed so far south before.

And three times more during that terrible night, the German squadrons did indeed attack the shattered remnants of FR 77. In the first assault—about 0545—there were two direct hits—one on a merchantman, blowing away most of the fo'c'sle, the other on the *Ulysses*. It sheered through the flag-deck and the admiral's day-cabin, and exploded in the heart of the sick-bay. The sick-bay was crowded with the sick and dying, and, for many, that bomb must have come as a godsent release, for the *Ulysses* had long since run out of anaesthetics. There were no survivors. Among the dead was Marshall, the torpedo officer, and the master-at-arms. Brooks had not been there.

The same explosion had also shattered the telephone exchange: barring only the bridge-gun phones, and the bridge-engine phones and speaking-tubes, all communication lines in the *Ulysses* were gone.

The second attack at 0700, was made by only six bombers— Heinkels again, carrying glider-bombs. Obviously flying strictly under orders, they concentrated their attack solely on the cruisers. It was an expensive attack: the enemy lost all but two of their force in exchange for a single hit aft on the *Stirling*, a hit which, tragically, put both after guns out of action.

The third attack just before dawn, was carried out by fifteen Heinkel 111s. Again the cruisers were the sole targets, the heavier attack by far being directed against the *Ulysses*. Far from shirking the challenge the crew of the *Ulysses* welcomed the enemy gladly, for how can one kill an enemy if he does not come to you? "Tell them," Vallery had said, "tell them they are the best crew God ever gave a captain." Vallery. *That* was what mattered.

And the crew hoisted the shells, slammed the breeches and squeezed the triggers, men oblivious of everything except the memory of the man who had died apologizing because he had let them down. Oblivious of everything except the sure knowledge that they could not let Vallery down.

The first part of the attack, however, was launched against the *Stirling*. Bombs struck her amidships, and exploded deep inside, in the boiler room and engine room. She was desperately wounded, on fire again, and listing heavily to starboard.

Then five Heinkels approached the *Ulysses*. One bomb exploded in mid-air, just for'ard of the after funnel and feet away from it: a murderous storm of jagged steel scythed across the boat-deck, and all Oerlikons and pom-poms fell silent, their crews victim to shrapnel or concussion. Another plunged through the deck and engineers' flat and turned the WT office into a charnel house. The remaining two smashed squarely into "X" gun-deck and "X" turret. The turret was split open around the top and down both sides as by a giant cleaver, and blasted off its mounting, to lie grotesquely across the shattered poop.

Briefly the *Ulysses* ran into dense black smoke from the *Stirling*, now heavily on fire, her fuel tanks gone up. Suddenly the *Ulysses* was out in the clear again, and the Heinkels, all bombs gone, were harrying her with cannon and machine-gun, desperate to finish her off. But still, here and there, a gun fired on the *Ulysses*.

There was a gun firing just below the bridge, for instance. Turner risked a quick glance over the side, saw a gunner pumping his tracers into the path of a swooping Heinkel. And then the Heinkel opened up, and Turner flung himself back, knocking the Kapok Kid who was standing behind him down onto the deck. Then the bomber was gone and the guns were silent. Slowly, Turner hoisted himself to his feet, peered over the side: the gunner was dead, his harness cut to ribbons.

He heard a scuffle behind him, saw a slight figure climb to the edge of the bridge. It was Chrysler, Chrysler who had neither smiled nor scarcely even spoken since they had opened up the Asdic cabinet; at the same time Turner saw three Heinkels forming up to starboard for a fresh attack.

"Get down, you young fool!" Turner shouted. "Do you want to commit suicide?"

Chrysler looked at him, his eyes wide and devoid of recognition, then dropped down to the sponson below, and with all his slender strength dragged the dead man from his Oerlikon. He was climbing into the cockpit as Turner saw the flame of the Heinkel's guns and flung himself backward.

Cannon shells and bullets smashed against the reinforced armour of the bridge—then he heard the twin Oerlikons opening up. Six shots the Oerlikon fired—only six, and a great, grey shape, stricken and smoking, hurtled over the bridge barely at head height, sheared off its port wing on the director tower and crashed into the sea on the other side.

Chrysler was still sitting in the cockpit. His right hand was clutching his left shoulder, shattered by a cannon shell. Even as the next bomber straightened out on its strafing run, even as he flung himself backwards, Turner saw the boy's bloody hand reach out for the trigger grip again.

Flat on the duckboards beside Carrington and the Kapok Kid, Turner pounded his fist on the deck in terrible anger. He thought of Chrysler, of the excruciating hell of the gun-rest pounding into his shattered shoulder. If he himself lived, Turner swore, he would recommend that boy for the Victoria Cross. Abruptly the firing ceased and a Heinkel swung off sharply to starboard, smoke pouring from both its engines.

Quickly, Turner scrambled to his feet, hoisted himself over the side of the bridge. He did it without looking, and he almost died then. A burst of fire from the third and last Heinkel whistled past his head. Then he was stretched full length on the duckboards again. They were only inches from his eyes, these duckboards, but he could not see them. All he could see was the image of Chrysler, a gaping wound the size of a man's hand in his back, slumped forward across the Oerlikons, the weight of his body tilting the barrels grotesquely skywards. Both barrels were still firing, would keep on firing until the drums were empty, for the dead boy's hand was locked across the trigger.

The attack was over. Turner rose to his feet. Behind him, he heard someone coughing. The Kapok Kid, with Carrington kneeling at his side, was sitting quietly on the boards, his back propped against the legs of the admiral's chair. From left groin to right shoulder through the middle of the embroidered "J" on the chest, stretched a neat, evenly-spaced pattern of round holes, stitched in by the machine-gun of the Heinkel. The blast of the shells must have hurtled him right across the bridge.

The Kid, Turner knew with sudden sick certainty, had only seconds to live. The vivid blue of his eyes was dulled already, the face white and drained of blood. Idly, his hand strayed up and down the punctured kapok, fingering the gashes. Suddenly he smiled, looked down at the quilted suit.

"Ruined," he whispered. "Bloody well ruined!" Then his head slumped forward on his chest. The flaxen hair stirred idly in the wind.

THE *Stirling* died at dawn. She died while still under way, still plunging through the heavy seas, her mangled, twisted bridge and super-structure glowing red, glowing white-hot as the wind and sundered oil tanks lashed the flames into a holocaust.

The Stukas came from the south, flew high over the convoy, then, in the classic Stuka attack pattern, they peeled off in sequence and fell out of the sky, plummetting each one arrow-true for its target.

Six bombs buried themselves in the cruiser, the lightened Stukas lifting away to port and starboard. From the bridge of the *Ulysses*, there seemed to be a weird absence of noise as the bombs went home. They just vanished into the smoke and flame, engulfed by the inferno.

No one blow finished the *Stirling*, but a mounting accumulation of blows. She had taken too much and, like a reeling boxer, she could take no more.

Turner watched her die. Cruisers, he mused in a queerly detached abstraction, must be the toughest ships in the world. No sudden knock-out, no *coup de grâce* for them—always they had to be battered to death. . . . Like the *Stirling*. Turner's grip on the shattered windscreen tightened. For fifteen months, now, the old *Stirling* had shared the burden of the *Ulysses* in the worst convoys of the war. It was not good to watch a friend die. Turner looked away, but he could hear the mon-strous hiss of steam as the white-hot superstructure of the *Stirling* plunged deeply into the ice-chilled Arctic. When he looked up, there was only the rolling, empty sea ahead.

There were seven ships left now—four merchantmen, including the commodore's ship, a tanker, the destroyer *Sirrus* and the *Ulysses*. All were damaged, but none so desperately as the *Ulysses*. Seven ships, only seven: thirty-six had set out for Russia.

At 0800 Turner signalled the *Sirrus*: "WT gone. Signal C-in-C course, speed, position. Confirm 0930 as rendezvous. Code."

The reply came an hour later. "Delayed heavy seas. Rendezvous approx. 1030. Impossible fly off air cover. Keep coming. C-in-C."

"Keep coming!" Turner repeated savagely. "Would you listen to him! Keep coming, he says! What the hell does he expect us to do—scuttle ourselves?" He shook his head in angry despair. "I hate to repeat myself," he said bitterly. "But I must. Too bloody late as usual!"

Heavy grey clouds blotted out the sky from horizon to horizon. But the snow did not come—not then. Once more, there came instead the Stukas, the roar of their engines as they methodically quartered the empty sea in search of the convoy—Charlie had left at dawn. Ten minutes from the time of the first warning of their approach, the leading Junkers 87 dropped out of the steadily darkening sky.

Ten minutes—but time for a council and plan of desperation. When the Stukas came, they found the convoy stretched out in line abreast, the tanker *Varella* in the middle, two merchantmen in close line ahead on either side of it, the *Sirrus* and the *Ulysses* guarding the flanks, a formation which offered at least a fighting chance. If the Stukas approached from astern—their favourite attack technique—they would run into the massed fire of seven ships; if they approached from the sides, they must first attack the escorts, for no Stuka would present its unprotected underbelly to the guns of a warship. . . . They elected to attack from both sides, five from the east, four from the west. This time, Turner, noted, they were carrying long-range fuel tanks.

Turner had no time to see through the murk how the *Sirrus* was faring, for thick smoke was blowing back across the bridge from the barrels of "A" and "B" turrets. In the gaps of sound between the crash of the 5.25s, he could hear the quick-fire of Doyle's midship pom-pom, the vicious thudding of the Oerlikons.

Suddenly, startling in its unexpectedness, two beams of dazzling white stabbed out through the gloom. Turner stared. The 44-inch searchlights! Of course! The great searchlights, still on the official secret list, capable of lighting up an enemy six miles away! What a fool he had been to forget them—Vallery had used them often against attacking aircraft. Even in daylight no man could look into those terrible eyes and not be blinded.

Turner peered aft to see who was manning the control position. It was

Ralston—searchlight control, Turner remembered, was his day action station.

Jammed in the corner of the bridge by the gate, Turner watched Ralston's utter concentration. There was not a flicker of emotion as the first Stuka weaved, seeking to escape those flaming arc-lights, not even a flicker as it swerved violently and crashed into the sea a hundred yards short of the *Ulysses*.

What was the boy thinking of? Turner wondered. His mother, his sisters, entombed under the ruins of a Croydon bungalow: of his brother, innocent victim of that mutiny—how impossible that mutiny seemed now!—in Scapa: of his father, dead by his son's own hand?

The face was inhumanly still. There wasn't a shadow of feeling as the second Stuka overshot the *Ulysses*, dropped its bomb into the open sea: as a third blew up in mid-air: not a trace of emotion when the guns of the next Stuka smashed one of the lights . . . not even when the cannon shells of the last smashed the searchlight control, tore half his chest away. He died instantaneously, slumping quietly onto the deck.

One bomb had struck the *Ulysses*, just for'ard of "A" turret, fracturing the turret's hydraulic lines. Temporarily, at least, "B" was the only effective remaining turret in the ship.

The *Sirrus* hadn't been quite so lucky. She had destroyed one Stuka— the merchantmen had claimed another—and had been hit twice, both bombs exploding in the after mess-deck. And during action stations the after mess-deck was always empty. Not a man had lost his life—not another man was to lose his life on the destroyer *Sirrus*: she was never damaged again on the Russian convoys.

Hope was rising fast. Less than an hour to go, now, and the battle squadron would be there. It was dark, and heavy snow was falling. No plane could find them in this, they were almost beyond the reach of shore-based aircraft, and it was well-nigh impossible weather for submarines.

"Maybe we'll make it yet," Carrington said.

"Maybe, maybe." Turner was non-committal. "Preston!"

"Yes, sir, I see it." Preston was staring to the north where the signal lamp of the *Sirrus* was flickering rapidly.

"A ship, sir!" he reported excitedly. "*Sirrus* says naval vessel approaching from the north!"

"From the north! Thank God!" Turner shouted. "It must be them!

They're ahead of time. I take it all back . . ." He broke off, looked to the north. Stilettos of white flame had lanced out briefly, vanished again. He saw shells splashing whitely in the water under the bows of the commodore's ship, the *Cape Hatteras*: then the flashes again, brighter this time, that lit up for a second the bows and superstructure of the ship that was firing.

He turned to his first lieutenant. "The answer to many questions," he said softly. "That's why they've been softening up the *Stirling* and ourselves for the past couple of days. The fox is in among the chickens. It's our old pal the Hipper cruiser come to pay us a social call." He shrugged. "We deserved better than this. . . . How would you like to die a hero's death?"

"The very idea appals me!" boomed a voice behind him. Brooks had just arrived on the bridge.

"Me, too," Turner admitted. "Have we any option, gentlemen?"

"Alas, no," Brooks said sadly.

"Full ahead both!" Carrington called down the speaking-tube: it was his answer.

"No, no," Turner chided gently. "Full *power*, Number One. Tell them we're in a hurry. Preston! General emergency signal: 'Scatter: proceed independently to Russian ports.'"

THE SNOW WAS still falling when Johnny Nicholls climbed laboriously up to the *Sirrus*'s bridge. He was deadly weary, and he winced in agony every time his foot touched the deck: his left leg was shattered just above the ankle—shrapnel from the bomb in the after mess-deck.

Peter Orr, commander of the *Sirrus*, was waiting for him. "I thought you would want to see this," he said. "Just look at her go!"

Half a mile away on the beam, the *Cape Hatteras* was blazing furiously, slowing to a stop. Some miles to the north, Nicholls could distinguish the vague shape of the German cruiser, still mercilessly pumping shells into the sinking ship.

Half a mile astern on the port quarter, the *Ulysses* was coming up, sheeted in foam and spray. Nicholls gazed, fascinated. This was the first time he'd seen the *Ulysses* since he'd left her and he was appalled. Both masts were gone, the director tower shattered and grotesquely askew: smoke still pluming up from the great holes in fo'c'sle and poop, the after-turrets, wrenched from their mountings, pitched crazily on the deck. The skeleton of the Condor still lay athwart "Y" turret, a Stuka was buried to the wings in the fo'c'sle deck, and she was, he knew, split right down to the water level abreast the torpedo tubes.

A messenger came to the bridge. "Rendezvous 1015," Orr read. "1015! Good lord, twenty-five minutes' time! Do you hear that, Doc? Twenty-five minutes' time!"

"Yes, sir," Nicholls said. He hadn't heard him.

Orr looked at him, touched his arm. "Bloody well incredible, isn't it?" he murmured.

"I wish to God I was aboard her," Nicholls muttered miserably. "Why did they send me—? Look! What's that?"

A huge red and blue and white flag, twenty feet in length, was streaming out below the yardarm of the *Ulysses*.

"The battle ensign," Orr shook his head in wonder. "To take time off to do that *now*—well, Doc, only Turner would do that. You know him well?"

Nicholls nodded silently.

"Me, too," Orr said simply. "We are both lucky men."

The *Sirrus* was still doing fifteen knots when the *Ulysses* passed them by a cable-length away as if they were stopped in the water, at a speed of just on or over forty incredible knots. Afterwards, Nicholls could never describe it accurately. He had a hazy memory of the *Ulysses* battering through waves and troughs on a steady even keel. He could recall, too, that "B" turret was firing continuously, shell after shell screaming away through the blinding snow, to burst in brilliant splendour over the German cruiser: for "B" turret had only starshells left. He carried, too, a vague picture of Turner waving ironically from the bridge, of the great ensign streaming stiffly astern, already torn and tattered at the edges. But what he could never forget as long as he lived, was the tremendous roar of the great boiler room intake fans as they sucked in mighty draughts of air for the engines. For the *Ulysses* was driving through the heavy seas under maximum power, at a speed that should have broken her shuddering back, should have burnt out the great engines. There was no doubt as to Turner's intentions: he was going to ram the enemy, to destroy the Hipper cruiser and take it down with him.

Nicholls gazed and gazed and felt sick at heart, for that ship was part of him now, his good friends, especially the Kapok Kid, they, too, were part of him, and it is always terrible to see the end of a legend. But he felt, too, a strange exultation; she was dying, but what a way to die! And if ships had hearts, had souls, as the old sailing men declared, surely the *Ulysses* would want it this way, too.

She was still doing forty knots when, as if by magic, a great gaping hole appeared in her bows just above the water-line. Shell-fire, possibly, but unlikely at that angle. It must have been a torpedo from a U-boat, not yet located. The *Ulysses* brushed aside the torpedo, ignored the grievous wound, ignored the heavy shells crashing into her and kept on going.

She was still doing forty knots, driving in under the guns of the enemy, guns at maximum depression, when "A" magazine blew up, blasted off the entire bows in one shattering detonation. For a second, the lightened fo'c'sle reared high into the air: then it plunged down and kept on going down, driving down to the black floor of the Arctic, driven down by the madly spinning screws, the still thundering engines her own executioner.

EPILOGUE

THE SKY WAS BLUE, with little puffs of drifting cotton-wool cloud. The street gardens spilled over with flowers, the birds were singing, clear and sweet above the roar of the traffic, and Big Ben was booming the hour as Johnny Nicholls climbed awkwardly out of his taxi and hobbled slowly up the marble steps into the huge hall.

The tip-tap of his crutches sounded unnaturally loud on the floor as he limped over to the counter. A trim young Wren, red-haired and shirt-sleeved, came up.

"Can I help you, sir?" The blue eyes were soft with concern. Nicholls caught a glimpse of himself in a mirror behind her, a glimpse of a scuffed uniform jacket over a grey fisherman's jersey, of sunken eyes and gaunt, pale cheeks. He didn't have to be a doctor to know that he looked in pretty poor shape.

"My name is Nicholls, Surgeon Lieutenant Nicholls. I have an appointment—"

"Lieutenant Nicholls . . . HMS *Ulysses*!" The girl gasped. "Of course, sir. They're expecting you. Just across the hall here, please.'

She knocked and announced him. There were three men in the room. The one he recognized, Vice Admiral Starr, came forward to meet him. He looked older, far older, far more tired than when Nicholls had last seen him—hardly a fortnight previously.

"How are you, Nicholls?" he asked. "Not walking so well, I see. Come and sit down."

He led Nicholls across to the big table. Behind it, framed against huge wall-maps, sat two men. Starr introduced them. One, big, beefy, red of face, was in the uniform of an admiral of the Fleet: the other was a civilian, a small, stocky man with iron-grey hair, eyes still and wise and old. Nicholls recognized him immediately. The Navy was indeed doing him proud: such receptions were not for all. . . . But they seemed reluctant to begin the reception, Nicholls thought—he had forgotten the shock his appearance must give. Finally, the grey-haired man cleared his throat.

"How's the leg, boy?" he asked.

"Not too bad, thank you, sir," Nicholls answered. "Two, three weeks should see me back on the job."

"You're taking two months, laddie. More if you want it. And if anyone asks, just tell 'em I said so. Cigarette?" He sat back in his chair. "Had a good trip home?"

"Very fair, sir. VIP treatment all the way. Moscow, Teheran, Cairo, Gib." Nicholls's mouth twisted. "Much more comfortable than the trip out." He paused, inhaled deeply on his cigarette. "I would have preferred to come home in the *Sirrus*."

"No doubt," Starr broke in. "But we were anxious to have a first-hand account of FR 77—and particularly the *Ulysses*—as soon as possible."

The grey-haired man nodded in confirmation. "Just tell us all you know," he said kindly. "Everything—about everything. Take your time. . . ."

Nicholls did his best, but here in the heart of London the tale he had to tell fell falsely, even on his own ears. It wasn't so bad when he stuck to the facts, of carriers crippled by seas, stranded and torpedoed; the storm; the gradual attrition of the convoy, of the U-boats and bombers sent to the bottom, of the *Ulysses*, battering through the snowstorm at forty knots, blown up by the German cruiser, of the arrival of the battle squadron, of the flight of the cruiser before it could inflict further damage, of the rounding-up of the scattered convoy, of the curtain of Russian fighters in the Barents Sea, of the ultimate arrival in the Kola Inlet of the battered remnants of FR 77—five ships in all.

It was when he came to the less ascertainable facts that he sensed the doubt. But he told the stories of heroes such as Ralston, Riley, Petersen and a dozen others as unemotionally as he could. For a second, his voice broke as he spoke of the half-dozen survivors from the *Ulysses*, picked up by the *Sirrus*. He told how Brooks had given his lifejacket to an ordinary seaman, who amazingly survived fifteen minutes in that water: how Turner, wounded in head and arm, had supported a dazed seaman till the *Sirrus* came plunging alongside, had passed a bowline round him, and then was gone before anything could be done: how Carrington, that man of iron, a balk of timber under his arms, had held two men above water till rescue came. Both men had died later. Carrington had climbed the rope unaided, clambered over the guard-rails dangling a left-leg with the foot blown off above the ankle. Carrington would survive: Carrington was indestructible.

But what the three men really wanted to know, Nicholls realized, was how the *Ulysses* had been, how her crew of mutineers had borne themselves. But what was there to tell? That Vallery had spoken to the men over the broadcast system: how he had gone among them and made them almost as himself, on that grim, exhausting tour of inspection: how he had spoken of them as he died: and how, most of all, his death had made them men again? For that was all that there was to tell, and such things could neither be explained nor understood.

Suddenly Nicholls was overwhelmed by the futility of it all, and his voice trailed into silence. Vaguely, he heard the grey-haired man ask something and he muttered aloud, unthinking.

"What did you say?" The grey-haired man asked.

"I only said, 'They were the best crew God ever gave a captain,'" Nicholls murmured.

"I see." There was no other comment. "Take things easy for a minute, boy. If you'll just excuse us...."

He rose to his feet, walked over to the other end of the room, the others following. Nicholls sat slumped in the chair. From time to time, he could hear a murmur of voices. Starr's high-pitched voice carried most clearly. "Mutiny ship, sir . . . never the same again . . . better this way." There was a murmured reply, too low to catch, then the

grey-haired man said something rapidly, his tone sharp with dis-
agreement, but the words were blurred. Nicholls looked up. Then
the deep, heavy voice of the fleet admiral said something about
"expiation", and the grey-haired man nodded slowly. Starr looked
at Nicholls over his shoulder, and he knew they were talking about
him. He thought he heard the words "not well" and "frightful strain",
but perhaps he was imagining it.

Anyway, he no longer cared. He was anxious only to be gone. He
did not belong here, where everything was so sane and commonplace
and real—and withal a world of shadows. Gradually, he became aware
that the three men were standing above him, their eyes full of concern.

"I'm damnably sorry, boy," the grey-haired man said. "You're a
sick man and we've asked far too much of you. A drink, Nicholls?
It was most remiss—"

"No, thank you, sir." Nicholls straightened himself in his chair.
"I'll be perfectly all right." He hesitated. "Is—is there anything
else?"

"No, nothing at all." The smile was genuine, friendly. "You've
been a great help to us, Lieutenant, a great help. And a fine report.
Thank you very much indeed."

Nicholls struggled to his feet, reached out for his crutches. He
shook hands with Starr and the admiral of the Fleet. The grey-haired
man accompanied him to the door.

Nicholls paused. "Sorry to bother you but—when do I begin my
leave, sir?"

"As from now. And have a good time. God knows you've earned it,
my boy.... Where are you going?"

"Henley, sir."

"Oh.... A girl, Lieutenant?"

Nicholls nodded.

The grey-haired man clapped him on the shoulder, and smiled.
"Pretty, I'll be bound?"

"I don't know, sir. I don't know at all. I've never seen her."

He tip-tapped his way across the marble flags, passed through the
heavy doors and limped out into the sunshine.

SURFACE AT THE POLE
by Commander James Calvert, U.S.N.

Surface at the Pole

A CONDENSATION OF THE BOOK BY **COMMANDER JAMES CALVERT, U.S.N**

The secret orders that Commander James Calvert studied as the US submarine *Skate* reached the Arctic ice pack in August 1958 were a challenge to him and his crew. A sister ship, the *Nautilus*, had just made her historic cruise under the ice at the North Pole. The *Skate*—if she dared—was now to make a still more dangerous attempt to test the strategic usefulness of the Arctic ocean: she must surface at the Pole! In this exciting book, the reader enters the inner world of a great nuclear submarine and shares the crew's suspense as they search agonizingly below and between massive floes of ice for openings large enough to take the huge craft.

JAMES CALVERT was twice awarded the Legion of Merit in recognition of his achievements in polar exploration aboard the *Skate*. He retired from the US Navy in 1972 with the rank of vice admiral, having been Superintendent of the famous Naval Academy, Annapolis. A company executive, he now lives in Darien, Connecticut.

CHAPTER 1

It was ten o'clock on a Sunday morning in August 1958. Around a small table in the center of a long, low, steel-walled room stood a group of four men, gazing intently at a moving pinpoint of light which shone like a glowworm through the glass tabletop and the sheet of chart paper that covered it. One of the men was following the path of the light with a black pencil.

A second knot of men were looking at a gray metal box suspended at eye level. Through a glass window on its face was visible the rapid oscillation of a metal stylus, inscribing an irregular pattern of two parallel lines, like a range of mountains upside down, on a slowly rolling paper tape. One of the men watching it broke the silence in the quiet room. "Heavy ice, ten feet," he said laconically. At the plotting table, the black pencil line continued to follow the path of the moving light.

Then the stylus pattern suddenly converged to a single narrow bar. "Clear water!" This time there was a poorly concealed trace of elation in the voice. At the plotting table, a small red cross was made over the pinpoint of light, completing a roughly rectangular pattern of similar crosses on the paper. And so the United States nuclear submarine *Skate*, cruising in the depths of the Arctic Ocean, completed preparations for an attempt to find her way to the surface deep within the polar ice pack.

As commander of the submarine, the next move was up to me. I studied the plotting paper. The moving light, showing the position of the submarine, was just entering the rectangle of red crosses indicating where ice ended and open water began. "Speed?" I asked.

"One-half knot."

"Depth?"

"One eighty."

"All back one-third," I said.

A slight quiver ran through the ship as her two eight-foot bronze propellers gently reversed. On the plotting paper, the pinpoint of light was no longer moving.

"All stop," I called out. The vibration of the propellers ceased. "Up periscope. I'll have a look."

A slim crewman pushed a lever, and a steel cylinder rose out of its well, moving sluggishly against the pressure of the sea. Finally the bottom of the cylinder, containing a pair of handles and an eyepiece, rose to eye level and sighed to a stop. I folded down the hinged metal handles and looked through the eyepiece.

The clarity of the water and the amount of light at this depth were startling, like the lovely tropical waters off the Bahamas. I turned the periscope to the right and a blob of color came into sight. We had company: an ethereal, translucent jellyfish was gracefully waving his rainbow-colored tentacles in the quiet water of a sea whose surface is forever protected from waves by its cover of ice. When I shifted the line of sight upward, I could see nothing but a blurred aquamarine expanse. There was no ice in view.

"Down periscope," I said, folding the handles up. I looked around the crowded control center of the submarine. Every face was turned questioningly toward mine. "Nothing in sight but a jellyfish," I said. There was a ripple of nervous laughter. "There's a good bit of light here," I went on. "We must be under an opening." At the plotting table, the pinpoint of light was resting squarely in the center of the rough rectangle of red marks. I turned toward the men around the ice-detecting instrument with its sweeping stylus.

"How does it look?"

The man in charge looked impassively at me. He held up his left hand with the index finger and thumb forming a circle and the remaining three fingers raised. Now was the time.

All eyes were on the men at the diving controls and on a blue-eyed lieutenant with short-cropped curly hair, the diving officer. He was responsible for holding the *Skate* in its present motionless position, one hundred and eighty feet below the surface—a delicate task, but nothing compared to what he would now be called upon to do.

With a note of confidence in my voice that I didn't really feel, I said to him, "Bring her up slowly to one hundred feet."

To the intricate commands of the diving officer, a crewman standing by a long bank of control valves started to lighten the ship. The whir of a pump filled the room as seawater ballast was pumped out of tanks inside the ship. The three-thousand-ton submarine began to drift slowly upward. Our depth had kept us safe from the ice; now we were deliberately taking the ship up where danger lay. My heart began to pound. I ordered the periscope up again. "Call out the depths as she comes up," I told the diving officer as I put my face to the eyepiece. There was nothing to see but water. Even the jellyfish was gone.

"One forty." This meant that the top of the raised periscope, sixty feet higher than the keel, was now only eighty feet below the surface—perhaps much less than that from the underside of the ice. I couldn't understand why the ice was not yet visible. The room was deathly quiet. The *whish* of the ice-detector stylus sounded strangely loud. I walked the periscope around in a complete circle. Nothing.

"One twenty." The top of the periscope was only sixty feet below the surface. Suddenly I saw an outline of heavy ice, rafted and twisted in huge blocks—and frighteningly close. I hastily turned the prism upward, but could see only the same blurred aquamarine. I could hear water flooding into the tanks—the diving officer was preparing to halt the ascent. The thought of what might happen if he could not bring the ship to a stop flashed through my mind.

"Secure flooding," the diving officer said, without moving his eyes away from the depth gauge. The submarine slowed and stopped at one hundred feet, as though on a gigantic freight elevator.

So far as I could see, there was no ice directly overhead, but we could only hope we were in the right position. The red checks on the plotting table told us that the lake in the ice was just large enough to hold us safely if we stayed near its center. Bringing the ship up too slowly could be dangerous, for it increased the chance of drifting under the edge of the surrounding ice. On the other hand, to blow

the main ballast tanks with high-pressure air and pop to the surface like a cork would be foolhardy. If the thin pressure hull of the *Skate* should strike the ice, the ship would be lost with every member of her crew.

A submerged submarine moving neither forward nor aft is like a huge, sluggish balloon. It normally uses its forward motion to control its depth. Deprived of forward motion, the submarine will drift upward or downward in accordance with its trim and buoyancy. Here, under the ice, we were staking our ship on the ability of the diving officer to make the *Skate* do something no submarine was ever designed to do—rise straight upward at a predetermined speed.

A bead of perspiration was starting on my forehead. I looked around the room; every eye was turned in my direction. No matter what my inner feelings, I must appear as calm and decisive as possible. I turned to the diving officer. "All right, bring her up, and just let her come out of the water as easily as you can. Call out the depths as you go." Again we slowly began to ascend.

"Ninety feet." The periscope was only thirty feet below the surface, and from here on we would have to go blind. If the periscope struck the ice, it could bend or shatter our vital and fragile eye.

"Down periscope," I said, and the slender tube hissed downward into the bowels of the ship to safety.

"Eighty feet," chanted the diving officer. "Seventy feet." How could he be so calm?

Without warning, the upward speed of the ship began to accelerate. I stepped forward, a cry of warning rising to my lips, but checked myself, realizing what was happening. The diving officer was already flooding the tanks in an attempt to slow her. It was no use. We had struck a layer of colder or saltier water, which was making us rise much too swiftly.

"Fifty-five feet," reported the diving officer. There was real concern in his voice now. If we were going to hit anything, it would be soon. But there was no shuddering shock against the ice. The submarine rose to about forty feet, hung there momentarily, and sank back to forty-five feet.

"Forty-five feet—seems to be hanging there," the diving officer reported, returning to his flat monotone.

Now it would be safe to look. "Up periscope!" The shiny steel

From the *Skate*'s control center the author gives orders to surface.
Photo © National Geographic Society

cylinder seemed to fly up now, in comparison with its sluggish action in the depths. I flipped the handles down and swept around. The light was dazzling. The top of the periscope was in clear, open air! I could see the huge slabs of rafted, broken ice that formed the edges of the lake. The ice seemed dangerously close on all sides, until I remembered that we are not accustomed to looking at things close by through a periscope.

As I twisted the prism downward, I could see rippling deep blue water between us and the jagged ice fields stretching as far beyond as I could see. I carefully measured the distances to the ice forward and aft. There would be room to surface, provided we did not move even a few yards in either direction.

"Stand by to surface!" The words went out on the loudspeaker system, electrifying the rest of the ship. None of the eighty men stationed outside the control center could know exactly where we were or how we stood until that word was passed.

The team went into action. Valves were opened and closed, switches thrown, reports made to the diving officer. Finally he turned to me and said, "All vents shut, ready to surface." I nodded assent, and he ordered, "Blow all ballast!" No need to hesitate now; we could see what we were doing.

The roar of high-pressure air in the ballast tanks was ear shattering after the strained silence of the past hours. The submarine leaped upward; yet so skillfully was the job done that the ship moved scarcely a yard ahead or backward.

"Open the hatch!" I shouted to the crewman poised by its locking dogs. He spun the handles and threw the vaultlike hatch open to the fresh air. As we stepped out I felt the slap of damp, cool air almost as a physical blow. The sky was lightly overcast and there was almost no wind.

We climbed quickly to the bridge. The first impression was of being in an infinite desert of ice, a flat patchwork maze of floes in every direction. Before us the black hull of the submarine contrasted with the deep blue of the lake water and the stark white of the surrounding ice. The *Skate* was on the surface of the Arctic Ocean, deep inside the polar pack. And she was safe. I let out a sigh that seemed to reach to the bottom of the ship.

My companion, who had been drinking all of this in with me,

pointed suddenly downward, near the port side of the ship. There, climbing slowly out of the water and up onto the ice, was a full-grown polar bear. He shook himself like a wet dog and gazed curiously at this intruder in his domain. No doubt he was seeing his first atomic submarine, and it was probably his first sight of man as well.

CHAPTER 2

I HAD COME A LONG way to meet this puzzled polar bear at the top of the world: this voyage was the climax of three years of hard work and careful preparation.

In the spring of 1955, I had completed more than two years in my first submarine command, the USS *Trigger*, operating from the base at New London, Connecticut. I had just received orders to staff duty in Pearl Harbor, and my wife, Nancy, and our children were looking forward to life among the palm trees and pineapples. I was not viewing the assignment with any aversion either.

Then, when only a few days remained until our departure, I received a summons to the office of Rear Admiral Frank Watkins, boss of all the submarines in the Atlantic Fleet. He told me that Admiral Rickover wanted to see me in Washington, D.C., and, if the interview was satisfactory, would want me to go to work for him.

I was thunderstruck. Everyone in New London knew who Admiral Rickover was. The submarine world had been electrified by the spectacular success of the nuclear-powered *Nautilus* and by the equal success of the outspoken, independent officer responsible for getting her built in the face of tremendous controversy.

I asked incredulously, "What does he mean come to work for him? What would I do? I'm not a specialist in engineering and I don't know anything about nuclear reactors."

Admiral Watkins looked at me steadily. "Jim, there's one thing you know how to do that could interest Rickover—that's command a submarine. I'd advise you to get the next train to Washington." I did.

THE NEXT DAY I entered a shabby gray Washington building labeled ATOMIC ENERGY COMMISSION and found myself in a bare anteroom. I announced myself and was asked to sit down and wait; and wait I did, for perhaps two hours. During this ordeal my trepidation grew. Stories about Admiral Rickover were being told in every submarine wardroom. He personally grilled every person who was a candidate to work for him—and no candidate ever forgot his interview. I was prepared for the worst when at last I was escorted into Rickover's office.

The admiral, white-haired and slight, was in civilian clothes. I later discovered that he never wore a uniform if he could possibly avoid it. He shook hands and asked me to sit down. I glanced around his office. A table in the center was covered with documents, letters, and a half-empty cup of coffee. Three sides of the room were lined with heavy-laden bookshelves.

"How old are you, Calvert?" the admiral asked abruptly.

"Thirty-four," I answered.

"Where did you go to school?"

I described my small Ohio high school, my two years at Oberlin College. Soon we were discussing the subject of my class standing at Annapolis. "About one hundredth out of a class of six hundred," I said with a bit of pride.

"Why so low?" snapped the admiral.

While I pondered this unexpected thrust, someone came into the office and handed the admiral a card. He looked at it with an expressionless face and picked up the telephone on his desk.

The conversation, which moved rapidly, was with the president of a company producing material for Rickover's program. It was all too clear that the admiral was displeased with the product, the company, and its president. I watched with dismay as the admiral's voice rose and his face purpled. He stood up and banged his desk until everything on it jumped.

My heart sank. After this outburst I was sure he would be exhausted or in too bad a humor to carry on an objective interview. The telephone went down with a colossal crash and the admiral returned his attention to me. In a perfectly calm voice he went on. "Now why did you say you stood so low at the Naval Academy?"

I leaned forward uncomfortably. "Well—" I began.

"I'll tell you why," Rickover snapped. "You're either dumb or lazy. Which is it?"

While the admiral probed mercilessly through the shortcomings of my Naval Academy career, I became aware of one reason why I was doing so poorly in this interview. Most of us observe certain routine amenities in our conversation and avoid the abrupt approach to an unpleasant fact. Rickover has trained himself to do just the opposite. He comes directly to the heart of the matter. The more unpleasant it is, the more swiftly he gets to it.

We went on to the subject of spare time. "How many books do you read a month?" he asked.

"About two," I answered truthfully.

"What were the last four?"

I told him, and he then discussed them with me briefly. He had read all four.

"Calvert, do you play golf?" the admiral asked, with the same inflection one would employ to ask a man if he used narcotics.

Sheepishly I admitted that I played occasionally.

"That's fine, just fine," the admiral said with biting sarcasm. "You admit time is a problem for you and yet you go out and waste hours on end playing golf." He looked at me narrowly. "Do you have a television set?"

I admitted hopelessly that we did.

"That's all, thanks," he said, rising with finality.

I walked out of his office a beaten man.

LATE THAT EVENING I was back in New London.

"It couldn't have gone worse," I told Nancy woefully. "You're always off-balance in the conversation. The guy thinks I'm just a golfing playboy."

"Well, it probably wasn't quite as bad as you think," she said consolingly.

"This is one time you're wrong," I said with conviction.

The next morning, as I stepped on board the *Trigger*, the duty officer handed me a message from the Navy Department. It read:

ORDERS OF JANUARY 22 CANCELED X WHEN RELIEVED OF COMMAND OF USS TRIGGER YOU WILL PROCEED TO WASHINGTON DC AND REPORT TO THE CHIEF OF THE NAVAL REACTORS BRANCH US ATOMIC ENERGY COMMISSION FOR DUTY

The message had been sent a few hours after I left Admiral Rickover's office.

WHEN I REPORTED TO THE Naval Reactors Branch in May 1955, the organization was six years old. It had already accomplished great things; and it was, as much as a government organization can be, built around one man.

During World War II, Captain H. G. Rickover had run the electrical desk at the navy's Bureau of Ships with devastating and often unpopular efficiency; and in 1946 he was one of the men invited to a meeting at Oak Ridge to discuss the peaceful applications of atomic power. Rickover had long been impressed with the potential importance of the submarine if it could be freed from its technical limitations. At Oak Ridge, it occurred to him that atomic power was the key to what he sought. Before long he was obsessed with the idea of a submarine driven by a uranium pile.

The scientific and political obstacles in the way of this project were enormous. When Rickover arrived back in Washington, he had no position, no money, and no authority. All he had was a great idea, ruthless determination, and courage. For eight years he talked, argued, bluffed, schemed, and fought. In January 1955 the *Nautilus*, the world's first nuclear-powered ship, went to sea.

Along the way, one of the most remarkable things Rickover had done was to create for himself simultaneous positions in the Bureau of Ships and the Atomic Energy Commission. In both organizations he was in sole charge of the development of atomic reactors for naval vessels.

Perhaps the strongest impression I have of Admiral Rickover is his abiding respect for things of the mind. His range of knowledge and interest is vast. In his search for competent people he has interviewed thousands of candidates, and always he has put heavy emphasis on their education. In addition, he has tried to instill in his subordinates a deep respect for the value of time, and a knowledge of the difference between spending it and killing it. He spent long hours going over with me not merely technical matters but his philosophy of what was ultimately important, for oneself as well as for the organization one worked in.

Lastly, Admiral Rickover is not afraid. In the world of pulling and hauling for power that is Washington, he does not quail easily. I remember that in his office hangs a familiar Shakespeare quotation I would often mull over:

Our doubts are traitors,
And make us lose the good we oft might win
By fearing to attempt.

Not often did he fear to attempt.

WHEN I REPORTED for duty, I was at once started on a review of mathematics, then went on to elementary nuclear physics, and later worked into other technical subjects necessary for a working understanding of nuclear power.

The skipper of the *Nautilus,* Commander Eugene Wilkinson, would occasionally drop into my office to see how I was getting along. "Dennis" Wilkinson is a husky, dark, energetic man. Vitality and enthusiasm mark everything he does.

We had a conversation in 1955 which marked a turning point in my life. We were talking about one of Dennis' favorite subjects, the Arctic Ocean. Leaning forward, he said vigorously, "There are only four oceans in the world and this is the one with the most powerful location. Just look where it is." He jabbed a finger at a small chart on my desk.

I understood this well enough. The Arctic Ocean is situated directly between the two heartlands of the world. Strategically, it is an area of destiny.

"It's huge," Dennis went on. "More than five times the size of the Mediterranean Sea."

"But how about the ice?" I asked. "Doesn't it make naval operations more or less impossible?"

"Some fairly good surveys have been made," Dennis said, "and we know the ice thickness averages only about ten feet—*overall,*" he added with meaningful emphasis.

If that were true, I realized, a submarine would have little trouble operating underneath it. Dennis went on to tell me that the sea ice in the Arctic is made up of flat sections called floes and that these sections butt up against one another with great force, forming pressure ridges that jut both upward and downward.

"How deep do these ridges go?" I asked.

"Not so much dope on that," Dennis admitted. "Probably not more than a hundred feet. But I think we could get under 'em all right!" he said with a grin.

It was obvious that he wanted to take the *Nautilus* into the Arctic Ocean under the ice—perhaps as far as the North Pole.

"Sounds pretty wild to me, Dennis," I said, shaking my head. Dennis grabbed a small chair, spun it around, and sat on it backward, resting his chin on its back as he looked hard at me.

"Listen, Jim, this isn't a brand-new idea. Sir Hubert Wilkins went up there at least twenty-five years ago in a converted navy submarine. Had to turn back because the ship gave out. Remember?"

"Vaguely. They had a pretty tough time, didn't they?"

"Things have come a long way since then," said Dennis.

American navy interest in the polar submarine, he went on, started when a young research physicist named Waldo Lyon persuaded the navy to send a submarine along on Operation Highjump, Rear Admiral Richard E. Byrd's huge Antarctic expedition of 1946–47. On this and subsequent expeditions Dr. Lyon perfected a machine which measured not only the depth of the submarine beneath the ice, but the thickness of the ice itself.

Nevertheless, it seemed that Lyon's dream of conquering the Arctic by submarine would never come about. An ordinary diesel-electric submarine could last only about thirty hours submerged, and then only if it went very slowly—say about three knots. This meant it would have only about ninety miles in which to locate one of the lakes of open water which open and close among the shifting ice floes. Although the odds were in favor of finding a lake within this distance—at least in summer—the penalty for failure was death. And no responsible submarine commander would ever sign up his crew for this kind of underwater Russian roulette.

But when the *Nautilus* went to sea, Dr. Lyon immediately realized that here was a submarine made to order for his work. Conventional submarines use diesel engines—which require enormous quantities of oxygen—for surface cruising, and electric motors—which run on short-lived batteries—when submerged. But a nuclear submarine requires no oxygen beyond the breathing needs of her crew, and with her virtually unlimited fuel supply can remain submerged under the ice as long as necessary to find suitable openings for surfacing.

Within a short time Lyon was talking to the skipper of the *Nautilus*. Dennis was soon an ardent advocate of a polar probe. He went at the business of selling *Nautilus*-under-the-ice with his usual vigor, and when he left my office that summer afternoon in 1955, he had made still another convert. Not only was I sure the *Nautilus* should go, I also knew that I wanted to go myself.

My aroused curiosity led me to books on the Arctic, and my reading soon introduced me to Fridtjof Nansen.

Nansen, a Norwegian, had read of the tragic voyage of the *Jeannette*, a steam-and-sail-powered U.S. ship which in 1879 attempted to reach the North Pole through the Bering Strait. At a comparatively low latitude the *Jeannette* froze fast in the ice. She drifted helplessly for nearly two years, while ice floes clawed at her. Finally she was crushed. Her thirty-three officers and men, led by Lieutenant Commander George Washington De Long, made their agonizing way one hundred miles to the southwest over the summer ice, dragging three heavy wooden boats. They were finally able to launch their boats, and somehow, through drifting floes, reached open water. On the way to Siberia, four hundred miles away, the boats became separated and one of them was lost with ten men. De Long's boat reached the Lena River, but he and all but two of the thirteen with him perished before they found a village.

One aspect of this tragedy fired Nansen's imagination. The *Jeannette* had sunk in the Arctic Ocean, north of Siberia, in 1881. But in 1884 some of her wreckage drifted ashore on Greenland, more than two thousand miles from where she had sunk! To Nansen this meant that a current must have pushed the ice floes with the wreckage across the Arctic Ocean and out through the Greenland-Spitsbergen strait. Here, Nansen thought, was the way to reach the Pole. If he could build a ship so strong that it would not be crushed, he could lodge it in the ice pack near Siberia and allow the drift to carry him all the way to the Atlantic.

In 1893 he launched his *Fram*, small, strong, and with a rounded hull so that the crushing squeeze of the ice would tend to force her up rather than hold and destroy her. That summer he sailed from Norway along the northern coast of Russia, and lodged the *Fram* in the ice pack north of the New Siberian Islands. In three years she drifted almost precisely as he had predicted. In the spring of 1896 she broke loose from the ice north of Spitsbergen and arrived triumphantly a few days later in Norway. But Nansen was not on her. He and one of his men had left the *Fram* in March 1895 and attempted to reach the Pole on foot. Food shortage made them turn back before reaching their goal, and it was only after a sledge and kayak voyage that makes a splendid adventure story in itself that they reached the Franz Josef Islands and safety. They were taken by ship from there to Norway, arriving only eight days earlier than the *Fram* herself.

To Nansen we owe a great deal of our basic information about the Arctic. He confirmed his hypothesis that the ice floes averaged only some ten to twelve feet thick. Using makeshift sounding equipment, he discovered that the polar basin itself was enormously deep, over two miles in some places. He established that the temperature averages about 32 degrees Fahrenheit above zero in summer and about 32 degrees below zero in winter. He also meticulously recorded his observations of the bears, seals, foxes, and gulls who make a permanent home in the Arctic. Nansen was accurate and objective; his ideals were high. If men like him could devote themselves to the Arctic, then I wanted to do all I could to add to the store of knowledge they had begun.

CHAPTER 3

NOT UNTIL THREE years later did I get the chance to fulfill what had become a deep desire: to see and explore the icy frontier at the top of the world. My two years of education and labor under Admiral Rickover had been rewarded with the command of the USS *Skate*, the country's third nuclear submarine. (Following the *Nautilus*, the *Seawolf* had been launched in 1955.) Now, in 1958, we were actually on our way to the frozen North.

We slipped our moorings at New London on a warm, moonlit July night, and stood down the quiet Thames River toward the open sea. In a few minutes we were nosing into the dark waters of Long Island Sound. But the calm of our departure was deceptive, for, within, the ship was tense with excitement. The whole ship's company of ninety-seven men, plus our nine volunteer civilian specialists, buzzed with speculation. I had not yet divulged all of our orders, but everyone had a general idea of them.

As the Connecticut shore receded, I stood on the open bridge with the officer of the deck, Lieutenant Dave Boyd. Dave is a sandy-haired Scot of rugged appearance and intense energy, the sort of trustworthy and capable officer any submarine commander likes to have. We remained on the bridge, silent, as the *Skate* began to plow into long ocean swells. Then the silence was broken by a loudspeaker: the radar operator was reporting a surface contact.

On the horizon, the lights of an approaching merchant ship, still more than six miles away, could be dimly seen. Radar had indicated that we would come no closer to her than two miles. Dave nonetheless studied the lights carefully through his binoculars, then spoke over the bridge microphone to the helmsman in the control center. "Come left," he said, "to zero nine five," and our bow swung left and settled on its new course, which would give the merchantman even more passing room.

This extreme wariness against collision is customary in submarines, since the slightest damage to the hull is likely to imperil the ship and her crew. The good submarine officer gives a wide berth to every object which he might run into. Yet I could not help thinking, on this balmy night, how our mission in the Arctic would require the very opposite. Our orders directed us to explore the possibility of bringing the *Skate* to the surface in the lakes or leads we hoped to find even in the heart of the ice pack. Instead of giving obstacles a wide berth, we would have to head straight for them. The *Skate* would be meeting few ships where she was going, but there would be an obstacle even more dangerous—ice. Instead of measuring our margin of safety in miles, we might have to measure it in feet.

Our job called for the exercise of more precise judgment, more delicate maneuver, than our duties had ever before demanded. Could we learn enough, become skillful enough, to accomplish this mission and return in safety? Now that we were actually on our way, I was not so sure as I had been.

I prepared to leave the bridge and go below, giving Dave orders to submerge when we reached the thirty-fathom curve. We would then set course to pass south of the famous Nantucket Lightship, the last beacon for ships leaving American waters for Europe—or points farther north.

I descended to the lower bridge, where a heavy watertight hatch, much like the door to a bank vault, led into the ship. To me it has always symbolized the private world of the submarine, isolated and self-contained within a hostile element. Through the eyeports of the lower bridge could be seen the calm, moonlit Atlantic.

I passed through the hatchway and down a long ladder, emerging in the control center, where the shadowy figures of the men on watch could just be made out in the near darkness. At night this room is illuminated only with a few red lights, to preserve the night vision of men going to the bridge. The two barrels of the periscope shone balefully in the eerie light. At the diving stand, only the end of a burning cigarette betrayed the presence of the helmsman as he steered by the faint red glow of the compass repeater in front of him. A few steps aft, a radarman sat silhouetted before the green fluorescence of his screen, watching the moving dot of light that was the merchant ship passing to the south of us.

I could not help being struck by the difference between the open bridge and this highly artificial environment, where men steered without being able to see where they were going and talked confidently about the distance and direction of ships they would never see. For weeks, perhaps months to come, we would have to trust the eyes and ears of electronic instruments. I stepped into the dark passageway leading forward and made my way more by instinct than vision to the small cubicle which is the captain's cabin.

A built-in bunk surmounted by a bookcase, a small desk, a chair, a washbasin that folds Pullman fashion into the wall, a small closet, an intercom phone, and course and depth indicators on the wall—these are its only furnishings. The pastel green color scheme gives only an illusion of airiness and space. Yet one attribute made this Spartan chamber seem like luxury accommodations. The captain's cabin is the only place on board a submarine where there is any privacy.

At the desk, I wrote the night orders for the officer of the deck. I passed the small leather-covered book to the control center, put on my pajamas, and turned in.

Before long I was awakened by the klaxon blasts of the diving alarm. The *Skate* nosed down slightly as Dave took her under—cautiously because of the still relatively shallow water. I could feel her level off and build up that slight hum of motion that makes her seem like something alive when she puts on speed.

It was good to be on our way.

NEXT MORNING, AS IS my custom at sea, I took a walk through the ship, visiting every habitable area from bow to stern. I learn all sorts of things on these trips—what shape the equipment is in, what small problems have arisen, and (most important of all) what frame of mind the crew is in.

People have often asked me what it is like to go to sea in a nuclear submarine. There is much to say in reply, but I think the most striking difference from any other sort of seagoing is that one is completely free from the surface of the water.

The ancient curse of the seagoer is that strangely nauseating motion of ships on the surface. Sailors (especially navy men) will always deny that it affects them. But it does. Even men who have gone to sea all their lives, and have long since gotten over any trace of seasickness, know the discomfort and fatigue that come from the surface of the sea. The British have an expressive term for it: sea-weariness. And no one knows sea-weariness better than those who take ordinary submarines to sea. Small and low in the water, forced to remain on or near the surface to get the air which their diesel engines consume in such huge quantities, they are miserable in rough weather and uncomfortable all the time.

In the *Skate*, however, we can travel three hundred feet below the surface day after day. We are almost devoid of any sense of motion, and the greater hull diameter required to enclose nuclear machinery allows more roomy and comfortable living conditions than those in conventional submarines.

The *Skate* is divided into two basic parts: the engineering spaces aft, and the control and living spaces forward. The extreme ends of the ship contain the torpedo tubes (she carries a total of twenty-two torpedoes and the tubes are always kept loaded).

Almost in the exact center of the submarine is the reactor compartment with its uranium-packed atomic pile. This reactor consists of a jug-shaped steel vessel, almost twenty feet high, containing a gridwork of metal-clad uranium plates, and filled with ordinary water under pressure so great that it cannot boil. When control rods which fit into the uranium grid are pulled out to the correct positions, a controlled chain reaction of uranium fission takes place, generating heat throughout the grid, which is transferred to the water surrounding it. This water is then circulated into the large cylinders of the steam generators. Here the pressurized water gives up some of its heat to another water system on the other side of a metal barrier. This "secondary water" turns to steam, which spins the turbines that drive the ship and generate electric power for use on board.

The pressurized water, which is pumped in and out of the reactor every few seconds, is of course heavily radioactive. It does not, however, transmit this radioactivity to the secondary water. All the radioactivity is confined to one compartment, which is safely shielded by lead plates and heavy sheets of polyethylene plastic.

I began my tour by walking aft through the control center and into the thirty-foot shielded passageway of the reactor compartment, with its gleaming banks of stainless-steel piping. The reactor is below the floor, the only evidence of its presence a faint hum from the giant centrifugal pumps which circulate the pressurized water. The waxlike smell of warm polyethylene filled the air. I stooped to lift the metal cover from one of the inspection windows in the deck. Almost twenty feet below me I could see the bottom of the well-lighted, deserted reactor-machinery space. All looked in good order; replacing the metal cover, I passed on into the engine room and came to the two turbine-generator sets that produce electricity for this small, self-sufficient city beneath the sea. They are the heart of the ship, manufacturing not only electrical power for lighting, cooking, heating, and air purification, but also the electricity required to control the reactor and to operate the main power plant itself. If these whirring giants should fail us, the *Skate* would soon become a lifeless hulk.

I continued aft into the maneuvering room, actually an instrument-filled corner of the engine room. In overall charge was Lieutenant Bill Cowhill. He stood back from the control panels so that he could see all of the instruments without moving. Bill is a thin, crew-cut young man who seems to exude calm and capability. His uniform is always pressed, his shoes always shined. A product of the Naval Reserve Officers' Training Corps program at Northwestern University—where he majored in English literature—he had remained in the navy as a career officer and graduated second in his class from the nuclear school at New London. He nodded to me as I entered, and after a glance at the panels before him wrote down several entries in his engineering log in a neat draftsman's hand.

The maneuvering room is the nerve center for the propulsion

plant, as the control center is for the ship as a whole. In an emergency—fire, steam leak, uncontrolled flooding—many things must be done here rapidly and accurately to prevent serious damage to the power plant and the rest of the ship.

The worst emergency for any submarine, of course, is collision. Its hull will rupture easily when struck, and the internal construction of the submarine is such that almost no one has an opportunity to escape. A special alarm is installed in each submarine for only one purpose—to warn of imminent collision. It is a piercing, whining crescendo that splits the ears and strikes instinctive fear into the marrow of those who hear it.

MY NEXT STOP was the aftermost compartment of the ship. At the extreme end are the vaultlike doors of the stern torpedo tubes; on either side, interspersed with spare torpedoes, are bunks and lockers for fifteen men. In one forward corner of the room is the ship's laundry, complete with a home-style electric dryer. In the other corner is a small radiation-testing laboratory, where I saw the ship's medical officer "reading" one of the film badges that each crew member is required to wear. The degree to which a film turns dark upon development indicates how much radiation the wearer has received. It is interesting that the man with the highest recorded amount of radiation received less than he would from a single set of dental X rays.

It was apparent that the *Skate* would find it difficult to shoot any stern torpedoes in a hurry. Set up in front of them was a working oceanographic laboratory, with boxes full of empty bottles for water samples, a spectrometer to measure the ability of seawater to bend light, and other complicated-looking instruments. In the midst of these gadgets was our senior civilian scientist, Dr. Gene LaFond of San Diego. A cheerful white-haired man of fifty or so, he was to establish himself as an absolutely ruthless poker player at our Saturday afternoon sessions.

I retraced my steps through the engine room and passed into the forward part of the ship. A conventional submarine is divided horizontally into two layers, the lower one of which is normally used for storage. The extra-large hull diameter of the *Skate* enables her to be divided into three layers: two living levels and one storage level. The upper living level contains the control center and the officers' wardroom and quarters; the lower level holds the crew's mess hall, bunk room, galley, and washrooms.

The crew's mess hall is literally never idle. As I entered it, about a dozen of the crew were sitting about reading magazines, playing cards, or studying. The mess hall is equipped with its own Coke machine, hi-fi system, automatic ice-cream machine, and—of course—a gleaming coffee urn to provide an inexhaustible supply of that essential elixir of navy life.

I stopped for a moment beside chief torpedoman Paul Dornberg, chief of the boat—the man in direct military charge of the crew. "Well, Chief," I asked, "have you found a bunk for everyone?"

"Not without looking in all the corners, Captain," Dornberg said. "You know we have better than a hundred people on board, with the civilians. Going to have over thirty of them hot bunking—but we didn't promise to bring them *Queen Mary*–style!"

Hot bunking is the navy term for the sharing of a bunk by two men or, more often, of two bunks by three men. When one of them is on watch, the other two can sleep. It's not the best of arrangements, but it works if everyone cooperates.

From the mess hall I stepped forward into the galley. This compact room, not more than twelve feet square, contains all the equipment necessary to turn out more than three hundred full meals every day, plus sizable snacks for men going on, or coming off, the night watches. The delightful aroma of roasting pork filled the galley as Ray Aten, the tall cook in charge, opened an oven and basted a browning roast. "For lunch?" I asked.

"Yes, sir, along with mashed potatoes and broccoli," Aten answered with a smile.

The preparation of meals was only one of Ray Aten's problems. It is navy policy to carry on board submarines enough food for sixty days, whatever the planned length of the cruise. This meant that Aten had been required to store enough food for eighteen thousand meals. This demands more than a little ingenuity.

Aten had another essential responsibility. A ship that travels submerged day after day must have some means of getting rid of its garbage. In the corner of the galley stands a bronze tube about four feet high, with a top like that of a pressure cooker. Several times a day garbage and trash are put in nylon mesh bags and dropped down this tube to a door in the bottom of the ship. When the top is tightly fastened, the bottom door is opened and the nylon bags are pumped out into the sea. The bags are always weighted to prevent them from floating up and thus betraying the submarine's presence in wartime. For this purpose Aten had to stow a thousand bricks.

I crossed a narrow passageway to the main bunk room. Here, in a room about thirty feet long and fifteen feet wide, are bunks and lockers for forty-one men, each isolated on three sides by metal barriers, and equipped with foam-rubber mattress and pillow and an individual reading light. A room with so many men living in it either is kept scrupulously neat or becomes a hopeless shambles. On the *Skate* this was the responsibility of Paul Dornberg, who saw to it that the first of these alternatives was followed. He had, however, made one concession to Ray Aten's storage problems. The floor of each passageway was completely covered with a single layer of bricks, with a cover of plywood neatly cut to fit over them. The ingenuity of submarine sailors in finding storage space is famous, but I had to admit that this went beyond the usual limits.

I now walked into the *Skate*'s forward torpedo room. At the far end the doors of torpedo tubes gleamed; along each side were racked the cigar-shaped torpedoes. Twenty bunks were located in this large room, some of them among the torpedoes. In charge was torpedoman Julian Buckley, a fresh-faced, stocky New Englander. He and a group of his assistants were busy with a torpedo which had been pulled into the middle of the room and opened like a giant robot patient on an operating table. Navy philosophy about torpedoes is the same as that concerning food: Be ready. Continual checks are made to assure that they are in working order. With flashlights, tools, and meters, Buckley and his men were performing intricate maneuvers deep within the weapon. I doubt that any group of surgeons more earnestly discussed a problem over an open patient, although the language in this case may have been more colorful.

"Good morning," I said. "How does this load of fish look?"

"Too soon to say, Captain," Buckley said, wiping his brow. "But you know how it is—those shops don't take care of them the way they used to."

I smiled. Even on one of the world's newest, finest ships, Buckley held to the navy belief that things were better in the old days.

I walked back through the mess hall, up a broad metal stairway, into the officers' wardroom. It was now nearly lunchtime; a crisp white cloth was on the table, set with shining silver and the plain, blue-trimmed china that has been traditional in navy wardrooms for more than a hundred years. Before long we were enjoying delicious roast pork as the *Skate* moved smoothly along at eighteen knots, three hundred feet below the stormy surface of the Atlantic.

The *Skate* was a magnificent ship. Everything that human ingenuity and national resources could provide had been included in her. Indeed, the ship itself tended to lull one into a sense of complete security. And yet every turn of our propellers brought us nearer regions for which the *Skate* had not been designed; regions fraught with danger for this ship. We knew that the *Skate* and her men were facing the challenge of their lives. Soon they would take the gravest risks ever asked of a peacetime crew.

CHAPTER 4

OUR SECOND MORNING out, I made my customary visit to the *Skate*'s navigation chart desk, checking on the night's run and examining the track that lay ahead.

Bending over his charts was our navigator, Lieutenant Commander John Nicholson, executive officer and second-in-command. Over six feet tall, with broad shoulders, blue eyes, and wavy brown hair, "Nick" is frequently teased—to his great embarrassment—because he looks like a "Hollywood naval officer." Nick, however, has never needed to get by on his good looks. He was one of the top men in his class at Annapolis and one of the first officers chosen by Rickover for training in nuclear power.

Navigation is always a troublesome task in a submarine, but navigating the *Skate* under the polar ice would pose special problems that, until now, had had no solutions. The basic means of navigation on every ship is still that which took Columbus across the Atlantic— dead reckoning, the determination of position by keeping an accurate record of directions and speed. At sea, there are two means of checking the accuracy of your dead reckoning: celestial navigation and an electronic system called loran (long-range navigation).

Celestial navigation depends upon the accurate measurement of the angle between some fixed celestial body, such as the sun, and the visible horizon. For centuries this angle has been measured with the sextant, but to use a conventional sextant Nicholson would have had to surface the *Skate*. This necessity was avoided by installing a special device in one of the *Skate*'s periscopes. Many a dark and stormy night I have watched Nicholson calmly snapping off sights through the periscope as the stars scudded in and out of the clouds. How different from the old days, when on stormy nights the submarine navigator had to brace himself on a swaying bridge, trying to shield his sextant from the blowing spray!

The loran system measures the minute time difference in the reception of radio signals from towers set up in various locations around the world. Special tables and charts then show the position of the receiving ship. A submarine needs only to expose a buggy-whip antenna briefly above-water to receive these signals.

These were the tools that Nicholson was using to find the *Skate*'s way from New London north to Spitsbergen. But under the frozen Arctic, loran and periscope sextant would be unusable, for the ice would make the briefest of surfacings impossible. Even without these two devices, however, the *Skate* might be navigated reasonably well by dead reckoning, were it not that in the Arctic Ocean a magnetic compass doesn't know whether to point south, north, or give up. Usually it just spins.

The Arctic Ocean is nearly twice the size of the United States. Lost under several million square miles of ice, a submarine could easily wander in drunken circles for days. Then, just as nuclear power was making the venture into the Arctic possible, another invention offered an answer to the problem of finding our way.

One spring day in 1958, a stocky, energetic, and businesslike young man with an engaging smile came on board the *Skate*. He was Zane Sandusky, an engineer from North American Aviation, sent to install an inertial-navigation set. He was especially interested in this job, he said, since he and an assistant were to go with the *Skate* to keep the machine running properly. The huge electronic marvel was an impressive sight, with its mysterious green-glowing tubes, banks of dials and meters, and rows of flashing dots which, when properly counted, revealed the information stored up in its mechanical brain.

How does it work? Well, a series of gyroscopes stabilizes a platform deep in the heart of the system. This platform tends to remain fixed in space—not just in relation to the *Skate* or the earth, but also in relation to the entire universe, to the fixed stars. By sensing, and remembering, the forces that attempt to move the platform out of its position, the system and its computers can determine the position of the *Skate* anywhere on the globe.

Now, looking over Nicholson's shoulder, I pointed to Spitsbergen, the traditional gateway from the Atlantic to the Arctic Ocean. "I want to make a good landfall here, Nick," I said, "to fix our position accurately before we duck under the ice."

"I'd like to get Wittmann's opinion on the ice boundary before we decide just where to try," he replied. "I'll give him a call."

Soon the lanky form of Walt Wittmann, our ice expert from the Hydrographic Office of the Navy Department, was bent over the chart desk. He drew a sweeping line reaching from the eastern shore of Greenland to the northern tip of Spitsbergen.

"That's about it, Captain," Walt said. "Of course, the wind can shift that ice boundary north or south a good bit."

Nicholson pointed to a long, thin island west of the main body of Spitsbergen. "If that's the ice picture, this should be the place to make our landfall—deep water close to the beach and a good radar target with these mountains."

Nicholson was pointing at Prins Karls Forland, where Nansen's sturdy *Fram* had put in after her three years in the ice pack. Her crew had also used its towering mountains for a landmark.

"Prins Karls it shall be," I said. "Let's head right for it."

It was our custom to leave the large ocean chart on top of the worktable, where everyone could see it, and as I turned to go to my room I couldn't help overhearing a couple of crewmen discussing our progress.

"Man," I heard a tall torpedoman say, "we're really roarin' across that ocean! We'll be at the Pole in no time."

"I don't care how fast we go," responded his shipmate, "as long as we get there first. *Nautilus* had *their* chance. This is *ours!*"

It made my heart sink to hear them. For there was one thing I couldn't tell them, much as I wanted to, and I dreaded their finding it out.

I WENT BACK TO my room feeling depressed. It's hard to explain the feeling a submarine skipper has for his crew and their spirit. I can walk through the *Skate* and tell in ten minutes the frame of mind of the crew. And their frame of mind now was all too easy to sense. They were—to use their own words—hot to trot.

People on a ship are fiercely loyal and develop a strong spirit of competition with other ships. The better the crew, the higher their morale, the more they like to compete.

This doesn't imply any animosity or lack of respect for other ships and their crews. A third of the *Skate*'s officers and many of her enlisted men, for example, had served in the *Nautilus* before coming to the *Skate*. They knew the *Nautilus* was a great ship, and they maintained their friendships with members of her crew. But right now they were in the *Skate*, and they wanted her to be great too. And so the *Nautilus* had become their foremost rival.

This rivalry had come to center on the North Pole. The autumn before, the *Nautilus* had reached for the Pole and had been turned back because of compass difficulties. The *Skate*'s crew hoped this was our chance. But fate was working against us. Some time before we sailed I was told that a second, top secret transpolar voyage had been planned for the *Nautilus*. The *Skate* would go too, to develop techniques for surfacing in pack-ice areas; but she would not be first at the Pole. I was cautioned that I could discuss this with no one—not even my executive officer.

The aims of the *Skate* cruise were scientific and military: to explore a little-known region and to test our ability to employ the Arctic Ocean as an operational area. Whether the *Nautilus* or the *Skate* was first at the Pole was of no real consequence. But that wasn't the view my men had—they wanted to be *first*.

There was nothing I could do, nothing I could say, to prepare them for their inevitable disappointment.

ON THE NINTH of August the *Skate* approached Prins Karls Forland cautiously in a light fog. Our buggy-whip antenna was out of the water, cutting a razor-thin wake in the calm sea. Several receivers were tuned to BBC as we gathered what might be our last news for many days.

The clipped accent of the announcer came in suddenly:

"The world was thrilled yesterday by news of the incredible feat of the American atomic submarine *Nautilus*. She has crossed from the Pacific to the Atlantic, passing under the North Pole en route. The world-famous submarine is expected . . ."

The rest was drowned out; but the word was over the ship in seconds. Now they knew.

It came at a bad time—a few hours before we were to go under the ice—but a great weight was lifted from me. Better that they should know now, than to think they had been first and learn later that they had not.

Things were worse, however, than I had expected. The spirits of the crew had been as high as the sky; now they were plunged into despair. Over the ship's announcing system I tried to tell them that we must keep in mind the *Skate*'s real purpose. We were attempting to demonstrate the military usefulness of an ocean area and the distinction of reaching the Pole first had no bearing on that. We were in the navy to serve our nation, not to make headlines for the ship.

I'm afraid they didn't hear much of what I said. Nevertheless, to their credit they soon picked themselves up and carried on resolutely. In a few minutes Nick appeared with a message which he suggested we get off before going under the ice:

TO COMMANDER ANDERSON AND THE MEN OF THE NAUTILUS X HEARTFELT CONGRATULATIONS FROM ALL OF US IN SKATE

I signed the message and told Nick to send it. It represented our true feelings beneath our momentary disappointment.

My thoughts wandered to a wintry day when Nick and I had visited the British Museum during the *Skate*'s stopover in England on her shakedown cruise. We came upon an exhibit of several pages from the diary of Robert Falcon Scott, the famous British polar explorer. One paragraph came vividly back to me now. It was written in January 1912, when, after a long struggle, Scott and his four companions were at last within striking distance of their aim of many years—the South Pole. Then, over the next rise, they saw the black tents and markers left by Roald Amundsen a few days earlier:

The Norwegians have forestalled us and are first at the Pole. It is a terrible disappointment and I am very sorry for my loyal companions. . . . All the daydreams must go.

The best thing to do at a time like this is to keep busy with something important. I intended to do my best.

The *Skate* continued toward Prins Karls Forland until we were able to get its green silhouette on the radar screen and could pinpoint the *Skate*'s position. There was, as yet, no ice in sight, but we went to a depth of three hundred feet and set our course straight for the North Pole, six hundred miles away. As we sped northward our topside Fathometer was pulsing away, sending chirping surges of sound up to the surface, feeling for ice. So far, it recorded only open water.

None of us could understand why we were finding no ice. Had a southerly wind blown the pack away from its normal line? By midnight I had had enough of this blindman's buff. I brought the *Skate* cautiously near the surface and, at very slow speed, poked the periscope above it. The fog had lifted, and in the half-darkness I could see over the still water. Suddenly my heart skipped a beat. Stretching across the northern horizon was a dim white line, ominous in the distance. It was the pack.

We submerged back to three hundred feet immediately. In a few minutes the ice detector showed blocks of ice floating by overhead, the machine's rapidly moving stylus sketching an exaggerated cross section of them. Then, under open water again, the stylus would trace a narrow black line. It was fascinating to watch. Rex Rowray, an assistant of Dr. Waldo Lyon's, the inventor of the machine, was operating the equipment, and he soon had a good audience looking at the ice with him—through the magic of the instrument.

As we drove northward at sixteen knots the ice began to grow heavier and closer together. Then there were no more openings: the stylus traced the underside of an icy ceiling, mile after mile. Occasionally it drew what resembled a huge stalactite as we passed under one of the pressure ridges formed by the grinding together of two floes. The idle conversation of the men around the machine slowed down and stopped, and an unaccustomed tension began to creep over us. We were now wholly dependent upon our ship.

The control center was lighted only dimly with the red bulbs used at night to preserve the night vision of the officer assigned to the periscope—we had not yet considered that there would be no use for the periscope for some time. In the dim red light the planesmen and helmsman held the ship on her depth and course, expertly and steadily. There was no talking. The ice-detector stylus made its quiet *whish, whish, whish* from the after part of the room.

We had reached the point where our charts no longer provided accurate soundings, and up forward, navigator Nicholson was closely watching the bottom Fathometer. The anguished whine of its ping rang through the control room; back came the faint echo from the ocean floor five thousand feet below. In a small room nearby, we heard faintly the long, purring impulses of still another device, the sonar, as it sent sound waves quivering out into the dark water ahead of us, probing for deep pressure ridges hanging down between the floes, or—chilling thought—the presence of a deep-draft iceberg.

I walked aft to have a look at the engine room. It was like entering another world. In place of the unearthly red glow of the control center was the harsh white glare of fluorescent lights. In place of eerie electronic noises were the honest whine of turbines and the throbbing grind of gears as power surged into our propellers—power from energy stored in uranium atoms before the ice pack was formed; perhaps before the earth itself was created.

ALONE IN MY ROOM I could not fight off the feeling that our propellers, driving us deeper and deeper into the ice pack, were taking us farther and farther from safety. If we had trouble, could we make it back to open water? I told myself firmly to put that sort of thinking out of my mind; but in spite of all my efforts, I finally had to admit something to myself that I could admit to no one else.

I was afraid.

Admitting it, even privately, I felt better. I had felt fear—the ugly child of ignorance and imagination—before. In 1943, on my first Pacific war patrol in the submarine *Jack*, I had feared that I would not measure up in combat. Once the unknown was removed, after our first desperate but successful action against a Japanese convoy, I had stopped worrying.

But there was a difference. In the *Jack* I had been a young fellow, with an experienced captain to look to in time of trouble. Here in the *Skate*, whatever my doubts and fears might be, I could never let them be shown. I had to do my best, as captain, to appear confident.

What a blessing, I thought, to have men like Nicholson on board. With him I could share my burden, even though neither of us would ever discuss it directly. I stepped into the control center and saw him working over his chart table.

"Nick," I said, "I'm going to turn in for a while. Will you keep an eye on things?"

FOUR HOURS LATER I went back to the control center to see how things were going. The *Skate* was still driving straight north at sixteen knots—about five hundred yards a minute. We were more than one hundred miles within the ice. Whatever befell us now, we would have to deal with it inside the pack. There could be no running for the edge.

I watched the ice detector as it steadily drew the profile of the canopy over us. Occasionally the stylus would trace the thin black line near the top of the tape that indicated we had passed under a stretch of open water—a lake. Then the line would plunge downward to begin the picture of the next ice floe.

Our ice expert, Walt Wittmann, had explained the origin of these lakes to us. The winds and currents of the Arctic Ocean exert considerable force on the crust of ice that covers the sea. The crust is broken up into floes (some several miles in diameter), which push and jostle against each other endlessly. Under the slow, implacable pressure of millions of tons of ice a pressure ridge may form between floes; or floes may just as mysteriously pull apart, leaving lakes of open water sparkling among the fields of ice.

Lake is the simplest word to describe these openings that pockmark the polar sea, but Walt divided them more scientifically into two basic groups: (1) long cracks called leads, which appear between floes at all seasons of the year; and (2) irregular lakelike areas, which usually develop from leads and are especially characteristic of the summer Arctic. This latter type Walt called a polynya, a Russian word meaning, loosely, an area of open water in the ice.

Walt told us also that the cracklike leads would vary in width from a few yards to perhaps several miles. They are often very long, sometimes meandering for miles across the ice. Polynyas also vary in size, from small ponds to lakes hundreds of yards in diameter. But beyond the first sixty miles or so of the pack, we had not seen a single opening that appeared large enough to be of any value.

My operation order read, "The military usefulness of an ocean area is dependent on at least periodic access to the surface." Developing accesses to the surface of the Arctic was our primary task on this cruise. A submarine deep beneath the ice cannot transmit or receive on her radio. She cannot observe weather, detect aircraft, or launch missiles. In short, she cannot act as a military agent.

The background of earlier attempts to surface was not especially encouraging. Waldo Lyon's successful surfacings in the 1940s had been made near the edge of the pack, where the openings were not really polynyas but rather gaps among loosely scattered floes. In the first attempt to surface a nuclear submarine in a polynya, the *Nautilus,* the fall before, had seriously damaged her periscopes colliding with a small block of ice, and had nearly been forced to turn back.

All of this was much in our minds as we sailed toward the Pole. How soon should we attempt to surface? An attempt now might result in damage that would force us to return, with nothing accomplished. I concluded that it was better to reach the Pole first, then experiment.

I glanced at my watch: nearly time for Sunday morning services. As the one who conducts these services, I have always found that they bring me much comfort and reward. Although I am a Presbyterian, I have found the beautiful and simple language of the Episcopal Book of Common Prayer the best guide for an informal service conducted by a layman. On this Sunday morning, hundreds of feet below the ice and thousands of miles from home and family, I thought we might find particular strength in the responses of the *Venite:*

> *In his hand are all the corners of the earth; and the strength of the hills is his also.*
> *The sea is his, and he made it; and his hands prepared the dry land. . . . .*

On my way to the crew's mess hall I passed the ice detector, where Walt Wittmann was watching the endless procession of floes and ridges overhead. "Captain," he said, "for the past few minutes we've been showing signs of coming into a loose area; there's been a good bit of open water. . . . There! Look at that one!"

A thin black line stretched on and on, then stopped as suddenly as it started. It had remained on the machine for nearly a minute—almost five hundred yards, at the speed we were traveling.

"That's the biggest one we've seen," Walt said eagerly. "I don't know how many more we'll see like it."

I thought how badly this crew needed something to shake them out of yesterday's disappointment. No submarine had ever surfaced so far north. I suddenly changed my mind.

"We'll have church later," I said. "Call away the plotting party."

For weeks we had been drilling a special group for this critical point in our cruise. They had not expected it so soon, but they all moved quickly to their positions: Bill Cowhill, the engineering officer, to the diving officer's stand; Lieutenant Al Kelln, our electronics officer, to the ice detector. In overall charge was Nick.

We moved slowly back and forth under the suspected polynya, plotting our motion as we went and attempting to draw a picture of the opening. We were new at the job, and our picture had flaws, but we got the rough shape. Finally we came to a stop beneath the center.

I raised the periscope against the pressure of the sea; and there was that graceful jellyfish I have mentioned, staring into the lens.

Lowering the periscope, I took one last look at the chart and asked if all was clear overhead.

Al Kelln, with an expressionless face, held up his left hand, with index finger and thumb forming a circle and the remaining three fingers raised.

CHAPTER 5

For nearly half an hour I enjoyed the fresh air of this first polynya. From the bridge, about twenty-five feet above the water, I was able to see other polynyas, some even larger than the one chance had guided us to. The impression, however, was one of an infinite sea of ice. Like the pieces of a gigantic jigsaw puzzle, the floes stretched on and on in all directions as far as I could see. In the distance, the white of the overcast sky blended with the ice to blur the horizon.

Walt Wittmann came to the bridge in his fur parka, bubbling with enthusiasm. He carried a can for ice samples, a thermometer attached to a long knotted line, and a pair of binoculars. Walt is devoted to the study of ice as a painter is devoted to his art. To be floating in

open water deep inside the ice pack, where no man had ever been before, was an experience he couldn't take calmly.

He was soon joined by Dr. LaFond; and in a few minutes, Wittmann, LaFond, and Paul Dornberg were on their way to "shore" in the inflatable rubber boat with which the *Skate* is equipped for just such taxi purposes. Soon after, we were joined by a pair of white seabirds, and I saw Dr. LaFond examining them through his binoculars. He later told me they were ivory gulls (*Larus eburneus*). It embarrassed me somewhat that while I stood idly on the bridge, reflecting on the puniness of man and his works in the midst of an overwhelming environment, our scientists were busy measuring and identifying, to gain that power over one's environment that knowledge brings.

Lunch that day was a festive affair. Accomplishment had taken the edge off disappointment, and a new confidence could be felt all over the ship.

After lunch Nicholson shot the sun several times through the periscope, which even on the surface is easier to use than a sextant. On the chart his resulting position was very close to the heavily marked circle that indicated our position estimated by dead reckoning. Close to it a lighter circle showed our position as reckoned by the magic of inertial navigation. All three techniques seemed to be checking. It was a comforting feeling.

I decided it was time for us to be on our way. The rubber boat was deflated and stowed. I went to the bridge for a last look at our surroundings, and gazed at the icy horizon to the north. The ice field seemed to stretch on forever. How far could I see? Perhaps six miles at the most. And the Pole—how far was it? Over four hundred miles.

I climbed down the narrow ladder into the control center, where Bill Cowhill had all in readiness. For diving, a submarine normally uses her forward momentum to plane herself under. But with almost no room to move, the *Skate* would have to submerge straight down.

The heavy watertight bridge hatch was shut. Cowhill rang the diving signal, and the raucous *ah-uu-ga* of the klaxon echoed through the ship. We could hear the roar of water as it rushed into the empty ballast tanks.

Through the periscope I looked at the bow and stern of the *Skate*, slowly beginning to settle into the calm blue water. I looked at the edges of the polynya. In two hours there had been no sign of change

A crewman ropes down the side of the *Skate*'s ice-covered hull.
Photo © National Geographic Society

in its oval shape. Not a ripple had marred the surface of our pond; no stray floating blocks of ice had threatened us. It had been a friendly place.

As we sank farther, only our periscope remained to show our presence. I saw the two seabirds circle the periscope just before the water closed silently over its top.

WHEN THE *Skate* HAD sunk far enough to be clear of any deep-reaching pressure ridges, I gave the order to head due north. Looking up with the periscope, I could see the darkness close in over us once more as we moved under the heavy ice.

I was anxious now to hold the postponed services, and we were soon assembled in the crew's mess hall. I thought of a passage in the 139th Psalm that seemed especially appropriate for this day, and at the close of the service I read it:

> "Whither shall I go from thy spirit? or whither shall I flee from thy presence? . . .
> "If I take the wings of the morning, and dwell in the uttermost parts of the sea;
> "Even there shall thy hand lead me, and thy right hand shall hold me. . . ."

In *The Age of Faith*, Will Durant commented that man must reason in order to advance, but that he must believe in order to live. The reason of man created the *Skate* and makes her work. But we who are in charge of this creature of reason must often lean upon our faith in a Presence beyond reason to find the strength of spirit to fulfill our duties *in the uttermost parts of the sea.*

I thought of the men—most of whom I knew—who had spent years designing this ship and this machinery. I thought of the gray-haired admiral whose relentless will had made it possible, and of the sign behind his desk:

> Our doubts are traitors,
> And make us lose the good we oft might win . . .

The thin blue folder containing our operation order lay on the green felt of the wardroom table. Gathered with me were all the officers not on watch. "Let me read this to you so we'll all know what we're authorized to do," I said:

"If the Pole is reached by the fourteenth of August you are authorized to proceed to the vicinity of Drifting Ice Station Alfa, attempt
to communicate with its personnel, and further to attempt to surface
near enough so that contact can be made."

The United States was at this time maintaining two survey stations
on the polar ice pack in connection with the International Geophysi-
cal Year. Carried along by the drifting ice at the rate of two or three
miles a day, the men at the stations were able to gather much data in
otherwise inaccessible parts of the Arctic.

Such camps did not originate with the IGY. In 1918, Vilhjalmur
Stefansson and his sturdy assistant, Storker Storkerson, conceived the
idea of camping on an ice floe in order to take scientific data as they
drifted through the polar sea. Storkerson established a camp two
hundred miles north of Alaska in which he and four men lived for
nearly six months while drifting some four hundred miles.

After World War II a Soviet drifting ice station discovered one of
the most spectacular features of the Arctic—a gigantic underwater
mountain range crossing from Greenland to the New Siberian
Islands. The Soviets named the mountain range the Lomonosov, after
the eighteenth-century Russian scientist.

The U.S. Station Alpha was, at this time, about three hundred
miles from the Pole in the direction of Alaska. The idea of finding
it—a pinpoint in five and a half million square miles of frozen waste—
from underneath the ice had seemed so fantastic to me that I had
never before seriously discussed it with my officers.

"There's nothing mandatory in this operation order," I said. "How
about it; do you think we ought to take a chance on Alpha?"

There was a unanimously affirmative shout in reply. Nicholson,
who as navigator would have to find the station, said, "I think we
can find Alpha. After we go to the Pole, we should try to surface
somewhere near and talk to them on radio."

Bill Layman, our chief engineer, asked, "Do we know where
Alpha is now?"

"I have their predicted positions during the next few days," I said.
"But I don't know how accurate the predictions'll be."

"If we surface even within a few miles of Alpha," said Nick, "we
can take radio direction-finder bearings on their radio signals. Then
we can submerge and run down the bearing line until we find them."

"How will we know when we're there?" asked Dave Boyd.

"Well, I'm not sure about that yet," Nick admitted. "We may have to have a little luck."

ALL THE NEXT DAY, August 11, tension and excitement in the crew built up. Navigator Nicholson announced on the loudspeaker system that if all went well we should be at the Pole shortly after midnight.

Everyone was up and about as the *Skate* drove northward at better than sixteen knots. The depth gauge read two hundred and sixty feet as we skimmed along under heavy ice with almost no openings. The goal of a year's work and planning lay just a few miles away.

The crew down in the inertial-navigation room studied the flickering green signals of the cathode tubes as the delicate sensing instruments of the system showed us approaching ever closer to that point on the globe where every direction is south. Carefully the men counted the dots winking by and plotted the resulting numbers, translating them into navigational terms.

"Only a mile to go now, Captain," Zane Sandusky commented as I approached his machine.

"This course look good?" I asked.

"You're right on the nose—you'll split it right in two," Zane said exuberantly.

I walked up to the control center and announced our distance to the Pole on the speaker system. Then I turned to Al Kelln, the officer of the deck. "Let's slow to five knots, Al—we want to hit this one right on the money."

The ring of the engine annunciators sounded loud in the quiet room. Nick called from the chart desk, "One minute to go."

Then he gave me the signal and I counted down over the loudspeakers, "Four, three, two, *mark*. At one forty-seven Greenwich time on twelve August 1958 the *Skate* has reached the northernmost part of our planet. My congratulations to each one of you, but this is only the beginning. Before we are through we are going to demonstrate that a submarine can come into this ice pack, operate at will, surface when it wants to, and carry out whatever mission our country requires." It was four hours earlier, August 11, in New London.

We immediately put the rudder over and swung slowly left onto the course for Drifting Station Alpha.

SELDOM HAD THE ICE seemed so heavy as it did in the immediate area of the Pole. For days we searched in vain for an opening to surface in. Walt Wittmann's ice log tells the dreary story:

> Roughest ice yet encountered . . . no openings of any size. . . . Ice very closely compacted with heavy pressure ridges on every hand. . . . First opening of any kind for some time but much too small to use. . . .

We crept along at five knots, investigating every possibility. At eight thirty Tuesday morning, Pat Garner, a new officer, called me aft to the ice detector. "I don't know whether you want to fool with this one or not," he said, "but I wanted you to see it."

A short black line had appeared on the tape, so short that previously we would not have considered it. But now circumstances were different and I decided to have a closer look. The plotting party was called away and we doubled back under the opening, carefully plotting its shape. It was small, no doubt about it.

Finally we halted under the center of the opening at periscope depth. When the periscope was raised, I could barely suppress a gasp of shock. On either side of us hung huge blocks of ice, jagged blocks turned on edge, rafted chunks ten feet thick piled on top of each other—monstrous frozen jaws, and all looking just a few yards away. "Flood her down, we're moving on," I said.

It was easy to read the disappointment on every face, but I could see no alternative. Twice more that morning we went through the same ordeal. The tedious weaving, the cautious halt, the tense ascent, observation with the periscope, the decision to go on.

Shortly after lunch we found another small stretch of water. Again the periscope presented the same terrifying vista. But this time I hesitated. Perhaps this was the only kind of polynya we would ever find this far north. If so, we should find out once and for all if it was possible to use it.

"Start her up slowly, Bill," I said to Lieutenant Cowhill. Immediately the control center quieted and tension gripped the room. Slowly, agonizingly slowly, we came up. On every side the ice seemed to be closing in about us, yet Nick assured me calmly that we had open water above.

Hopefully I tilted the prism of the periscope upward. There was only heavy gloom to be seen. The ice on our port side was so heavy it was dead black, like an enormous velvet curtain hanging down in dark folds. My heart was hammering and my mouth was dry. I looked at Nicholson and Cowhill. Both were perfectly calm outwardly. Did they feel the same apprehension?

Finally I could see the surface of the water lapping the edges of the ice. Now I had to lower the periscope to protect it. "How close *is* that ice to port?" I asked as the scope went down.

"Pretty close now, Captain," said Louis Kleinlein, our senior sonarman, who had been estimating the distance. "But I can't really tell anymore."

Bill Cowhill said quietly that we were hanging at forty-five feet. I raised the periscope quickly and focused it on the menacing cliff of ice to port. There it was—less than ten yards away! There was nothing to do. We were slowly drifting down upon it. For the first time, we were going to hit.

I thought immediately of the propellers and rudder; with a damaged rudder we might never get out of the ice pack; and we could not repair it under the sea. Quickly I turned the periscope aft. Everyone could hear my sigh of relief. By the greatest good fortune the wall of ice we were being set against curved slightly away from the stern of the *Skate*—as though it had been designed to accommodate her without injury.

With a gentle thud the side of the ship struck the wall of ice. No harm was done. We hung like a whale awash, with just the periscope and the hump of our sail, or conning tower, out of the water, at the edge of a small polynya. It appeared doubtful that it was large enough to hold the *Skate* safely when completely surfaced.

To hold on was dangerous; but this was the top of the world, where no submarine had ever surfaced before. If we gave up, no one might try it again for years. I wanted desperately to hang on.

I decided to remain where I was, partially surfaced. In this position we could accomplish most of the things we wanted to do; we could use our radio, take sights with our periscope sextant, and put up our ventilation piping.

Nicholson took over the periscope. A low whistle was his only comment before he started snapping hasty sun elevations through the intermittent clouds. After he turned the periscope back to me, I looked at the thermometer we had wired to a radio antenna so that we could read it through the periscope. It was 33 degrees above zero. The ice was in motion, and it occurred to me that the polynya we were in might close with little or no warning.

I immediately drafted a message to be sent to the Navy Department. They had not heard from us since we entered the pack:

REACHED NORTH GEOGRAPHIC POLE AUGUST ELEVENTH X NOW IN PO-
LYNYA ABOUT FORTY MILES FROM POLE X ALL WELL

Chief radioman Dale McCord sat down in the radio room and tapped out the signals for:

ANY SHIP OR ANY STATION X THIS IS THE USS SKATE X WE HAVE A MES-
SAGE TO SEND

Almost immediately came this reply:

THIS IS RADIO MANILA X HEAR YOU LOUD AND CLEAR X REQUEST YOU
REPEAT YOUR NAME

It was the U.S. Navy operator in the Philippines. He couldn't understand what the *Skate*, supposedly stationed in the Atlantic, was doing in his ocean!

A few moments later, after Radio Manila had taken our message for relay to Washington, Nick handed me a message he had drafted to Station Alpha:

REQUEST YOUR EXACT POSITION X ALSO REQUEST INFORMATION ON
NUMBER AND SIZE OF POLYNYAS YOUR VICINITY

"That ought to do it, Nick," I said, scribbling my signature.

I felt deeply tired, and Nick looked tired. He had gotten less than four hours' sleep in the last seventy-two. I had done better than that, but not much.

"Nick, this is where you and I both get some sleep," I said. Leaving instructions for the officers of the deck, I went to my room and slept for fourteen hours.

During all that time the normal, busy routine of the ship kept up just as though we were traveling under the sea: reactors and turbines running, the galley giving steady service, a torpedo opened for servicing. But the *Skate* herself hung motionless, perched just below the surface of the water between two cliffs of ice, her periscopes, antennae, and ventilation pipes piercing the still surface like the pales of a picket fence at the edge of our small lake.

When I awoke I read the answer we had received from Alpha:

NO OBSERVATIONS FOR SEVERAL DAYS SO POSITION NOT KNOWN X BEST ESTIMATE NEAR EIGHTY-FIVE NORTH ONE THREE SIX WEST X MANY POLYNYAS IN VICINITY BUT BEST ONLY FIFTY YARDS FROM OUR MAIN BUILDINGS

Dave Boyd was sitting in the wardroom and I handed the message to him. He chuckled and said, "How do you go about finding a place that doesn't know where it is? But wouldn't that be something if we could find the polynya only fifty yards away? It'd be like surfacing right in their camp!"

At nine thirty a.m. on August 13 we finally prepared to leave our hard-gained position at the top of the world. It was the morning of our fourth day in the ice pack, and our awe was diminishing. Down we drifted, much faster than we had dared come up. I looked at the walls of ice as we dropped away and wondered if I would have the nerve to get into such a tight place again. Soon the aquamarine and black of the ice walls gave way to the deep azure of the Arctic water, and we turned once more in the direction of Alpha.

Until we reached the Pole, our Fathometer had traced the ocean floor of the North Eurasian Basin, which averages close to twelve thousand feet in depth. To picture the *Skate* in this ocean, imagine a kitchen matchstick suspended about two inches below the ceiling of a ten-foot-high room. The ceiling would be the ice, the floor the bottom of the sea, and the humble matchstick our submarine. It is a vision which makes man and his works seem pretty minute.

Almost as soon as we had left the Pole, however, our Fathometer began to record a gentle rise of the ocean floor toward the Lomonosov Ridge. Now, as we resumed our journey, we could watch the profile of the mountain chain taking shape on the traveling tape of our Fathometer. I could envision the lofty range below us, dwarfing into insignificance the tiny steel egg cruising above it.

What a magnificent sight this Lomonosov would be if set out on dry land! More than one thousand miles in length, it soars in places to heights more than ten thousand feet above its surrounding plain. In its size and the sharpness of its slopes and peaks it could be compared with the dramatic Andes in South America. But only through the vicarious sight of instruments will man ever feel its presence and know its form.

By breakfast time on Thursday we estimated that we were within thirty miles of Alpha. Our location was roughly halfway between the North Pole and Alaska; we had penetrated to a part of the Arctic that explorer Vilhjalmur Stefansson named the Zone of Comparative Inaccessibility, because it was the region most remote from approach by ship—more remote than the North Pole itself.

We found a promising opening in the ice and floated cautiously underneath it. The periscope showed a polynya like that we had found our first day in the ice pack. I told Bill Cowhill to blow the tanks, and in a few minutes the *Skate* rose quickly to the surface.

In August the ice fields are dotted with thousands of puddles of melted water ranging from a few feet in diameter to sizable ponds, and in depth from a few inches to three or four feet. The water in them is surprisingly fresh, and the color is an aquamarine of gemlike purity. As I stood on the bridge, these bright jewels were scattered everywhere over the ermine white of the floes. Other polynyas were also visible, looking almost black beside the cheerful blue of the ponds. I passed the word for the deck hatches to be opened so that everyone could come out on deck.

The crew began to appear from the hatches to gaze in wonder at the sparkling blue lake in which we rested. Their high spirits became immediately apparent. Quartermaster John Medaglia, a short, dark young man with an infectious sense of humor, called up to the bridge, "Looks like just the place for swimming call, Captain!"

"We've just had it—you're first!" I shouted back. Four men grabbed John without delay and started to swing him toward the icy water. Medaglia's screams, or reason, eventually prevailed, and finally, in no wise chastened, he was put back laughing on his feet.

Below, in the wardroom, I found Nicholson working over a huge chart spread across the table. The position of the *Skate* was marked and a pencil line extended for about ten inches from it. "Got the bearing on Alpha with no trouble," Nick said, pointing to the line. "By the way, his call letters are I-C-E. Pretty good, eh?"

"Yes," I said with a smile, "but how far away is Alpha on that line?

There could be five polynyas inside a square mile—and only one right one."

As we sat eating lunch a message came in from Alpha:

WILL RUN OUTBOARD MOTORBOAT CONTINUOUSLY IN POLYNYA NEAREST CAMP

There was our answer—if only we could hear the motorboat far enough away. In a few minutes I was asking the sonarman, Louis Kleinlein, how far he thought he could hear an outboard motor underneath the ice.

A smile of understanding spread over Kleinlein's cheerful face. "We wouldn't hear it at all unless we were submerged," he said, "but submerged we might be able to hear it five miles or so off."

After lunch I went to the bridge for some fresh air. Wittmann and LaFond were over on the ice getting their customary samples of ice and water. Before long they were back, late for lunch, but as usual bubbling with enthusiasm. I asked the men rowing the rubber boat to give me a lift to the ice. When they dropped me off, I struck out across the floes for a bit of exercise and solitude.

I made my way over a small pressure ridge and lost sight of the ship. After the constant, unnoticed background noise of the *Skate*, the dominant impression was one of stillness. In the melt ponds the water was as transparent as the air, and at the bottom the lovely aquamarine blue of the ice was revealed. I thought of what lay under this tranquil surface. A foot of water, perhaps nine feet of ice, and then thousands and thousands of feet of black, icy seawater, reaching down to a bottom so remote that man would probably never know its real nature.

I walked on toward a low hummock. The rough snow was like mush underfoot, and even the slight exertion of my walk left me damp with perspiration. When I stopped to rest, the cold of the air penetrated my clothes and chilled me to the bone. What misery it must have been for De Long and his men from the *Jeannette,* crossing this ice that summer of 1881, dragging three boats with them! What chance would my men from the *Skate* have if we found it necessary to trek across the ice? At least De Long's men had had dogs, sledges, and furs, and provisions for overland travel. I recalled William Bolitho's memorable remark about Columbus. The glory of

Columbus, he said, was that of all adventurers, "to have been the tremendous outsider."

That was the phrase that expressed it. We were outsiders, able to exist here only for a few hours without the slim black hull that floated a few hundred yards away from me.

Suddenly I felt very lonely. I hurried back to our polynya and called for the boat. Climbing down the long steel tube into the interior of the ship, I entered another world. Warmth, light, noise, and companionship were everywhere. This was home.

THE AIR HISSED out of the ballast tanks as we started to submerge. Slowly the still water lapped higher and higher on the black hull until it disappeared. The outsider was gone.

The *Skate* moved gently ahead, settling into her element. Soon, Kleinlein broke into a slow grin at the listening apparatus. He handed his earphones to me. The soft *put-put-put-put* of an outboard motor was unmistakable, apparently directly ahead.

We steered on down the bearing line. Al Kelln saw many polynyas on the ice detector that looked large enough to use, but it was not just any polynya we wanted now. We were shooting for one out of thousands. The sound of the outboard grew steadily louder, but it became harder for Kleinlein to give us an accurate bearing. His readings swung from right to left and Nick began to look concerned.

Then without warning the sound disappeared. Although we searched carefully in all directions it was not to be heard. Only one thing could have happened—we had passed the Drift Station, and the bulk of the *Skate*'s hull blocked off the sound astern. Ponderously the *Skate* swung her three thousand tons around and headed slowly back. Once more the *put-put-put-put* came into the earphones.

Now we had to go more slowly and see where the noise cut off and a polynya showed up simultaneously. The noise cut off again, but the ice detector showed nothing but solid ice overhead. We turned slowly and made another pass. Now Kleinlein reported that the noise was all around—we couldn't be far away.

"Open water overhead!" shouted Kelln. But his joy turned to dismay as he saw that the opening was not long enough to hold us. This couldn't be it. They said it was a big one.

Nevertheless, we marked its position on the plotting sheet and turned back to pass under it again, in a different direction. And this time the open water stretched on and on and on. It was a long, narrow polynya.

"Port ahead one-third, starboard back one-third, right full rudder," I said, and the *Skate* obediently swung slowly to the right to align herself with the open water above.

"All stop, rudder amidships." We were just right. As we rose, I could see ripples on the water above the periscope. The ice was the same distance away on either side; I could see none forward or astern.

Slowly the periscope came out of the water. Small brown huts dotted the ice around us. A high radio antenna rose over them. The squat silo shape of a radar dome lay farther astern. Near it stood a tall pole with the American flag.

Our polynya, as we had thought, was long and thin but of good size. And around the edge of it, as though on a racetrack, cruised a small outboard motorboat. Its occupant was waving his hat wildly.

CHAPTER 6

Hardly had the *Skate* reached the surface when the small boat was tied up alongside and its passenger was welcomed on board. He was Major Joseph Bilotta of the air force, the senior military man at Alpha. "I've never seen an eerier sight in my life," he exclaimed, "than your periscope coming up in this empty lake! It was weird!" Bilotta was cold and tired, and Nick hustled him down to the warmth of the wardroom for coffee and cake.

With the prospect of a longer stay than usual, iron stakes were driven into the ice and mooring lines made fast. The *Skate* lay secure fifty yards from the main camp—and less than a hundred miles from the center of Stefansson's Zone of Inaccessibility.

Down in the wardroom, I found Bilotta, a short, rugged man of about forty with an enviable thatch of brown hair, wearing no sign of rank except a major's gold oak leaf pinned to his Arctic-style wool hat. He was telling Nick the history of Alpha.

The drifting station had been established in April 1957, about five hundred and fifty miles north of Barrow, Alaska. The floe was chosen by two famous Arctic authorities, Father Thomas Cunningham, a Jesuit priest in Barrow, and Colonel Joe Fletcher of the air force. Fletcher and Father Cunningham flew over the ice pack until they found a sturdy floe so located that the drift of the ice would carry it through regions of interest. By now the station had drifted in a slow clockwise circle to a point about nine hundred miles northeast of Barrow.

There were twenty-nine men at the station; they had been there since the early spring of 1958 on a six-month tour. Half civilian, half military, they were all volunteers. Bilotta explained to us that no airplane landings could be made in the summertime; no one could be evacuated under any circumstances until the autumn freeze.

It had been a full day, to say the least, and now I suddenly realized I was bone-weary. So after arranging with the major for an exchange of visits the following morning, we called it a day.

Friday was cloudy but warm, and we spent the day on shore leave, Arctic-style. Major Bilotta took three of us for a tour of the station. It was a striking contrast with the feeling of aloneness, quietness, cleanliness I had had the day before. Here the mark of man was everywhere. A fuel dump of barrels dropped by plane made an olive-drab blotch against the white snow. The same aquamarine melt ponds dotted the tops of the floes, but their pristine loveliness was marred by bits of trash and dirt.

The station consisted of about a dozen huts that were used variously as mess hall, recreation hall, quarters, and laboratories. As we walked along I asked, "Why do you have ice blocks under all of these huts?"

"Those aren't ice blocks," Bilotta replied with a smile. "That's where the ice used to be. When we brought the huts here last spring, the ice level was two or three feet higher. A lot has melted off since. except where the huts have insulated it from the sun."

Mounted on their pedestals of ice, the huts resembled sadly misshapen toadstools. As the summer progressed and the ice pedestals grew higher, the wooden stairways to the huts gradually became longer and more rickety. Furthermore, a large melt pond had grown under each ladder, so that quite a leap was required to clear it.

In the mess hall, we had coffee with Dr. Norbert Untersteiner, the Viennese-born senior civilian scientist, a tall, dark, impressive man in

his late thirties, who was doing research on the rate of growth and decay of the ice pack for the University of Washington.

He explained the scientific work of the station: research on the current theory that the pack is diminishing; studies of the ocean bottom from samples and photographs taken by flashbulb at depths of more than ten thousand feet. We could not help but be impressed by the devotion to learning which would lead men like Untersteiner to isolate themselves in this lonely and forlorn place for half a year. All of us want to understand our world. But in these men the drive is strong enough to send them out to places like Alpha to gain knowledge for which they thirst.

Major Bilotta rejoined us and asked me if I'd like to come over to the radio station and make a phone call to the States. At the hut, a cheerful air force operator in a fluorescent red shirt asked whom I wanted to call. I decided on Rear Admiral Frederick Warder in New London, the man who had replaced Admiral Watkins as commander of Atlantic Fleet submarines.

Bilotta's operator swung into action. In rapid, singsong tones he started calling: "Hello, any operator in the U.S., this is Station KL7FLA near the North Pole calling. . . ."

Over and over went the call as he changed his transmitting frequencies, attempting to make contact with some interested amateur more than two thousand miles to the south. Finally a faint voice came over our speaker. It was an amateur operator in Portland, Oregon. After much shifting of frequencies we managed to receive him fairly well. We asked him to patch his radio circuit into a long-distance telephone call to Admiral Warder in New London.

It wasn't until after I'd returned home that I learned how Admiral Warder received my call. He was at a formal luncheon with several special guests when the telephone rang in the next room. In a few moments a puzzled steward beckoned Lieutenant Thomson, who was the admiral's aide, to come to the telephone.

Thomson is a young man who takes pride in remaining unruffled in a crisis. With an absolutely straight face he came back to the door and said, "Admiral Warder, telephone for you. It's Jim Calvert and he says he's calling from somewhere near the North Pole."

Toward the end of our conversation, which ran mostly to questions and assurances about families, the signal became weaker and weaker until we could scarcely hear. Finally the signal was lost altogether.

Leaving the radio hut, I made my way back to the ship for a brief nap before dinner. I was awakened by the phone buzzer. It was Guy Shaffer, the officer of the deck. "Sorry to wake you, Captain," he said, "but I think this ice is starting to move."

I was on my way up in an instant. All that I had read about swiftly closing leads that caught and crushed ships like pecans in a nut-cracker flickered through my mind. As I reached the bridge, the dull boom of what sounded like distant thunder struck my ears. Shaffer pointed toward a long ridge of ice. "That pressure ridge has come up within the last hour," he said.

The wind was still gentle, the sky only lightly overcast. But some-where in this great ocean of ice, pressure was building up. We ran the risk of being squeezed to death in a slow but irresistible grip. Though the motion was almost too slow to see, there was no doubt that our polynya was getting smaller. Suddenly, with an ominous crack, a chunk of floe ice thirty feet across broke loose not far from our bow and started drifting toward the ship.

"Recall the crew, Guy," I said grimly. "We have to leave."

Many of our people were visiting the station, and we had a number of Alpha men on board visiting the *Skate*. But the word had not far to travel, and soon people were hurrying back to the ship from all directions. My necessary but hasty decision disrupted all our plans. Since Alpha had no facilities for making ice cream, we had arranged to send over ten gallons of our best mixtures in exchange for some polar-bear steaks, and this trade had yet to be consummated. I told the negotiators to hurry up and get the ice cream over while there was still time. Then I sent notes over to Bilotta and Untersteiner apologizing for departing so abruptly.

The minutes ticked by and still not all of us were back. I began to get more than a little worried. The distant boom of the ice furnished a sinister reminder of our danger. Finally the polar-bear steaks came aboard, wrapped carefully in waxed paper. Quartermaster John Me-daglia took them as they were handed up from the Alpha's motor-boat. "*Caramba!*" he exclaimed. "They were certainly generous with these! Maybe they didn't want them so much."

Everyone was back now but Walt Wittmann, and I began to think he might have to wait for the fall freeze-up to leave Alpha. The polynya was down to half its former size, and the *Skate* had moved to its center. At last we saw Wittmann bounding across the ice. He was ferried out to the *Skate*, and we waved good-by to the Alpha men lining the edge of the lake. I went below to look through the periscope before commencing our dive. Glancing around at the men standing by the edges of the polynya, I thought how well they embodied Fridtjof Nansen's meaning when he said, "Man wants to know—and when he ceases to do so he is no longer man."

WE TRAVELED THE night quietly, running two hundred feet beneath the ice at sixteen knots. The next day was Saturday, the sixteenth of August. We had been in the ice pack for six days.

We had decided to return to the Lomonosov Ridge to survey it more thoroughly, proceeding back across the polar basin to a point north of Greenland where we could intersect the huge underwater mountain chain and follow it back to the Pole. By suppertime it seemed likely that we would intersect the ridge during the night, and at about eleven Art Molloy, our specialist on the ocean bottom, called me to the control center. "She's beginning to show now," he said, pointing to the sweeping stylus of the Fathometer. An outline of the Lomonosov foothills gradually appeared on the tape as we cruised far above them. Within an hour we had crossed the ridge and come about to head once more for the Pole.

We spent the night and the next morning zigzagging over the backbone of the range humping northward toward the top of the world. Once more the Fathometer needle drew dramatic profiles of soaring crags and spectacular valleys as they passed beneath us.

As the Lomonosov range nears the Pole it veers off slightly to the left. Since we wanted to revisit the Pole to confirm some of our readings there, we left the ridge Sunday and headed north. The memory of our difficulties in reaching the surface near the Pole was still vivid as we lazed along at twelve knots, on the lookout for a good spot to try again. But the Arctic, as though it had inflicted its final persecution upon us for the time being, suddenly opened up. Only forty miles from the North Pole we found the largest polynya of our cruise—nearly half a mile in diameter.

We surfaced in it easily, and Wittmann and LaFond took samples of the water at various depths. For twelve to eighteen feet from the surface, polynya water is surprisingly fresh and warm; then a sharp transition occurs, and the water becomes salty and cold. There is a great difference in density between these two layers, and some objects that would sink in the light, warm fresh water float on the heavy, cold ocean water below. When we looked down, we could see tiny white Arctic shrimp crawling along at the surface of this cold layer as if it were the bottom of the sea. Wittmann told us that the layer of fresh water in the polynya used to trouble the Eskimos and early northern explorers. A seal, when shot, would sometimes sink through the fresh water at the top of the polynya, then float tantalizingly on the cold salt water, just out of reach of the hungry hunters. Walt said that the Eskimos had taken to attaching skin floats to their harpoons to hang on to their catch.

I suddenly recalled an interesting phenomenon during two or three of our surfacings. Just as the periscope approached the fresh-water zone, my vision would become clouded. I couldn't understand what was happening until I realized that tiny organisms in the water were responsible. Nansen had discovered the same phenomenon. He found that in the summertime diatoms and algae, growing in the layer of fresh water at the top of the polynyas, sink to the bottom of this layer. These were what had clouded the periscope, and possibly they were what the shrimp we had seen found so interesting. Then, of course, the Arctic seal eat the shrimp, and the bears eat the seal— and men eat the bears.

While Wittmann, LaFond, and I were talking on deck, we were interrupted by a sudden commotion at the forward torpedo-room hatch. "Get it out of here!" a voice shouted. "I don't care what you do with it—just get rid of it!"

The voice belonged to Ray Aten. Soon the laughing face of John Medaglia appeared above the hatch. He was clutching the package of polar-bear steaks we had been given the day before. "We tried to get Aten to cook 'em," chuckled Medaglia, "but he threw us out of the galley." Medaglia put the waxed-paper package down on the deck and opened it. The gamy odor was overpowering.

"We're just not hungry enough," said Wittmann encouragingly. "These things are great when you are."

"Yeah," said Medaglia. "I just hope I *never* get that hungry." He dumped the steaks over the side.

They drifted down about fifteen feet and hung there suspended as though in midair. "Look at that!" exclaimed Medaglia. "Even the ocean won't have 'em!"

WE FLOODED DOWN and continued north. By eleven that evening the *Skate* was back at the North Pole for the second time in a week. After taking careful readings of the depth, transparency, and temperature of the water, we pulled two miles away from the Pole and made a trip around a roughly twelve-mile circle in one hour, probably the fastest around-the-world trip ever made. The purpose was to enable us to take soundings in the vicinity of the Pole for a detailed chart of the area. I had not given up the idea of surfacing right at the Pole, and we closed in for one last check before departing. When we were almost precisely at the spot we saw a very encouraging stretch of apparently open water, and we were soon on our way up. Everything looked fine through the periscope until we got close to the surface. Then I gulped in astonishment and alarm. The surface of the lake was frozen solid. I could see cracks in this ice, and light penetrated it quite well, but it was there.

This had been our constant fear—that we might smash blindly into ice when we thought we had open water above us. To crash through even thin ice would mangle our delicate radio antennae, depriving us of contact with the outside world.

"Take her down, ice above!" I snapped to Bill Cowhill. First hesitating, then dropping as though she had been yanked with a wire, the *Skate* sank away from danger above. I turned angrily to Al Kelln. "Didn't you show ice on that machine of yours?" I asked.

Al looked completely mystified, and beckoned to me to come and look. The tape clearly showed open water, and we concluded soberly that the echo from thin ice and open water could look much the same. But what a difference it would make to us!

We set our course away from the Pole and toward the Greenland-Spitsbergen strait. We were headed for home.

As the great ice drift of the polar sea moves toward the channel between Greenland and Spitsbergen, it jams millions of tons of ice against the northern coast of the two islands. The pack in this region is treacherous, but for the ninth time in our nine days in the ice pack we found a usable opening and surfaced safely.

Already we were passing out of the Arctic overcast. The sun shone brightly through a mackerel sky, brightening the pale azure glints of the melt ponds and the ermine of the snow, and turning the protruding ice edges to flashing diamonds. The Arctic was putting on her most dazzling face for her good-by. As we sank out of our last lake I felt genuinely sorry. I was sure I was seeing the Arctic for the last time, and I had come to love it.

By six thirty p.m. the next day, Walt Wittmann announced that he thought we were clear of the ice. I brought the *Skate* to periscope depth and raised the lens to find a gently rolling swell. The sun was setting in a burst of rose-colored clouds, and the ice was only a faint white line to the north.

Air hissed into the tanks and the *Skate* rolled to the surface. Soon she was dashing along, burying her nose in the swell and then shaking herself high and free, the white water cascading gracefully from her bow. It was as though she was exultant to be in the deep swells of the Atlantic again, free of the confining Arctic ice.

AFTER SEVERAL RADIO messages were sent, we submerged once more and set off for Bergen, Norway, according to orders.

When we dived, I took a walk back to the engine room. The affection men feel for ships and machinery that serve them well can never be explained. It is a totally irrational thing, but that does not make it less real. As I walked between the gleaming rows of pipes and heard the deep-throated throb of power running through the turbines to our propellers, a shiver of awe ran up and down my back. This machinery, upon whose integrity our very lives depended, had never faltered, never missed a beat. How could I help feeling that it was a living presence?

Bill Layman was on watch in the maneuvering room. His expression told me I didn't have to explain what I had been thinking.

"It's a good ship, Captain," Bill said with simple finality.

For taciturn Bill, that was truly outspoken.

I SHALL NEVER FORGET our entry into Bergen. Waving families stood by storybook cottages, resplendent in red, yellow, and blue paint, along the water's edge. All had Norwegian flags flying proudly, and one family even fired a skyrocket in salute. With deep pride I recalled that, just sixty-five years before, Nansen and his sturdy *Fram* had departed for the North from these same fjords, and the same bright cottages and flags that now welcomed us had wished him Godspeed.

A few days later, in Oslo, a ceremony was held at the museum which now houses the *Fram*. We placed a spray of flowers at the base of Nansen's statue, and a bronze plaque commemorating our visit was placed on board the *Fram*. Plaques from the *Skate* are mounted in many places in America and Europe, but none gives me more satisfaction than the one on this small wooden ship.

As the days went by, messages of congratulation for the *Skate* poured in from many places. They meant a great deal to us, but I kept thinking of the fjord at Bergen. Deep in its shadowy water lies rusting, largely forgotten, the hulk of another submarine that once sailed proudly for the North Pole—the *Nautilus* of Sir Hubert Wilkins'. One of his many Norwegian friends, Dr. Odd Dahl, gave me a copy of Wilkins' *Under the North Pole*. I was unable to put it down until I finished it. Again and again the book forecast accurately what we had just experienced.

I thought of the hulk beneath the waters near Bergen, and I wanted to express my admiration for the spirit and vision of this man. I sent a message to Sir Hubert, whom I had never met:

REQUEST PASS TO SIR HUBERT WILKINS X THE EXPERIENCES OF THIS SUM-
MER : . . . HAVE LEFT US DEEPLY AWARE OF THE ACCURACY OF YOUR
INSIGHT AND VISION . . . X THE MAJORITY OF YOUR AIMS AND PREDICTIONS
OF NEARLY THIRTY YEARS AGO WERE REALIZED THIS SUMMER X THE MEN
OF THE SKATE SEND A SINCERE SALUTE TO A MAN WHO HAS MANY TIMES
SHOWN THE WAY

On our way home across the Atlantic we received answering congratulations and thanks from Sir Hubert. On September 22 we arrived in Boston amid the roar of helicopters and the tooting of tugboats. While we were still in the harbor, a launch bearing Dennis Wilkinson and Admiral Rickover came out to meet us.

It was the will and imagination of these two men that had made our venture possible. Naturally I was glad to see them. But as the *Skate* drew near to her berth, I could see in the crowd on the pier the softly smiling face of the one who had had the hardest job of all— she who had the courage to remain at home and wait.

LIFE IS SELDOM so sweet as for the sailor freshly home from the sea. The cycles that make up the patterns of our lives—night and day, winter and summer, hope and realization—all seem to be echoed in the cycle of the long sea voyage and the return home. Never had our hundred-year-old white frame house seemed so attractive, and never had the problems of our three children seemed so interesting. Thoughts of the Arctic soon faded into the background.

But in October, a few weeks after our return, I received a visitor who rekindled all my interest in the Arctic. Sir Hubert Wilkins came to spend a day on the *Skate*. The old explorer was still vigorous and alert, and curious about all the intricacies of the nuclear submarine.

As we discussed the *Skate*'s voyage north he suddenly said, "Now that you have everything you need to do the job, you must go in the wintertime."

I was startled. In winter the polynyas would be frozen over. "Not much use in going if we can't get to the surface," I said dubiously.

"I think you can," he replied. "Maybe you'll have to bore a hole, maybe blast. I don't know—but you'll find a way." He sighed and sat for some time with a faraway look and a half smile. I'm sure he found it hard to face the fact that the years were past when he could take active part in such an adventure.

A week or so after the visit of this gallant man, I received a letter from him saying, "I . . . have given considerable thought to the idea of a winter expedition. You must attempt to bring this about. Do not be discouraged by apathy and resistance, press for it. . . ."

On the first of December, I learned of his death from a heart attack.

IN LATE JANUARY, Nancy and I drove to Hanover, New Hampshire, where I gave a talk on the cruise of the *Skate* at Dartmouth College. The next morning I visited Vilhjalmur Stefansson, who was a member of the faculty, in Dartmouth's Baker Memorial Library, where the large Stefansson collection of Arctic literature is housed in a special section.

Stefansson was one of the great authorities on the northlands, and it was heartwarming to find him rugged and vigorous in his old age. As I came into his office, he riffled through his desk drawer and found a thin piece of paper which he handed to me. It was a copy of the message I had sent Sir Hubert Wilkins from Europe. Sir Hubert had passed on this copy to Stefansson with the note, "Wrong addressee—should have been sent to you.—W."

We discussed at length Wilkins' suggestion that we go to the Arctic in winter. "He would, of course," Stefansson said. "He always wanted to press into the thick of things."

"What do you think about it?" I asked.

"You'll find it a lot different from what you saw last August," Stefansson replied. Open water, he went on, would be very scarce. But water with thin ice—that might be a different matter. In still air and at 30 below zero, seawater will freeze six inches the first day, four more inches the second, and so on—a foot and a half or so in a week. "Do you think," Stefansson asked, "you could break that much ice with the *Skate?*"

I said, in all honesty, that I had no idea.

"Let me show you something," said Stefansson, reaching for a copy of his book *The Friendly Arctic*. He thumbed through it briefly. "Here. Read this," he said, handing me the open book.

Stefansson and two companions, on a trek across the ice more than one hundred miles north of Alaska, camped near a recently frozen lead. They were suddenly awakened by the barking of their dogs. Then they too heard the noise that had upset the dogs. It was the blowing of whales. A school of beluga whales were swimming along the lead, breaking the ice as they passed. "It was interesting," Stefansson had written, "to see the six- or eight-inch ice bulge and break as they struck it with the hump of their backs. A moment after the noise of breaking ice would come the hiss of the spouting whale and a column of spray."

"If the beluga whales could do it, why not the *Skate?*" asked the smiling Stefansson.

BACK IN NEW LONDON, I learned that while I had been talking about the Arctic, the Navy Department had been doing something about it. The Skate was scheduled to return to the polar sea in March and investigate the possibility of wintertime operations.

If we were to break our way through the ice, the *Skate*'s sail would have to act as our battering ram. This sail is filled with nearly a dozen hydraulically hoisted masts, radar, radio antennae, periscopes, and ventilating pipes—devices vital to the safe operation of the submarine.

Could they stand the splintering shock as the three-thousand-ton ship drove them into the ice?

The sail structure, which had been strengthened for the summer expedition, must now be altered further. Powerful floodlights would be installed in the deck to illuminate the ice from underneath in the darkness of winter. To help us examine it, a television camera would be embedded in the deck in a watertight container.

In my mind's eye I could see the *Skate*, groping silently in the dark, searching with floodlights and television for a place to break through the ice. Had our good judgment been carried away by the successes of one ten-day period in the most favorable season of the year? My doubts notwithstanding, workmen swarmed over the *Skate* from one end to the other, installing new equipment.

One day, while all this work was going on, a phone call summoned me to the office of Admiral Warder.

"Jim," he said, "I know you thought a lot of Sir Hubert Wilkins. How would you like to do a last favor for him?"

The admiral told me that after Sir Hubert's visit to the *Skate* he had expressed to Lady Wilkins the hope that when he died his ashes might be carried to the North Pole by submarine and there distributed.

"The *Skate* would be honored, Admiral," I said. "But to surface right at the Pole is a pretty big order. We couldn't do it last August, and I don't hold much hope for the winter."

We finally decided I would take the ashes along. Somehow, I felt, we would have to find a way.

SAILING DAY WAS set for the third of March; the lowest Arctic temperatures occur from January through March. In December, John Nicholson had been ordered to his own command; Bill Layman moved up to take his place. Big, cheerful, redheaded Guy Shaffer replaced Bill Cowhill as diving officer; Dave Boyd became new chief engineer. The rest of the crew remained essentially the same. For this I was thankful. We would need all the confidence and team spirit that we could muster.

Meantime, the civilian specialists began to gather, including Waldo Lyon. Hard at work on our television installation was Cramer Bacque, a rotund, jolly, and highly competent young engineer from the Bendix Corporation. No one had ever put a movable television camera into a submarine before, and Cramer had his hands full with the technical difficulties involved.

Several times during the fall, Dave Boyd and Dr. Dick Arnest, our medical officer, both skin-diving enthusiasts, had said that they thought we ought to have equipment along so that we could examine pressure ridges from underneath, in the hope of unraveling some of the mysteries of their formation. Finally it was arranged for Boyd, Dr. Arnest, and two others to go to diving school in Washington for a rigorous two-week training period.

They returned with quarter-inch-thick black sponge-rubber suits which completely covered all but their faces. The sponge rubber would absorb and hold water, which would become warm from body contact and act as an insulator against the icy sea. It was hoped that the divers could stay in near-freezing water for up to half an hour with no ill effects.

A few days before our departure, Walt Wittmann rejoined us, armed with a mountain of Arctic literature.

Finally the television system was installed; a new ice Fathometer had been put in; our sail structure had been modified for better protection; and the new floodlights seemed bright enough to illuminate the whole Arctic basin. What the wealth of our country could do for us, it had done; the rest was up to us.

FOR THE SECOND time in seven months the *Skate* was leaving for the North Pole and beyond, and all that remained were the good-bys. Nancy and I had been married for seventeen years, but the partings seemed harder each time. The last days are only made bearable for husband and wife by the solace which the perspective of experience brings. Time does pass, and returns are sweet.

But not so for the children. Good-by for them is good-by, though in their brave young way they don't talk much about it. It was three-year-old Charlie who nearly broke my heart. When all the farewells were said, he came toddling out to the car. His trusting face looked up at me. "You won't be gone so long *this* time, will you, Daddy?" he entreated. "Back *soooon?*"

And then Nancy, standing behind him, could no longer keep back the tears.

CHAPTER 7

As the *Skate* sped northward for Prins Karls Forland, her crew handled her with veteran skill and confidence, but as we approached the wintry North Atlantic, gale-driven seas began to toss the ship about whenever Layman brought her to periscope depth to shoot the sun. The periscope would be clear one minute, submerged under tons of cascading green water the next. It was a real relief when we could drop back to the deep, quiet waters below.

Inside the ship, the usual good-natured banter of men at sea went on. In the crew's mess, the veterans made preparations to initiate the few new hands as we crossed the Arctic Circle. When the day arrived, elaborate ceremonies were held; the neophytes were brought before a judge, who was dressed gaudily in red-dyed long underwear. Each victim, blindfolded, was brought in and required to sit in a puddle of ice water, completing an electrical circuit that gave him a mild jolt. This brought roars of laughter from the veterans.

Saturday afternoon, the fourteenth of March, the periscope broke the water in a choppy sea and I peered out into murky weather. It was almost dark, although it was only two o'clock. Navigation showed us to be just off Prins Karls Forland. I could see no land, but radar soon confirmed our position, so we dived to four hundred feet and set our course northward. Within a few hours our new ice detector—devised by Dr. Lyon—began to sketch sudden dips. The ice pack—its boundaries much farther south than last summer—was upon us.

The ice machine, however, was no longer the main attraction for the curious crew. Instead, a fascinated group was clustered about the television screen. Even with the poor illumination of the Arctic twilight, shadowy images of the huge ice blocks drifting overhead were outlined plainly. The instrument barrier had been broken—at last we could see!

By nine in the evening, however, the ice had closed solidly overhead; the television screen showed nothing but solid black. We were running along smoothly when, about midnight, Dave Boyd called me to say that the seal around one of the propeller shafts was leaking.

I went hastily to the engine room, where I found Dave crouched worriedly in the crowded corner aft. As he shone his flashlight into the dark corner, I could see a steady jet of water streaming in where the spinning shaft penetrated the hull. Water was collecting in the engine-room bilges. It was still not rising very fast—our pumps could easily keep up with it—but it might get worse. For a moment I thought of turning back before we got any farther under the ice.

"What do you think?" I asked Dave.

"Well, we can try backing the shaft," he replied. "Sometimes that seats the seal."

I nodded. "Starboard back two-thirds!" I shouted above the roar of machinery. The shaft hissed to a stop, then began spinning swiftly in the opposite direction. As the huge propeller bit into the water, the submarine shuddered and shook from one end to the other.

Suddenly we recoiled from a shower of icy salt spray which exploded from the seal in all directions. What had gone wrong? The ship continued to shake as the great propeller chewed the water just outside the hull, and the noise was deafening.

Then—as suddenly as one turns off a faucet—the water stopped. "Stop the shaft!" I shouted. The shuddering ceased; all was quiet. Only a trickle of water came from the seal.

I was limp with relief. "Wow!" I exclaimed weakly.

"We've still got to be careful," Dave said. "When that seal shifts, it sometimes jams, and then you're in real trouble. Ready to try her ahead?"

I nodded, and called out the order to the maneuvering room. Slowly the shaft started to turn, spinning faster and faster as the *Skate* regained speed. Finally we reached sixteen knots. The seal held.

Still deeply disturbed, I walked slowly forward through the reactor compartment to my room. Everything had gone so well on the first cruise under the ice—almost too well. Now, returning under circumstances when everything *had* to work absolutely perfectly, was our luck to turn against us?

That night, for once, I could not sleep.

BEFORE BREAKFAST NEXT morning I walked into the control center, where Walt Wittmann stood by the ice detector.

"How's it look, Walt?" I asked.

Walt shook his head. "Not one bit of open water during the night. Over a hundred and ninety miles and nothing but ice."

I whistled in amazement and walked over to the television screen. Huge black patches of floe ice could be seen, outlined in the dim light which filtered through the thinner ice surrounding them.

We were now extremely anxious to make a practice surfacing before we got too far north to find any open water. Almost as an echo to my thoughts, the officer of the deck soon reported that he was turning around to investigate possible open water. *Possible* open water—that sounded strange. Last summer it either was or it wasn't.

When I went to look at the trace on the ice machine, I saw what had everyone confused. Hour after hour the stylus had been tracing an unbroken ceiling of heavy ice—mile after mile of thick floes, with an occasional pressure-ridge stalactite. Now the stylus had jumped up and was drawing out a long, flat line. But there was a faint hint of fuzziness—the line was not clean and sharp, as last summer's open-water traces had been. Was our new ice machine faulty, or was this the sign of thin ice?

We stopped under the suspected opening, and television showed nothing but murky gray. Through the periscope I could make out only a faint aquamarine light coming through from above. I told Guy Shaffer to raise the ship to one hundred feet, but as we drifted up, I looked in vain for the heavy blocks and jagged edges which had been so familiar a part of the polynya icescape. There was only a faint greenish blue glow from above as far as the eye could see.

"I think we're under a large lead that has frozen over," I announced. "Don't believe the ice is too heavy—I can see some light coming through from above." I turned to Al Kelln at the ice detector. "How thick do you think it is?"

"Can't tell for sure," he replied, "but it has to be less than three feet, and it could be as thin as four or five inches."

It was Sunday morning. It had also been a Sunday morning last August when we took our first big step—and a mighty successful one it had proved to be. As long as men go to sea, I suppose, a thread of superstition will run through the things they do.

"Stand by to hit the ice!" I called out. "Bring her up," I told Guy.

The whir of the trimming pump filled the room as the *Skate* began to rise out of the dark depths. "Snap on the floodlights," I ordered.

"Up periscope." I was disappointed to see that the lights were of little help. It was like turning on car headlights in a fog. However, even in the hazy yellow glare I could see our friends·the jellyfish.

I finally turned off the floodlights. We were now so close to the ice that the periscope had to come down for safety. We decided to train the Cyclops eye of the television camera on the part of the ship which would take the initial shock—the sail.

"Turn on the sail floodlight," I ordered. A ghostly cone of light appeared on the upper part of the screen. Far above we could see a faint disk where the floodlight illuminated the ice. The cone of light became smaller and brighter as we rose. Everyone instinctively braced himself for the shock.

Suddenly there was a sensation like that of being on an elevator stopped too quickly. My stomach turned over. There was no noise of collision, but on the television screen the cone of light was growing longer—we were dropping away!

I glanced at the depth gauge. We had passed one hundred feet and were still falling. Desperately, Guy pumped out water to regain our stability. Blowing the ballast tanks would have been faster, but with ice overhead it was unthinkable.

Guy checked our downward motion at one hundred and fifty feet. By television we examined the sail for damage. None was apparent.

"We'll hit it again," I said with determination. "Harder this time." Again we started up. Again the cone of light narrowed as we neared the ice. Holding my breath, I braced my back against the periscope stand, watching the television screen as though hypnotized.

Again a sickening lurch as we hit—but now the television screen was filled with the image of splashing water and bits of shattered ice. A heavy, grinding crunch shook the control center. The top of the sail disappeared from the screen. We were through!

"Up periscope." I gripped the handles and put my face against the eyepiece. It was as though I were looking into a freshly laundered white pillowcase. I shifted the prism of the optics in the hope they would clear. Nothing.

Then I understood what had happened. As soon as the wet periscope reached the frigid Arctic air, a film of ice had formed on the lens. I folded up the handles of the useless scope. I assumed that we were floating with our sail out of the ice and the rest of the ship underwater. The television camera, embedded in the main deck, was still submerged and could help us no more.

I hesitated. What to do? Blowing the tanks to surface might be dangerous, especially if the delicate rudder were under heavy ice. But we had to take the chance. We would not have any clear idea of our surroundings until I could reach the bridge.

"Blow the main ballast, Guy," I said. "But take it easy."

The hiss and chatter of high-pressure air filled the room. Nothing happened for a few moments, then the *Skate* again started to move slowly upward. We listened carefully for the sound of breaking ice or crunching metal, but could hear nothing over the noise of the air.

Finally the *Skate* was high enough so that I knew the hatch was above the water. I told Shaffer to stop blowing the tanks.

Quartermaster John Medaglia climbed the ladder leading through the tube to the hatch. "Open the hatch!" I shouted up to him. Medaglia went up at once. Ordinarily he crosses the platform at this level and climbs a second ladder to the bridge, but I found him standing on the platform, arms akimbo, looking at the small ladder opening. It was jammed with huge pieces of ice!

I shouted down for a man with a heavy crowbar, and in a few minutes a husky fireman was chopping away at the obstruction. At last I went up the ladder, squeezed past several ice blocks, then climbed on top of one for a better view.

Last summer's pale blue melt ponds and black patches of open water were gone and in their place was a world of stark whiteness. The black sail of the *Skate* was poking up through the center of an enormous flat plain—a frozen lead that wandered to the horizon. There was no wind, but the air was biting cold. Setting off the white of the snow-covered ice was a beautifully soft sky of rose and lavender to the southeast, where the sun peeped above the rim of our frozen world. There was no sign of life, and the stillness of the air seemed in keeping with the beauty of the scene.

Medaglia joined me on the bridge and neither of us spoke. Nothing we could say could express the wonder of what we felt.

Finally I ordered Guy to blow the tanks. The *Skate* began to press against the underside of the ice along her entire length. Faint bulges appeared. For a moment the ship stopped rising. Then, without warning, she began to break through like an enormous cookie cutter.

Up she came, staggering under the heavy load of ice that remained on her deck. Aft, the rudder punched a neat hole for itself; protruding from the ice, it looked like the fin of a gigantic shark. There was no open water visible at the edge of the ship. No need to worry about drifting; we would stay where we were.

Bill Layman joined me on the bridge and, after a moment of awed silence, suggested that I put on something warmer. Only then did I realize that in my excitement I had come up on the bridge with nothing heavier than a parka and that I was getting colder every minute. It was 20 degrees below zero.

BEFORE LONG I RETURNED to the bridge encased in bulky trousers, a jacket of nylon quilted over foam rubber, and a helmet. Several men with crowbars were removing ice blocks from the deck. It was a simple matter to slide down the *Skate*'s superstructure and onto the ice. The ship did not appear to have suffered any damage. The whale-backed sail had taken the original impact without harm, and then it had been a matter of slowly pushing the rest of the ship up.

Elated, I walked farther away from the ship to gain some perspective; not many skippers have the opportunity, this far from land, to stroll out and take a look at their ships. Her black hull looked as though it had been dropped gently on the surface of the ice like a confectioner's decoration on a white cake frosting. It seemed inconceivable that she could ever move again.

When I returned, our official photographer, Lieutenant Bruce Meader, was getting ready to go out on the ice. Bruce looked like a well-stuffed teddy bear in his heavy Arctic clothes. He had cameras slung over both shoulders and was trying to slide down the side of the ship without damaging his equipment. "Better get a lot of pictures, Bruce," I told him. "No one'll believe this unless you do!"

Later, when he brought his chilled cameras back inside the warm ship, moisture from the air condensed and froze on them. In minutes his elegant Leicas and Nikons were encrusted in white rime like the coils of an old-fashioned refrigerator.

WHEN WE SUBMERGED about five that afternoon, we could see on the television screen a long, cigar-shaped hole in the ice above us. It was a perfect outline of the *Skate*.

We set our course for the North Pole, and all through the night as we sped northward the ice detector and television scanned the surface in vain for patches of thin ice. Our plan to surface precisely at the Pole began to look hopeless.

I had not said much to the crew about the service for Sir Hubert Wilkins, mainly because I had become increasingly unsure there would be any. However, on the morning of the seventeenth, as we were nearing our destination I told them over the announcing system what our task was and how we hoped to accomplish it. When we reached the Pole, we would start a slow and patient crisscrossing search of the immediate vicinity. The ice cover was moving constantly at about two and a half miles a day, and the new ice coming over might be better. The test would be of military value in showing whether submarines could surface at a *given* geographic location in the Arctic—not a place like Drifting Station Alpha, which shifted with the ice.

At the breakfast table we began discussing what we should call these vital areas of thin ice. Actually they were newly frozen leads, but that seemed an awkward way to put it. Dr. Lyon said, "Why don't you just call them skylights?"

That is what they resembled: stretches of blue-green glass in an otherwise black ceiling. Skylights they would be.

We cruised slowly, adjusting our course carefully as Bill Layman finally brought us into the spot where every direction is south. The *Skate* had returned to the Pole.

I made a brief announcement to the crew, reminding them that almost fifty years ago, on April 6, 1909, Robert Peary had first reached the Pole. How different his circumstances from ours! Accompanied by four Eskimos and his steward, Matt Henson, Peary had had no scientific marvels to guide him. He measured distances with a crude wheel attached to one of the sledges, and determined his position by observation of the sun. When he was certain he had reached the Pole, he planted his flags and took his pictures. And then, in a few hours, the drifting ice of the Arctic had carried his flags away. The shifting signs of fame!

Thanks to the marvels of inertial navigation, we had reached the Pole with little difficulty, but there was not a sign of a skylight. With the ship stopped two hundred feet under the sea directly at the Pole,

I raised the periscope. But not the faintest glimmer shone through the ice above; we were sealed in.

We began our crisscross search in the immediate area, proceeding at very slow speed and using the periscope as well as the ice detector and the television. Several hours went by with no results. And then we saw it. At first it was just a faint glimmer of emerald green, visible only through the periscope. It looked too small for the ship, but we maneuvered under it. The trace on our ice detector showed thin ice.

We drifted up to one hundred feet. The skylight was dogleg in shape and treacherously small; we had never attempted anything like this. However, if we could once break through the ice, the *Skate* would be held as tightly as in a vise, with no danger of damage from drifting. "Stand by to hit the ice," I said. "Bring her up."

We had barely started up when Kelln, standing at the ice detector, called out, "Heavy ice overhead—better than twelve feet!"

I could see what had happened. The ice was moving, and the skylight was simply drifting away from the submarine.

"Flood her down, Guy!" I said. Reluctantly the ship began to sink back into the black depths. Patiently we realigned her under the opening and tried again; but again we missed.

"We'd better try an offset," said Bill Layman. He quickly calculated how far to the side we should position ourselves in order to come up and find ourselves in the right position. Painstakingly the *Skate* was maneuvered into position.

But again, as we started upward, Kelln reported heavy ice overhead. The top of the sail was only fifty feet below the ice, and I was forced to lower the periscope, leaving us blind except for the television camera, which showed only the fuzzy edge of the heavy ice.

Now the top of the sail was only twenty-five feet under the ice. "Heavy ice, still heavy ice." The strain was apparent in Kelln's voice.

We could wait no longer. "Flood her down—emergency!" I snapped. The wave of air pressure slapped into my ears as Shaffer opened the negative tank and sent tons of water into the ship. Quickly we fell away from the ominous ice cliffs.

"Blow negative to the mark," Shaffer ordered, trying to regain control of the *Skate*. The roar of high-pressure air filled the room.

"Blow secured; negative at the mark," reported chief torpedoman Dornberg.

"Shut the flood, vent negative, pump from auxiliaries to sea," said Guy. Slowly our downward momentum slackened, and finally, far deeper than we had intended to go, we were motionless.

Beads of perspiration were on my brow, and I could sense the feeling of strain through the ship. With grim determination we started all over again.

Once more Bill Layman calculated the offset required, this time allowing for a little less drift, and the whir of the trimming pump announced our slow ascent.

"Heavy ice, still heavy ice," intoned Kelln, like the voice of doom. Time for the periscope to go down.

"Thin ice! There she is! Looks good!" he exclaimed.

The television screen showed us very close. We braced ourselves. With a sickening lurch we hit and broke through.

"Don't let her drop out, Guy," I warned. I was most reluctant to surface blind, but when the periscope went up, it revealed nothing but a field of blank white. Frozen. I glanced at the diving instruments; we were holding our position well. If we could break through completely, we would make history. "Stand by to surface at the Pole," I announced over the speaker system.

Preparations were made swiftly, and Shaffer turned to me with a smile. "Ready to surface," he said, "at the Pole!"

Slowly we blew the tanks and the *Skate* moved reluctantly upward. It was apparent we were under the heaviest ice yet. After what seemed an eternity, the upper hatch was far enough above the ice to be opened.

"Open the hatch!" I shouted, and raced up the ladder.

I leaped to the bridge, and was struck by the first heavy wind I had experienced in the Arctic. It howled and swirled across the open bridge, carrying stinging snow particles which cut like flying sand. Heavy gray clouds hung in the sky. We had broken through almost exactly at the bend of the dogleg. The lead was narrow and meandering, and on either side were hummocks eighteen feet high—the tallest we had yet seen.

We seemed to have a clear path in which to surface the rest of the way. The tanks were blown, and with loud cracks that sounded like gunshots, the deck began to break through. Finally the *Skate* lay on the surface—the first ship in history to sit at the very top of the world.

In every direction—ahead, astern, to port, to starboard—was south. The planet turned ponderously beneath us. The lodestone of the Arctic, which had lured brave men to their deaths for over a century, had fallen to the modern submarine.

AFTER A WALK out on the ice, Walt Wittmann warned me that he did not like the looks of our surroundings. With the wind blowing a stiff gale, there was every reason to expect heavy ice movement, and he advised us not to stay longer than necessary.

We made immediate preparations for the service. Sir Hubert had been born in Australia, had performed many of his finest deeds for the United Kingdom, and had made his final home in the United States; we flew the flags of all three nations from the *Skate*. They made a brave sight snapping sharply in the wind.

On a small table on the ice beside the ship we placed the bronze urn. About thirty of the crew formed ranks on either side in the 26-below-zero cold. We were in the lee of the *Skate*, but our breath froze on our chins like white beards. The wind blew snow into our noses and mouths, and it was difficult to breathe. It was dark, so men held red flares on both sides of the altarlike table. Their shimmering light glared through the blowing snow, giving the scene an unearthly atmosphere.

The remainder of the crew lined up on the deck of the *Skate*, and a rifle squad formed near the bow. In a few words I tried to catch the essence of the man: "On this day we pay humble tribute to one of the great men of our century . . . [who] spent his life in the noblest of callings, the attempt to broaden the horizons of the mind of man. . . . This [is a] prayer which he himself wrote: 'Our heavenly Father, wouldst thou give us liberty without license and the power to do good for mankind with the self-restraint to avoid using that power for self-aggrandizement. . . .' "

Lieutenant Boyd then picked up the bronze urn and, followed by me and the two torchbearers, walked about thirty yards away from the ship. The bitter-cold wind made it physically difficult to hold and read the prayer book, but I began the committal: "Unto Almighty God we commend the soul of our brother departed, and we commit his ashes to the deep. . . ."

Dave took the urn and sprinkled the ashes to the wind. They

quickly disappeared in the half-darkness and the swirling snow. The rifles cracked three times in a last salute. Sir Hubert Wilkins had reached his final resting place.

DINNER THAT EVENING was a sober gathering. The service had seemed a tribute not only to Wilkins but to all of the men who had spent their lives in the conquest of the North.

That night we built a small cairn of ice blocks and planted a steel shaft in it to which we attached an American flag. In a waterproof container buried inside it we left a note recording the event. In due time this message may, like the wreckage of the *Jeannette,* be carried along in the ice drift and cast up on the shores of Greenland far to the south.

There had been no sign of the ice movement that Wittmann had feared, but the gale was increasing and the temperature dropping. It was time to return to the warmer environment of the sea.

The diving alarm sounded, the vents opened, and we began to sink slowly into the canyon of ice. The wind roared and whipped over the jagged hummocks. Our cairn was plainly visible through the periscope a few yards to port. The last thing I saw was the American flag whipping proudly in the swirling, windswept snow.

CHAPTER 8

BY THURSDAY THE nineteenth we were in uncharted waters, more than twelve hundred nautical miles from open water, and we could find no place to surface. What would we do if we had trouble with the ship now? For the first time on either of the *Skate*'s expeditions I seriously considered turning back. But we were eager to check on conditions in this remote part of the Arctic. Walt Wittmann and I were discussing our chances of finding looser ice when suddenly we felt the ship heel sharply to starboard as the officer of the deck doubled back to have another look at a possible skylight. I went immediately to the control center and asked about it.

"Small, but worth a look," said Bill Cowhill laconically.

In a few minutes, through the periscope, I could see a faint emerald streak across our roof of black. In the deep gloom the floodlight on the sail made a brilliant spot on the underside of the ice as we came up. Suddenly the light disappeared and all was darkness. For a moment we were baffled. Then with triumphant relief we realized what had happened—the light was shining up into thin air! We had broken through ice so thin we had not felt it.

The scene outside was different from anything we had experienced. There was not a cloud in a sky brilliant with stars. A three-quarter moon, reflected by the snow and ice, gave a surprising amount of light, and the fantastic moonlit landscape and the cloudless star-filled sky combined to create a scene of fragile beauty. Our position seemed safe, so I decided we would remain awhile to relieve tension and give everyone a chance to see the scenery.

After supper the sun began to rise, as sharp and clear as if a red paper disk were being pushed above the horizon. The ice fields became flooded with the vermilion glow. Dave Boyd joined me on the stern. "How about trying out the skin diving here?" he asked.

"Good *night*, Dave!" I exclaimed. "It's twenty-three below!"

He laughed. "Soon's we get in that warm water we'll be fine."

So closely did the *Skate* fit into the ice that we had to break a new hole for the aqualungers to enter the water. Dave and three others clustered about it in their martian costumes; then, giving a thumbs-up signal, Dave stepped off the stern into the water. He bobbed in the ice hole a moment and then went down. A light line was tied to his waist for safety, and the sight of this cord paying out like a fishline into the small hole was odd indeed. In a short time he reappeared and pulled the breathing piece from his mouth. "This is *great!*" he shouted. "The water's warm and clear as crystal!"

Two other divers went under the ice in an attempt to reach a pressure ridge that rimmed our lead. After they had been gone nearly ten minutes I was getting more than a little concerned, when their heads appeared simultaneously in the hole. I crouched down to talk to them. "Any sign of life?" I asked.

"Coupla jellyfish, nothing else. The light's good. Looks like you're swimming under a glass ceiling."

When the men stood on the deck being helped out of their heavy aqualung rigs, the water absorbed by their spongy suits froze. With every step, as they headed for the warm interior of the ship, they tinkled and crashed with a sound like breaking glass.

WE SUBMERGED RELUCTANTLY from our skylight on the other side of the world, and by next morning were roughly one hundred miles from the New Siberian Islands. Here we took a sharp turn to the right to continue our exploration of the polar basin.

The day passed quietly, with everyone working hard to bring reports up to date. About nine in the evening there was a sharp rap on my door. Dave Boyd popped his head in.

"Captain," he said grimly, "we've developed a pretty serious leak in the engine room. Will you come and have a look at it?"

On our way to the engine room Dave explained, "It's the starboard circ pump, at the seal where the drive shaft enters the pump."

Steam from the boilers comes into the engine room of the *Skate* at high pressure. It hisses through the blades of the turbines, making them spin at blinding speeds, and then drops into a large condenser where it is chilled back to water, to be returned again to the boilers. A centrifugal pump circulates seawater to chill the steam. The men in the engine room simply call it a circ pump.

We hastily clambered down into the lower level of the engine room. In the beam of a flashlight I could see the faulty seal spraying water in every direction. Water ran across the steel deck plates and into the bilge below us, sprayed up to spit and sizzle on the bare steam pipes of the air ejector, splashed against the metal doors of an electrical switchboard.

"Isn't there any way we can tighten up on it?" I asked.

Dave shook his head. "This is a new type of seal—there's no way of adjusting it."

"Won't you have to shut the condenser down to replace the seal?"

He nodded. But shutting down the condenser would mean that half our turbines would also be shut down, and it was most undesirable for us to operate under the ice without all of our turbines.

"Looks as though we'll have to repair this on the surface," I said.

"There's a chance the thing will reseat by itself," Dave said dubiously. "They do sometimes."

I looked at the huge electric motor. Water was already starting to splash up into its windings—a little more of that would ruin the motor, and we had no replacement.

"All we can do is put a canvas cover around the seal to keep the water from spraying, and hope it reseats itself," said Dave.

"Right," I replied. "And when we find a place to surface, we'll decide what to do."

We pressed on at high speed for the rest of the night. At intervals we would drop down into the depths and then rise in stages while Dr. Lyon measured the temperature of the water. On one of these excursions the variation of pressure on the circ-pump seal caused it to reseat perfectly. It didn't leak a drop. However, neither Dave nor I was convinced the trouble wouldn't reappear.

While we were discussing it, the ship banked sharply to starboard as the officer of the deck turned back for some thin ice. It looked worth trying, and sure enough, we passed through easily, finding ourselves in a narrow lead winding off into the distance.

Now what to do? Fix the pump or not? We were scheduled to remain in the pack for nearly another week. We had many hundreds of miles to travel, many jobs remaining to be done.

I called the officers together for a conference. Finally I said, "We'll take a chance on it. I believe it'll hold."

On Sunday, March 22, about seven in the evening, my telephone buzzed urgently. "The circ-pump seal has just broken loose again!" Dave Boyd reported. "Much worse this time—spraying water all over the place. We'll have to get up and fix it as soon as we can."

I went directly to the control center, where Guy Shaffer was on watch, and explained the emergency to him.

"This ice has been really heavy for hours," said Guy grimly. "No point in doubling back."

An air of tenseness and gloom settled over the control center. I thought to myself what a fool I had been not to make the pump repair the last time we surfaced. Two hours dragged by. Thirty-two miles of heavy, solid ice without a trace of a gap.

Reluctantly I went back to my room. I was not helping matters by staring at the ice machine and television. And then, within an hour, the ship heeled to starboard and began a rapid turn. They'd found something! I immediately returned to the control center, where Al Kelln had relieved Guy Shaffer.

"It's a big one!" exclaimed Al, with a smile from ear to ear.

I looked at the ice detector. Sure enough, we had passed under several hundred yards of thin ice. The light was strong enough to be clearly visible on the television. We were soon under the skylight, ballooning slowly upward. Through the periscope, the now familiar jade green was sharply outlined against the jet black of the pack. At ten thirteen p.m. we hit the ice with an impact which brought butterflies to our stomachs. But on the television we could see the ice bow and then shatter. We were through.

As I climbed to the bridge, I could see the faint glow of sunrise on the horizon. We had surfaced in a long, straight lead, its smooth snow-covered ice heavier than any we had yet broken. Once up, we were gripped fast. There were tall pressure ridges to port made of husky slabs ten to twelve feet thick. Dave immediately wanted to know if he could go ahead with the pump repair. I said to get on with it and asked how long it would take. "About twelve hours," he said.

We had not been on the surface that long at any time this winter. I decided to have a look at the heavy ridges to port, and went below to put on my heaviest clothes and get my binoculars and camera.

The edges of the rafted ice blocks were sharp, showing that they had recently been broken. The ridge itself was about fifteen feet high and stretched for hundreds of yards along the side of the lead. I climbed to the top of a hummock. Nothing but endless ice fields stretched to the horizon. I frankly do not know how men live in temperatures like that, week after week, with no protection. Those who have done it have my heartfelt salute.

When I returned to the ship, the engine room rang with the voices of men and the clatter of tools. Engine-room chief Charles Whitehead was in charge of a group who were removing lockers, wires, and small pipes above the motor. Another group prepared a wire sling and block and tackle to hoist it. In designing the *Skate*, Admiral Rickover's engineers had spared no effort to ensure that every piece of machinery that might have to be repaired at sea could be reached and hoisted out. Every pipe, wire, and fitting had been mocked up life-size in wood and then moved around like furniture in a new living room to make sure nothing was inaccessible. That effort was paying off for us now.

My presence here could contribute nothing. I went forward to my room. Shortly after, my phone buzzer rang. "Captain," said Al Kelln in a tense voice, "I'd like to have you come up here."

I pulled myself into my warm clothes again and climbed to the bridge. As I neared the top of the ladder, I could hear a dull boom like distant thunder. "What's up, Al?" I asked.

In his calm, deliberate manner he handed me his binoculars. "Look over to port, in the ice fields beyond the hummocks."

In the distance, moving with ponderous slowness, huge ice cakes rose up on end like giant green billboards, then slowly slipped back into the surrounding white. The dull, thunderous boom grew louder. The ice was on the move. I looked at my watch. It was eleven twenty-five p.m. The engine-room job had been under way for about an hour. Near the ship there was still no sign of movement.

From close by came a noise like the report of a rifle. Startled, I spun around but could see nothing. Kelln pointed beyond the bow, where a new crack ran diagonally forward. Somewhere in the closely packed ice floes stretching to the horizon, gigantic forces must have been at work to tumble ten-foot blocks of ice like a child's building blocks. To port, the rise and fall of the ice gave the appearance of sluggish waves, all moving inexorably toward the *Skate*. As the noise of the grinding, tortured ice grew louder, the ice in the lead started to creep slowly up the sides of the ship. Pieces of it caught on protruding parts of the superstructure, screeching like banshees as they forced their way past the protesting metal.

I could hardly believe what I saw. This was the fifteenth time we had surfaced in the Arctic and the first time we couldn't submerge easily and quickly.

"Is anyone out on the ice?" I asked.

"I got them down below before I called you," Al answered.

We were all on board and ready to leave this treacherous place—except that we were one hour into a twelve-hour repair job.

"Permission to come up?" It was Layman and Wittmann. I waved them up. "This pressure is making an awful racket inside the ship," said Bill in a worried tone. "I wanted to see what it looked like."

By now the ice had been forced up over the deck far enough to cover most of the hull. With binoculars Wittmann studied the ice beyond the steep hummocks to port. "That's mean-looking stuff," he commented. "Can you get out of here?"

I shook my head. "Not now, Walt. Do you think it will stop?"

"You just can't tell with this sort of thing," he said cautiously.

The pressure ridge on our left was now at least ten yards closer than when we had surfaced. The lead was closing, and when it did, the *Skate* would be caught between the two floes like a walnut in a nutcracker. The noise was terrifying as the heavy boom of the moving floes mingled with the high-pitched shriek of the ice being crushed in the lead. We had to shout to make ourselves heard. I asked Bill Layman to go below to get me a report on the pump repair. The ice was now being forced up over the deck from both sides, forming a tent-shaped canopy along its length.

From behind the ridge to port, a huge slab of ice rose slowly on edge and hovered ominously as though poised to strike. It was not more than thirty yards away. The noises increased in intensity.

At eleven thirty-five, Bill Layman came back and told me that the men in the engine room were ready to hoist the big motor. Everything was disconnected. "The noise is pretty bad inside the ship," he said. "I think you ought to go down and listen to it."

My mouth feeling dry as cotton, I went down the ladder to the control center. I immediately discovered that the noise of the ice scraping against the thin metal shell of the ship was immensely amplified, as if we were in a steel barrel being dragged along a rock road. Even more disturbing than the noise was the vibration. The ship fluttered and shook as the ice pressed around her, seeming to protest in agony.

With a convulsive shudder she suddenly took an alarming list to starboard. We would have to dive. I was deeply worried lest ice might be pressed so tightly against the sides of the ship that she could not submerge.

I ran to the engine room and beckoned to Dave Boyd. "We have to go down," I said. "Secure things as quickly as you can and let me know when you're ready."

Dave nodded and turned to his men to order them to undo what they had done. I started back to the bridge, but even as I walked into the control center, the noise diminished. By the time I reached the bridge it had almost stopped.

"It just stopped," Al Kelln said. "All of a sudden."

The narrow lead in which we lay was now about half its original width, its ice tumbled crazily in every direction.

"It's going to start again in a moment," Wittmann said, looking out to port with his binoculars. "The ice out there is still moving."

In a few minutes, building up like music composed in hell, the moaning and screeching reached an even higher level than before. The vibration could be felt through the deck plates of the bridge. The ice all around the *Skate* was in slow movement, all the more awesome in its deliberate ponderousness. The fragile rudder was buried under a pile of rafted ice, and could not be seen.

Everything I had read and heard about ships trapped in the ice went swiftly through my mind. The *Jeannette*, in these very waters; the *Karluk* of Stefannson's, lost near Wrangel Island; the *Endurance* of Ernest Shackleton's, lost in the Antarctic . . . The accounts of the ice which destroyed them had a striking similarity to what we were now seeing. The men of the *Jeannette, Karluk,* and *Endurance* had waited beside their crafts—stores, sledges, and dogs already evacuated to the ice as the ships went through their death throes. Their crews had, with great hardship in each case, made their way to land. But our safety lay only in the ship.

In a few minutes Dave reported that the engine room was well enough secured to submerge. We had only half our engineering plant; we would have to accept the risks involved in operating under the ice this way. Everyone but Al Kelln hurried below. I shouted to him to come down as soon as he had checked everything for diving.

A circle of gray, tense faces greeted me at the bottom of the ladder. I went to the periscope stand to wait for Kelln to shut the hatch and come down. Why was he taking so long?

"Captain, pick up the phone, please," grated the intercom from the bridge.

I snatched up the phone and said irritably, "What's the delay? Let's go!"

"There's not a sound up here. Not a sign of ice movement. Wish you'd come up and take a look," Al said.

Nothing is worse on a ship in danger than a captain who vacillates. A bad decision made and stuck to is usually better than indecision. Nevertheless, I went back to the bridge.

The silence was deep and complete. Not a sound could be heard. Was it a temporary respite? I looked at my watch: it was eleven fifty-five. It seemed that the pressure had started an eternity ago, but it had been only a little more than half an hour.

I decided to wait, unavoidably keeping one hundred men below in an agony of suspense. Ten minutes went by. I asked Wittmann to come to the bridge. He looked at the ice carefully and said nothing. All three of us scanned the ice fields beyond the pressure ridge for any sign of movement. None.

About twelve twenty, a sudden crash of noise nearby convinced me it was starting again, but this time it was the easing of pressure. We suddenly recovered from our list and floated naturally. A few inches of water were visible along the bow.

I leaned over and called down the hatch for Dave Boyd to come to the bridge.

When he arrived I told him to start the pump repair again. All Dave said was a quick, "Aye, aye, sir," and he was on his way.

I resolved to stay on the bridge and watch the ice myself. Illogically, I felt that by my very presence I could prevent it from moving again. As the hours crept by, with no further sign of ice movement, I began to see the foolishness of what I was doing. It would be important for me to be fresh in the morning, when many of my officers would be half dead of exhaustion.

I went below to my room and lay down on my bunk to rest. I fell asleep before I could turn my light off.

It was six thirty in the morning when Dave knocked on my door. His eyes were bloodshot and his face haggard.

"Repair completed. Ready to submerge, sir."

The job had been done in less than seven hours.

CHAPTER 9

"O Eternal Lord God, who alone spreadest out the heavens, and rulest the raging of the sea; Vouchsafe to take into thy almighty and most gracious protection our country's Navy, and all who serve therein. Preserve them from the dangers of the sea. . . ."

A SMALL GROUP was assembled for evening prayer in the mess hall of the *Skate*. The day was Sunday, the twenty-ninth of March, exactly a week after our experience with the moving ice. During that week we had made four more surfacings and ranged far and wide through the eastern half of the polar sea.

On Friday the twenty-seventh we had passed Prins Karls Forland and headed for New London. We sent a message to the Navy Department describing our results briefly. We knew that it had gotten through, because we began hearing the story of the *Skate* in the news broadcasts each time we came to periscope depth.

Messages of congratulations began coming in. One of the shortest arrived first, from the Chief of Naval Operations. It said simply:

WELL DONE X ARLEIGH BURKE

And indeed we had the sense of a job well done. We had been pioneers in what we knew would be an ocean of destiny.

We left the Arctic with deep regret. The first time we surfaced outside the ice pack marked the end of a great adventure, the end of a supreme effort to which we had all given at least two years of our lives. Now we were going home. The members of the team would disperse to go their separate ways—not only the navy crew, but also the dedicated band of civilians who had become shipmates in the truest sense of the word. In the past year they had faced the unknown and made it the familiar. The dark ocean forever covered by its frozen sheath of ice had become their element; they had learned to love its austere beauty. They had been the tremendous outsiders.

Machinery and instruments had been their sword and shield. But it was not the machines that won the victory; it was the men. To watch them rise to the challenge of the unknown, fulfilling and even surpassing my belief in them, had been one of the finest experiences I had ever had. Their triumph particularly encouraged me, because I have always believed that the men who serve in the navy simply reflect the nation as a whole. They represented their country in every sense of the word, and their achievements strengthened my confidence and pride in the nation that produced them.

We would always be bound together by the special bond that grows between men who have shared danger and aspiration together. Our feelings were expressed in the words of exultation and thanksgiving which ended the service:

"Lord, now lettest thou thy servant depart in peace, according to thy word.
For mine eyes have seen thy salvation. . . ."

ACKNOWLEDGMENTS

The condensations in this volume have been created by The Reader's Digest Association.

ENGLAND EXPECTS, copyright © 1959 by Dudley Pope, is used by permission of the author.

HMS ULYSSES, copyright Alistair MacLean, first published by William Collins, Sons & Co. Ltd. in 1955.

SURFACE AT THE POLE, copyright © 1961 by James Calvert, originally published in the UK by Hutchinson & Co. (Publishers) Ltd.

Page 6: the poem "Sea Fever" by John Masefield, is used by permission of The Society of Authors as the literary representative of the Estate of John Masefield.

ILLUSTRATION CREDITS
Cover: Background photograph: Picturepoint. Page 1: A. J. Hartman/Photofile Ltd. Pages 2/3: D. James/Zefa. Pages 4/5: James Randklev/Shostal Associates. Page 6: Beken of Cowes. ENGLAND EXPECTS: Pages 12/13: *The Redoutable About to Surrender* by A. Mayer, Musée de la Marine, Paris; photo by J. P. Germain/SRD. Pages 21 (left), 76, 86/87: National Maritime Museum. Page 21 (right): painting by Lemuel Abbott, National Portrait Gallery. Page 27: Mary Evans Picture Library. Page 36: drawing by Thomas Baxter, National Maritime Museum. Page 37 (left): painting by Schmidt, National Maritime Museum. Page 37 (right): after a painting by Bone; photo by Art-Wood, National Maritime Museum. Pages 46, 92, 123: Greenwich Hospital Collection, National Maritime Museum. Page 47: painting by Nicholas Pocock, National Maritime Museum. Page 52: painting by H. Howard, Greenwich Hospital Collection, National Maritime Museum. Pages 53, 68, 126: by kind permission of the commanding officer, HMS *Victory*, and Pitkin Pictorials. Page 60 (left): Picture Collection, New York Public Library, Astor, Lenox and Tilden Foundations. Page 60 (right): Musée de la Marine, Paris. Page 69: drawing by Christine Warburton, by kind permission of the commanding officer, HMS *Victory*. Page 80: Portsmouth Royal Naval Museum. Page 82: National Maritime Museum; photo courtesy of Weidenfeld and Nicolson Ltd. Pages 92/93: Nelson Museum, Monmouth; photo by D. H. Jones. Pages 98/99: courtesy of the Trustees of the Tate Gallery; photo by Derek Bayes. Pages 122/123: Museo de Bellas Artes, Cádiz; photo by Fernando Fernández Fernández. YOUTH: Pages 188/189: *The Missing Steamer*, from *Harper's Weekly*, General Research and Humanities Division, New York Public Library, Astor, Lenox and Tilden Foundations. SURFACE AT THE POLE: Pages 350/351, 384, 398, 420: James F. Calvert/© National Geographic Society. Pages 353, 356: J. Baylor Roberts/© National Geographic Society. The portraits of the authors on Pages 14, 130, 190, 220, 353 were drawn by Claire Davis.